ISBN 13: 978-1-63489-022-9
eISBN: 978-1-63489-023-6

Library of Congress Catalog Number: 2016931949
Printed in United States of America
First Printing: 2016
20 19 18 17 16      5 4 3 2 1

Cover and interior design by Aurora Whittet
Headshot photography by Stacy Kron

Wise Ink, Inc.
53 Oliver Ave S
Minneapolis, MN 55404
www.wiseinkpub.com

To order, visit www.itascabooks.com or call 1-800-901-3480. Reseller discounts available.

# Bloodmoon

# Endorsements

"A unique urban fantasy world of werewolves and magic."
—**Aileen Erin**, *USA Today* bestselling author
of the Alpha Girl Series

"This was an action-packed book from the first chapter to the
end. . . . happy and sad moments, but a great end for Ashling
and her story. Fun, fast-paced, and all the loose ends were
wrapped up nicely. . . . I loved it, and I would
recommend the whole series!"
—**B. Kristin McMichael**, Amazon bestselling author
of the Blue Eyes Trilogy, the Day Human Trilogy, and
the Chalcedony Chronicles

"Readers dying to know what happens to Ashling and Grey will
not be disappointed by *Bloodmoon*. I know this reader wasn't.
What a thrilling conclusion to the trilogy!"
—**Andrew DeYoung**, author of *The Girl from Beyond*

# Bloodmoon

Aurora Whittet

*Life is unexpected and ever changing,*
*always follow your heart,*
*trust in yourself and jump.*

*For my son, Henry:*
*With every sunrise, you show me the world anew.*

# Contents

1 *In the Wind*     1

2 *Secrets*     17

3 *Mycenae*     23

4 *Sacrifice*     39

5 *Broken*     47

6 *Haunted*     53

7 *One Love*     61

8 *Freedom*     67

9 *Ripped Apart*     75

10 *Grey Storm*     87

11 *Blood Sacrifice*     95

12 *Riddles and Plans*     101

13 *Broad Daylight*     109

14 *Werewolves*     119

15 *The Crone*     133

16 *Blood River*     147

17 *Branded*     159

18 *Divine Animal Right*     175

19 *Lies*     183

20 *Vargr*     197

21 *Stonearch*     207

22 *Ghosts*     219

23 *Homecoming*     227

24 *Starry Sky*     239

25 *The Mother*     249

26 *Racing*     257

27 *Watched*     265

28 *Army*     273

29 *A Mother's Stand*     287

30 *Vercingetorix*     301

31 *War for the Rock*     311

32 *Faith*     325

33 *Mirror*     331

34 *Cemetary*     341

35 *Carrowmore*     355

36 *Crimson Queen*     365

37 *Promise*     373

# 1

## *In the Wind*

*"Eamon, I give* you back to Old Mother; I give you peace," I said.

As I lit the fire to release Eamon's spirit, tears burned in my eyes. The flames cracked and spread quickly, circling him in flame. I could feel the heat from the fire caressing my own skin.

"Watch over us, as we look up to you, for we are one pack, one people, one world." My voice broke. Mother wept and Shikoba whispered prayers to the wind. Eamon, whose face I'd grown to fear, was gone. Gazing upon him, I felt as though I was watching a stranger. I had never truly known him when he was alive, but his loss cut deep in my soul.

I was surrounded by the faces of my pack, what was left of them. Mund, Brychan, and Dilara surrounded Grey and me. Mother, Father, Tegan, Nia, Gwyn, Cara, and Fridrik huddled close in darkness. Kane, Quinn, Channing, and Marcius clustered close together and whispered to one another. I could feel their strength and their sadness. Their emotions felt like a storm colliding inside me.

As the ceremony ended, most of my pack retreated away from the fire.

"What have I done?" I whispered.

"You set him free," Grey said.

Grey's shoulders, back, and face were stoic, but I could feel his fear for Baran. Grey held my hand and squeezed it a little tighter. I knew he could feel my every emotion; we were one soul in two bodies. We said our vows before Old Mother Earth and made love under the stars in the depths of the Bloodrealms. Our hearts and bodies were one. No one could separate us now. The tiny pieces of ourselves that we had once kept hidden from each other now belonged to the other. There was no piece of my soul that wasn't his, and I could feel him drowning in all the emotions inside of me. They weren't just my emotions, but the emotions of everyone in my pack. I felt all their pain. My powers grew stronger every day. My eighteenth birthday was less than a year away, and I could feel myself changing, growing more into the leader I would become.

Mund, Brychan, and Dilara came back to my side. As we watched the fire, my mind wandered back to Eamon's wife, Grete. I'd seen her on the balcony before the fighting started. She'd been beaten and enslaved.

"Vigdis will find pleasure killing Grete," I said. "Now that Eamon is dead, she no longer serves a purpose for them. And she's human. Grete won't stand a chance down there." I looked to Grey, Mund, Brychan, and Dilara, wishing we could somehow devise a plan to change the past and the future. "And they will kill Baran, too."

I felt sick saying the words, but I could feel the truth in them. It was like a dead weight in the pit of my stomach. Eamon was dead, and Baran and Grete were in danger. It had all been so I could survive. The wind swept past me, blowing my red hair like flames around me as my tears streamed down my face. I couldn't lose Baran. He was more of a father to me than my own father had been. I couldn't leave him to his death.

"Bastards," Brychan muttered.

"We'll save Baran," Grey said. He sounded so sure, so confident.

Verci had taken Baran, and we all knew, even if no one would say it, the torment Baran would be enduring. I was certain they wouldn't kill him yet. They needed Baran because I needed him, but they would make his life a living hell until my claiming on my eighteenth birthday. Just the thought of what Baran had to endure made my stomach roll.

I glanced back toward the secret entrance of the Bloodrealms above the Seven Sisters waterfall. We were a mere mile from that hell. Being that close to Vigdis and Verci made me nervous. I knew Dagny's warriors stood guard, but I still felt as if at any moment, Vigdis would come hunting for me. We would wait for the flames to dwindle, then we would sleep for the night and flee from this place at first light.

I'd killed Vigdis's daughter, Æsileif. I didn't regret protecting myself and my pack, but I hated knowing I'd destroyed another life, even one as dark as Æsileif's. I wondered if Vigdis would burn Æsileif's body as we burned Eamon's. Did she even believe in Old Mother, or had she completely cast her faith away? It pained me to think of yet another soul who would be trapped on this earth.

"All this death . . . it's because of me," I said.

"Verci attacked Eamon because he wouldn't kill Grey in the Bloodrealms," Brychan said. "You didn't have control over Eamon or Verci. This is not your fault, Ashling."

"No one knew Verci had taken Eamon's wife and son captive. Hell, we didn't even know he had a wife and child. He never came to us for help. There was nothing you could have done to save him," Mund said.

I knew he was right. I couldn't stop Eamon's uncle from killing him, but the regret swirled through me. I hadn't realized until the last precious hours what he'd truly given up to protect me.

I saved Eamon's baby from the bowels of the Bloodrealms, but really Eamon saved me. He had burned his Bloodmark into my skin; what I had thought was malicious became my weapon against the Draugr. He saved Fridrik, Dilara, and me from death. He could never truly have known what giving me his Bloodmark would do in the Realms, but it saved his own son.

"Eamon gave up his own life and any chance he had left to save his wife, Grete," I said. "He did it to protect his son, Fridrik, me, Grey, the prophecy . . . he sacrificed everything." I wondered if he'd done it as repayment for me saving Fridrik. There was so much more to Eamon than I would ever know, so many questions I longed to ask him.

"Ashling, he made the right choice," Dilara said. "Don't regret and mourn it, because then his sacrifice is belittled. He saved all of us, and he saved his son, too."

"I know," I said. He deserved a hero's honor, not pity. I looked up to the sky, to the smoke swirling in the wind. "Eamon, I will protect your son and I will destroy your murderers. This I swear."

"Damn right," Brychan said.

"He protected you, and you protected everyone, Ashling. You called to the Stone Wolves and they fought for you. No one else could have woken them. You are more than my little sister. You are the Crimson Queen," Mund said.

I smiled, though I was sad. It had truly been a miraculous moment when the Stone Wolves came to our rescue. I remembered howling in desperation, never knowing the help that might answer when the stone statues came to life to save us. Without them, we'd all be dead. Except for me. Vigdis would have kept me alive until my eighteenth birthday; she had a special death planned for me.

"Why don't we just storm in there, mess up some Draugr, and save our friends?" Brychan said.

"We can't just walk back into the Bloodrealms all vigilante style," Dilara said. "You'll be the bloody mess in the sand. Besides, we barely made it out alive last time. We need a stronger force."

"Mother Rhea will help save Baran," Mund said.

"What good can Mother Rhea do to help us in this war? She may be wise, but I'm not sure why we should be traveling hundreds of miles to save Baran when we are only a mile away at most right now," Brychan said.

"She's an Elder God. Speak with some respect," Dilara said. The tension between them was so thick it was almost a visible haze.

"If we don't know where to find Baran in that labyrinthine blood world, we'll die without ever saving him or seeing the light of day again," Mund said. "That world is too vast. We need to know where they are keeping him, have a plan, and have much more support before returning."

"I can help us get there," Dilara said. She'd lived a lifetime in the Bloodrealms; if anyone could find their way through it was her.

I looked around at my patchwork renegade pack. We'd fought and barely survived against Vigdis's Garm wolves. My pack looked worn and broken, yet there was still hope in their hearts—I could feel it.

"It isn't over, Ashling," Grey said. "We can win this."

"We fight together," Dilara said.

They still had a lot of fight in them. Praise Old Mother for that, for I had so much more to ask of them. The war for good and evil had only just begun. Verci and Vigdis would stop at nothing. They murdered their own nephew for the allure of power. They didn't see me as all the parts that made me, Ashling Boru, the Crimson Queen: a wolf, a human, a daughter, a wife, and a friend. They only saw blood power, a pawn to their pursuit of power. They wanted to claim me and my power at Carrowmore, and I knew they would kill every last one of my pack members to get to me. Then I would die, too.

I watched all their faces scattered around the shack. Mother, Father, Tegan, Nia, Cara, and Fridrik all sat together as Mother softly sang a Celtic mourning song. Gwyn and Quinn talked with Kane and Shikoba. Channing and Marcius sat comparing scars. Dagny stood far off getting constant reports from his warriors. I watched as the warriors would appear almost out of thin air and disappear almost as quickly.

I glanced over to my Bloodsuckers, the newest members of my pack, Rhonda, Jamal, and Paul. They leaned against the shack and watched us. It was obvious by how they separated themselves that they didn't feel comfortable.

Grey, Mund, Brychan, and Dilara still surrounded me. My warriors. My protection. They had all risked their lives for me.

I looked into their tired faces, and I knew my face looked the same as theirs: beaten and broken . . . so broken. We'd lost too much already, and our war was only beginning. I looked down at my bloodstained hands and closed my eyes. My heart filled with rage.

"I'm just so bloody furious," I said. "None of this was necessary. No one should have had to die, but for some sick, twisted need for power, Verci and Vigdis have made war," I said, fuming with anger.

"This isn't a new war," Mund said. "This fight for power is centuries old and is far deeper than the prophecy. It is like a disease has taken hold of our people. But the prophecy, beyond predicting you and your birth, predicted the end of this conflict and infinite power to whomever claims you. Vigdis and Verci have decided that power belongs to them and will stop at nothing and kill anyone in their path to rule over the world."

"Grete and Baran are both captives in this war, and somehow I have to save them," I said. I just didn't know how. How could one little girl save the world, much less my own friends?

"You two are the cure," Brychan said, winking to Grey and me.

Brychan knew and accepted that I'd secretly given my heart to Grey, and he had stepped down as my betrothed. I was grateful for Brychan's friendship. It didn't matter who wanted to claim me now; I belonged to Grey, and I wasn't afraid for anyone to know it. But Brychan also knew I could feel Grey's physical pain; this was unusual in our world, and it was a secret I desperately needed Brychan to keep. If anyone found out, they could hurt me by hurting Grey. The rules of this terrorism would change.

"We just have to keep Ashling and Grey alive that long," Mund said. Mund knew how dangerous everything was, and he wasn't a big fan of taking risks, especially with his baby sister. I used to hate his overprotective big brother thing, but it was kind of endearing.

Mother stopped singing and rocked back and forth, making almost no sound at all but a slight whimper. Father stood next to her. I could see he wanted to comfort her, but he didn't seem to know how. Grey and I walked over to where my mother sat with Fridrik in her arms. I sat with them and wrapped my arms around them both.

"I will save him," I whispered in her ear.

Her sadness slammed into me. She mourned for Baran. The little pieces I knew of their story told me she loved him still. I just wanted to protect her from pain. I felt so helpless.

I scooped Fridrik into my arms as I gently pulled Father to kneel next to Mother. He wrapped his arm around her shoulders, weaving his thick fingers into her strawberry-blonde hair, and she crumbled into him. His posture was stiff and awkward. Maybe one day he would be more than a great man; maybe he could be a great husband and father, too.

"Da! Da-da!" Fridrik cried, reaching toward the fire.

I looked into Fridrik's innocent face. I saw Eamon in his eyes, but I could also see Fridrik's mother, Grete. I brushed back his dark curls and whispered, "I will protect you for all of my days, and I will stop at nothing to save your mother." Fridrik stopped crying and held on to my cheeks, smooshing my face. Somehow, I knew he understood. Fridrik crawled out of my arms and back onto Mother's lap. I stood and walked to Grey.

Grey wrapped his arms around my waist and rested his chin on my shoulder. His breath tickled my skin. Despite everything, all the horror we faced, I smiled, knowing he was mine.

I pulled the Tree of Life amulet that Eamon had given me from inside my pocket and slid it around my neck. I didn't know why I needed it, but I trusted him. Eamon had saved me in the Bloodrealms with his Bloodmark on my wrist. He'd given his life for me. This symbol had to mean something, too.

"What do you suppose that is for?" Grey asked.

"I don't know, but Eamon went to a lot of trouble to get it for me," I said.

I considered every choice I had made in the last year. Some of my choices had been selfish, some regretful, and others naïve, but all came from a place of the deepest love. All my choices had led me to this moment, both the good and the bad. My choices had led me to be the woman I was today and the woman I would be tomorrow.

It was nearly dark when a new wave of tears flooded me. I wasn't only feeling sadness, but a strange sense of joy as well. Eamon's soul finally had peace. He was free of Adomnan and Verci; he belonged to Old Mother now. I cried for Eamon, Emil, Baran, Grete, Svana, and even Odin and Æsileif; some dead, some missing, but all victims of a war for hope.

My people had the hope for a balanced and unified earth filled with one people. There was truly no difference between any of us. Wolf or human, black or white, rich or poor, we were all the same. We all deserved love. If Verci and Vigdis won and claimed me at Carrowmore, the world would fall into a deeper ruin, and the war over race and power would destroy everyone. There would be nowhere for the good to hide, and evil would reign.

"My sweet Ashling. We will survive this pain," Grey whispered.

I nuzzled into his neck. I always felt safe with Grey by my side. Grey's love was so big that I almost felt like we were in the center of the sun.

I clung to him. It felt good to touch him and not have to worry who might see. I didn't want to hide anymore. Love was pure and beautiful and meant to be celebrated, not hidden away and judged.

Soon the anger and sadness drained from my body and a calm

settled over me, like Old Mother herself was holding me. Or maybe it was Eamon. Old Mother had claimed him now . . . I could feel it. It was incredible. I could feel so much love and hope flow through me. I knew none of my pack could feel this. It was a sacred power, and I had never felt it this strongly before. I wanted to hold it forever, but I sent the energy out to all of my pack. I wanted them to have it. They needed Old Mother's love more than I did. With Grey, I had all the love I would ever need.

As I sent out Old Mother's love, I watched my pack begin to embrace the joy and the freedom of the open air, and their sadness dissipated. I watched as they began to dance around the fire, feeling Eamon's happy, loving spirit surrounding them. Eamon was free, and there was beauty in that.

Gwyn scooped Fridrik from Mother's arms and spun him around the fire with Tegan and Nia. The sounds of children's laughter filled the night sky. There was no sound more beautiful or captivating than that of children laughing. Even the darkest night could glow with their laughter.

Grey lightly kissed me, leaving my skin tingling. His touch was healing for me. "I love you, my wife," he whispered. His voice was deep and sexy. I couldn't help but smile. I loved the sound of those words on his lips. I could smell his earthy scent, and I buried my face into him. He pulled me to my feet as my pack danced around us.

"I love you too, my wolf," I said, kissing the tip of his nose.

"I will protect you," he said, smiling that mischievous smile I loved so much.

I touched his cheeks and looked deep into his green eyes. "And I will protect you. With all my love, I am yours."

I laid my head on his chest as he caressed my neck and back. His strong hands massaged every aching muscle, easing my tension. I loved Grey with all of my soul. It was crazy. I still couldn't believe he was mine forever. Every possible obstacle once stood in our way, and yet our paths crossed and changed us both forever. I didn't believe in coincidences. Every choice we had made, good and bad, brought us both to the same moment in time. We were meant to be one love. *One unstoppable love.*

My mind drifted back to Baran, alone in the darkness of the Bloodrealms. I felt sure they were torturing him. We were right here, so close to him and yet so far from finding him and saving his life. I put my hand on the earth, wishing I could feel him down there. The Realms were immense, and there was no way to know where they had him imprisoned.

"I will get Baran back," I said quietly.

Grey lightly tilted my chin up to look at him. "We will save him."

I searched his face and said, "He's alive, right?"

"He'll fight to stay alive," Grey said. "He'll always fight for you, Ashling."

"What about you and Willem?"

"He'll fight for us, too. We are Baran's kin. But you, Ashling, you are his queen."

"I'm not sure I deserve Baran," I muttered.

Grey smiled. "From what I hear, he chose you."

I laughed. Grey was right. From the very first moment, Baran had chosen me. He knew what I was and what trouble I would cause him. He may have even known he would have to sacrifice himself for me, and yet he still chose me. His choice said so much about his character. He was as good as they came. Baran once told me to work on my strengths as a wolf. Hearing, scent, my visions, all of it. I didn't think then that he was asking me to hone the skills I would need to claim my power as the Crimson Queen. He had known more about me than I had known about myself. He always believed in me. I would prove to him that he was right.

I noticed Rhonda, Paul, and Jamal still sitting away from us by the shack. They were Bloodsuckers and we were wolves. They spent their lives killing us and seeing us as the enemy. Now they saw us mourning and celebrating our dead; it had to be surreal for them to truly see the other side of us.

I pulled Grey with me over to them and knelt in the grass.

"This is how we say good-bye to our people," I said. I turned to look at what was left of the flames that had consumed Eamon and turned him to ash. The wind swirled around, Eamon's love flowing with it. "The flames set us free."

I studied their faces. Paul couldn't meet my eyes, yet I could see the tears on his cheeks. Jamal looked scared; he clearly didn't feel safe here. Rhonda looked remorseful. Even she had a hard time looking me in the eye.

"What happens . . ." Rhonda paused and cleared her throat. I looked into her piercing blue eyes. "What happens when we collect your skulls?"

I shuddered, remembering Grey's father's trophies. I remembered hearing all of their cries in that dark room, feeling their sorrow. How long they had waited for us, for their freedom, I didn't know, but just thinking of it made me sad. We'd burned them all. We set each one of those lost souls free that night.

"When we die, we need the flames to cleanse us, to burn us to ash so that we may again be free. If we are not burned to ash, our souls are trapped. It is painful. Our souls yearn for Old Mother to take us home, but our cries are never answered until we are returned by flame. Without the healing flame, we are left to suffer alone," I said.

None of them would look at me. They knew what they had done. Bloodsuckers had been hunting werewolves for centuries. They mercilessly killed us, drank our blood, and kept our bones. But none of us were innocent. We killed them, too. Our fatal rivalry had been passed on for generations, and until now, no generation had chosen to release the hate and forgive.

I touched Rhonda's hand, and she looked up at me with her regret-filled eyes. I sighed. There was nothing I could say or do to erase the past.

"We all fought a war we didn't understand. We killed each other never knowing the truth," I said. "But we have a choice. We don't have to blindly do what we are told and hate each other because of our ancestors. We can choose to be one and protect all life. We can win this war together."

Rhonda nodded. "Yes we can." Her energy shifted; she was no longer filled with sadness—she was eager. "I am a warrior, and I will fight for my own purpose. I will fight with you."

"Our fathers will kill us for this betrayal," Paul said. I could smell his fear.

"We will protect you," Grey said.

Jamal snorted. "We can protect ourselves."

"I believe that," Grey said, "but fighting your own father isn't a battle that can be won easily. Believe me."

Jamal nodded. They had all known Grey's father, Robert Donavan; before Robert died, he had been their leader. Grey was supposed to be his successor.

Sadness settled over Grey. I gasped. What had happened with Grey's father was something we had both pushed away from our thoughts. Grey had poured his energy into loving me for so long and ignored the pain he carried for his father. I was surprised to feel a longing from Grey; through it all, he still missed his father.

Robert died in a fight while he was trying to kill me. He would have murdered me, drank my blood, and kept my skull as his prize, just like he had done to Grey's mother. He would have killed Grey for loving me. The only reason I wasn't dead was Adomnan. It was weird to think that my tormentor was also my savior in this case. The world was always full of surprises.

"Jamal, we were meant to be brothers as Bloodsuckers; we still are brothers as we fight for the humans. That is and always has been your purpose. That hasn't changed," Grey said.

"Brothers," Paul said as he and Grey slapped each other on the back.

Jamal smiled. "Brothers in life and death."

"We are one in life and death," Rhonda said.

"We leave for Mycenae in the morning," I said. "We are about to wage war."

"Who are we going to see?" Paul asked.

"My grandmother, Mother Rhea. She is an Elder God, and she has the power to help us find Baran."

"Are you sure she can help us?" Grey asked, wrapping his fingers with mine. I always drew such comfort from his presence. I put my head on his shoulder for a moment and breathed in his scent.

"No," I said with a shrug. "But she's the best hope we have."

Mother Rhea had always been kind to me, but I didn't know if she could help us find Baran. If it hadn't been for her kindness when she allowed Grey to be one of my suitors, my own pack would have splintered apart and sides would have been chosen. She saw something in us and she knew our truth. Hopefully she could see Baran's as well.

"Will she kill us?" Paul asked.

I pictured Mother Rhea; she appeared to be in her eighties, with white, beautiful hair and startling blue eyes. She was regal in every way. I couldn't imagine Mother Rhea hurting a fly, but I knew better. She was an Elder God, a warrior—she'd killed many to protect her family, and I knew she'd do it again. Though I knew she hadn't engaged in war in over a century.

"Do not be deceived by her appearance. If you were to threaten her in any way, without a doubt she'd take your life," I said. "Otherwise, she's quite grandmotherly."

"So we're gonna get our asses kicked by a grandma?" Jamal chuckled.

"You just might, boys." I laughed.

I left Grey to talk with Jamal and Paul and walked over to my father and mother. Mother held Nia and Fridrik, one sleeping in each arm. Despite all the pain and fear that nearly consumed her, when she was surrounded by children, the smile on Mother's face could outshine the sun. Father, on the other hand, looked endlessly uncomfortable.

It felt strange for me to realize that my father, the mighty King Boru, didn't know his place yet in my world. My father's time to rule over me for my protection was over. As the Crimson Queen, it would now be up to me to protect him.

Calista prophesized that I would bring balance to our people. Though I still didn't understand how standing in a circle of stones and having someone claim me would make me a queen.

My father's once-red salt-and-pepper hair and full beard, with his stocky build, made him look like a fierce man, but I had seen tiny pieces of his kindness buried in his hardened exterior. Despite feeling his rejection of me for the first seventeen years of my life, I still yearned for his approval and love.

"Father?"

He looked at me with his stoic expression. It didn't soften as his hard eyes studied my face. I knew he was hard because of all he'd lived through, all he'd lost, all he had protected. But it didn't make it easier to talk to him.

"What, child?" he asked.

Instantly he made me feel powerless. I'd have spat back, I'm not a child, but that would have only made me look childish. I took a deep breath and pretended I didn't notice the slight. Maybe he didn't even notice he'd done it.

"Father, I need you by my side," I said. "I need to know you're with me in this war. I don't want to do this without you."

I felt like a child asking a god for a favor. It felt ridiculous. What right did I have to ask a warrior to stand on my team, to protect my pack? I looked up into his unwelcoming face and stared back. Eye to eye.

"Ashling, you are my youngest, my baby, and my only daughter. You are headstrong and wild and completely unreasonable. You have never obeyed a rule in your life, and I don't even begin to understand your choices." He glanced at Grey and shook his head. "But, you are still my daughter, and I will protect you with my life."

My breath caught and I wanted to cry with joy. His words were overwhelming. "Will you help me rescue Baran? Will you fight with me?" I asked.

Mother watched him. I knew she loved Baran, and saving him meant as much to her as to me. Maybe even more. The vein in Father's forehead started to bulge, like it always did when he was upset. I forced myself not to cringe away from him. I stood my ground. I didn't want to plead and beg, but I would if I had to. I needed him. If I lost his support, I would lose the support of those at the Rock of Cashel, and I might lose the support of many in my pack. He was vital to securing a unified army, and we needed to be united if we were going to survive Vigdis and Verci's wrath.

"Against my better judgment," he said. He stalked off.

I felt relief as well as anger, but it was the best agreement I would ever get from him.

Mother sighed. "It's the best he can do," she said. "One day, I hope he has the strength to show you all of his love. He does love you, Ashling, he just doesn't know how to show it and still be a fierce leader. He cannot easily live in both worlds as you can, being both fierce and loving. And it is a challenge for him to break out of our old ways."

"I know," I said. My father wasn't all bad—nor was he all good. Perhaps one day he'd love me like I always hoped he would, but for now, this tiny bit of grace was worth celebrating.

My worry shifted to my next unknown. "Do you think Mother Rhea can truly help us find Baran?" I asked.

"If she can't, he is lost," she said.

# 2
*Secrets*

*I curled up* with Grey near the embers of Eamon's fire and rested my head against his chest. I breathed him in deeply, and his scent filled my lungs with need. I remembered the pond in the Bloodrealms, the way his hands caressed my skin. Just thinking about it brought every nerve in my body to life. He wrapped his arms around my small body and pulled me close. Our bodies fit perfectly together, like we were truly made for one another.

"Are you concerned they can all see us together?" Grey asked.

I looked up and saw the silhouettes of my pack talking and sharing food across the fire from us. In the darkness and smoke it was hard to make them all out. Some may have noticed us, but none were blatant enough to stare. At this point, if I was to be the Crimson Queen, it would be up to me to create a new world. The silly little rules of old didn't matter.

"No. You are mine and I am yours."

"I like the way that sounds," Grey said.

"Me too," I said. "You are my future."

"The future is now." He smiled.

I leaned up and captured his lips with mine. I knew anyone who wanted could see, but I didn't care. I loved him.

Still, I felt we had to hide our secret marriage and physical connection. If anyone knew that our souls had bound, they could hurt me by hurting Grey. It would change the rules of this game we played.

I let myself melt into his touch as his hand went over my entire body. I was losing control and loving it. I felt my skin flush and my pulse race with every move of his tongue on mine. He grabbed my bottom and pulled me tightly against him, and I could feel his hardness. I softly moaned.

"Not here, love," he groaned. "You're too much."

"I'm sorry," I said, pulling away and hiding my face.

He touched my chin. "Never say sorry for that." He smiled. "Just not here."

I laughed, glancing around. No one seemed to notice us, but he was right. I was getting carried away in the romantic feeling of the stars and the fire. Grey was shifting his pants, trying to hide the bulge. I smiled as I watched. There was something gloriously powerful about turning him on. I allowed a little space between us, mostly so I could control the urge to push him over, crawl in his lap, and kiss him again.

Mund walked over to us with an all-knowing smirk on his face. At least one person had seen us. I blushed. Mund punched Grey in the shoulder and Grey grunted from the pressure, but my eyes instantly watered from the pain.

"Still my baby sister," Mund said.

Grey punched Mund back. "Yeah, well she's my wife."

As soon as the words left his lips I gasped. Grey's eyes grew huge. I felt his cockiness instantly be replaced by fear. The color drained from Mund's face as he looked at us. I met Mund's gaze with my eyes and waited for his disapproval. I waited to be punished and rejected. Even though Mund had never done those things to me, I was terrified that my secret marriage to Grey would break my bond with my brother.

Mund cleared his throat and sat straight, almost rigid as he watched us. Grey reached out and wove his fingers with mine. I was thankful for his touch.

"What have you done?" Mund whispered.

"It wasn't a choice to love Grey—it was always going to be him. We thought we were going to die in the Bloodrealms. So we said our vows for Old Mother Earth and committed our souls to one another," I said.

"Did you consummate the marriage?" Mund asked.

I nodded.

"Twice," Grey said.

I nearly choked. Either Verci would kill us eventually or Mund would kill us right now. Mund's face was a grotesque mix of rage and dumbfounded humor. I almost laughed, but I didn't dare. I glanced at Grey; if I hadn't been mortified, I'm not sure I would have been able to resist the naughty smirk on his lips.

"If anyone finds out that you married Grey in secret, you risk destroying the delicate allegiances you've worked so hard to create." Mund's brow wrinkled and he rubbed his eyes. His fear swirled around us and filled my nostrils with its potent scent.

"Mund, I'm sorry, but I won't justify our love. I don't have to. Our love is real," I said.

"Of course it's real," he said with a sigh. "Just . . . don't tell Mother. Or anyone else. But especially Mother . . . you'll break her heart."

Mund was right. Mother had always dreamed of my wedding. I couldn't take that away from her. She had even handmade a wedding veil for my birthday present. Grey and I would still celebrate our union with her and all of our pack when the time was right. We all deserved a celebration after this unending war.

Mund frowned and punched Grey in the shoulder, but with gusto this time. I grimaced with pain. "That's for marrying my sister without permission. This is for blurting it out." Mund punched him again. This time I flopped over in the grass and waited for the pulsing ache moving down my arm to subside. Mund didn't seem to notice. "Now, learn to keep your mouth shut, because if you hurt Mother's feelings and destroy the alliances we've made, I'll personally flog you."

"Mund, don't be so barbaric. And would you please stop punching him? It is starting to hurt," I said. "Now what did you actually come over here to say?"

"Oh, sorry about that," he said. He looked confused for a moment and then laughed. "I don't actually remember why I came over."

"Too busy being a big brother, huh?" I laughed and rolled my eyes.

I stood up and dusted myself off. I looked around and studied my pack. Mother, Tegan, and Cara sat playing with Fridrik and Nia. Father and Brychan sat off by themselves, but they didn't seem to be talking. Dilara and Rhonda drew scenarios in the sand, talking of strategies to get back into the Realms. Marcius, Quinn, Channing, Jamal, Paul, and Dagny shared a bowl of smoked goat jerky. Shikoba, Kane, and Gwyn stared up at the rising sun.

I loved them all; they were part of me as I was part of them. Each one was as different as the scent that came from their skin, but all were perfect as themselves. Not one of us knew how it would end. We all had hopes, but I could also feel their fear. It was hard not to let the doubt creep in. They all believed I was the one Calista had named in the prophecy, that I was the one with the crimson curls and the snow-white skin who would unite our people, but even I had doubts at times. It was impossible to be infallible. I'd watched too many die on both sides. It wore me down, but I had to give them more of myself. I had to give them hope.

One by one they noticed me watching them, and a silence filled the air. They all came closer to Grey, Mund, and me. It was like they knew I had something I needed to say.

"We embark at daylight for Mycenae, Greece, to seek counsel with our Elder God, Mother Rhea," I announced. "We have very little time to save Baran and Grete and destroy Verci and Vigdis before they destroy us. Do not mistake what I say—this is war. Verci and Vigdis will never show us mercy. They will kill every last soul who stands between them and power. They mean to claim me at Carrowmore and steal my blood and reign over you. But we will be *victorious*." I watched them absorb my words. "In less than a year, I will be claimed at Carrowmore before Old Mother Earth and all of you. We will take back our people and our lands. We will become one pack as I become your Crimson Queen," I said. "I will lead you to freedom."

Hoots and howls came from all around me. I didn't feel as confident as my words suggested, but they needed to hear them, and they needed to see me strong, even if I still felt like a seventeen-year-old girl.

"Rest and gather your things and your strength," I said. "Our journey will be long."

I turned back to Grey and Mund. Their strength and pride filled the voids in my heart. I looked from one to the other, waiting for them to say something. Instead, Mund crushed me in his arms and held me tight. When he finally let me go, I saw tears in his eyes.

"You're a strong leader, Ashling. I still can't believe my baby sister grew up. And she rules us all." He smiled and shook his head. "But there is no doubting your strength to love. It flows from you like sunlight, surrounding all that you see."

"Mund," I said.

"Yeah?" he said.

"I love you."

He smiled. "And I you, Ash."

He walked off to join Tegan and Nia, wrapping them in his arms as they walked into the shack. Something inside me knew this might be the last rest any of us got for a while. This semblance of peace would soon be gone. Evil was rising.

# 3

## *Mycenae*

*We all woke* with beacons of hope in the morning light as the sun rose in the east. Some of my pack had slept out under the fading stars near Grey and me. I knew Rhonda, Jamal, and Paul would; they were certainly uncomfortable surrounded by wolves in a secure underground fortress like Dagny's. I watched as Gwyn and Quinn finished their run. I assumed from the swagger in their gait that they must have caught a nice breakfast for themselves.

I couldn't help but smile at Brychan and Dilara as they both grumbled and stretched. I wasn't looking forward to the two-thousand-mile journey either. By planes, trains, and boats, we would cross from Norway to Greece. With any luck, Verci and Vigdis wouldn't be tracking us.

I hadn't fully worked out how we would get where we were going. Moving this many people without notice from Verci and Vigdis's allies would be very difficult. Dagny walked over to me as I stretched.

"Do you know which path you will lead us on?" Dagny asked.

I half-smiled and shook my head no.

He nodded without judgment or question. "The safest way is underground when you reach Hungary. Verci has too many allies in Serbia and Romania. If we were attacked there we would surely be overtaken," he said. "I will contact my friends in Hungary so they will be ready for us, and they can take us through to Greece."

"Thank you for your counsel, Dagny. You are ever loyal," I said.

He nodded and took his leave.

I knew Dagny and Baran had been lifelong friends; saving Baran meant a great deal to him. Even though he didn't show his pain and suffering, I could feel it. He wasn't my true pack, yet I felt his emotions. I felt all of their emotions.

Baran had told me once to hone my senses. I think he knew something about me that he wanted me to discover on my own. I was more than a normal wolf—I could feel the emotions of everyone around me. I could dream the future. I could feel Grey's physical pain. What else I was capable of, I had yet to discover.

"Gather your things; we hike down the fjord, where we will rent cars in Geiranger," I said. "We move in ten minutes."

The hike was easy for all of us, even the humans. But they weren't really human—they were Bloodsuckers. Our blood changed them. They were stronger, but not immortal. I would have to make sure I didn't push them too hard.

Geiranger looked like a deserted bar brawl after the beer festival had ended and all the vendors and gypsies moved on to the next city, leaving this one in ruin to clean up the mess. I remembered seeing Eamon here.

"Mund, Brychan—please acquire the cars," I said. They grinned and walked away. "Legally," I added.

I heard them both mutter under their breath. And I smirked.

Minutes later everyone started piling into various sedans, and we began our journey to the coast. Father drove and Mother sat in the front while Grey and I sat in the back. It was awkward and silent, but I kept my attention on all that we passed to make sure we weren't being followed. Our car was in the middle of all the others. Like they were guarding a great treasure. I was beginning to understand what I truly meant to everyone. I wasn't just family—I was their hope for the future.

From Denmark we flew to Prague, pretending we didn't all know each other. Moving a group this large was difficult. I constantly worried we'd be noticed and Vigdis would find out where we were, but we landed safely in Prague.

As I walked next to Mund and Grey through the airport, I looked into the face of every person who passed me, wondering who of them was a spy. I spotted the car rental booth with relief.

"Mund?" I said.

He nodded and returned shortly with five sets of keys in his hand. He handed one to Grey, Channing, Brychan, and Kane and kept one for himself. "Let's go." He grinned.

We followed him outside to five matching black cars. They were sleek and sexy, I had to admit, but a bit showy. "Tesla Model S?" I questioned.

Mund smiled so big I thought his face might break. "Electric."

I shook my head. Grey slid into the driver's seat. Dagny opened the door and slid in with us. He didn't say a word, but I knew he was there to protect us. He was one of Baran's, as were we.

We raced as fast as those boys could push the cars from Prague to Budapest. The landscape was covered with beautiful old cities. The architecture was stunning. I wanted to explore it all or even get a chance to just look at it. The drive should have taken nearly five hours, but they got it done in only three and a half.

"Slow down," Dagny said. "We've arrived."

Grey dropped down to the speed limit, and the others matched our speed. "Slower," Dagny said. Grey did as he was asked, but it made me nervous to crawl into this residential community drawing attention to ourselves. "Third house on the left."

"Park out front?" Grey asked.

"Drive into the garage."

"There isn't room for all of us in there," Grey said.

"Never mind that. Follow the order," Dagny said.

Slowly Grey pulled into the fancy three-stall garage. Mund and Brychan pulled their cars in too. I looked outside at Channing and Kane and their passengers and was suddenly filled with dread.

"Dagny, are you sure about this?" I whispered.

The garage door started closing us in and the rest of my pack out. Panic raked through me. Men started dropping from the ceiling all around us and coming out from the walls, painted like they were part of the room. They wore skintight clothing in the same color as the light gray walls and their skin was painted to match. Some of their skin and bodysuits bore the pattern of wood grain to match the beams. When they blinked, my skin chilled. They had been there the whole time—I hadn't seen any of them, and we were surrounded.

I heard screams from the other cars and my pack banging on the garage door from the outside.

"Dagny, how could you betray us?" I said. I was angry and heartbroken.

He looked at me, surprised. "Betray you? Never, my queen. These are the Steel Wolf guard. They protect the entrance to the city." He opened the door and stepped out before them. "*Megáll!*" He spoke Hungarian as fluently as Norwegian and English.

Each of the men bowed and backed away back into their hiding spots, disappearing into the surroundings except for their eyes, which they kept open, watching us. It was unnerving. As though the walls were watching our every move.

I held Grey's hand tightly, like it was my lifeline.

"*Család,*" Dagny said. It meant "family"; as the word flowed off his tongue, the floor collapsed into ramps going underground. He pointed outside to our other two cars and said, "*Család. Köszönöm.*"

He slid back into our car, and I took a deep breath. "Where are we going?"

"Underground, my queen. Welcome to Szabadság."

"What does it mean?"

"Freedom," he said as the ramps closed behind our cars.

"They will let the others through, won't they?" I said.

"Indeed."

We drove into the narrow metal tunnel, one car after the other. I looked back and could see the headlights of the other two cars lower into the tunnel behind us. There was a comfort in knowing we were all together, yet it was one of my greatest fears. If we were to be discovered, it would mean the ruin of my entire pack. I shook the thought from my mind.

"Where will it let out?" I asked.

"We will come out near Mycenae, Greece. The rest of the journey we will make on foot," he said.

The narrow tunnel opened into pockets of wolf cities. None as poor as the Netherworlds, nor steampunk as the Bloodrealms; this was elite. Their homes were made of varying types and textures of steel. It was utterly refined and minimalistic. There were so many wolves down here, every few miles another city rose.

"Who are these people?" Grey asked.

"Have you not heard the bedtime stories of the steel warriors?" Dagny asked, smiling.

Grey looked up suddenly. "My mother told me a story once."

"What of it?" Dagny said.

Grey shook his head. "It was just a bedtime story," he said.

Dagny laughed. "We are all bedtime stories." He was right; we were werewolves, creatures of myth and song . . . legend.

"Grey, will you tell it to me?" I asked.

"Well, I don't remember it all, but I guess she started it like this. Once upon a time, in a small, peaceful village in Hungary, a pack of werewolves lived among the people. One day, an evil emperor came upon them and took over their lands and murdered their people. The survivors were condemned to death. Every one of them—men, women, and children—were to be encapsulated in steel, to exist forever as statues for the emperor," he said.

"Why?" I shuddered.

"Mother said that everywhere the emperor went, he left deserted cities of metal statues to intimidate any who might come across his territory," Grey said.

"Did they die?" I asked.

"I don't know," Grey said.

"Some did," Dagny said. "But as the liquid steel burned and boiled the flesh of the werewolves, they shifted from their human forms into wolves, and neither killing nor encapsulating them into statues, the steel became part of them. With the burning hot metal still liquid on their skin, they tore their oppressors apart, protecting their humans."

"Mother said the steel wolves can still be seen glimmering in the light of the full moon," Grey said.

"These are your steel wolves. They are your people, my queen," Dagny said as he motioned out the window.

A young girl, maybe about thirteen years old, stood by the edge of the tunnel watching us. Across her face, a metal mask almost concealed her identity in the most beautiful asymmetrical pattern. Her blonde hair was stick straight around her face. Her expression was unchanging, but as my car passed, she shifted into a wolf with steel covering her face in the same way, and it pooled over her back. Steel spikes grew from her body like armor. She raced with us for a time, matching the pace of the car. There was a calm energy to her, but it was her curiosity I felt the most. A distant howl brought her to a stop, and she returned from where she came without giving me another glance, but I was sure I would never forget her.

The trip through the tunnel took a day. Everyone was growing weary, but we emerged into the breaking dawn. So far, there had been no sight of our enemies, and I was relieved of that, but just because I didn't see them didn't mean they didn't see us.

I felt childish, but the question remained the same no matter how I thought about it. "Are we there yet?" I asked.

Dagny smiled. "Nearly. We will make our final trek on foot into Mycenae."

"Why?" I said.

"Mycenae is holy ground to our people," he said.

"Can't we run as wolves?" Grey asked.

"A pack of wolves this large would alarm the humans that reside here," Dagny said. "We just look like tourists if we walk in on foot."

The exercise would feel good after being cooped up so long in cars, planes, and boats. We parked our cars, and I stared in wonder at the enormous climb ahead of us. The ruins of Mycenae stood atop a tall hillside commanding over the surrounding plain. It was once the home of Agamemnon, who was the king of all the Archaean Greeks. A once impressive fortified city now stood only as forgotten ruins, but what the humans had forgotten was still the home of Mother Rhea, the only living Elder God of our people.

Mother held Fridrik in her arms while he slept. I couldn't look at him without feeling the weight of Eamon's death, but there was a time for sadness and reflection, and now was not it. Now was the time for action. Not only did Baran and Grete's lives rest in my hands, but so did the lives of all of my pack, all the innocents. I didn't have time for a pity party. Without a word I started hiking up the rocky terrain as black rain poured down over us as though Old Mother was trying to cleanse the earth.

Despite the warm air, I shivered in my wet clothes. I would have liked to stop and admire the splendor of the lands, but the cold rains changed my mind. I just kept hiking up and up and up. The rocks shifted under my feet, and with every step the air became harder and harder to breathe. It seemed unending.

"Gracious," Mother whispered as she lost her footing for a second. "This is harder than I remember."

"What was it like growing up here?" I asked.

She looked around. "Beautiful," she said. "I explored every inch of this land. It left a mark on me. There is a peace that I only find here. We watched over these people with love and sacrifice."

I smiled. I'd never been to my mother's home before. As a child she had spoken of it with joy as though it were a member of her pack. It was even more beautiful than she had described.

"When was the last time you were home?" Brychan asked.

"Since I was home to the Treasury of Atreus?" Mother sighed. "Over a century."

"Well then, welcome home," Brychan said as he bowed to her.

She smiled.

I looked back over my pack, all cold and wet, and yet they followed me. Even after days of traveling and uncertainty, I could feel their hope and excitement for the future that Calista promised in her prophecy. I smiled at them, feeling myself fill with the love I held for each of them. I felt light and unstoppable.

All too soon, the smell of blood filled my nostrils through the cold rain. It was faint at first, then suddenly overpowering. The smell of human blood and werewolf blood filled the air. My hair bristled, and I wanted to run the other way. I didn't want to see what lay just inside the city ruins of Mycenae.

"There is death here," Mother whispered.

"I know," I said, my voice just a whisper in the wind as I forced myself to continue walking.

Mycenae came into view, and my breath left my body. I stared in horror at the blood-soaked earth. Bodies lay in pieces around the doorway of the earthen tomb. By the way their broken bodies lay, it appeared as though they had been trying to seek refuge in the sacred tombs where Mother Rhea lived.

Though the people of Mycenae didn't realize she still lived, they were running to her for their lives and shelter. I could hear all their cries. All their souls weeping at once, like a hundred voices entering my heart. They had sacrificed their human lives to protect a memory, a legend, a wolf. It was a warning cry. Even now, the dead were trying to protect us.

"What happened here?" Tegan said.

"Why are they still here? Why has no one come for them?" Rhonda asked.

"Because they are all dead, and there is no one left to call for help," Shikoba said.

The weight of sadness and death was debilitating. The pain from my pack soaked into me and mingled with the voices of the dead. I felt like chains were pulling me down into the bloody mud to die with them. It was too much sadness. I closed my eyes and let the rains wash away my tears.

"Who would do this?" Jamal asked.

"I think we know," Mund said.

"But why?" Gwyn asked. "What did Mother Rhea have that Verci and Vigdis could want?"

I took a deep breath and said, "I have to find Mother Rhea."

"We should flee," Dilara interrupted. "Only death awaits us here."

"I agree," Rhonda said. "She's probably already dead."

But something pulled me inside. Something was waiting for me, and I had to know what or who it was. I took a step forward, letting go of Grey's hand.

"I'm with you, my love," he said, twining his fingers with mine once again.

"As am I," Mund said.

"And I," Brychan said.

"The rest of you, stay alert; Verci and Vigdis could still be here.

Dagny, you're in charge. Be ready to fight and keep the babes safe," I said. I looked at Mother and Tegan holding our future, Nia and Fridrik, in their arms. I needed to find safety for my pack before this war stole more innocent lives. War was no place for babies. I couldn't keep moving the innocents around with me. They were in danger with me; a pack this large made all my actions stand out to my enemies. I would have to send them away. The thought chilled my heart, but I knew it was true.

"Look for the Vanir Bloodmark; give your breath, and it will lead you to Mother Rhea," Mother said.

I nodded and entered the stone, pyramid-like tunnel into the Treasury of Atreus, into the earthen tomb where Mother Rhea lived. Grey, Mund, and Brychan walked with me as my guards. I was thankful not to be alone in the dark.

The door was broken open, and the pieces lay shattered on the ground. We walked down the steps to a dead end. I studied the large stone wall and spotted a golden trinket in the wall; it was a carving of the Vanir Bloodmark. It was no larger than a dime. I blew my breath on it and a secret door opened. Only a Vanir could open the door, and I was half Vanir.

Mother Rhea's home was an underground fortress filled with glittering gold treasures of immeasurable wealth. I looked around in the darkness, letting my eyes adjust to my new surroundings. The floors were littered with the dead. I nearly drowned in the weight of the souls' desperation as we stepped over their bodies.

"Only a Vanir could have opened that door," I whispered.

"Vigdis," Mund snarled.

Grey squeezed my hand tighter. "I'm with you in life and death," he whispered.

We didn't know which way to go, so we followed the bodies deeper into the tomb. The four of us came to an enormous door covered in deep claw marks, but it was still barred closed. A Vanir pack warrior lay dying in front of it, and seven dead Garm wolves surrounded him. He wore the golden armor of the Vanir. His silver hair was matted to his skin with sweat and blood, and his wide nose was clearly broken.

When I kneeled beside him and touched his bloody face, his eyes snapped open. "You came," he gasped. "My queen."

"What happened here?" I said.

"Vigdis," he whispered through clenched teeth.

"Did she get to Mother Rhea? Is she safe?" I asked.

He gagged on his own blood as he whispered, "She will destroy everything you love."

"No, she won't," I said.

He looked at me as though he saw into my soul. Perhaps he was a watcher and could read souls. Perhaps this near-death state gave him new eyes. Either way, I was certain he saw my soul and my heart. I felt as though he were deciding the truth of my words from inside of me.

He nodded as blood seeped from his lips. I wanted to heal him. I wanted him to live. "Shift into a wolf," I demanded. "Live."

His lips curled into a sad smile. "I can't my queen, but I did my duty. Mother Rhea is safe. She is waiting for you. And now I've had the chance to look upon the face of my queen before I die."

I smiled at him, knowing mine would be the last face he saw in this life. I glanced at the door and was too frightened to go inside. Had Vigdis gotten to her? Was it a trap? I looked back at the warrior to see only death in his eyes. I closed his eyelids with my fingertips.

"Ashling, you should wait outside," Brychan said.

I stared at him. "Maybe you should stay outside," I said.

He shrugged at Mund, shaking his head. "Worth a try."

I stood and Grey followed as I slammed my fist into the doors. "Open the doors," I commanded.

I didn't know what waited on the other side of the door for me, but I was going to find out. My heart was in the pit of my stomach and rage filled my veins, but still no answer came from behind the doors. Not even the sound of someone moving. Were they all dead?

"You will open these doors to your queen," I said so firmly it even scared me.

"Old Mother, please let Mother Rhea be alive when I find her," I whispered. I needed Mother Rhea, and I loved her. I held my breath as the sounds of doors opening echoed in the halls.

"It could be a trap," Mund said.

Brychan nodded and they positioned themselves to fight. One stood on each side of Grey and me as the heavy doors swung open with a creak. I waited for Garm wolves to rip us to shreds, for Verci to slice his sword through my neck, yet nothing came. Only silence.

"Come, my child," Mother Rhea's soft voice called. "It is safe."

I looked to my companions and they all nodded. We moved as one into the tomb. Mother Rhea sat on a golden throne surrounded by the Vanir pack. She looked completely untouched; her golden robes were smooth and unwrinkled, and her hair was piled perfectly on top of her head. I was thankful and angry to see her. Was it not our duty to protect the humans? She let Vigdis kill them while she stayed hidden in here.

I walked toward her as her people stepped aside, and I knelt before her. She was my grandmother, an Elder God. Mother Rhea was so many things in the humans' legends and so very many things to me.

"I need your help, Mother Rhea," I said. "I need you to help me save Baran, and we need to unify our people."

She looked down on me, and I could feel her pity, but I didn't understand it. "No, my child. There is no salvation for Baran of Killian. He is lost to us," she said.

"No . . . no, please! He can't be dead," I begged. "I'd know. I'd feel it."

"He's not dead yet, child, but he will be," she said.

"Then help me save him," I said.

"No one can beat Verci, and I will not fight Vigdis, my own daughter," Mother Rhea said. "It is not proper."

"Mother Rhea, we have to stand against Vigdis and Verci. This is not just to save Baran, but to help me claim my throne as the Crimson Queen. If we do not stand against them, I cannot bring balance and love to our people, " I said.

"We are not getting involved," Mother Rhea said. "Baran is not of my pack. This is not our war. I will not send any more of my people to die for it."

"This is everyone's war," I said.

I smelled my parents as they entered the tomb, but I couldn't look at them. I was losing. If I couldn't persuade my own grandmother to fight with me, how could I expect anyone else to join me?

Mother Rhea turned her attention to Mother and Father and spoke to them as though I weren't there, as though I were that tiny wolf pup in the family painting from so long ago. "We have to hide the child until she's eighteen," she said to them. "Then she can be claimed at Carrowmore and no one else important need die," Mother Rhea said. The calmness and conviction in her tone was unsettling.

"Everyone is important," I said, but she didn't turn her attention back to me. Her home was surrounded by the Vanirs' humans. All slaughtered. Every last human life smothered out, and their families didn't even know yet. They lay dead right outside these walls. Did she not realize she had failed her people? Anger filled me, and I stood before her. Elder God or not, I would never stand aside while humans died.

"Whether you stand with me or not, a war has already begun and death is coming. Even for those who stand aside. Do you think you can just hide behind your big walls and the storm will pass?" I said. Rage seethed in my veins.

"My child, you will understand one day that this is what is best," Mother Rhea said.

"The hell I will," I said. I grabbed Mother Rhea's hand and pulled her from her throne. Her guards lunged forward to protect her, but

Grey, Brychan, and Mund snarled at them, holding them at bay.

"Stop this at once," Mother Rhea said.

"You will see what you have done," I said.

I pulled Mother Rhea from the safety of her tomb into the rain. Mother and Father followed closely behind; her guards twitched with the need to save her, but they didn't dare when they saw the size of my pack that waited for them outside.

The sun shone through the clouds onto the dead that surrounded us. It was almost as though Old Mother was shining her love onto each body and illuminating them.

"Do you think Verci and Vigdis will spare any life . . . after this?" I pointed to the dead bodies of men, women, and children and shook my head. "Your people died running for their lives and desperately trying to get into your tomb for safety, never even knowing you were right there the whole time listening to them die. We are meant to protect them. Couldn't you hear their screams as Vigdis's Garm tore them apart?"

She stared at them all. They were her people. I was sure she knew all their faces.

"We are all dead if we do not stand together. I need every one of my pack fighting by my side. I am not asking you, Mother Rhea; I am telling you. We all fight together and we die together. I will not hide while humans are murdered!" I screamed.

Mother Rhea stared at the lost souls around her, and tears ran down her cheeks. She crumpled to the ground, and the mud and blood soaked into her gown. She scooped a child into her arms and wept.

"I stand with you, as do my warriors," Mother Rhea whispered.

I knew she was trying to pretend that no one had been brutally murdered outside her own doors. The sounds of them dying would likely haunt her for the rest of her life. Just as looking upon their bodies would haunt mine, but I needed everyone to see what had been done here. These weren't just bodies, they were souls.

"Thank you," I said.

We walked back inside the tomb, my entire pack following us. Mother Rhea sat on her golden throne, hair soaked through and her dress covered in blood and mud, yet still she looked somehow regal. Her eyes followed me as I paced back and forth. The tomb was filled with my pack and hers. I could feel the tension in the air and the anger of her guards.

"Dagny, lock down the chambers and leave no sign of our kind," I said.

He nodded.

"Mund, will you please report the slaughter outside to the authorities. These people deserve to be put to rest," I said. "The humans will likely blame wolves." I shook my head, hating everything. The bodies had been torn by teeth and claw, and despite our innocence, wolves would be to blame; humans could never understand the mythical world they lived in.

Mund pulled out his phone and walked away.

"You will help me save Baran Killian," I said to Mother Rhea. "He is my pack; he is mine to protect."

I stopped pacing and turned to face her. My golden eyes locked with hers. I remembered my sweet grandmother and her riddles, her soft hands and warm heart. I was asking her to fight. I was asking her to once again be a warrior. I wasn't sure if what I was asking was fair, but it didn't matter; nothing in life was fair. We couldn't control what happened to us, but we could control how we reacted. I took a deep breath and let it out.

"Mother Rhea, you are the only wolf powerful enough to help me find Baran in the Bloodrealms," I said. I wanted her to understand.

"I know," she said. "But do you understand what you are asking for?"

"I am asking you to help me save my friend."

She smiled sadly. "Then you do not understand."

I crossed my arms, suddenly frustrated with her riddles. "Then explain it to me," I said.

She stood and a hush grew over everyone. "With everything you ask for, there is a sacrifice. You may not feel it today, but it has been promised. And everyone who follows you knows the risk. If you continue on this path, someone will die," she said.

"We fight together," I said. "We fight for freedom."

"I know you would die for them as willingly as they would all die for you. I see it in their souls and yours," she said.

The idea of any of them dying made me hurt. I didn't want to accept that they were all risking their lives for me. Just as I had made her acknowledge her dead, I had to face this reality too.

"But the truth is, Mother Rhea, all of our lives are at risk whether we stand together or not. But when we stand together, we are stronger than when we stand alone. Together we have a chance."

She nodded. "This is true. You've grown into quite the warrior."

I smiled.

"Why is Baran Killian so important to you?" she asked.

"He gave everything for me," I said.

It was true. He protected me from Adomnan and Robert. He fought for me in Iceland. He gave up so much for Grey and me. He was the support and love and the father figure I had always needed. He risked his life again and again to protect me . . . to protect all of us. If I didn't save him, he'd die for his sacrifice.

"I have to consult the stones to find him," Mother Rhea said. "And then your bargain will be made."

I didn't know what kind of bargain I was making to save him, but I wasn't sure I cared. I owed him his freedom. I owed all the people of the Bloodrealms freedom. Without Baran by my side, I wasn't sure I could save all those people.

"Please," I said. "Help me save him."

She nodded solemnly.

# 4
## Sacrifice

*Mother Rhea swept* out of the room with her golden skirts swirling behind her. Even soaking wet and covered in blood, she still owned the room; every eye was upon her. She retired to her room and left us all to sleep in the main hall. I didn't mind sleeping on the ground, but I felt sorry for everyone else. I walked slowly around to where Dilara sat with Khepri, Willem, Quinn, and Gwyn.

"Dilara, would you join me in the hall?" She smiled and stood to follow. I found Rhonda in another group. I could feel Rhonda's unease. Even still, she didn't like being separated from Jamal and Paul. "Rhonda, would you please speak with us in private?" She nodded and followed us into the hallway.

I drew them in close as we sat on the cobblestone floor. The floors were worn down by the centuries. I wondered how many children ran on these floors over the years and how many stories these walls could tell.

"I would like you two to be my counsel and my guards," I told them.

"My queen," Dilara said bowing. "It is my honor and pleasure."

Rhonda smiled from ear to ear with pride.

"Mother Rhea is consulting the stones. When she has her answer, we will begin this war. I need both of you by my side. Grey, Mund, and Brychan are too emotional to lead if something were to happen to me. We protect each other, we protect our packs, and we protect the humans. We are above no one, we fight for one another," I said. "Do you accept my terms?"

"With my life," Dilara said.

"I will fight with you and for you," Rhonda said. "No matter who the enemy."

I knew she spoke of her own father. Being a Bloodsucker meant she was in a hierarchical system similar to a wolf pack, and Rhonda stepping out of the order and joining the enemy would mean her life, but Dilara and I would protect her.

"Good." I smiled. I needed strong warriors to win this war. "Get some rest. Something tells me you'll need it."

From outside, I heard the humans beginning to collect what was left of their dead. I wanted to go to them, help them, and mourn with them, but it would only add to their questions and accusations. They had no way of getting into the Vanir chambers. We were hidden deep in the earth. Instead, we all waited on Mother Rhea . . . waited on our future.

After hours that felt like days, Mother Rhea rushed back into the room, blood dripping down her arm as she clutched her sacred stones above her head. All secrets came with a blood price. Blood dripped down her arm in red streams.

"I have spoken to the stones," she called out, waking everyone. She turned her attention on me. "Ashling Boru. At Carrowmore on the Bloodmoon, you will need the Triple Goddess. You, my dear, are the Maiden. You will need to find the Mother and the Crone to stand by you for the prophecy to be fulfilled."

"What about Baran?" I asked. I would worry about the Triple Goddess and the prophecy later, but my immediate concern was Baran's life . . . which I feared was closing in on him.

"To save Baran," she said, "all you need is to look inside yourself."

Look inside myself? What did she mean? I looked at her hard, stoic face. "Why is everything a damn riddle?" I said.

"The stones do not give names or places," Mother Rhea said.

"How can I find Baran inside myself?" I said.

"Only you can seek that answer," she said. "And find the Mother and the Crone."

"Mother Rhea, you are the only remaining Elder God. Are you not the Mother?" Father said, pointing to her.

"Pørr Boru, things are never that simple," Mother Rhea said.

I let the riddle flow through my mind again. The Triple Goddess was a symbol of our people—the Maiden, the Mother, and the Crone. If Mother Rhea wasn't the Mother or the Crone, who was? Could it be Lady Faye or my own mother?

"How do I know who the right people are?" I said.

"They are Elementals. They create current, energy. When they are near, you will feel their energy and you will know," Mother Rhea said.

I visualized Baran and placed my hand on Mother's shoulder, hoping and praying she was the one, but the energy was the same as in my childhood. Nothing was different. She wasn't the answer to my riddle.

"*Arragh*," I groaned in frustration.

Mother wrapped her arms around me, "*M'eudail*, you will find them," she said. "And we will save Baran." Those simple Gaelic words on her lips, which meant "my dear," always made me miss home.

"How?" I asked, my voice barely a whisper. "How do I look inside of myself to find him?"

I closed my eyes to stop the tears and my anger. I couldn't show weakness in front of my people, not now, at the brink of war. I was embarrassed that I had taken my pack two thousand miles away from Baran for an answer only to hear that I supposedly had everything I needed inside of me all along. I was terrified that as the seconds and minutes dragged on, the likelihood that Baran would die became stronger and stronger. I wouldn't give up on Baran; he'd never give up on me. But Mother Rhea's damn riddle . . . what did it mean?

I looked to my pack around me, and their faces eagerly watched mine as though they were waiting for something profound. "I need time to think," I said. I walked away and left them in my wake.

I wandered the dark halls and sat with my back against one of the cold stone pillars as I let my fear leak from my eyes. Stupid tears were a weakness. I hated myself for crying. I smelled him coming. Musky, earthy, delicious, and all mine. Grey sat down next to me and held my hand, but he didn't say a thing. I was thankful for that. I didn't want to be given false hope. I needed to think; I needed a plan.

Grey pulled me into his arms, cradling my head against his chest. I ran my fingers over his scarred chest, remembering everything we'd been through. We survived his father, my father, Adomnan, three other suitors trying to win my hand, the Bloodrealms, and so much more. We were a stronger couple because of everything. When we said our vows before Old Mother Earth we became one, our minds, bodies, and souls. I blushed thinking about it. I wanted him again. Every moment that passed my desire for him grew. Our bodies fit together; we were made to be together.

He ran his fingers through my hair, playing with the snarly red curls. I looked up into his emerald green eyes and searched for my salvation, but instead I was flooded with love.

"Oh, my sweet," he said. "I wish I knew how to help you."

I smiled. "You already are."

He captured my lips with his and his tongue plunged into my mouth. I turned, straddling him, giving his hands full access to my body. I was his and he was mine. All mine. In this one stolen moment, we were all that mattered in the world.

I shivered as his rough hands slid down my long neck and down my chest. He stopped when his hand was over my heart. I burned with need everywhere he touched me. He stared into my eyes, seeking something.

"What are you looking for?" I asked, breathless.

His lips curved into a mischievous smile that his sexy sideburns always drew my attention to. "An invitation."

My breath caught. I wove my fingers into his messy brown hair as I kissed him, letting my yearning flow into him. I rocked my hips against him, feeling his urgency grow stronger. As I nibbled on his earlobe, he moaned and pulled my hips harder against him. I wanted to feel his bare skin against mine, but this tomb wasn't private, and many eyes could find us here in the dark.

I slowly pulled away, trying to catch my breath.

"You are so sexy," he said, biting his lower lip.

That simple gesture made me want to kiss his luscious lips again. "You're supposed to be helping me find solutions, not distracting me with your wonderful self," I said.

"Oh my," he said. "I guess I've been bad."

I laughed.

I leaned forward and whispered in his ear, "I shall keep you."

He swatted me on the bottom. "Good."

I squeaked. "You shall pay for that."

"I hope so." His smile was devilish and so inviting.

I leaned my forehead against his. "Grey?"

"Yeah?"

"How do I find the Mother and the Crone?" I sighed.

He looked at me thoughtfully for a minute. "Well, divide and conquer, right?" he said. "You have so many here who would do anything for you. Let them help."

I never was good at asking for help. I was independent to a fault, but he was right; I didn't have to do everything on my own. I had a pack.

"But . . ." he said.

"Hmmm?"

"I go where you go."

"Always," I said.

He lightly kissed my cheek and held me a moment longer. Finally we stood and walked back through the long and forgotten halls into the throne room. Everyone watched me. I once was nervous with so many eyes upon me, but I was growing accustomed to it.

"I have made my decision," I said. "Father?"

"Yes, Ashling," he said, studying me with his hard eyes.

"I am charging you and Mund with the safety of Mother, Tegan, Nia, Fridrik, and Mother Rhea. You shall return to the Rock to Flin and Felan and protect Carrowmore," I said. "It is of the utmost importance that the sacred stones of Carrowmore are protected for the claiming."

He nodded.

Out of the corner of my eye, I saw Mund pacing. He hated my idea. I could smell it on him. But Mund was the one person I trusted to protect my family. I ignored his movements and continued.

"Dagny, you will resume your post in Norway; however, on your journey home, you will gather warriors to join my fight in the Blood-realms. Wait there for me at the Seven Sisters Waterfall, where our war will begin."

"My lady," he said with a bow. "An army you shall have."

"Grey, Brychan, Dilara, and I will journey to Maine. Rhonda, Jamal, and Paul will join us as well. We will protect the humans there while I seek answers for finding the Mother and the Crone," I said.

"Willem, Khepri, Kane, and Shikoba, you will go to Canada and seek Lady Faye. I believe she may be part of the prophecy. You will find her in the Netherworlds and bring her to me in Maine," I said.

"Quinn, I need you, Gwyn, Channing, and Cara to go to the ancient Library of Celsus in Ephesus. In the underground catacombs,

research translations, meanings, and legends of the Triple Goddess, especially the Crone and the Mother. We need to know who they are if
the prophecy is to be fulfilled, and we have less than a year to find out
who they are and get them to Carrowmore."

They all nodded and accepted their charges. My missions would
be daunting, and I was thankful for everyone in my pack. There was no
way I could find the remaining pieces of the Triple Goddess, protect
humans, build an army, save Baran, and defeat Vigdis and Verci by
myself. All of this was possible because my pack believed in me.

"Ashling, it is my job to protect you," Mund protested.

"Mund, you have always been my knight, but now you must protect us all," I said. "And I must return to Maine. Verci and Vigdis must
not realize that I am searching for the Triple Goddess, so it is imper-
ative that I am known to be elsewhere. Further, by calling Maine my
home, I have caused the town of York Harbor to be in great danger. If
we don't return to protect the town, we leave those people at great risk."

My mind flickered to all my human friends. Beth, Emma, Lacey
. . . I couldn't imagine losing a single one. I knew Vigdis would likely
target them to hurt me, regardless if I went to Maine or not. I had to
protect them. I had to be there when Vigdis unleashed her evil.

"Ashling?" Mund said, interrupting my thoughts. "Don't do this."

I looked to Nia and Fridrik. Their sweet, innocent faces solidi-
fied my decision. They were our future. "War is no place for babes," I
said. "And I trust you to protect them more than I trust anyone in the
world."

I looked at my sweet mother and all the grace and love that flowed
from her. The thought of never seeing her beautiful face again made
my stomach knot and churn with desperation. The thought of never
hearing her voice again was more than I could bear.

Mother rushed over and hugged me tight. "Come back to me, my
daughter, for if you die, I die with you. My heart beats in your chest as
only a mother knows," she whispered in my ear. "I need you."

"I need you, too. I cannot have all of my treasures in one place," I said, hugging her back.

# 5
## *Broken*

*As everyone started* to break off and make their plans, Father pulled me aside. He grabbed my elbow as he would when I was a child and escorted me out of earshot of the others. I wanted to be annoyed with him, but the look on his face made me listen. His voice was raw and hushed.

"Ashling, you must change your mind and come with us to the Rock of Cashel. You will be safest there," he said.

I looked into his weathered face and saw only concern, no anger or hatred. It was strange yet comforting to see him so unguarded. "Father, I have made my decision."

"You are only a child yourself. War is no place for my daughter," he pleaded. I could hear the strain in his voice. He wanted to command me to do his bidding, despite the fact that it had never worked for him in the past.

"Father," I said, "I have never understood why you pushed me away, why you withheld your love from me, why you wouldn't brand me and claim me as your child. I hated you for it all, yet I yearned for your love and affection and approval. But now I'm nearly grown, and whether we like it or not, I am the Crimson Queen. I am the very center of this war. Verci and Vigdis will stop at nothing to claim my power as their own, and the only way for them to secure their power is to claim me and kill everyone I love. I cannot be removed from this war . . . it will follow me wherever I go until it is won."

His eyes welled with tears for a moment, but his tears disappeared so quickly I wasn't sure they had been there at all. "A son is a son until he comes of age; a daughter is a daughter all her life," he said.

I knew the phrase; it was a Gaelic phrase, one of protection and love. One only a father could utter.

"The safest place for Mother, Nia, and Mother Rhea is with you, but that is not the best choice for me. I have to draw the attention away from all of you while we search for the Triple Goddess. I have to appear as though I have accepted Baran's death and resumed my life. We need time. If I am the one to search for the Mother and the Crone, they will figure out what I'm up to. But if all my pack scatters to the wind, that may just give us the time and distraction we need," I said. "Father, you have to see that this is the only way. No army will ever follow me if I hide behind walls and ask them to die for me."

He cleared his throat and put his hand on my shoulder, the most comforting thing he'd ever done for me. "It is not the only way," he said. I was readying myself for an argument. "But I see it is the best way."

"Thank you, Father," I said. My heart ached. I wanted desperately to hug him, to hide in the safety of his arms, but I stood still.

"Ashling, you proved yourself in the Bloodrealms. You are fearless and you call to the Gods themselves. I believe in you," he said. Before we could sink into the moment any further, he stalked off. I smiled as I watched him go. Mother was right . . . in his way, he loved us all.

My pack began to organize themselves. It was impressive. They were all so strong and independent. I could feel all of their emotions, but it was Mother's that I noticed first. She was scared. I couldn't blame her—I was afraid, too. I would feel uneasy until they were safe at the Rock.

Every day that ticked by meant Baran spent one more day being tortured. I had no doubt Verci and Vigdis would keep him alive as a bargaining chip or a way to punish me—there was a common war strategy in that—but I also knew Baran and Verci had a history that ran deeper than getting revenge against me . . . and it was a bloody history. Verci raped Baran's sister, Brenna, a violent act that produced Baran's nephew, Willem. Verci slaughtered the rest of Baran's family. Vigdis tried to kill my mother, her own sister. They were pure evil. Wherever they kept Baran, I knew he couldn't escape alone. He needed us, and time was slipping through my fingers.

I walked over to Mother as she sat alone by the fire. "Mother, I love you," I said.

"*Tá grá agam duit*," she said. It meant "I love you." She gave a small smile, but the worry on her face was clear.

"I know you love Baran," I said. "I know your heart is torn. I see it on you."

She opened her mouth and closed it again. "I already lost him. I can't lose you, too," she said.

"You won't. I'm as pigheaded as Father, and you know that sort of stubbornness is hard to beat." I smiled, but my joke didn't soften her fear. "Mother, I will save Baran, and I will be the Crimson Queen. I will make you proud of me."

"I'm already proud of you, Ashling. I've been proud of you since the first time I saw your tiny face and your pretty red curls," she said.

I smiled. "I will survive this war."

"You'd better," she said, hugging me. "Because no mother should ever outlive her babies."

I felt her softly weeping as she clung to me. She smelled of summer . . . the smell of my memories. It made me miss my time on the cliffs by our home in Dunmanas Bay in Ireland, where she and I hid out for most of my life. I missed the simplicity of it, and I missed having her near always.

"Mother, I need you to look after Fridrik. Will you do that for me?" I asked.

I knew her answer would be yes. She was already so in love with that little boy. But if I gave her a task that she felt was important, it might ease her worry while we were apart.

"As though I were his grandmother, he will be spoiled and loved," she said.

Willem, Khepri, Kane, and Shikoba were the first ready to make their journey. They were headed to Canada to the Netherworlds to find Lady Faye. Before they left, I turned to face my entire pack. It was the last time we would likely be whole until the claiming.

"As we enter the darkness, may I be your star on a dark night," I said. "May hope fill your hearts, and may we destroy the evil who fights against us."

They cheered and I felt the room fill with energy and determination. I hoped it could last. They needed hope. Darkness loomed before us all.

Soon, Quinn, Gwyn, Channing, and Cara were ready to leave for Ephesus. Channing grabbed my hand and bowed before me. I still thought he looked like he could be James Bond with all his swagger and muscles. The idea almost made me laugh.

Channing kissed my hand and looked up at me. "If you decide you're bored of the little boy," he said, looking at Grey, "and want a man by your side, I'll be waiting."

Barf.

"Channing Kingery, did I not give you a task? Are you not supposed to devote your attention to research?" I said calmly.

He smiled, not even missing a beat. "Anything you wish," he said.

He was trouble. That much was for sure, but I couldn't tell if he was just kidding around or if he was truly as loyal as he attempted to show me. He was so over the top that it was impossible to know.

"My queen," Dagny said. I turned and he was kneeling before me, his blond hair draping in his eyes.

"Yes, Dagny?" I said.

"I will take my leave and build your army. When you are ready to fight, we will be behind you," he said.

I leaned down and kissed the top of his head. "And I will be ready to lead."

Finally it was time. I had to watch Mother Rhea, Mother, Father, Mund, Tegan, Nia, and Fridrik leave for Ireland. I'd dreaded this moment. I wasn't sure I was strong enough to watch them all go, but it was my duty and it was my choice.

"I love you," I said to them, looking at each of them. Trying to memorize their faces. "Protect each other; I need you all."

Mund hugged me so tight I thought I might burst. "I love you, Ash," he said. When he pulled away he shook Grey's hand. "And if you let anything happen to her I'll . . ."

"I know, you'll kill me a hundred different ways," Grey interrupted.

"You should be so lucky," Father said, his eyes cold and his threat very real.

"Yes, sir," Grey said.

Tegan darted toward me, wrapping her tiny self around me. "Be careful," she cried. "I don't like this, you know."

I laughed. "Neither do I," I said.

"*Tá mo chroí istigh ionat*," Mother said.

"And my heart is with you," I said.

Mother Rhea stood before me. "We look to you to save us all," she said. "It is time for you to come into your power as the Crimson Queen. All you have to do is look inside yourself."

I nodded.

"And you, dear boy, best behave yourself," Mother Rhea said to Grey. He blushed so deeply, and I giggled at his expense.

"Brychan," Father whispered, not knowing I could hear him, "if those Bloodsuckers give you any doubt, kill them."

"I will keep her safe," he said.

I glared at them.

"Dilara, it is your duty to keep Grey and Brychan away from my daughter's virtue," Father said.

I couldn't believe it. He was actually talking about my virginity in public. In front of Grey, who had already taken my "virtue"—as though it meant my value had been squandered. It was ridiculous. I nearly died of embarrassment.

Dilara bowed to Father. As soon as they were gone, she leaned over to whisper in my ear. "Your virtue is up to you. I protect your life, you protect your heart."

"Agreed," I said with a smile. I liked her attitude. When she stood next to me, sometimes her height made me feel like a child again. Everything about her spoke volumes of her being a warrior, but when she smiled, her face brightened and she was endlessly beautiful. I envied her.

"What now?" Rhonda asked.

"We travel home to Maine," I said. "It is time to protect our humans."

# 6
## *Haunted*

*Time passed quickly* with my pack shattered apart. It took us more than a week to travel home from Greece, making sure we weren't being followed. I had peace knowing that many of my loved ones were safe at the Rock in Ireland, with its tall walls and underground fortress. They were all safer far away from me. And frankly, after the battles in the Bloodrealms, it was nice to have the quiet presence of Grey, Brychan, and Dilara. It was calmer. When we landed in Maine, we rented a car, and the four of us drove to Baran's house in silence.

Rhonda, Jamal, and Paul decided to take up their post in Grey's old house in the woods, which meant they would be at the former home of a Bloodsucker in case any more came to town. If they could convince other Bloodsuckers to join our pack, we would be stronger for it. Living in Grey's old home would also give them some privacy as they acclimated to York Harbor. It was a sweet little town, but it took a little getting used to for outsiders. I still remembered when I was new to town and I met Grey and Beth and all my human friends. I cherished all of them and this place, but it was hard to get used to, and I often missed Ireland. But America was my home now.

We'd listened to the news reports from around the world of the massacre at Mycenae. The authorities had labeled the attack as rabid wolves. With every day that passed, a new devastating story surfaced somewhere around the globe. They called it a wolf epidemic. Was Vigdis trying to find the Triple Goddess? Did she mean to strike fear into us, or was she trying to make it harder and harder for us to hide as the humans began to fear common wolves?

Grey and I had to go back to school on Monday. We only had a few more days of freedom before we joined our classmates for our senior year of high school . . . a few weeks behind schedule. Somehow, the thought of returning to high school seemed as bleak as returning to the Bloodrealms. I knew that was silly, but I didn't exactly love school. It felt like a waste of time, but we had to keep up appearances and protect our friends.

When we arrived at Baran's house, I stood staring at his front door, unable to open it. It looked too big, too daunting, and too empty. There wasn't anything on the other side of that door that I truly wanted-ed. Baran was lost somewhere in the dark depths of the Bloodrealms at the mercy of Verci and Vigdis, and this was just an empty shell of my memories.

As I stepped inside, the house smelled of dust mingled with Baran's musky scent. It seemed like yesterday when we were all together here. I missed the gravelly sound of his voice and the way his long, silvery hair shone in the light. I missed our banter and watching him practically fly on his motorcycle. He saved me so many times, and he loved me when my own father couldn't. I'd never forget that. I thought of when I first saw him in the shadows at the Rock of Cashel and he stole me away. I was certain he was going to end my life. He was a dark stranger, but he was really my savior. I remember the ferry he crashed his motorcycle into to keep Adomnan from getting me, and all his ridiculous warnings to stay away from Grey. I smiled at that.

Baran fought Bloodsuckers and protected me time and time again from Adomnan. He came after me through Canada and Iceland, crossing the earth for me. He chose me over my father to protect my choice in Grey. He trained Grey to fight to earn my hand in the Bloodrealms, and he fought alongside us all to save me. He gave Grey the diamond that Grey used to make the ring to offer in claiming me. I missed Baran so much my heart ached. When I tried to imagine the ways he was being tortured in the Bloodrealms, I felt sick.

I wandered the halls of his house, not knowing where I was going, but I found myself sitting in his office staring at his abundance of books. Several lay open just how he'd left them, covering the surface of the desk. I laid my head down on a stack of open books, smelling the mix of their musty pages and Baran's earthy scent, and cried myself to sleep.

*I stood at the edge of the gold mines, looking at the treasure of the Bloodrealms. It all looked the same as the day Grey and I had been there. When I had punched Vigdis's apparition in the face. I smiled at the memory, but why was I here?*

*"Makes you envious, doesn't it?" Verci hissed.*

*I jumped at the sound of his voice and turned to see Verci holding his silver sickle sword at Baran's throat. Neither he nor Baran were looking at me—it was as though they didn't know I was there. Baran was covered in blood, and his armor was destroyed.*

*"All the wealth of the Dvergar. And if you look closely, that small pile way over there, coated in old blood, that's the Killian treasure," Verci said. "That is the blood of your pack and a symbol of how far you have fallen."*

*"Screw you," Baran said through gritted teeth.*

*Verci slowly scrapped the tip of the blade across Baran's cheek, and a bead of blood dripped down. I knew the pain of silver, I knew it too well, but Baran only breathed harder. He didn't give in to it. I had to stop this—I had to save Baran.*

*I knelt and picked up a small stone and threw it at a stack of gold gob-*

lets. *The ringing sound vibrated through the enormous chamber as the cups toppled over. Both Baran and Verci turned to look at the falling goblets, but neither seemed aware of how they fell. I picked up a gold coin and held it in my hand.*

"*I'll get the answers I want from you, Killian, one piece of flesh at a time,*" *Verci hissed.*

*I started to step toward Baran . . .*

Suddenly, I awoke to being shaken.

"What, what?" I gasped.

"Ashling, are you all right?" Grey said.

My eyes focused on Grey's face. I glanced around Baran's office to see Dilara and Brychan, both as worried as Grey.

"What's going on? What happened?" I said.

"I could feel your fear and I came out to check on you," Grey said, glancing at Brychan. "You were so still, as though you were dead. When I tried to wake you, it took minutes before you came out of it. Like you were possessed or in a trance or something."

"I wasn't breathing?" I asked.

"It looked like you were holding your breath," Dilara said. "I've never seen anything like it."

Brychan stood back, arms crossed over his chest. "Brychan?" I asked.

"You didn't wake up, Ashling. He shook you hard, and you didn't wake."

"I don't know what happened," I said. "I was dreaming about Baran."

As I tried to sit up, I realized something was in my hand. I opened my fingers and stared at the gold coin from the dream. I dropped it from my hand and it hit the floor with a thud.

"What is that?" Dilara said, but I knew she recognized it.

"How is that possible?" I said. "I picked that up in my dream."

I looked down at the coin again; it was about an inch and a half, solid gold, and pressed with Uaid Dvergar's face. I'd heard of these coins, but no one had seen them for hundreds of years . . . until Grey and I saw them in the Bloodrealms. How did it come through a dream?

"What happened in your dream?" Grey asked.

I stared at my shaking hands, unable to look away. "I was in the treasure room—the one we rode through, remember? Baran was there, and Verci cut him with his silver sword. So I threw a stone to cause a diversion. Just before I woke up, I picked this up. I was going to throw it to distract Verci so I could attack him," I said.

"It was just a dream," Brychan said.

"But it wasn't, Brychan—it felt real."

"It was probably one of your visions of the future," Dilara said. "So it is something that could come to pass."

Grey picked up the coin, holding it in his hands. "It wasn't just a dream. Somehow, you brought a piece of it back with you."

I looked down at the books I had been sleeping on. A patch of drool was spread over the notes. I wiped it away and the wetness spread over the page. As I did, a different message was underneath. Only parts of the letters showed in the streaky saliva, but something had been covered up. I shoved the other books onto the floor, crashing things all around me, but I didn't care. I started spitting all over the page.

"What are you doing?" Dilara said.

I spit again and started smearing it over the page, soaking it into the paper.

"Gross." Brychan cringed.

I ignored him and kept spitting and wiping. As I did, the words fully appeared. The others drew near.

"What is that?" Grey asked.

"I don't know yet," I said, "but this page was left open in Baran's book, and there's a hidden message underneath the words. It has to mean something."

When I had wiped away as much as I could, I began to read. Grey came behind me to read along.

*Ashling, if you are reading this, I have perished. I am sorry I couldn't stay by your side, but if you are safe, then I have done my duty. You are the daughter I never had, the pride in my heart, and I love you.*

My eyes welled with tears as I read Baran's words.

I sobbed, unable to continue reading. I wrapped my arms around myself as Grey stood behind me, holding me together. I thought I might fall apart. Baran had known . . . he had always known he'd die for me.

Dilara took the book and began to read aloud. "*It is time for you stop playing their games. Don't let them claim you.* But . . . don't you have to be claimed for the prophecy to come true?" she said.

I stared at her in bewilderment as I wiped my tears away and tried to focus on the words on the page, but they'd already begun to fade. Dilara spit on the page, but nothing happened. He'd made the message just for me. I had no idea how he managed to hide the message so only I could read it. I felt a sad smile creep onto my face. I was deeply touched—even in death, he would still try to protect me. I wiped my tear-stained hands across the book, and the last words reappeared.

*Don't let them claim you.*

"What does that mean?" Brychan said.

I blanched. "I have no idea," I said. He couldn't possibly mean I should turn my back on the prophecy? On my family, on my pack, or on the world? Was he afraid that Brychan or Channing would still try to claim me? Or a thousand times worse, Vigdis and Verci?

"He doesn't want me to claim you?" Grey said. I could hear the hurt in his voice and feel it in my heart as though it were my pain.

"He can't mean that," Dilara said. "Maybe it's a trick and someone else wrote that."

I studied the handwriting. "No, it is his handwriting, but what does he mean? Does he not want me to go to Carrowmore? Or does he not want . . . " I paused, looking to Grey. "Does he not want anyone to claim me, even you?" I shook my head.

Did he want me to push Grey away? Didn't he know how much I loved him? Was this all just a game? I didn't know what to think, but between Baran's message, the dream, and that evil coin, I knew something bad was happening.

"This is only going to get worse," I said. "Much worse."

# 7

## *One Love*

*"I need time* to think," I said. I hung on to Grey's hand. I needed him. "Brychan, Dilara, would you mind?"

Brychan closed the door behind Dilara and himself. I turned away and set the coin on the desk and closed my eyes. "What am I?" I said to Grey, to myself. "How is it possible for me to bring objects through dreams while I lay nearly dead in this world?" I turned and wrapped my fingers with Grey's and let his soul soothe my worry. Letting his love in was like opening the curtains and letting in sunlight.

"I don't know . . . it's terrifying and amazing. Do you think dream traveling is a gift many other wolves have?" he asked.

"If there are other wolves who do this, I have never heard of any."

"If you brought that coin back, it wasn't just a dream of the future; that was the present," Grey said. "You may have truly seen Baran in the Realms."

"I left him there," I whispered

"Maybe this is what Mother Rhea was talking about; maybe this is how you look inside yourself to save Baran," he said. "If you found him once, maybe you can do it again."

"I hope you're right," I said.

"We can figure out anything together," he said. "We are one."

I smiled. "One love."

He was quiet for a moment. "I'm sorry if I hurt you when I shook you awake," Grey said. "I just had to make you open your eyes. I could feel your fear and rage, but your body didn't move. I thought if I couldn't get you to open your eyes, I might lose you forever."

"Oh, my love," I said, wrapping my arms around his neck, pulling him close.

I ran my fingers through his messy brown hair and breathed in his scent. I wanted my touch to fix him, to save him from his fear and pain. I wanted to be his sunlight as he was mine. He buried his face in my neck, and with each breath he took my skin tingled. I wanted him. He ran his fingers over my neck and collarbone, caressing me. Just a simple touch, but my body screamed for more. The warmth and roughness of his skin against mine took my breath away.

Grey picked me up, wrapping my legs around his torso as he pushed my body into the wall of Baran's office. He ground his body into mine as he layered kisses down my chest.

"I missed the way you taste," he said.

His hands were rough and urgent as he touched all of me. His touch was my salvation, drawing me into his love, filling me with need. I writhed in his arms, wishing we could join our bodies, right then and there.

"Baby, I want you," he whispered.

"I want you, too," I moaned. "So badly."

I sucked on his earlobe, making him groan and his heartbeat race. He rested his forehead against mine with our bodies still pressed into the wall. "Oh, my wife, you have me all worked up." His mischievous smile consumed his handsome face.

"I love the sound of that," I said.

He laughed. "You love that I'm wanting you?"

"Well of course I love that you want me, need me, desire me, but I meant the sound of the word *wife* on your lips," I said. "That will always make me smile."

He put his hands on my cheeks and guided my face to his lips. His tongue met mine as his hands crept down, caressing my body, making me moan with pleasure. He pulled away and watched me with his green eyes.

"You, Ashling Killian, are my wife, and I am your husband, and we are in love," he said.

I nearly giggled hearing his wolf surname with my name. He had chosen Killian. He was no longer a Donavan in his heart—he was a Killian, and so was I. All I needed was his Bloodmark on my wrist, and we'd be one forever.

"Are you sure you don't want to be Grey and Ashling Boru?" I smiled, challenging the tradition.

His hands roamed over my body, filling me with warmth. "I will take any name as long as you're mine." He smiled.

"If you keep touching me like that, we're going to make love right here," I panted. "You'll have your hands full, sir."

"Mmmmm. Well, I like the sound of that."

I slowly unwrapped my legs and slid my body to standing. He was still pressed so close I could feel his rock-hard body. I wanted him, but I shook my head.

"Not here."

I had to smile—he looked pained. "Soon?" he half-begged.

I was desperate for his touch, too—I knew exactly how he felt. "I hope so," I said. "Now come on. We better get back before we are noticed." I started pulling him toward the door to the hallway, but he didn't budge. I turned back, searching his face.

"Sorry, love. I need a minute." He smiled, pulling me gently back into his arms and simply holding me.

Just a hug. Something so simple as that and yet it meant every-thing. It was sweet, private, and sensual. Just thinking like that made me tingly all over again. He sighed as he lightly rubbed my back.

"Do you think they've found Lady Faye yet?" he said.

It took me a moment to direct my thoughts to something other than him.

"I hope so," I said. "But I still don't know who the Mother and the Crone are or whether Lady Faye is one of them or will even help us. Or how to bloody save Baran."

"I guess we just have to wait to hear from them and what the oth-ers can find at the Library of Ephesus. That will give us better clues, right?" he said. "It's like a game."

I could feel the color draining from my face as I stared at him. "It is not a game." I started walking away, but he caught up in the hallway.

"I know," he said. "I was just trying to lighten the load. I'm sorry."

Grey's eyes glistened with tears, but none fell. I knew he missed Baran as much as I did. I could feel his regret and fear. Baran was his uncle, his blood.

"I'm sorry, Grey. I know you miss him, too. I just want to save him," I said. "I need to."

"*We* need to," he said.

Brychan rounded the corner and saw us. "Oh, stop being so gooey. It will ruin both of your reputations."

His tone was jovial. But I could feel his tension. I knew he'd given me up, but emotions didn't just stop. They so often flowed on long after we wished they would. That's how I felt with Father. I wanted to stop wishing he'd show me his love, but I couldn't stop. I assumed this was a similar pain. Brychan had planned for years to marry me, and now his future was uncertain. Brychan was patient, respectful, caring, and strong . . . he had so many things one desired in a partner. But just as he couldn't make himself stop loving me, I couldn't make myself fall in love with him. He deserved love. It just wasn't mine to give him.

Grey had my heart, mind, body, and soul. All I could offer Brychan was my friendship.

I still felt guilty for kissing Brychan in Wales. I knew all along that I loved Grey, but there was something about Brychan that drew me in. Maybe in another life we were meant to be, just not in this one. I had hurt both of them as well as myself. Maybe it was rebellion or fear. I still didn't know, but I hoped one day I could forgive myself; thankfully, they had both forgiven me. I should have had more honor, but life was full of mistakes. Maybe I was to be one of Brychan's scars.

Brychan had so many scars. He was born a fighter and spent nearly every day of his life training and fighting. He'd been a leader in nearly every war since he was old enough to fight. He was a grown man, and in truth, Grey and I were still children. We weren't even eighteen yet. Neither of us had seen war like Brychan had . . . but we were about to.

"Brychan," Grey said.

Brychan paused and looked at Grey. The odd tension between them always made me uncomfortable. I was terrified they'd fight and I'd lose everything.

"Thank you for being here with us," Grey said.

Brychan nodded and walked away.

"Grey, I feel bad for hurting him," I said.

"Me too," Grey said. "But I can't give you up. I'd die."

The idea of not being with Grey made me sick to my stomach. Knowing that a love this deep could be mine and I was choosing to live without it seemed like a disgusting waste. Love was many things, but none of them could be ignored.

We walked into the kitchen, where Dilara sat at the table. Her posture was impeccable. She glanced up at us as we entered.

"Some kid named Ryan called," she said. "He said practice is at seven." She studied us for a while, mulling something over in her mind. "What kind of practice do you do with humans?"

I laughed. "They have a band."

"I'd like to see that." She smiled, sitting back and crossing her arms to watch Grey. I wasn't sure what she thought of him yet. She seemed suspicious. I suppose that was fair; he was half Bloodsucker, and his father had been particularly dedicated to his lineage.

"Fun!" I said. "You and Brychan can both come."

"Where am I going?" Brychan asked.

"To garage band practice at Ryan's house," I said.

He looked to Dilara. "Really, you want to watch that?"

Dilara smiled her most brilliant smile. "And why wouldn't you, Lord Brychan? Are you intimidated?"

His eyes narrowed, but before he could respond, Grey said, "If you behave, I'll give you each your own tambourine."

The thought of it was so absurd that even Brychan chuckled. "Yeah, fine. We'll go watch kids playing instruments in a garage, but after dark, I'm hunting."

Just the word made my skin tingle with excitement. I needed to eat. "All of us?" I asked eagerly.

He smiled at me. "All of us."

# 8
## *Freedom*

*I couldn't wait* to hunt. It made me want to skip band practice and run free. I always found my calm and Old Mother's love when I was in nature. I craved the feeling of it; being on my four feet felt like peaceful solitude and infinite connection all at once.

But I missed my friends, too. I wanted to hear all about what they'd been up to and how the school was, even what new crazy rumor was going about Grey and me since we missed the first few weeks of school. There was a chaotic simplicity to human life that I found so intriguing. Their lives were complicated by choice; they almost seemed to need the drama. Admittedly, I missed it all.

I called Beth, Emma, and Lacey to make sure they were all going to be there. I missed those girls so much. Beth and Emma helped me when Grey broke up with me, and Lacey and I had grown to be friends after Brychan and I saved her from her ex-boyfriend. I was eager to see them.

"Let's go!" I said.

"It's only six forty-five, and the band practice is right across the street," Brychan said. "What is the rush?"

"They're my friends! Now hurry up!"

Dilara and Brychan shared a look. I was sure it was one of either confusion or annoyance for my excitement, but I didn't care. Grey slung his guitar around his back and took my hand as we walked out the door.

We walked into the garage to see Eric and Ryan setting up. It was like the first night I met them all. They were all the same—older, but the same. There was a comfort in that. I remembered being so scared of them then and how rottenly jealous Lacey was of me. I loved to think how far we'd all come and how close we'd grown. I had always liked humans, but these were my first friends.

"Ashling!" Emma yelled as she ran over. Beth and Lacey were right on her heels. I smiled so big I thought my face might crack. I grabbed them all in a big hug.

"I love you girls," I said.

"We missed you," Beth said.

"I missed you all, too."

Emma stared past me, and I turned to look behind me to where Dilara and Brychan stood. Even though I'd convinced Dilara to wear casual clothes, she still looked like a runway model with her smooth, pitch-black skin, beautiful almond-shaped eyes, and long limbs. She was strikingly glamorous.

"Everyone, you remember Brychan, and this is Dilara. She's . . ." I paused, trying to define her, but there was no label that even remotely fit. Warrior, goddess, queen, friend, guardian, and protector all felt too small for Dilara.

Dilara interrupted my thoughts. "I'm a family friend here to keep an eye on Ashling and Grey while Baran is traveling for business," she said.

Emma just stared. "You're beautiful," she whispered.

"So are you," Dilara said.

Emma looked at her feet. I could smell her emotions, doubt or fear maybe, but I wasn't sure why. Dilara, Brychan, and Grey could smell it too; it was potent. Dilara walked closer to Emma and me.

"What's your name, child?" Dilara asked.

"Emma."

"Never ever doubt yourself, because if you let even the tiniest bit of doubt in, you invite everyone else to doubt you, too."

"Thank you," Emma said quietly.

"What? Didn't anyone miss me?" Grey asked as he leaned against the side of the garage door looking like the bad boy I had fallen in love with. Though I knew his sweetness.

Snorts and laughs broke out around the garage as we mingled in with the rest of our friends. Grey and Ryan started chatting and tuning their guitars while Eric warmed up on his drums. It was a racket. I glanced at Brychan, and he looked utterly out of place. What was I going to do with him?

Dilara poked him in the side. "Lighten up," I heard her say.

He crossed his muscular arms over his chest. I had to laugh—he looked so disapproving. She rolled her eyes but leaned against the wall next to him. They both had tragic pasts. Maybe that would be their bond of friendship, I hoped. As soon as the thought crossed my mind, Brychan walked away and sat out on the curb.

"Where were you this time?" Beth asked.

I turned back to my friends, smiling at their eager faces. "Norway and Greece," I said. "Saw my grandmother."

"Oh, it must be so dreamy in Greece," Emma said.

"It was more frightening than I expected," I said.

"Oh I heard about the rabies outbreak in Greece," Emma said.

"Yeah . . ." I replied. "It's nice to be home."

"Where's Channing?" Lacey asked.

I wondered if she was still crushing on him. "Channing and his little sister, Cara, are on a trip with Quinn and Gwyn."

"I'd like to go on a trip with him," Lacey sighed.

"I bet you would," Beth teased.

It was nice hearing them all laugh and knowing they were looking out for each other. A year ago these three weren't friends. From what I had come to understand about high school, their friendship was a pretty amazing feat—to get three girls of different social hierarchies to bridge the gap and be friends was amazing. I was proud of them. I could feel lifelong friendships forming right in front of my eyes. I hoped they'd keep me, too, but I knew one day I'd have to leave them. I would stop aging, and eventually it would be noticed. I would have to watch them all from afar. That was the curse of immortality. One day, far sooner than it seemed, I would have to let them all go.

My heart felt heavy, and suddenly Grey's voice pierced the night sky and filled me with desire. He started to sing an entrancing love song I'd never heard before. When I met his eyes, I knew the lyrics were about us making love in the water.

I blushed instantly and looked away only to catch Dilara's eyes. They gave none of her secrets away, but she watched me and seemed to know all of mine. Somehow, I knew she knew the truth of Grey and me. Had Brychan broken my confidence and told her? Or had she figured it all out on her own? I avoided her stare for the rest of the night, preferring instead to chat with my friends and catch Grey's eyes when I could. I knew Dilara would have questions for me eventually, and I'd have to answer for myself, but for now I just wanted to savor this moment with my friends.

Eventually, the band stopped and everyone started going home. Watching them all filter out in the crisp fall air made me yearn to run. The excitement of hunting started to pulse in my veins. It was time.

"Let's all meet at the beach tomorrow," Ryan said. "One last dip before the cold weather settles in."

"Hell yes," Grey said, smiling at me.

Damn, I loved his smile. It made me melt every time. The thought of swimming with him again made me remember the last time we swam together, alone in a waterfall, when we'd made love for the first time . . . and the second time. I shivered.

"What time?" Beth asked.

"How about three?" Eric said.

Everyone seemed to agree. I was excited, and I could feel Grey's excitement. It was our last day before school started on Monday. We deserved a little freedom.

"Good night, everyone," I said.

"Later," Grey called as we walked back to Baran's house. I was too eager to go hunting to chitchat any longer. I wanted to hunt. I wanted flesh. I wanted my true body, my four feet and connection to Old Mother. I wanted it all, and I wanted it with Grey.

"You're not bad," Brychan said to Grey.

Grey half-smiled. "I'll take that as a compliment."

"Best one you'll get from him," Dilara said.

Brychan stomped off ahead of us. He was definitely struggling with something. Was it my rejection of him and my obvious love of Grey? Or was it something else?

"Don't mind him," Dilara said. "He's just being stodgy."

"Is he okay?" I asked.

"Just let him run and he'll be fine," she said. "Warriors have a hard time conforming to human life."

"Why aren't you upset then?" I asked.

"Because I'm better at hiding it," she said. "Now put your crap in the house and let's hunt, because I need blood, and you don't want me to get moody like him."

When she smiled, the moonlight glinted off her perfect white teeth. She threw some stuff on the table and walked out the back door after Brychan. Grey set down his guitar, and we walked out on the back porch. There were clothes strewn everywhere, and I could see their wolf silhouettes in the moonlight.

I licked my lips and began to strip, and Grey matched me shirt for shirt, pants for pants until we were naked. I took in the sight of his golden skin. As the moonlight basked over his naked body, I burned with delight. I wanted him.

"Damn, you're sexy," he said.

I smiled, loving the way I felt with his eyes on my body, and I jumped into the air as I shifted into a wolf. He landed as a dire wolf next to me and nuzzled his nose into my red fur. It was so simple, primal, and perfect.

My blood pumped with Old Mother's love, and my paws touched the soft earth, bringing me closer to her. In less than a year, I would be claimed at Carrowmore in her name.

Brychan howled, calling us to them. We began to run. Old Mother's energy pulsed through me each time one of my four feet hit the ground. Electricity flowed through my paws with every step. The moon and the cool ocean breeze filled me with memories.

I watched Grey running beside me. He was enormous, even larger than Brychan, but the strength and precision of his movements was incredible. The Killians were dire wolves, much larger wolves than the rest of us. I wanted to watch every muscle in his body flex and move, but I'd likely run right into a tree.

We followed Dilara and Brychan deep into the woods. The smell of the wet earth floated around us like a dream, and all my memories of running through these same trees with Grey felt so far away. The forest felt different now. So many things had changed here. The Bloodsucker cages were gone; no more wolves were being captured. Still, a chill settled over me as I neared the waterfall.

I should have died here. Grey's father had lured me here to kill me, eat my heart, drink my blood, and keep my skull as a trophy. His son's girlfriend. It was so twisted and repulsive. If it weren't for Adomnan, my other tormenter, Robert Donavan would have succeeded. I'd be nothing more than a skull in his home.

There was still a piece of me that hated myself for Adomnan's attack on me. I didn't fully understand the guilt. It didn't make sense. There was nothing about what he did that I had caused. He violently beat me and tried to rape me. Those were his crimes, not mine. And yet I felt gross about it, like I'd caused it or asked for it. But all those thoughts weren't mine. They were evil crawling through me. They were pieces of Adomnan's sickness that still held court in my mind. They were parts of him I had to learn to let go of, so I could live free.

I slowed to a walk as the others raced on after the scent of deer, but I had penance to pay here and memories to face. I heard Grey stop. I knew he was still with me.

The water surged down into the pond below, creating such chaos in otherwise still water. As I watched the water react and ripple away from the source, it strangely reminded me of the war in my own heart.

I shifted to a human at the water's edge, dipping my bare feet into the pond. Letting the cool night waters coat me in their innocence.

I would leave Adomnan behind now. I was done carrying the weight of his evil, his crimes, and even his death with me. He was no longer my weight to bear. I closed my eyes and walked into the water. I let the water envelop my body and soothe my skin. When at last my body was consumed by the waters up to my neck, I looked up at the moon.

"I am forever changed, but I am forever my own, and no evil can live inside my heart," I said as tears I didn't know I had yet to shed flowed down my cheeks. "I am innocent and I am loved. I belong to Old Mother, and her soul flows in my veins . . . so I am free."

Grey howled to the moon and joined his prayer with mine.

I smiled at him and let my head slip into the blue water, cleansing myself of all evil. Every drop of blessed, cool water offered a chance to be free. I felt lighter than ever before. As I held my breath, I felt Old Mother's love. I was one of her children; she would always care for me; she could wash away this sadness and pain.

I swam up to the surface of the water, and I breathed in the beautiful night air as though I'd never breathed before. I saw three wolves—Grey, Brychan, and Dilara—standing at the edge of the pond. They howled and a peace settled over me. I was finally free of Adomnan. He couldn't hurt me anymore; I wasn't going to give him that power over me. I was free to live.

I leaped out of the pond, landing as a wolf once again. The water dripped from my red fur. I looked at each of them and knew how lucky I was to have them in my life . . . how lucky I was to have love and friendship.

A branch cracked and Brychan's ears perked. We were downwind from deer. My mouth watered at their scent. I tore after them with an insatiable hunger. I knew Grey, Brychan, and Dilara ran with me through the trees even though our footsteps were silent in the night.

We closed the distance as seven deer came into view. We startled them and they began to run. Brychan and Dilara each took one down in mere moments. Grey and I took one down as a team.

The taste of warm flesh made me primal as Grey and I bit into our prize. This doe was a gift from Old Mother Earth, and we honored her spirit and the spirit of the doe. All creatures were of her love, and every one of us was part of the circle of life. We each had something to give and something to receive. Today was her turn to give us sustenance.

One day, it would be my turn to sacrifice.

# 9

## *Ripped Apart*

*I lay on* the ground watching Grey finish off the deer we'd caught. My belly was full and my mind was content. I'd never seen Grey feed before; there was something intimate about us taking down our first kill together. Survival was intimacy.

With nothing but bones and small bits of meat left, Grey curled up next to me on the musty ground as Dilara and Brychan finished their meals and scrounged for other food. I nuzzled my nose under Grey's neck and let rest take me.

After several hours, voices roused me from my peaceful sleep. I recognized Brychan and Dilara's voices, so I stayed still and kept my eyes closed. Grey was still cuddled close to me; I couldn't tell from his breathing if he was awake or asleep, so I just listened.

"They are pretty cute together," Brychan said.

"If you believe in that sort of thing," Dilara said.

"What do you mean?"

"Love," she said.

"You don't believe in love?" Brychan said.

Dilara laughed and said, "It didn't work out that well for you, did it?"

Brychan grunted. "Well, whether you choose to believe in love or not, you cannot deny that love emanates from her. That everyone that comes near her feels it pouring out of her. Human, wolf, Bloodsucker—all are drawn to her."

"And she gives her love to that boy."

I could feel Grey's anger flow into me. He was awake and listening.

"And he gives it right back to her," Brychan said. "They are quiet, and if you aren't paying attention you'll miss it, but they are one being. One love."

"Love is a dangerous thing for her right now. He can become a weapon against her," Dilara said. "I'd separate them."

Brychan laughed so hard the ground vibrated around me. "Good luck with that," he said. "Besides, she is our queen. We follow her rule."

"Well, it's our job to make sure neither of them die," she said. "Part of me wants to lock them away until her eighteenth birthday, but when I look at her, I know that she's a fighter like me, and I know she needs to be seen by her people if they are to follow her."

"Do you think Baran is dead?" Brychan said.

My anxiety boiled to the surface and fear filled me. If she thought he was dead, I wouldn't give up. I'd still go after his body. He would have peace. I held my breath waiting for her answer.

"No. Bloodied and broken, yes, but they need him alive." She sighed. "I know all too well what that torment looks like. Truly, only she can save him now."

Silence settled over them. All I could hear were the sounds of Grey's breathing and an owl hooting off in the distance.

"What did they do to you down there?" he asked.

"Everything you can imagine," she said. "And far worse."

I didn't want to hear any more. I fake yawned and stretched, drawing attention to myself. Grey followed suit. I wondered if he knew I wasn't sleeping either. Brychan and Dilara shifted back into wolves, and we began to run for home in the breaking dawn. So many emotions filled my heart.

Brychan and Dilara let us pass them and run ahead. I knew they were close behind, but the separation felt good. I quickly shifted back into a human and pulled on my clothes.

"Come on," I said. "Let's get some more rest."

Grey wrapped his fingers with mine, and instantly my heart quieted. Our connection was spiritual and necessary.

I closed my bedroom door. "Lie with me?" I asked.

Grey smiled. It wasn't his usual mischievous smile; something darker was behind his eyes. He was worried, too. I could smell it on him. We lay down and he pulled the covers over us, and we wrapped our limbs together so tight that our entire bodies connected.

"I don't want you to go after Baran," Grey said. "I'm afraid I'll lose you. Let me go in your place."

"Grey . . ."

"I can't lose you, Ashling," he interrupted. "I won't."

"Grey Robert Killian, don't you dare push me aside like some little girl that needs saving. If we die, we die fighting, but we do it together. We are one," I said.

He sighed and kissed my forehead. "You're right," he said quietly. "Besides, I think Dilara is right, too. Only you can save Baran now."

"I hate that," I said. "It feels so lonely. What if I fail him?"

"I believe in you. I always have," he said, caressing my skin.

He lazily ran his fingers through my hair, playing with the curls. The silence was nice. Just being together. No plans or rules or prophecies, not even lust. Just being was nice.

"Do you still want to swim with everyone?" he asked.

"Yeah. I missed all of them."

"Me too," he said. "They are as much a part of our pack as the others."

"Whether we like it or not," I said with a laugh.

"Do you think we endanger them by being around them?"

"Yes." I sighed. "But I think they'd be in more danger if we didn't come back. We would be leaving something we love completely un-protected."

He nodded.

"I worry about them all. Whether the threat is Verci and Vigdis or my father's clan of Bloodsuckers, everyone we care about is in danger because of us," Grey said. His voice was raw with emotion. "I'm glad we picked the beach. Even though the waterfall has always been our place to jump, I don't think any of our friends would ever go back because they all know it was where my dad was killed. I think it scares them," he said. "And I hate it because you almost died there, too. There are too many memories for me—both good and bad," he said.

The pain raged through me, and I gasped at his inner struggle. "You don't have to feel guilty for missing him, Grey. He's still your dad."

He nodded again.

I propped myself up, looking into his green eyes. "Grey, I won't love you less for missing him."

"He killed my mother. He nearly killed you." He shook his head. "I will always hate him and love him equally, but I will never forgive him."

A single tear rolled down his cheek. I gently wiped it away.

"Grey, don't let your father's choices haunt you, or it will consume you. I know, because I nearly let Adomnan consume me. It is a choice, a damn hard one, but it is a choice. You have to let go of hate so Old Mother's love can fill you again."

"I don't know if I can. I should have protected you from my father and Adomnan. It was my job," he said.

I hadn't realized how much blame he put on himself, how much healing he had yet to do. We were both victims in this, not just me.

We both lost our innocence that day, and I finally understood what it cost him.

"Grey, I love you with every fiber of my being. You are in my thoughts always, and I am connected to Old Mother more deeply than I ever thought possible because of your love. You did everything to protect me. And I feel your love in everything you do. Please don't punish yourself for something I am so thankful for. I am thankful for you." My voice cracked. "I love you, Grey."

He crushed me into his chest. "I love you, too. I just wish I could have protected you from it all."

"My love, those were parts of my journey. I had to live through them to be who I am today. They changed me, they became part of me, and they will help me lead. They will help me win."

"Baby, I believe that." He smiled and nodded his head. "You will win."

A beautiful silence settled around us as we held each other. Our love felt deeper every day, every moment, and every conversation. Every hug and kiss and touch powered my soul. This was how love was meant to be, full and overwhelming and perfect.

"I want to invite Dilara and Brychan to the beach," I said as we were waking. The sun was shining brightly through the window. I could feel Grey chuckling as he reluctantly released me from his strong arms.

"The beach . . ." he laughed again. "Brychan at the beach?"

"Yep." I smiled. "I think he needs to learn to relax."

He kept laughing as we wandered down to the kitchen. Brychan and Dilara were sitting at the table, obviously in conversation.

"Do you guys want to come with us to the beach?" I asked Brychan and Dilara. Both looked skeptical.

"You want us to go swimming with a bunch of kids?" Brychan said. "We're wolves, not babysitters."

"What are you afraid of?" Dilara teased. "That they will have better abs than you?"

There was a strange tension between them. I looked from one to the other. It was possible they liked each other, but they were both too pigheaded to admit it. I mused at the idea. Maybe I could play matchmaker.

"Oh, stop being poops," I said. "You're both coming. We'll pick you up swimsuits at the store on the way. So let's go."

"Fine," Brychan muttered. "But I'm driving."

I chuckled as I ran upstairs to change. As I took off my clothes, I could hear Grey's breath catch and his pulse speed up. I turned, facing him in all my naked glory. My husband.

He breathed out slowly. "You better put some clothes on," he said.

"Or what?" I teased.

"This," he said, lightly running his fingers over my body. I shuddered at his touch, yearning for more.

"You win," I gasped. "I'll behave."

I watched him undress as I slipped on my teal bikini. His rock-hard body was a delicious temptation. I knew exactly what he meant. Just the sight of him made my body ache for him.

Grey took in the sight of me in my bikini and sighed. "This is going to be a long day if I have to restrain myself with you wearing that. I hope the water's cold."

"Me too," I said, kissing him on the earlobe. I was going to need that cool water to calm my desire.

We piled into Brychan's beat-up, old, military-style Humvee and drove to the beach with the wind in our faces. The warm sun and the smell of the ocean surrounded us. I spotted our friends all parked on the beach with a bonfire. They'd already made themselves at home.

We parked and jumped out onto the warm sand. "I should have brought s'mores for later," I said.

"Already got you covered!" Beth said.

"You're awesome."

"Let's get in the water!" Lacey said. "We didn't come all this way just to look at it."

I ran into the cool water with all my friends. We laughed and splashed each other. It was carefree being with them. Truly innocent. I wanted them to stay that way always, but after what happened to Lacey last summer, I knew some of her innocence was already gone.

I lay on the beach applying yet another layer of sunscreen when I spotted a police officer approaching us. I caught his scent on the wind and knew him instantly. It was that cop from when I'd saved the girls from getting assaulted after we shopped for formal dresses. As he got closer I recognized his face and blond hair. His name was Officer Gavin Thilges, and he had offered to take me to the hospital.

"Officer Gavin?" I asked.

"I've been looking for you, Ms. Boru," he said.

He stopped about ten feet away; his posture was rigid, and I could smell his fear. Was he afraid of me? I hadn't seen him since that day, and I'd thrown away his business card and really never thought of him again.

"Can I help you?" I asked.

"I am leading an investigation into some murders, and you have been found to be a common thread in all of them," he said, studying my body in my tiny teal bikini. I suddenly wished I were wearing more clothing for this conversation. "Let's go talk in private, Ms. Boru."

"She didn't do anything!" Beth said, jumping up. I looked at her and rolled my eyes as if to say, "Don't worry about it."

I followed Officer Gavin to the edge of the beach and the grass. "The suspects were all interrogated and said some pretty interesting things about you," he began.

"Okay, what does that mean?" I said.

"There is evidence leading me to you for the murder of Robert Donavan and the attack on James Pieks at the carnival on July ninth." I glanced over at Lacey, who was watching intently . . . they all were. I remembered how Brychan and I protected Lacey from James, or "Jimmy," when he attacked her for leaving with us. I could smell Lacey's fear. She was terrified. We both knew what happened at the carnival, and Lacey knew what I truly was. "There's also the unexplained disappearance of your guardian, Baran Killian. All of the witnesses and evidence lead me to you, Ms. Boru. Why do you think that is?"

He stared at me, waiting for me to crack, cry, or beg. "I'm sorry, Officer Gavin, but I don't know what you're talking about. Baran is traveling; he does that quite often. When he calls again, I'll mention to him that you're looking for him," I said. Officer Gavin didn't break his stare, so I continued. "We were all attacked the day you saved us, and thank goodness you came—I can't imagine what would have happened to us otherwise." I shook my head and sighed. "And it is horrible about Grey's dad; we are all still mourning his loss. I'm not sure what you're talking about at the carnival though . . . did something happen there?"

"Would you care to take a ride downtown with me to discuss this further?" he asked.

Dilara was suddenly at my side. "Do you have a warrant, officer? Are you interrogating a minor without a legal guardian or lawyer present?" He started to reply but Dilara talked over him. "I am Ashling's guardian while Mr. Killian is out of the country. She will not be going anywhere with you."

The firmness in her statement left no one to question her intent. She'd kill him before he took me. His hand unconsciously went to his gun as he studied her. Brychan and Grey walked over.

Officer Gavin looked back to me. "Ms. Boru, I know you are involved with these cases. I'm not sure how yet, but I will find out. You will answer my questions—maybe not today, but you can't escape this investigation," Gavin said. "I'll see to that."

"Don't be ridiculous," Beth said. "Ashling didn't hurt anyone!"

"And she was with us the day Grey's dad died," Lacey said. "I'll never forget that day." Tears came to her eyes.

The others all nodded. Did they even realize they were lying? They were protecting me. They were putting themselves in harm's way for me. It was so selfless I was speechless. If they all knew what I was, would they still protect me?

Brychan held his hand out and shook Officer Gavin's hand. "Officer Thilges, best of luck with your investigation, but I'm sorry to tell you that you've been highly misinformed. Baran Killian is visiting family in Norway on a hike to the pilgrimage of his faith. Dilara and I have all the legal paperwork as Ashling and Grey's guardians until Baran's return. If you have any further questions, they will go through us first," Brychan said.

Officer Gavin looked at them for a while. "It seems I have more investigating to do."

"I'm sorry you wasted your time with us, Officer Gavin," I said. "But I'm just one little girl. I'm not what you think I am."

If he only knew . . . he'd be terrified.

He nodded wearily and walked away.

When he was far out of earshot, I looked to my friends and studied all their faces. Each one innocent, each one of them my shield.

"Why did you do that?" I asked, sitting down in the sand next to Lacey, Emma, and Beth. Grey, Brychan, and Dilara followed and sat down with us. I looked to the water, where the rest of our friends still played.

Emma looked at Brychan and Dilara and back to me. Her voice was barely a whisper. "We know you aren't like us," she said.

"You're not a human," Beth said. "Are you?"

I was shocked. Beth and Emma didn't know what I was. Did Lacey tell them? I searched her face, but she shook her head, stunned.

"What do you think I am?"

Beth shrugged, "Our friend."

"A guardian angel," Emma said.

"It doesn't matter, you're ours," Lacey said. "We are a little band of misfits, but we look out for each other. That's what friends do."

I hugged them. Even when I thought secrets separated us, they saw me. They knew me.

"I love you all," I said.

Beth looked up at Grey, "Something is wrong with him, too."

"What, that I'm inhumanly strong?" he joked. He picked me up, running with me into the water while my friends laughed behind us.

"Hey! Hey! NO!" I shrieked, laughing.

Grey tossed me into the water with ease. As I surfaced, he was smiling so big I felt the need to seek revenge. I dove under the water and swam to his ankles and pulled them out from under him. He splashed into the water next to me, and I swam to him and kissed him while we were still submerged in the water. I kept my eyes open and watched him in that surreal moment. Loving him. There was something so sensual about kissing him underwater. We were pure and protected from the world around us.

"That was hot," Grey whispered, panting for breath as we surfaced.

I smiled at him as he pulled me tight against his wet body. My friends all watched us, and I could feel their love, even Lacey's. It was so good to see how she had grown . . . how we had all grown. I never thought I would be able to have my friends know the truth, or at least enough of the truth for me to feel truly accepted. It was a new feeling, and I could get used to it. I finally understood; I'd always thought our duty was to love them, but their love for us was equal to our love for them. I thought it was our duty to Old Mother, but it wasn't a duty at all. It was a choice. We all chose to love. When we did, love was unstoppable and immeasurably beautiful.

"They all love you," Grey said. "Why are you so surprised?"

"I have no idea. It was there all along; I just didn't see it."

He laughed. "Well, start seeing it. Wolves, humans, Bloodsuckers . . . we all follow you."

"Now if I can just find the Mother and the Crone to join me at

Carrowmore, I can claim my people," I said.

"Soon, my love. Soon," he said. "It's nice to at least pretend to have a carefree day, though, isn't it?"

The wind whipped around us, and a scent swirled in the salty air. It was so subtle I didn't catch it at first, but it was there. I looked at Grey with wide golden eyes, and my hair stood on end.

"Do you smell that?" I asked, suddenly alert.

# 10

## *Grey Storm*

*We raced home* as fast as we could, and the scent grew more potent with every mile we covered. I was eager and excited.

"Drive faster!" I said.

"I'm not getting pulled over when that cop is already on your tail," Brychan grumbled. "Now is a good time to work on your patience."

Before Brychan even had the car in park, I leaped out the door and was running into the house with Grey on my heels.

"Wait!" Brychan yelled.

"Ashling!" Dilara yelled.

I could hear the worry in their voices as they chased after me, but I couldn't stop. I had to know. I had to see with my own eyes. I ran through the house, but there was no one to be found. I smelled the air again. Was I mistaken? Frustration filled me.

"Ahhh," I growled.

Grey wrapped his fingers with mine. I looked up into his bright green eyes, and his worry flooded me. Did he think they were dead? Or had we imagined them? No, the scent was real enough. They were here . . . somewhere. I just had to find them, but why were they hiding?

I searched the house and they weren't inside. I opened the back door and Grey and I walked slowly around the house, followed by Brychan and Dilara. Terror inched me forward step by step. What if they were dead? What if other Bloodsuckers murdered them?

I swallowed down my nerves and turned to the side of the house. They stood below my bedroom window: Willem, Khepri, Kane, Shikoba, and the unmistakable Lady Faye. They were all sitting at the spot below the tree where I had held the little boy Adomnan killed.

I watched in wonder as Lady Faye swirled her hands over the ground as she chanted so quietly I could barely hear her. "Old Mother Earth, cleanse this place and these people, for their hearts still ache with every step they take. A loss of a child is the loss of hope. Give us the strength to return love and hope to your people." Her voice was so smooth.

A branch snapped under my foot, and she looked up at me with her black eyes. She was as startling as I remembered her in the Netherworld. Her hair and skin was almost pure white, lacking pigmentation, but her eyes were black as night, with no difference between her pupils and irises.

I could smell Grey's fear, and he stopped walking. He just stared at her. She was unnerving, but she was also beautiful. She stood and faced us.

"I hear you destroyed the cloak I made for you," she said.

I felt guilty and looked at my feet. "I used it to save people," I said.

She nodded. "Magic like that can't be replaced or manufactured. Use it wisely," she warned me.

"I did," I said. I felt a little bit stubborn but also right. "Every one of those people needed Old Mother's love, and every one of them deserved it."

Her expression didn't soften. She just studied Grey and me. Grey's grip on my hand was firm. He didn't want me any closer to her than we already were.

"As you showed Old Mother's love on Adomnan and Æsileif?" she asked.

She took my breath away. I felt as though I'd been kicked with her words. She was questioning my choice to kill. Did they truly deserve to die? Did I deserve to live? I thought of Adomnan's sinister smile as he touched my skin, as he tore off my clothes, and as he lashed my flesh. I thought of every horrible break of my bones, of the sweet girl he killed to prove a point to me, of every moment with him. I thought of Æsileif's trickery and her burning Dilara's flesh. The way Æsileif caressed me and wanted me to be her pet . . . it made me sick.

The sickness of my own memories crawled over my skin like a disease waiting to devour me. It made me want to question myself and my feelings and my worth, but most of all, it made me mad.

"Their deaths were mercy. They were given back to Old Mother and their souls are free, which is more than I can say for those they murdered. Did they deserve to die? That isn't my right to judge, Lady Faye. Only Old Mother can see such things. But I had a divine right to protect myself and my people, and I will not regret living," I said.

Anger rippled over me, washing away my doubt with every shiver. I'd lived through hell, and no one, not even Lady Faye, was going to make me feel guilty for choosing to fight.

She moved so fast that she was right in front of us in an instant. Grey put his body between her and me, and her black eyes fixed on him.

"And what of you, boy?" she said.

"You will not come any closer," he said pushing me farther behind him. "I love Ashling, and nothing you say or do will ever hurt us. Our love is infallible, and I would fight you to the death to protect her."

"I know all that, boy," she said. "But why do you love her?"

Grey looked startled. He looked at me for the first time since we'd spotted Lady Faye, taking his eyes off someone he viewed as a threat to look into my eyes. He searched my face, looking for his answer.

"You are my breath when I swear I can't breathe," he said. "My heart follows your every move, and I am a better man with you by my side. You're my best friend."

I leaned up and lightly kissed his delicious lips. The moment our lips touched, I felt my love pour into him and cycle back into me, but stronger. His love had joined my stream of love. Together, our current was so strong that it made me feel weak in the knees and invincible at the same time.

I looked back to Lady Faye and her face had softened. She wasn't smiling, but there was sweetness in her features.

"I have read of you and heard your tales. Long before you were born we knew you'd both come, and we knew if you found each other, your force would be unstoppable," she said. "But I had to know for sure."

"Know what?" Grey said cautiously.

"Why do you think the Killians were targeted so long ago by Verci? Do you think it was a coincidence? Happenstance that a creature as evil as he would stumble on Brenna Killian?"

"I don't understand," I said.

"You will," she said. "Only Mother Rhea and I know the truth of that fateful meeting, and it is more than you know."

"Would you like to come inside?" Brychan interrupted.

Lady Faye looked up at him for the first time, as though he'd just come. She nodded and followed him inside, and we filed in after her. We settled into Baran's living room. If only he were with us.

"He is alive," she said suddenly.

I stared at her in wonder. She knew. She knew everything, it seemed, even my thoughts. "Tell me what really happened to the Killians," I said.

Her expression was solemn and distant. "It is true that my sister Vigdis and Verci conspired to eliminate the Killians. It is true that Vigdis despises your mother above all creatures in the world, and Baran did break Vigdis's heart, but what you don't know is where jealousy breeds from." She pointed her long, pale finger at me, and I shuddered as I met her gaze. "Lady Calista foretold of you, my Crimson Queen, of your reign in a new order. None of us knew which of Mother Rhea's daughters would bear the child who would one day rule the earth and bring Calista's prophecy to life, but we knew it would be one of us— Althea, Calista, Vigdis, Nessa, or myself. The child was said to have hair as red as blood and skin as white as snow.

"When this knowledge spread through the royal packs, my sisters and I were auctioned off to the highest bidders. We were desirable mates, for one of our daughters would change the world, and that kind of power is known to breed evil in men. Power is intoxicating.

"Uaid Dvergar wanted Calista. He wanted to control her power of sight and the heir to be his, but she refused him. Not only because she loved Ragnall Boru, but also because she saw the evil that lurked inside him. He killed her for her insult to him. As you know, he died for his sin. Vigdis wanted the babe to be hers, so she fought to find a suitable husband; when Baran rejected her and fell in love with Nessa, Vigdis's heart grew dark with jealousy.

"Vigdis's jealousy tainted her soul, and she went as dark as one could go. She wanted you for herself, and she believed eliminating her sisters would mean you would be born to her. Vigdis murdered Althea on her wedding night, leaving only Nessa and me. She wanted to punish Baran and Nessa, so she wrapped Verci around her finger, twisting his soul darker and tighter to her until he obeyed her every whim.

"Verci carried out her desires and killed the Killians—all but Brenna and Baran. This is where the prophecy is also about you, Grey. There is more to the prophecy than the Crimson Queen—there is a Grey Storm by her side."

"What?" Grey said.

"We knew you would come for her," Lady Faye said.

"Grey," I whispered. "You were always meant to find me."

He leaned his forehead against mine and clung to me like a lifeline in the storms that raged around us.

Lady Faye continued, "He was foretold to be a dire wolf, born to protect, born to love her. Only the Killians are dire wolves, so only a son of Killian could fulfill the prophecy. Vigdis knew, so she wanted all the Killians exterminated, but what she didn't anticipate was Verci's desire for Brenna. He raped her and gave her a son," she said, looking at Willem. "But he is not the seed we seek. Before Verci could kill Brenna and Baran, King Pørr Boru rescued them. Do you understand?" she asked.

"No," I said, shaking my head. It was too much, too many deaths, too many prophecies. "What are we supposed to learn from this tale of blood?"

"If Vigdis and Verci had not interfered, Brenna would not have fled to America and married Robert Donavan, and Nessa would have married Baran and been very happy. But neither of you would have existed, and the prophecy would never have been fulfilled. It was from Vigdis's hate that Old Mother Earth finally created true love in you," she said.

My heart pounded. It wasn't fate at all; it was a series of choices, even my very existence. Vigdis tried to stop the prophecy, but it was she who truly created it. Grey. I stared at him. He wouldn't be here . . . I tried to imagine a world without him. I shook my head. It was unthinkable.

"Damn," Grey said.

"You can say that again," Brychan muttered.

"We'd still have our pack and our lands . . ." Willem shook his head. "Baran would still be here."

"True Willem of Killian, but you wouldn't be here," Lady Faye said.

"Lady Faye?" I said.

"Yes, my queen."

"Are you an Elemental?" Instinctively I reached out and touched her arm, but I felt nothing.

"No, my dear," she said. "I am not whom you seek."

"Will you join my pack at the Rock?" I asked.

"With honor and my blood," she said.

"Thank you," I said. A sense of relief washed over me; even though she wasn't the Mother or the Crone, I'd feel stronger with her on my side.

"There are books I seek in Baran's library. May I have leave?" she asked.

I looked to Grey and Willem; those books belonged to them until Baran's return. They were the heirs to the Killian name. Willem nodded his agreement. I looked to Grey for his decision.

"Of course, Lady Faye," he said. Grey bowed to Lady Faye.

"Thank you, Lords Killian." She bowed and swept out of the room, leaving the weight of her words behind. I felt numb.

As I turned to walk upstairs, I saw Grey and Willem embrace. I hadn't actually considered it before, but they were half brothers. Grey would finally have a pack his own . . . a family.

I walked slowly up the stairs, almost in a trance. I felt like I couldn't even control my own mind. I crawled into my bed. It seemed oddly large and cold without Grey in it. I was used to having him with me; even though he was just downstairs, I felt so far from him. I desired his touch, his smell, and his comfort. Sighing, I closed my eyes.

I could feel Baran's pain, and I could smell him.

# 11

## *Blood Sacrifice*

*I'd been here before. It was all too familiar. I leaped from this very room into a waterfall for my life. This is the place where they separated the women from their children, where I first saw the love Grete had for Fridrik.*

*Baran's beaten body was hunched in the center of the room. He appeared to be barely breathing; his forehead was on the ground, against the stones. Two guards stood off to the side. What had these monsters done to him? I recognized one of the guards; he was the one who had hesitated when I was a captive in the Bloodrealms. Was there good in him? Could he be trusted?*

*I looked up to the balcony and saw so many familiar faces. Hatred radiated from me just looking at them; in the center was Selene, one of Gwyn's closest friends, and a flesh trader. Selene wore a beautiful black-and-purple dress and stood out from the surroundings, drawing attention to herself. If I didn't know how black her heart was, I'd think she didn't belong down here. How could Gwyn trust her for all these years knowing what Selene did for a living?*

*The air left my body as I spotted Grete, bruised and in rags. Selene kept her on a leash like a slave, a pet. How could Selene look at a human and see so little value, like they were lesser beings? At least now I knew Selene kept Grete and that Grete was still alive. Killing Selene would almost be a pleasure after all the evil she had done. I had promised Eamon I would save Grete. I would do whatever I had to in order to save Fridrik's mom.*

*Vigdis walked into the room wearing a floor-length, black lace veil, like a floating demon. The guards moved farther away to avoid her. They knew to fear her.*

*She caressed Baran's cheek. "Not quite broken yet," she said.*

*His eyes opened and he watched her like a hawk. The look in his eyes told me all I needed to know—Baran was holding back, biding his time. Making them think he'd given up, but he had a plan. I wish I knew what it was. I wish I could help him, but all I could do was watch in horror. Why did my dreams bring me here to watch him suffer?*

*Vigdis looked to the balcony. "Do you think he has another fight in him? Is there more blood to shed today?"*

*They erupted with cheers.*

*"Pick him up," she said.*

*The guards did as they were told. Baran's body hung like a rag doll. Vigdis watched the audience from the other side of the room. She thrived on their need for blood like she was a mother feeding her young.*

*I softly walked up to Baran and stood right in front of him. I knew he wasn't aware of my presence—in fact, no one seemed to notice me. I wanted to just close my eyes and set us both free from this nightmare, but I knew Old Mother wouldn't lead me where she couldn't go. The dreams had to mean something. If only I knew.*

*I slowly reached out and placed my hand on his cheek. Be still my heart. I could actually feel his warm skin and the soft stubble of his beard. His jaw tensed.*

*Could he feel me?*

*I put my other hand on his face and he looked up, looking right through me. Blood seeped from a gash on his cheek. I licked my finger and ran my finger over it, and the wound stopped bleeding. Was it possible he could feel my touch? Could I heal him? I ran my hands down his arms, and the pain from his breaks jolted into me, but with each move I made his body seemed to repair itself.*

*I leaned so close that my lips almost brushed his ear as I whispered, "I will save you; I promise."*

*Baran nodded.*

*How was this possible? I could affect his reality through my dreams. Just as Vigdis had been in mine . . . my dreams were a link between souls.*

*Vigdis turned back to Baran. "I will break your spirit, Baran. You will wish you'd chosen me."*

*He looked back to where I stood and stared at me as though he could actually see me. "You can't hurt me, Vigdis, for I am surrounded by my queen's love."*

*She walked right up to his face, and I nearly had to jump to get out of the way. I couldn't let her touch me. If Baran could feel me, she could as well. "Your false little queen can't protect you here. She's given you up for dead."*

*"You can't stop love," he said.*

*Vigdis was mere inches from his face, and she screamed like a banshee. Baran didn't flinch.*

*Murmurs came from the balcony. This sign of strength and defiance was noticed. I could feel the tension in the room.*

*Vigdis turned. "Quiet!" she hissed.*

*They all stood stiffly, and not a single sound came from the balcony. She turned back to Baran. "Do you think you're so strong, Baran? Do you think me so simple and so weak?" She smiled the sickest smile I'd ever seen. "Do you really think I intend for you to live through this?" She didn't wait for him to answer as she stabbed a thin silver knife into his side.*

*I grabbed my mouth, clenching my nails into my face to stop myself from screaming at the horror before me. I gagged on my tears, but I forced myself to watch.*

*"I will cut out her heart and drink her blood,"* Vigdis hissed to him. I shivered with fear. It was my heart she sought. *"Throw him in his cell. If he lives, we'll punish him for it,"* she said, then stormed out.

*I followed as the guards brought him into a tiny cell no more than four feet by two feet. He couldn't even lie down. They slumped him against the black, ragged stone in a dried puddle of blood. His fresh red blood poured out, coating the ground.*

*I said a silent prayer.* Old Mother, give me the strength to tear this world down to save him. I will stop at nothing. I will bring him back to you. *I let the words run through me over and over again.*

*The cell door slammed shut, and I knelt down with Baran. Tears ran over his filth-stained cheeks from the pain that radiated through him. I spit in my hands, coating his wounds in my saliva to numb the pain. Wolf saliva had a numbing quality, and from what I had seen, mine was the most healing of any wolf I had ever known. I peeled his fingers away from his side and placed my palms over the seeping wound. Blood coated my hands.*

*I pressed so hard on the wound that he gasped and passed out. I sat holding his skin closed for hours. I didn't shake or waiver. I knew my task, and I wouldn't let him down.*

*Every moment with him flashed through my mind as I poured that love and support into him. I let it all rush out of me and into him. He needed it more than I did. I felt exhausted and broken, but I couldn't give up. I couldn't stop. I blinked away my exhaustion.*

*When he started to rouse, I moved my hands and studied his wound; it was nearly healed.* "Thank you," *he said in barely a whisper. He couldn't see me, but he knew I was there.*

"I'm coming back for you," *I said.*

"Don't you dare," *he said.*

"Like I ever listened to you," *I said.*

*His mouth curved up into a smile. How I missed his smile. I felt lightheaded after my long night of holding his flesh to heal. Old Mother was glorious to give us this moment so I could heal him. He had been my protector . . . and now I was his.*

*"I have to go for now, but my strength is yours," I said. I knew as I said the words it was true; I had given him all of myself. "Grey and I will find you."*

*He nodded. I quickly kissed him on the cheek and willed myself to wake up. . . .*

I blinked over and over again to take in the darkness of my room. I was so tired. I wanted to go back to bed, but I somehow knew sleep wouldn't give me the rest I sought. I sat up and wandered downstairs to tell Grey what had happened.

I walked into the living room and saw Brychan, Dilara, Grey, Willem, Khepri, Shikoba, Kane, and Lady Faye all sitting around talking. As they turned to me, Dilara gasped. The room went silent.

"Ashling? You're bleeding," she whispered.

I looked down at myself. Blood coated my hands. I couldn't stop my mind from going back to Adomnan's torture chamber, but I forced myself past the memories back to reality. It was Baran's blood. There was so much of it . . . it was all over me. He would certainly have died without me last night. My knees buckled and I fell; Grey leaped across the room and caught me.

"What happened? Who hurt you?" Grey said. "Are they still upstairs?"

"No one," I said, still mystified. "It's Baran's blood. I found him in my dream. I healed him." I stared at the blood in wonder.

Lady Faye stood. "You can get to him in your dreams?"

I nodded.

"Then, my queen, you can save him."

# 12

## *Riddles and Plans*

*"I don't understand* . . . how can I save him? He's there and I'm here," I said.

"Through your dream," Lady Faye said.

I closed the distance between us and pulled her closer. "You must help me save him. He is mine to protect." I felt strong and calm in my conviction and suddenly confident that I could save him. I didn't know how, but I would bring him home if it were the last thing I ever did. "Please, Lady Faye, help me."

"You can touch him? See him? Hear him?" she said.

"Yes, and he can hear me and feel me," I said.

"Do you know where he is?" Brychan asked.

"As of last night, he was in a cell near the slave sorting area, by the waterfall. I was brought there last time I was in the Realms, but I don't know the way. They had been torturing him there, and Vigdis stabbed him and left him for dead," I said.

"I was there once, but I came in blindfolded and left unconscious," Dilara said. "No one knows how to find it."

"In your dream state, you are closer to Old Mother, closer to the afterlife. That's what gives you the ability to heal," Lady Faye said.

"But how do I get him out?" I asked. "Can Baran leave with me? Can I take him back with me when I wake from my dream, like I did with a coin?"

"No. His body would stay and they would kill him," she said. "You have to get him out whole."

"What if we went in?" Grey said. "What if we're there, and you're in a dream, and you guide us and heal us? This way, you don't actually have to go into the Bloodrealms. It will keep you safe."

Lady Faye held up her arm. "No. There is no safety for her in a dream. She can die there, but her spirit will be lost, and not even Old Mother can claim her soul then."

"If I die in the dream, my soul will never return Old Mother?" I whispered.

"You would risk your eternal soul to save Killian," she said as she searched my wide eyes. Was she looking for doubt or fear? Because it was all there swimming inside me, churning my stomach in knots.

Grey looked terrified; Brychan looked sad. A lot of help they were. Kane and Shikoba didn't make eye contact, choosing instead to concentrate on the floor. I looked to Dilara, and she was the only one who didn't seem to be saying "*Don't do it.*"

"If you are searching for fearless strength and a perfect plan, you'll be disappointed," she said.

"I'm afraid. I don't want to end my life without a promise of Old Mother's love, but I would do it to save Baran. I love him," I said. "Lady Faye, what should we do?"

"I am not a warrior, my queen. You should seek Brychan and Dilara for that. For strategy, trust Grey. And survival, look to yourself," she said.

I sighed. "Why? Why is everything a riddle?"

Her face softened. "Because even if I told you what to do, you'd do it your way."

Brychan laughed and tried to cover it with a cough. I rolled my eyes at him.

"Okay. Don't tell me what to do. Tell me the mysteries of the dreams. Can Vigdis see me? Does she know I'm there?"

"She could hear you if you spoke. She could feel you if you touched her. But she doesn't *sense* you," she said. "So never let your presence be known in front of her. The others aren't smart enough, but she'll know."

I thought of the rock I'd thrown in the first dream. The things I'd done. She would have known my presence then. I would have risked it all. I needed to be more careful.

"What if we flew back to the Bloodrealms?" Brychan said. "What if we did go back in? Could you get him out to us?"

I nodded. "Dilara, do you know the labyrinth?" I asked.

"Yes. I've been there many times. We often hid children there so the reapers wouldn't find them," she said. "I could find it easily."

"The slave selection chamber isn't far from the labyrinth," I said. "What if I found Baran in my dream and brought him to the labyrinth? Could you get us all out from there?"

"Yes," Dilara said. "I'm certain. There are a few hidden paths we could take to escape without being seen. But you'd have to get him to us."

"Ashling, you'd have to break him out and away alone," Grey said. "Are you sure you'll be safe in your dream?"

"None of us are safe," I said.

"It is the only way to save Killian," Lady Faye said.

"Then it is decided," I said. "Brychan, Kane, Dilara, and Shikoba, you will all fly to Norway on the next flight. Shikoba, can you deliver messages from Baran and me to Brychan, Kane, and Dilara?"

"I can find you anywhere in the Realms," Shikoba said. I shook my head, remembering all the times she moved through the Bloodrealms last time. Shikoba wasn't a living being anymore; she was a spirit. Being in spirit form, she could disappear and reappear at will.

"Okay," I sighed. "I will enter through my dream and get Baran to all of you at the labyrinth, and we will save him together."

"Where do you want me?" Grey said. I could feel the hurt flowing through him, but he was hiding it well from the others. There was a smirk on Brychan's face, like he thought I'd forgotten Grey, but I hadn't forgotten him. He was the most important piece of the plan.

"You stay with my body," I said. "I need you to protect me. If my spirit dies, I die. If my body dies, I die. I need you by my side."

Grey shook his head. His indecision and fear mixed inside me like napalm.

"You protect my body," I said. "Baran will protect my spirit."

Grey touched my hand, and electricity shot up my arm to my heart. I loved the current our love and connection generated. His touch could heal me.

"Love?" he asked.

"I need you with me," I said. "I need it like the air I breathe. I need it like Old Mother's love. Love protects, so protect me."

He sighed and gave me a half smile, though he looked a little sad underneath. "I will, with my life and my love," he said.

"Thank you," I whispered.

Knowing he would be protecting my body gave me a sense of safety that no other soul could give me. He was my one true love, my one true protection in this cruel world, as I was for him. I looked up at him, and I was lost in the sea of his eyes, always so beautiful and yet endlessly turbulent today. Knowing he would be with me gave me the strength to do what I had to do.

"Lady Faye, I will be sending you to the Rock of Cashel for your safety and to keep you close to Carrowmore for the claiming ceremony. You will be joining Mother Rhea and Nessa and the others. You will be safe there."

She smiled. "I knew where I was destined before I came to you, my queen. You have a long way to go, but I will meet you at the Rock. I see you standing there, and I see your infallible strength."

"You're my favorite riddler," I said.

She laughed.

"Willem and Khepri, I want you to escort Lady Faye to the Rock on the way to the Bloodrealms. She is in your protection," I said.

"We will see it done," Khepri said.

"Start booking flights, and I will reach out to Rhonda. We'll need them here with Grey and my body," I said.

"Do you trust them?" Brychan asked.

"I do."

I wasn't sure if Rhonda could protect me or even herself against her father, but I trusted her not to hurt me. I couldn't show them my doubt or my plans would fail. I had to believe in my plan.

"Then it will be done," Brychan said, but there was reluctance in his voice. I studied him for a while as the others dispersed.

"Brychan?"

"I don't like leaving you alone," he said.

I smiled. "I won't be alone."

"I'm leaving my queen alone with half a wolf and three and a half Bloodsuckers. This is against everything I've been taught in all my years. Ashling, they were the enemy, and you're asking me to leave you here unprotected," he said.

"You don't trust Grey?"

"I trust him not to kill you, but I don't trust him to be enough to protect you if the Bloodsuckers turn on you while your soul is in the Realms," he said. "Your father would kill me if he knew I was allowing this."

"He's killed many people for many stupid reasons," I said, dismissing the idea. "And through all the years, you've survived."

"I've never endangered his baby girl before," Brychan grumbled. "And Mund . . . what do you think he'll do when he gets wind of this?"

he said, shaking his head. He leaned in close to me, leaving only a foot between us. "You do know that even though you aren't mine that I would die to protect you? I still consider it my duty to keep you safe."

I nodded. I felt his sadness flood over me like a hurricane. "Brychan, that is why you must protect my soul in the Realms. I cannot live through this without all of you. My trust and love is with every one of you. You are just as important to my survival as any of the others," I said. I took his hand in mine. "And just because I am not yours does not mean that I wouldn't die to protect you, too. You are one of my people, my pack. I am your queen. And Brychan Kahedin, I am your friend."

I felt his pulse quicken from my touch. He still loved me, possibly more than he should.

Brychan cleared his throat and pulled his hand back. "As long as we're clear on the plan," he said. Brychan turned and walked off.

"He still has a thing for you, huh?" Dilara said, crossing her arms over her chest.

I studied her closed-off body language. "I think a warrior who is used to being a champion may not know how to accept defeat. And though his heart is true, I think he fears loss more than he mourns me."

She uncrossed her arms. We sat down across from each other at Baran's kitchen table. There was something on her mind, but she didn't seem ready to share it.

"I think he will accept it soon, and his heart will be open again," I said. "He lost his first love many years ago, and I think he may still be mourning her."

"I knew her," she said. "She was breathtaking . . . kind, soft spoken . . . like you in a lot of ways."

"I think I'm anything but soft spoken nowadays," I said.

"No . . . but your kindness, the love that emanates from you . . . she was much like you in that way."

"Perhaps he's ready for a woman who can match him in battle?" I said.

"Men don't love women who are equals." She scoffed and stood to leave.

"Dilara," I said. "I think for the first time in your life, you're wrong."

She stared at me with wide eyes. I laughed. She hadn't known that I could see her secrets just as she saw mine. I knew she was beginning to love Brychan. He was beginning to feel for her, too, but he wasn't really aware of it yet.

"Well, I've never . . ." she said.

"Get used to it," I said.

She laughed. "You weren't at all what I expected from the prophecy."

"Let me guess . . . I'm shorter," I said.

She shook her head and walked off smiling.

Dilara was so brilliant and strong, yet I loved her most for being as full of human emotions as I was. Sometimes, even after everything I had lived through, I felt doubt, fear, and loneliness. Seeing strength and imperfection in others gave me a sense of balance. I knew that we were not created to be alone. Old Mother created us as a pack, as a people to protect and be the companions to the humans. We were all meant to experience this journey together.

Yet I had sent my pack away . . . Mother, Tegan, Mund, all of them. Now Brychan, Dilara, Kane, Shikoba, and Lady Faye would leave. I reminded myself that we all had a duty to fulfill. A destiny.

Saving Baran wasn't even the greatest destiny that awaited me. My claiming at Carrowmore loomed ever closer as my eighteenth birthday approached, but I was no closer to the Mother or the Crone.

# 13

## *Broad Daylight*

*I stood on* the front porch, barefooted and wearing a strapless dress on one of the last warm days of the season. I watched Kane, Shikoba, Brychan, Dilara, Willem, Khepri, and Lady Faye climb into the car, and with them, my hope. I needed them as much as I needed my own strength to save Baran. Our plan was delicate at best. We had to keep faith, love, and trust in each other if we were to have a chance at surviving in the Bloodrealms.

"Be safe, and keep Old Mother's love in your heart," I said as Grey and I watched them drive away.

I wanted to go back to bed, to stay dreaming all day and night to be with Baran. I needed to heal him and keep him safe, but I also needed to keep my strength up for when we did go in to save him. For now, I just had to bide my time. I was going to be on pins and needles until I received word that my team made it safely to the Rock and then to Dagny in Norway. I was sending my pack out on a mission that terrified me. I supposed this was the challenge of being a leader.

"Ashling?" Grey said, interrupting my thoughts. "They're gone."

I blinked and realized I couldn't see their car anymore. They really were gone. I sighed. Was I truly ready for what was to come?

"Are you all right?" he asked.

"Will we survive this, Grey?"

He cupped my face. "Oh, my love, we will thrive."

I rested my forehead on his, letting his love pour into me. "You're mine," I said.

"And you're mine."

With his hands on my skin, I breathed him in, and my body filled with tingles and calmness. There was no power greater than love. He lightly rubbed his lips against mine, and my body ignited. I looked into his eyes as we kissed, filling me with his need and my own. I desperately wanted his hands to explore my skin . . . all of my skin.

"We're alone," he whispered.

I bit my lower lip and studied him as my pulse quickened. Every inch of his delicious face, messy hair, and golden skin was mine to admire, and I yearned for his touch. I licked my lips just thinking about it. Aching with need.

"Mmmmm . . ." I smiled.

"What should we do about that?" he said mischievously.

"I've got a couple good ideas."

His hands ran down my body over my breasts, making me groan. I leaned into his touch, wanting it so much more. Needing it. His scent warmed, and his body was hot to the touch as I let my own hand wander over his muscular arms.

"Maybe we should go for a walk," I said.

Grey looked at me with confusion all over his face. I took his hand in mine and brought his fingertips to my lips, kissing each one. Finally I took his forefinger in my mouth, sucking it lightly.

"Come, my husband," I said. I felt my face flush.

He lightly patted my butt. "Anywhere you go, I go, my beautiful wife."

We walked hand in hand into the forest on the dirt path. We walked in silence with the lust building between us. I wanted him. Needed him. And he needed me. I was looking for the perfect spot . . . somewhere secluded where we could make love in broad daylight without getting caught. I finally spotted a thick grouping of low pine trees off the path. We would be easily concealed there.

I pulled him toward them into the chest-high weeds as we waded our way to our sexy hideaway. I looked back at him with a smile on my face. I was eager to get him alone and share my body with him.

Once we were hidden among the trees and out of sight from the path, I stopped in a small clearing between the pines. I took hold of my dress and pulled it down, letting it fall to the ground to expose my bare skin to the warm fall air. Grey took in a breath and smiled. His expression was so handsome, but I couldn't quite figure out how he felt in that moment as looked upon me.

"Grey?" I asked, suddenly feeling shy.

"You're beautiful . . . more beautiful than the stars, and I still can't believe you're my wife. You're my forever," he said. "Fate put you in my path, and I am thankful every day."

"I insist you take off your clothes," I said as I walked into his arms, pressing my naked body against his clothed one.

He pulled me close to him and nuzzled my neck, nibbling at the delicate skin. My head fell back and I gave him full access to me. His hands ran over my bare skin as I pulled his shirt over my head. I captured his lips with mine, and our tongues danced. I fumbled with his belt buckle . . . I desperately wanted what was hidden inside. Finally, his pants fell to the ground around his ankles and he kicked them aside. He wrapped his arms around my tiny body, and his warm breath tickled my neck.

"You're mine," he said.

"Yes, please," I moaned. He gracefully lowered us down to the soft grass.

Grey nibbled at my lips and his body pressed into mine, and we made love so passionately that I had to stifle my moans against his neck. Our bodies became one in the glorious sunlight. We had nothing to hide, only to be completely open in each other's arms. Each movement brought me closer to euphoria. Finally, he collapsed into me. Grey pulled me tighter to him and cuddled me close as he breathed me in. Our scent was glorious together.

There was something freeing about having sex under the open sky and cuddling after. It felt sensual and even more connecting to be naked in broad daylight. I felt closer to him and to Old Mother, like nature and our faith made our love deeper than we had even thought possible. I kissed his collarbone as I lay naked on his chest.

"We're good at that," he said. His voice was raw with passion.

I licked his lower lip and ground my hips into him. "Yeah, we are."

"Mmmm, baby . . ." he groaned. "You want some more?"

"I want you forever," I said.

"Than you shall have me." He grinned and rolled on top of me.

After satisfying each other again, we reluctantly got dressed and tried our best to make ourselves presentable.

We started walking back to the trail when we spotted two people walking toward us. They eyed us so closely it felt like the Spanish Inquisition. I felt my face burn hot, and I wanted to start fidgeting and adjusting my dress, but I was afraid that would give away what we'd just done. So instead I stared.

"Enjoy the nice weather," Grey said. The pair nodded and kept walking.

When they were finally out of earshot, I said, "Thank goodness they didn't catch us."

"Yeah, I'm sure they didn't suspect a thing," he said, pulling a twig from my hair. We both burst out in laughter.

"Maybe that was a bad idea," I said.

"Rebellious, maybe," he said, kissing my neck. "But definitely not a bad idea."

We walked the rest of the path back home to Baran's house, smiling at each other and laughing at the amazingness of our afternoon. We'd waited weeks to be together again, and now that I had him, I wanted more.

As we walked up the street, I saw Rhonda, Jamal, and Paul lounging around the porch and chatting with Ryan and Eric. All of my worlds were combining—my wolves, my humans, and now my Bloodsuckers. I didn't do anything to connect them other than being in their lives, yet they made friendships all on their own. That was the true power of acceptance and love.

"Hey, guys!" I yelled.

Rhonda smiled. "Brychan said we should keep an eye on you." She studied us for a bit. "Now I can see why. Clearly the two of you are troublemakers."

She knew. She was a watcher, a tracker; there were no secrets with Rhonda. I almost had to laugh, but I knew she wouldn't call us out in front of the others.

"Isn't she clever?" Grey muttered.

Rhonda chuckled at that, but the other guys were oblivious. "What are you guys all up to tonight?" I asked.

"We live for the weekend," Ryan said.

"Wanna jam?" Eric asked Grey.

"Sure," Grey said. I could feel his excitement. He loved to play guitar. It was part of who he was, just as much as his motorcycle. "Ashling, do you wanna come hang?"

"I think I will actually call some of the girls to come watch a movie over here," I said. I was craving a little girl time. There was something beautiful and empowering about being surrounded by my best friends.

Grey smiled and kissed me on the cheek. "Sounds great. See you tonight?"

"You know where to find me." I winked. "Rhonda, do you want to watch a girl movie and eat cookie dough?" It was a human pleasure I had grown fond of during my time in York Harbor.

I laughed when Rhonda looked at me like I was an alien.

"I'll take that as a yes," I said, pulling her into the house.

Jamal and Paul went over to watch the guys play, leaving Rhonda and me alone. I picked up the phone and called Beth, Lacey, Emma, and Kate and asked them all over.

"So what is the purpose of this?" Rhonda asked before the others arrived.

"Just to hang out and laugh," I said. "Haven't you ever done that before?"

"My father raised me to be a fighter with men. I wasn't allowed time to rest or laugh or do anything with other girls," she said. "You're actually the first girl I've ever spent time with."

I stared at her, unable to hide my shock. I hadn't expected her to understand much about my life as a wolf, but I suddenly realized that she had more in common with me than most of my family. Like me, Rhonda had been sheltered and alone, without friends. My father did it to protect me; her father wanted to make her a competitive warrior. Both fathers had been wrong.

"Well, both of our fathers were stupid," I said. "I didn't have any friends until I came here either. So let's learn to have a little fun."

She smiled. "I can agree with that."

I ordered pizza and made cookie dough as the girls arrived. Everyone flopped around Baran's living room, draping themselves on his leather sofas. I wondered if he had ever imagined his home would be filled with teenage girls who were human, wolf, and Bloodsucker. I shook my head. This would probably make him pull out his hair.

I missed him.

"What should we watch?" I asked as I pulled up the streaming video menu.

"Something romantic," Emma said.

"No. Something funny," Beth said.

"I'm up for a period film," Rhonda said.

"How about a classic?" Kate said.

Lacey took the remote. "I got this," she said.

She cruised through the movies until she found *Pride and Prejudice.* I instantly swooned. It was by far my favorite book, and I was eager to see this movie adaptation. We all settled in to watch the movie as we ate cookie dough from the tub with spoons and devoured the pizza.

It was so simple and yet exactly what I wanted. A sexy afternoon with Grey followed by treats and friends that evening. It was the best thing for my soul.

The phone rang and I jumped up and ran to the kitchen to answer it.

"Hello?" I said.

"Ashling Boru," Mund said over the phone. "They just got here and told me your plan. Have you lost your mind?"

"Mund, please . . ."

"You can't save Baran from the Bloodrealms. You can send Brychan, Dilara, Kane, and Shikoba in there, but you cannot go in through your dreams. If you die there, you die. Nothing and no one can save you," he said.

I could hear the fear in his voice, the pain. I knew that I wasn't just his queen or even his sister; I was his friend. I hated that his fear made me feel guilty, like I'd disappointed him, but I knew it came from a place of love.

"Don't do this, Ashling. It's too dangerous," Mund said.

"Mund, you have to trust me," I said. "Do you trust me?"

I heard him exhale slowly. "With all my heart."

"Then accept that I have to do this. If I don't go into the Blood-realms to save one of my own, how can I possibly be worth following? How can I be trusted to protect everyone else? If I'm going to be queen, I need to start acting like one," I said. "I know you're scared, and so am I, but this is my path."

"I know."

"I love you, Mund. You're the best brother a girl could ever ask for."

"Better than Quinn?" he asked.

I laughed. "You've always been my favorite, and you know it."

"I'll see you soon, Ashling," he said. I could almost hear the bittersweet smile on his face. I missed his face.

"Give my love to everyone there. I miss you all so much." Just thinking of Mother and Nia made me want to cry.

"I will."

With that, he hung up the phone. He never was good at saying good-bye, but neither was I. My thoughts wandered to Eamon, and sadness slammed into me so hard it was nearly crippling. I hardly knew him and his loss was still devastating. If I lost Mund, Mother, or Grey, I couldn't imagine what I'd do. I shook my head, trying to get my worst fears back out of my head. Something happening to one of them was far worse than anything that could happen to me.

I wandered back into the living room. I hadn't heard the boys come in, but now the room was full. I saw Grey's green eyes glowing in the dark, and I knew mine were too. It was probably time to turn on a lamp to make it less obvious to my human friends. Even though they knew we were different, I didn't want to scare them. I clicked on a side lamp on my way over to Grey and snuggled into him.

"We thought we'd come enjoy the last few bites of cookie dough," Grey said, "but I have to say, you girls did quite a good job scraping the bottom of the bowl. There aren't even any chocolate chips left."

"What can we say . . . we're women who love to eat," Lacey said. "I think there might be a couple of pizza crusts left."

We all laughed. I remembered how I had judged Lacey unfairly for being so stick thin and loving pink, and it was all because she was a girl who once happened to like the same boy. And really, what was so wrong with being skinny and loving pink, anyway? How was it was so easy for me to use those things against her? Lacey hadn't been an angel, either—far from it—but that didn't mean I had been right to hate her. I looked at Lacey; she smiled at me as if she was thinking the same thing about me. I loved that we were able to become friends—she was so much more than what I first assumed.

The movie ended with swagger and kisses. I couldn't help but think how simple their lives really were. Elizabeth Bennet and Mr. Darcy didn't know about werewolves, Bloodsuckers, the Draugr, or Garm wolves. Jane Austin told a story of love. I envied that simplicity. My story was much more complicated than a simple story of two people falling in love. We had to save the world.

Everyone started getting up and wandering toward the door to head home when Beth darted over and threw her arms around me.

"It feels so good having you home again," Beth said. "I like seeing you all the time."

I smiled but my heart wasn't in it. Someday I'd have to leave her. I'd probably have to live at the Rock in Ireland or something. I never wanted to leave my friends.

"I missed you like crazy, too," I admitted.

"See you at school," she said.

Finally all who remained were Rhonda, Jamal, Paul, Grey, and myself.

"Do you want us to stay?" Jamal asked.

"No, thank you. I think we will be good here," I said. "You're still staying out at Grey's old house, right?"

Rhonda nodded.

"Perfect," I said. "We will talk to you tomorrow."

"Are you sure?" Rhonda said.

I knew she was thinking it was risky having just Grey and me here. If we were attacked, we'd be easy to kill. She was right.

"Maybe we could take turns guarding the house?" Paul suggested.

"How about you guys stay here for now. There are some extra beds down the hall, and we can protect each other better this way," I said.

"I'd feel more comfortable knowing you guys weren't alone out in the woods," Grey said. "And I'd sleep better knowing you guys were here in case someone came for us."

"Then it is settled," Rhonda said. "We'll stay here tonight. We will take turns staying awake to guard the house."

"Sounds good to me," said Jamal.

"Me too," said Paul.

"Then it's settled," I said. I felt the scratchiness of my eyes, and my head felt light. I hadn't slept well in ages.

"I think I'm going to head up to sleep. Good night to you all," I said.

Grey followed me upstairs to my room, and he closed the door behind him. His mischievous smile spread across his handsome face.

"Ready to cuddle, my love?" he asked.

More than anything, I yearned for his touch. I pulled my dress off, pulled on a pair of plaid pajama shorts and a white tank, and hopped into bed. Grey stripped down to his underwear and hopped in. He pulled me tight against his bare chest. He kissed my right cheek and then the other, followed by my forehead, nose, and lips. "Sweet dreams, my love. Be safe in your sleep," he said. "I will be here with you."

"Goodnight, Grey." I kissed him and snuggled in deeper into his arms. I felt a wonderful yet false sense of safety. I knew where I would go as soon as I drifted off to sleep.

# 14
## *Werewolves*

*I opened my eyes in the dark Bloodrealms. It was jolting every time. I was in Baran's cell again, but this time he was lying on the floor, and his limbs were twisted so grotesquely that I was almost sure he was dead. I wanted to scream in horror as I stared down at him, but the guards would hear me.*

*I held my breath as I bent down and touched his skin; his flesh was on fire, and he was sweating from either pain or infection, but with silver in his veins I knew he couldn't shift to heal. If I hadn't found him now, he would have certainly died. Even now my chances of saving him were slim. The amount of sticky blood on the floor was more than a mortal could lose and survive. His heart was beating so faintly that I almost couldn't feel his pulse.*

*I started moving his arms back into place. The cracking and snapping sounds of his bones and muscles made me want to gag and vomit, but I swallowed down the bile and kept straightening and rubbing his flesh to heal him. I spit into my hands and rubbed my saliva all over the cuts and tears in the flesh of his arms and legs. I could feel Baran's body relax. The power of my saliva to numb pain was unmatchable.*

*"I'm here, Baran. I'm here," I whispered into his ear.*

*I massaged the bones and muscles until they healed. The only wounds left would be mental . . . I couldn't heal those. I still carried the scars of Adomnan, and though I'd diminished his power over me, I'd never forget. When experiencing something that terrible, as Baran and I had, forgetting wasn't an option. And I knew Baran would always remember this sacrifice. I wondered if he regretted his choice to protect me?*

*I wished we were rescuing him tonight, but I knew he'd have to survive another day or two in the Bloodrealms before we could get him out. I didn't dare try to free him before the others were inside or it would alert Vigdis of my presence before I had the backup I needed for any of us to survive.*

*His eyes opened and he looked in my direction. Though he had been tortured to the brink of death again, the spark in his eyes was just as fierce as the day I'd met him. I wiped his bloody hair out of his face and smiled down at him. Though I knew he couldn't see me, he knew I was there.*

*I whispered, "I remember the first time you saved my life. You crashed your motorcycle onto a moving ferry to save me from Adomnan. You risked everything for me. You have every day since the moment I met you. I can't repay you for all you have done to protect and care for me. You were the father mine didn't know how to be,"*

*"My queen, you are the daughter I never had, and I love you as though you were mine. For all of my days, I will protect you," he said. "And not just because I love your mother, but because of you."*

*Tears streamed down my face at his words. He was so kind to comfort me in his time of need. He was truly selfless and gracious, and I was thankful to be by his side, even in the darkest place on earth. The color was returning to his face, and I was thankful for that. I knew I had healed his body, but to see his liveliness come back was more glorious than I could explain. I hadn't lost him yet. He still had a lot more fight in him.*

*"I have a plan to save you in a few days, but for now I will come for you and heal you every night until I can set you free. But you must hang on until then," I said.*

*"I can do that . . . in the meantime, I will keep annoying them," he said with a smile.*

*I looked at his arms and legs, "Maybe you should be a little less annoying."*

*He chuckled. He reached out to touch me and found my cheek. I could feel him and he could feel me. I wished he could see my face. I wrapped my arms around him, hugging him as tightly as I could.*

*"I love you, Baran," I said.*

*When I pulled back I saw tears on his cheeks as he hastily wiped them away. He smiled. "I love you, too, ylva."*

*I had missed his pet name for me. I missed everything about him. "I will see you tomorrow night," I said.*

*He nodded, but I wasn't ready to leave him behind. It was unnatural, but I reluctantly forced myself from the dream.*

I woke in my bed with Grey next to me; he'd been watching me sleep. His green eyes glowed in the dark, and his brow was furrowed. He lightly brushed my curls out of my face.

"Are you okay, love?" he asked.

"Yeah . . . weak, but okay," I said. My body felt weak and drained. It took a lot to find Baran in my dreams and even more to heal him.

"How is he?" Grey asked. I could feel his anxiety before he even asked.

I held his hand. "Grey, they are torturing him. This time, his arms and legs were all broken and dislocated. They had cut him with a silver blade so he couldn't heal himself, and they left him to die in a tiny cell, like he was nothing. It was one of the most horrible things I've ever seen."

Grey sucked in air so violently I jumped. He had been holding back tears for a long time, and now they were running down his cheeks.

"Sorry," he murmured, squeezing my hand.

"You don't have to be sorry for crying. He's your family," I said.

Grey nodded. Watching him cry made me feel so small. I wanted to help him, but I knew he had to let it out. "I just wish I could have saved him in the Bloodrealms. I should never have let him out of my sight," he said.

"I know. I wanted to try to save him tonight, but I had to leave him in that cell . . . I left him to be beaten again." I shuddered. "Grey, we have to save him."

He crushed me to his chest, holding me so tight I was sure we were one body. "I know, love, I know. We will save him. As soon as the others are with Dagny, we'll save him."

I nodded my head, wanting desperately to believe we'd succeed and that by the time they were in Norway, there would be something left of Baran to save.

"What time is it?" I asked as I gently wiped his tears away.

"Four in the morning," he said. "Plenty of time for you to fall back to sleep in my arms and actually rest this time."

"You're not the boss of me," I teased.

He gave a soft smile. "True, but you know I'm right." He kissed the tip of my nose.

I lay my head back on his chest and listened to the rhythm of his heart; it was my very own lullaby. I was safe in his arms. With his scent, the warmth of his skin, and his arms wrapped around me, all I could do was succumb to sleep. This time, I rested knowing that Baran was uninjured, if only for the moment, and I didn't return to the Bloodrealms in my sleep.

A few hours later, I woke to Grey kissing my cheek. "Good morning, love," he said. "I brought you some breakfast."

He held a little tray with two bagels, a pile of bacon, and a wild sprig of wolf's bane. It was the cure for silver poisoning, and it happened to be wild here. The delicate purple flower was one of the most powerful and sacred symbols of our people. Though extremely dangerous to humans, werewolves used it as a cure.

Grey sat down on the foot of the bed and grabbed one of the bagels, biting into it. I went for the bacon. "What's the occasion? Did I forget something?" I asked.

"Can't a guy just do something for his lovely wife?" he asked, but there was something in his body language. I raised my eyebrow and waited for him to tell me what he was hiding. "Okay, it's because I love you and because it's Monday and we have to go to school."

I groaned. I had completely forgotten. I didn't want to go to school. I wanted to save Baran. I wanted to save the world. Going to school seemed so irrelevant.

He laughed and it was so contagious that I smiled back.

"Thank you for breakfast," I said.

"You're welcome," he said as he began wandering around the room to pick out something to wear, his bagel sticking out of his mouth.

I snagged another piece of bacon and did the same. We munched and got ready for school while the wind howled outside. I looked out the window at the trees, and they bent and rattled to the power of the wind. It was remarkable, really; we couldn't see the wind, but it had the power to change everything. The wind was just like faith—untouchable and yet very real.

I quickly dressed. I put on a black-and-gray, loose, lace dress and a light-brown sweater with thick-cuffed socks that rolled over my charcoal boots. Grey tossed on a black t-shirt with a charcoal button-up sweater over it. The brown leather elbow pads made him look like a sexy hipster. He slipped on some dark jeans and his biker boots and we headed downstairs.

"Good morning," I said to Paul.

"Not really," he grumbled.

Rhonda laughed. "I made him get up."

"Not a morning person?" I asked.

"Hmmm," he said.

"Okay, okay," I said, retreating to the door. "I will see you guys after school."

"Later," Grey said.

"I'm totally driving," I said, bouncing around in front of Grey as we walked out the door.

He laughed.

"Sweet." I jumped in my red vintage 1965 Ford Mustang and clicked my seatbelt. "Let's go!"

He smiled. "You're cute."

"Huh?"

"You just are," he said.

I leaned over and kissed him on the cheek as I started the engine and my car roared to life. Baran had given me this car last year when Grey had broken up with me. He didn't want me to be dependent on anyone for transportation. Mund had shown me his love of vintage cars and taught me how to drive them. I missed both Baran and Mund terribly. I would find a way to make our pack whole again. I pulled out of the driveway and onto the road. I loved the freedom of driving. Every curve, every mile was mine. Our culture didn't allow women to drive, but Mund hadn't cared and neither had Baran. They treated me as an equal . . . well, most of the time.

We rolled into the parking lot far more quickly than I would have liked, but I spotted our friends all rushing into the school through the cold wind.

"Ashling," Grey said as I turned off the car.

I turned to look at him, and he captured my face in his gentle hands and my lips with his and kissed me so passionately I thought I might burst into flames. I wanted to crawl onto his lap and straddle him right there in my car in the school parking lot. All I could see in that moment was him—nothing and no one else existed . . . only our love.

When he pulled away, I felt a zap as our connection broke. "What was that for?" I asked breathlessly, trying to regain my composure.

"I needed to power up for the hours we'd be apart." He smiled.

I giggled. "I love you."

He winked at me with his sparkling green eyes. I was such a sucker for his green eyes. With that, we walked hand in hand up to the school.

The first few classes of the day were a breeze. As I was studying the chapters we'd missed in chemistry, I heard the door open. The aid, Mrs. Knute, walked in to whisper something to the teacher. When I glanced up, they were staring at me. I suddenly wished I had been listening to their conversation, because it was clearly about me.

"Ms. Boru, you are needed in the office," Mrs. Knute said.

A smattering of curious responses came from my classmates as I walked to the front of the room.

"What am I needed for?" I asked when we were alone in the hall.

"You have a call," she said.

The hair on my neck stood on end, and an exciting chill settled over me. Brychan, Dilara, Kane, and Shikoba were finally in Norway. This was it. It was time to save Baran. I wanted to run to the office, but I knew Mrs. Knute would yell at me. So I forced myself to match her waddling pace.

I walked into the office and grabbed the phone. I needed to know my pack was in position.

"Hello? Hello? This is Ashling," I said. My voice quivered with anticipation.

Mrs. Knute watched me as I listened to the silence on the other end of the phone. She was nosy; I supposed it came with the job. It would be hard to be an office aid without knowing everyone else's business, whether you liked it or not.

"Brychan? Dilara?" I said.

"No, Ashling, this is Channing." I recognized his voice instantly.

"Channing?" I repeated his name. "Are you okay?"

"Yes. Sorry for calling you at school, but I thought you'd want to know that we've searched all the records in the Library of Celsus in Ephesus. Though the Crone is mentioned throughout our history, there was no information about where you are going to find her," Channing said.

"I don't understand."

"They describe what she does, but never where. What she looks like, but not who she is," he said. "She's small and hunched over, she helps the souls of our kind get to Old Mother from the darkest place on Earth, but that's it," he said. "Over and over again she's mentioned, hunched and tiny; some say she carries a staff, but that's it. We don't know where to go looking for her."

I sighed and closed my eyes in frustration. "She could be anyone anywhere in the world. For all I know, she's already dead. I'm sorry, Ashling," Channing said. "I know we disappointed you . . ."

"No, Channing, you did as I asked."

"Oh, and Quinn wants to talk to you," he said. I could hear him pass the phone.

"Ashling? It's Quinn. I think we should search Father's library. He has some pretty rare artifacts there that might give us more clues."

"That's a great idea," I said.

"There's more, Ashling. We've been noticed here. We need to leave before Verci discovers what we've been looking for."

"Oh no . . ." I said. I had hoped spreading out would lead Vigdis and Verci off the scent, but they had discovered my pack's whereabouts sooner than I had hoped. "Get Gwyn, Cara, and Channing all safe to the Rock, and let me know if you find out anything else," I said. "I'm going to check everything I can think of here, like Baran's library."

Then it dawned on me: the bookstore in Bar Harbor! I nearly screamed it out loud. There were so many old books in that hidden room. The clue I needed might have been right under my nose the entire time.

"Ashling? Are you all right?" Quinn asked.

"Yeah. Just thinking," I said. "Hurry to the Rock and let me know you are safe and if you find anything."

"Will do," Quinn said.

"Thanks," I said. We hung up and I headed slowly back down the hall to my classroom. Thankfully, lunch was next. I needed time to think. And Grey and I needed to get to the bookstore in Bar Harbor as soon as possible.

As I walked into my class, the bell rang. Beth grabbed my books and met me at the door. "You okay?" she asked.

"Yeah, it was Quinn. He just wanted to let me know their travel plans."

She looked at me expectantly and I laughed. "They are on their way from Turkey to Ireland."

"Why?" she said.

"Apparently they love traveling." I smiled, knowing they were doing what I asked of them.

"Your family is weird like you and Grey, right?" she asked, studying me again.

I laughed. "Yes, they are."

"Explains a lot," she said.

"What explains a lot?" Emma asked.

"Her family is weird, too," Beth said.

"What about Channing? Is he . . . weird?" Emma asked. "Because Lacey seems to think they are getting married, but I'm not sure they've ever even spoken to one another."

"Oh gosh, you two!" I shook my head and started down the hall to meet Grey in the lunchroom. I could smell him with every step I took. His scent was easy to detect, even over the disgusting, unnatural smell of school lunch that permeated the halls.

Lacey joined us as we walked. "Lacey, are you really in love with Channing?" Beth asked.

"What if he's . . . you know?" Emma said, pointing at me.

I burst out laughing and pulled them close. "I'm a wolf," I said, and I studied each of their faces. Confusion, disbelief, and uncertainty stared back at me.

Lacey already knew. She'd seen me. I think she was more shocked I actually told the others. It wasn't an easy thing to swallow. I remembered all too well the terrible shock it put her into; without Baran's cunning, I'm not sure we could have saved her.

"No you're not," Emma said. I could sense her resistance to it.

"Yeah, she is," Lacey said. The others looked at her, shocked. "I've seen her." Lacey looked back down at her phone nonchalantly.

Beth looked me dead in the eye with that sharp look of hers. "You are, aren't you?" she said.

I nodded.

"Well shit . . . that's badass," Beth said. She smacked Emma on the back. "I'm hungry, so let's get in line so we can get out of here."

"You do know they aren't feeding us real food, right?" Lacey complained. "The crap they serve us for lunch will kill us one day."

"Yeah, you're probably right," Beth said. "But we are trapped on school grounds, I'm hungry, and if we don't feed *that one*," she pointed at me, "she might eat us."

I laughed. I loved Beth. She was so outspoken and truly didn't filter herself. She was pure thought and pure emotion. I liked that.

"Only on a full moon," I said with a wink.

"Really?" Emma asked.

"No. I'm just teasing," I said.

Grey walked toward us. He looked so calm, but there was something about the natural swagger in his hips that made me swoon. I was sure he didn't even realize it, but he exuded confidence. I wanted to wrap myself around him. I noticed many other girls watching him, but I wasn't worried. I knew he was mine. There was something so sensual about knowing I didn't have to worry—he only had eyes for me.

"Hi," I half-choked. Even now I ridiculously swooned for him. It was somewhat embarrassing. He winked at me as he lightly caressed my neck. I leaned into the touch like a cat begging to be petted.

"Oh quit, you two," Beth said.

Grey chuckled that deep, sexy laugh of his. As we went through the lunch line, I kept glancing up at him and catching him watching me. I still melted at every smile; I hoped that feeling would never go away. He leaned over and his lips grazed my ear as he whispered, "I missed you."

"I love you," I whispered back.

We gathered at our back lunch table, out of earshot of the younger classmen. As soon as everyone was sitting, I pushed my tray of unhealthy mush aside. "Grey. Channing and Quinn called. They didn't find anything in the Library of Celsus. Nothing of use, anyway. They are headed to the Rock to search Father's libraries, but I fear that it is hopeless."

"Is Channing coming back soon?" Lacey asked.

I felt bad for her. Channing was kind, but I wasn't sure he'd ever consider a human for a mate. As wolves, choosing a human for a mate was a guarantee that we'd have to watch our love die one day. "Probably not until next summer," I said.

She silently pouted as she poked at her mashed potatoes and sludgy gravy. I hoped she'd find love one day. She'd been through enough in her life.

"Where do we look now?" Grey asked.

"Oh, I want to check the bookstore in Bar Harbor," I said. His eyes grew wide, and I knew he understood what I was telling him. "Maybe it's been right under my nose the whole time."

"We could drive up after school," he said.

"Or now," I said with a smile.

"Can we come?" Beth asked.

"You all want to cut class?" I said. Emma looked nervous. She hated it last time, too, when she and Beth cut class to glue my broken heart back together.

"Not really," Emma confessed.

"I do," Lacey said.

"Me too," Beth said.

Emma sighed. "Oh fine, I'll go. I don't want to be left out."

I grinned. "Okay, you three go out the side door in five minutes. Grey and I will pull up, and you guys jump in and we'll be out of this place."

"Perfect," Beth said.

Grey and I stood and wandered off down the halls, looking as innocent as we could. Which probably didn't look innocent at all. As we turned the corner, the main doors came into view, but our freedom was blocked by Officer Gavin.

"Hide me," I whispered to Grey.

The football team was walking by and Grey whispered something to them and they started talking loud and shoving each other as they got closer and closer to Officer Gavin. Grey ducked down, pulling me with him as we cut through them to the doors.

We darted out across the parking lot, and I could still see the guys messing with Officer Gavin as the principal ran out and sent them all on their way. Grey ran to the driver's door and opened it for me.

Grey slid in the passenger seat, and we sped off to the side of the school. I saw the door open, and Emma, Beth, and Lacey slipped out and ran toward my car.

"Let's get out of here," Beth said as they all crammed into the backseat.

I hit the gas and we flew out of the parking lot and onto the highway. "I can't believe we just did that," Emma said. "I'm never going to get into college now."

"Sure you will," Beth said. "Every teenager gets a few rebellious freebies, and cutting class as a senior is one of them."

"I agree," Lacey said. "Besides, you're the valedictorian. You're going to any school you want. So relax a little."

"It is simply a best friends' mental health day," I said. I felt wickedly smart—we'd gotten away with it.

Emma laughed. "Well, mental health is important," she said. She was adorably cautious, but that was one of the reasons I loved her so much. "So what are you really looking for?"

I looked at Grey for a moment before deciding to tell them the truth. "I am searching for references to the Triple Goddess in our mythology, so I can locate the Mother and the Crone before my eighteenth birthday," I said.

"Like the original Mother and Crone from the legends? Like, you think they are still alive after all these years?" Beth said.

"Yep," I said, smiling over my shoulder. "We are immortal."

"Baran would flip if he knew you were telling them this," Grey said. "And Mund would poop his pants."

Everyone laughed. We all knew it was true. Whether the girls could fully believe me or not, Mund and Baran would be furious I was putting their lives at risk by telling them the truth, but they already knew we weren't human. Besides, I wanted my best friends to know me, really know me. And they had proven to me that I could trust them with my life.

"So let me get this straight . . . you're wolves, you can't die, and you are looking for ancient people who are living somewhere among us?" Beth said.

"Yeah, that pretty much sums it up," I said.

"Wolves?" Emma repeated.

Lacey smiled at me. "The prettiest wolf in the world. You should see her."

"Well, whatever you are," Emma said, "you won't find what you're looking for in that bookstore. They only carry new releases."

I just smiled.

"Damn," Beth said. "We know nothing about the creatures that surround us, do we? Your kind is everywhere isn't it?"

"We used to be. We surround the daily lives of humans to protect them from harm. Of course, we can't prevent every horrible thing from happening, but we try. That is our duty," I said.

"So, you too, Grey?" Emma asked.

"Yep. We're both werewolves," Grey said. His green eyes sparkled with danger.

# 15
## *The Crone*

"*Umm . . . my friends* are real werewolves," Emma said.

I turned to look at her with the kindest expression I could. I didn't want to scare her or any of them. "Yes, your legends call us werewolves. We are shape-shifters; at any moment I can shift into a wolf. We were created to protect Old Mother's children, her humans," I said. "So we do our best to protect humanity. With so few of us left serving, it makes it impossible to protect everyone, but you're my humans, and I protect you with my life."

"Who is Old Mother?" Beth asked.

"The Celtic goddess of creation," Emma said. "We know her as Mother Earth in this country. I've read about those legends. It's actually a similar story in many different cultures."

I should have known Emma would be the one to know pieces of our history. She was a huge history and mythology nut. It was possible she knew more about my people than I did, but she thought they were all silly bedtime stories instead of my family tree.

"Old Mother is our creator, and she made us to protect humans and be their companions. She isn't a legend—she is everything. She is the air you breathe and the ground beneath your feet," I said.

"So, the Triple Goddess?" Emma said. "Like the Celtic symbol with the waxing, full, and waning moons?"

I nodded.

"And you're searching for the Mother and the Crone?" she asked.

I nodded. It was impressive how smart she was. Maybe her research would lead me to the Mother and the Crone.

"What do you really need them for?" Beth asked.

I took a deep breath before telling them. "A prophecy was spoken, of the girl with the crimson hair and snow-white skin who would come of Vanir lineage. She would save the earth from destruction. She was the embodiment of love and would bring balance to humankind and unify all wolf packs for the greater good of humanity," I said.

They all stared at me, their eyes wandering up to my hair and back to my face. "Embodiment of love? How is that possible?" Beth said. I appreciated and loved Beth for her skepticism. It wasn't that she doubted me; understanding before believing was in her nature. Asking questions was her way of showing that she cared.

"A prophecy about you? That is so dreamy," Lacey said.

"And the Triple Goddess is the fulfillment of the prophecy?" Emma said.

"They are a huge part of it. All three must stand at Carrowmore on the Bloodmoon while the Maiden is claimed," I said.

"If you are seeking the Mother and the Crone, then . . . who is the Maiden?" Beth asked.

I pursed my lips nervously. "I am."

Lacey smiled. "I knew it!" she said. "I could feel the truth in everything you said. You are here to protect and love us, and you are going to change the world, aren't you?"

"I hope so," I said.

"Well then, we have you," Emma said. "Now we go in search of the

Mother and the Crone."

"You guys are going to help me?" I asked.

"Duh," Beth said. "Was there ever a question?"

"I love you girls," I said.

They continued to ask questions about our history and how old my family really was. It was wonderful to finally stop keeping secrets from them. Emma and Beth wanted to know everything, and Lacey was nearly swooning at the idea of it all. The nearly four-hour drive went by pretty quickly, and at last I pulled into the alley behind the bookstore, parking in the shadow of the dumpsters.

"Why are we parking here?" Lacey asked. I could hear the disgust in her voice.

"My car is a bit conspicuous," I said.

"Being a bit subtle might be in our benefit when we are out skipping class," Grey said.

"Still gross," Lacey said.

"Why here?" Beth asked.

"They have a nice collection of artifacts in preservation here that may have the answers I seek," I said.

"Ladies?" Grey said as he held out his hand to my friends in the backseat and started opening his door.

Suddenly the smell of blood hit me. My hair stood on end. Wolves. Something bad was happening here. I grabbed Grey's arm, pulling him back inside the car.

"What?" Grey asked, surprised.

"Do you smell that?" I whispered.

Grey smelled the air. "Blood," he said.

"I don't like it here," Beth said.

I locked the doors even though I knew it wouldn't protect my friends from the wolves inside the bookstore, but I thought it might give them a sense of security. The back door to the store was ajar. I closed my eyes and tried to hear the voices in the store. Just those voices. I had to drown out the sound of my friends' racing hearts, of the ocean waves, of the people on the street. Everything seemed so normal, but then I heard it.

The soft whimper of the old woman that worked in the store. I remembered everything about her. Her voice; her white, starry eyes; the curve of her back.

"Tell us where to find the Crone," a man said. The threat in his words was clear. He was interrogating her. His voice had a thick Japanese accent.

"You shall not see her, even if she is before your eyes," the old woman croaked.

"Then you will die with your secrets," a woman said.

"They are killing her," I whispered.

"Who?" Emma said.

"How many?" Grey asked.

"The old woman," I said. "I only hear two others, a man and a woman."

"Bleed her out," the man said. "And hurry up; I'm bored."

"What evil is this?" I whispered to Grey. "We have to save her."

"I can take two," Grey said. "Stay here and guard them. I will try to save the old woman."

I didn't want him to go in alone, but I wasn't sure what choice I had. We couldn't leave our friends unprotected, and I couldn't bear the idea of that sweet woman dying when we were right here to help her. "Be careful."

He nodded and leaned forward to kiss my cheek. Grey hopped out the door and shifted into a dire wolf, tearing his clothes apart. Grey was enormous, making the doorway look miniature as he ran into the bookstore. I watched him disappear and I felt like my heart left my body.

Behind me, my friends' hearts were beating fast, but they held their breath. I reached back and held their hands. "We have to stay hidden," I whispered. "Duck down as low as you can."

I listened from the car, feeling helpless as Grey snarled.

"Who the hell are you?" the man asked.

Grey growled in return.

"Looks like he's here to protect the old bag of bones," the woman said.

The man laughed. Without a word, I heard him shift into a wolf and attack Grey. I wanted to scream and rush into the store. I wanted to be by his side, but the heavy breathing and soft crying from the backseat kept me in the car.

I heard them fighting, but I couldn't make sense of any of it. But as long as they fought, I knew for certain Grey was okay. His adrenaline rushed through me like fire. I twitched with the need to shift.

Suddenly, the woman screamed and rushed out into the street. I recognized the black-jeweled eye patch immediately. I recognized her from the Bloodrealms. She hurried into the woods and disappeared.

Grey's dire wolf slammed through the door and chased after her. I nearly fell out of the car in my rush to open the door.

"Grey, no!" I called.

He stopped and turned back toward us. Emma wouldn't look at him; her fear was consuming her, but Lacey and Beth watched him with interest. Lacey had seen me as a wolf, but never Grey.

"Is the man dead?" I asked.

Grey nodded his wolf head. He nudged toward the store, telling us to go in.

"Hurry," I whispered to my friends. We made a dash from the car and went into the store.

The bookstore was in disarray. Bookshelves were broken and knocked down all around the store. The smell of wolf blood was stronger now. I saw the torn body of a black wolf lying in the debris of the store. I knew it was the Japanese man; I recognized his scent.

I heard her before I saw her, a soft gasp for life. I rushed over to her side and knelt down beside the blind woman as she stared up at me. Her eyes were like a starry sky of cataracts, and her face was bleeding and swollen. Grey was by my side . . . my wolf.

"Beth, see if there is a fridge and find something cold," I said. I wrapped my arms around the old woman. "I'm so sorry," I said, not knowing what else to say.

She smiled at me so kindly. I thought for a moment she was here to soothe me. There was a beauty and kindness to her that filled the air. Beth returned with a bag of frozen beans and handed it to me. I gently placed it on the woman's face as my friends sat down next to us on the floor.

"Are you going to be okay, ma'am?" Emma asked.

"Should we call for an ambulance?" Lacey asked.

"Oh, sweet children, thank you for your concern, but I am well now with all of you," she said.

Emma glanced at the dead wolf again. "The police, maybe?"

"Animal control." Lacey laughed.

"They won't be coming back here again I suspect," she said as she patted Grey's thick, furry neck. She reached out her hand to me. "Help me sit up, please."

I gently helped her sit up, and she smiled. "I knew you'd come," she said.

"What?" I asked.

"There's time for all of that, but first let's get that poor boy some clothes," she said.

I glanced over at Grey, who was still standing guard as my wolf. I laughed at the predicament he now found himself in. If he shifted back, he'd be naked. Though I loved the idea, I didn't want him naked in front of my friends, and admittedly, I didn't want him naked in front of Lacey, his ex-girlfriend.

The old woman wrapped her arm through mine as she pulled herself to standing, and I walked with her. "Behind the counter, dear," she said, and she pointed to a small trunk. "Inside there you'll find what he needs."

I opened the trunk and inside was a pair of black sweatpants, a t-shirt, underwear, socks, and boots all in his sizes. I looked up at her. There was some kind of magic in it, but I could feel that she wasn't going to explain it. I pulled out the things for Grey and set them in the bathroom for him.

"Girls, could you help me make some soothing tea?" the woman asked.

Emma and Beth followed her to the barista counter and helped make tea for all of us. Lacey and I flipped the table back upright and pushed the chairs all back in. The old woman walked over and sat down closest to the fire. Soon Grey emerged in his new clothes, looking so dark and dramatic. Emma and Beth brought over the tea for everyone and we all sat down.

I studied the dainty cup in my hands with ginger floating in the steaming water. It was a healing herb. I swirled the cup around in my hands as I swallowed a sip of ginger tea.

"What's your name?" I asked the woman.

"Oh my dear, you can call me Caoimhe," she said. Her accent was heavily Irish.

"How long have you lived here?" I asked.

"I've only been here about a year," she said, looking up at me with a twinkle in her eye. "What are you seeking here today instead of attending school?"

I blushed. "I'm searching for the Triple Goddess. I am trying to find the Mother and the Crone. Do you know where I can find the Crone?"

"What do you know already?" she asked.

"That she is an older woman, hunched from time, she delivers our souls to Old Mother," I said, studying her for the first time. She was an old soul and hunched from time. "Are you the Crone?"

"Goodness no, dear," she said. "The Crone dwells in the darkest, most evil place on earth."

"That's what Channing said he found in our mythology, but there was no hint at where that might be. What do I do?"

"Do you not already know where the earth's darkest place might be?" she said. "Have you not already seen the home of true evil?"

"The Bloodrealms," I said as my mind finally caught up. "The old woman who fed me the rat! She is the Crone!"

Caoimhe smiled as she patted my hand. "That is her, kindly and hunched into the tiniest woman, but do not underestimate her power. Even the smallest creatures can make the biggest explosions."

"Grey, we have to get her out of the Realms with Baran," I said.

Grey nodded. "But what about the Mother, Caoimhe? Can you tell us anything about her?"

"You will find her as you look upon the stars," she said. I stared at her, trying to make sense of her words. "Oh, and when you find the Crone, you should give her that pendant of yours." I looked down at the Tree of Life pendant hanging around my neck that Eamon had given me.

"Thank you. I will," I said. I pondered her riddle and the meaning of it all as I noticed my friends sipping their tea almost in a trance. "You guys okay?"

Emma nodded and Beth snort-laughed.

"A little surreal, but I kind of love it," Lacey said.

"Now that you know what we are, it is your secret to keep," I said.

"Fear not, child, they are true," Caoimhe said, patting their hands. "Now, my dear ones. It is time for you to make your journey."

"What about . . . " Emma trailed off, staring at the dead wolf's body.

"I will see him safely home." She nodded.

There was something about her words that gave me pause, but I didn't know what.

"Can we help you clean up before we head home?" Grey asked.

"No, dears. I will set this all back to order."

"Are you sure?" Grey asked.

"My Grey Storm, you have a greater duty than to clean my store. You protect the Crimson Queen. Always remember that," she said.

"I will," he said.

The girls said their thanks and good-byes, and we made our way out to my car. I felt weird leaving Caoimhe behind unprotected, and not helping her clean up. It felt unnatural. Shouldn't I protect her, too?

"Wait a minute," I said as I jumped back out of the car and ran back inside. I stopped dead in my tracks as I turned into the storefront. Everything was back as it was, perfectly in its place. The store was immaculate and organized and the dead wolf was gone. Caoimhe was magic, and though I didn't understand it, I knew she was on our side. I looked around the store for Caoimhe to invite her to stay with us, but she was nowhere to be found.

I walked slowly back out to the car and got in. "Everything is back to normal," I said.

"What?" Emma said.

"The store is perfectly back in order, and Caoimhe and the dead wolf are gone. It's impossible," I said.

"Nothing is impossible anymore," Emma said.

Beth shook her head. "Ain't that the truth," she said.

"I'm sorry, this must have been hard for all of you. Are you guys okay? I don't want you to fear us," I said.

"Yeah," Grey said. "When I shifted, I only wanted to protect you all. I'm sorry if I scared you."

"We weren't scared," Beth said.

"More shocked," Lacey said. "I'd seen Ashling, but you were surprisingly huge."

Grey laughed as he started driving us home. "I'm a dire wolf," he said.

"*Canis dirus*," Emma said.

"What?" Lacey said.

"That's your scientific Latin name," Emma said.

"Nerd," Beth said with a giggle.

Emma laughed. "I know."

"So, you're a queen?" Beth asked.

"I'm supposed to be, but sometimes I still feel like a little girl," I said.

"That's because you are; we're seventeen years old. How can you be expected to rule the world?" Lacey asked.

I smiled at them. "With the help of everyone I love."

"That's why friends were created," Beth said. "So we could hold each other up."

I loved those girls. They meant the world to me. We were created to be friends and support each other through love and community. Old Mother was glorious to have given us that chance at life.

The drive home was quite reflective. The girls became quiet and thoughtful. I held Grey's hand so tight, like a lifeline. My world changed with Caoimhe. Now I wasn't just saving Baran from the Realms; I had to somehow get the Crone out, too. And what was I going to do about the Mother?

We dropped all the girls off at their cars in the high school parking lot and made our way home to Baran's house.

"I'm sorry I left you today," Grey said.

"Don't be. I'm proud of you," I said. "You protected Caoimhe. You saved her life."

He smiled. "I don't know why, but I knew I had to save her."

We pulled into the driveway; every light in Baran's house was on, and I could see Rhonda pacing in the living room.

"We're in trouble," I whispered.

"Can't wait," Grey said.

"I don't think we told them we'd be late."

Grey laughed.

"It's not funny," I said, but it kind of was. As we walked in, we were faced with three very angry Bloodsuckers.

"Do you have any idea . . ." Rhonda started. She clenched her fists and shook her head, turning away from us.

"What is wrong with the two of you?" Paul said. "Just give us a head's up if you're not going to be coming home from school like normal. We can parole the perimeter of the school all day, but we're not magicians. We can't be on your every move."

"We thought you were dead," Jamal said as he sat down on the leather sofa. I could smell his sadness.

"I'm so sorry. I totally forgot. I got a call from Quinn, and we had a lead on the Crone . . ." I said. "But I know where to find her now."

Rhonda turned around and the energy of the room shifted. I could smell their excitement. "Where is she?" she asked.

"The Bloodrealms," Grey said.

Rhonda sat down next to Jamal. "Shit. Really?"

"Now you have to get two people out of there without getting caught?" Paul said. "I don't know, man."

I sighed and sat down. They were right. It was terrible odds to get Baran out, but to find and get the Crone out would make this rescue mission even more difficult. "I know," I said with a sigh. "I bloody know."

The phone rang and I jumped.

Grey leaned over and grabbed it off the receiver. "Hello?" he said. "Yeah, okay." He handed the phone to me. I looked at him for answers as I took the phone but didn't see any clues.

"Hello?" I said.

"Ashling, we're here," Dilara said. Just hearing her voice made me feel calm. "We made it to Dagny. You should see the army he's built for you . . .. there are so many wolves here. It's glorious."

My heart swelled with pride. My wolves. My people.

"You're going to win," she said. "They all believe in you . . . every last one of them."

"Oh, thank Old Mother," I said. "Should we go into the Blood-realms tonight to save Baran?"

"We need time to get into the Realms so we are in position when you bring Baran, but I think twenty-four hours should be enough time for us to get where we need to be. We need to be there to protect you both before you move him. I don't want you in there any longer than necessary. And once Baran is with us, you leave."

"Dilara, I can't just leave you guys," I said. "I'm going in tonight to heal Baran. Besides, I need to find the Crone."

"What are you talking about?" she said.

"I know where to find the Crone," I said. "She's in the Bloodrealms and I have to get her out. I need her with me at Carrowmore."

"Damn," she said. "You want to get two people out of the Blood-realms at the same time from different locations . . . that's going to take . . ." she trailed off. I could hear the doubt in her voice. She had lived in the Bloodrealms world for who knew how long, suffered with those people, and nearly died trying to get me out. Now I was asking her to go back in to save not just one but two people . . . for me.

But I couldn't choose between Baran and the Crone. I needed them both for entirely different reasons. I needed Baran for love and family and the Crone for the survival of all my people. It wasn't mutu-ally exclusive; to me they were a packaged deal. I couldn't be claimed at Carrowmore without the Crone, but Baran was my family.

"How are you planning to do that?" she finally asked.

"I don't know," I admitted. "Could you get Kane, Shikoba, Bry-chan, and Dagny on the phone? I'll have everyone here on with me. If we all talk it out, I'm sure there is a solution," I said.

She sighed. "Hang on," she said.

I heard shuffling on the phone and muffled talking in the back-ground. I walked into the living room with Grey, Rhonda, Jamal, and

Paul and sat down in the middle of them and put the phone on speaker.

"You're on speaker," Dilara said.

"We're all here," I said.

"You don't like to make things easy, do you?" Brychan said.

"Hi, Brychan." I was happy to hear his voice again.

"Ashling, do you know where to find the Crone in the Realms?" Kane asked.

"Not really. I stumbled on her down by the river after I jumped from the selection chamber. Really, I think she found me." I hadn't realized it until that moment, but as I said the words, I knew they were true.

Kane cleared his throat, and I just stared at my hands. I knew what they were all going to say. It was a lost cause.

"Do you think you could find her in your dream like you do with Baran?" Grey asked. "Like if you concentrate on her long enough you'll find her?"

"I don't know," I said. "I'm not sure I control my dreams at all."

"Then how are you going to find either of them?" Dagny asked. "What if they get all the way into the Realms and you can't even find Baran again?"

"I don't know," I said, suddenly terrified. What if I was leading them all to their deaths? What if this was all a mistake? "I don't know what to do."

I felt weak and ridiculous. What if I failed them all?

"What now?" Dilara asked.

I didn't know how to answer. How could I ask them to risk their own lives in the Realms when I didn't even have a plan to get them to the Crone and Baran and get everyone out safely? I sat in silence and Grey held my hand. I could feel his love and warmth pouring into me. He believed in me, even when my heart was filling with doubt.

"Ashling, what would Baran tell you to do?" Brychan asked.

I snorted. "He'd tell me to let him die and go save the Crone."

"And what are you going to do?" Brychan said.

"Save them both," I said.

"Because you never listen to anyone." He laughed. "Which should be, by all logic, your demise, but somehow it is your secret charm. We will all follow you to the ends of the earth because we know what you are and we know who you are. You are not just our queen, Ashling— you are our everything. Now, what would Baran do?"

I felt my heart swell. "He'd tell me to learn to control my powers and instincts." I laughed. "He told me that a year ago. Like he knew even then that his life depended on it."

"Well, it does," Dilara said. "You have twenty-four hours to locate the Crone and Baran and get them to the labyrinth. We will meet you there."

"I will not fail," I said.

"We know," Brychan said.

# 16

## *Blood River*

*The phone went* silent, and I sat quietly surrounded by Grey, Rhonda, Jamal, and Paul in Baran's living room. I wasn't sure if I could look at any of them. I felt nervous. I had to find the Crone and Baran by the time my pack was in the Realms or they would be risking their lives for nothing. We hadn't talked about a contingency plan. What if I never made it to them with Baran and the Crone? How long would they wait for me before they were discovered and killed? I knew the answer—they'd search for me. There was no room for error.

I felt Rhonda wrap her arms around me, and she hugged me tightly. "You know what to do and I believe you know how. It's time to woman up and save some lives," she said. "Now go sleep and find the answers while we protect you."

I laughed. "Thanks, Rhonda."

"Yeah, yeah. Now get to work! You have to save the fricking world!" she said. "There isn't time for all this mush."

"Good night," I said as I ascended the stairs. Grey chuckled as he followed me.

"I like Rhonda," he said. "She's delightfully weird."

"We are all weird. That's why we all make sense together," I said.

"Are you scared to close your eyes?" Grey asked suddenly.

I stopped on the stairs and turned to look at him. "Terrified," I said. "But my fears can't rule me. Love will prevail."

He winked. "That's my girl."

I walked cautiously to my bed, as though I was afraid it would hurt me. It looked so innocent in the corner of the room, but the truth was that sleeping could cost me my soul. I sat down on the edge and held my face in my hands. Grey knelt down in front of me and pulled my hands away from my face.

"So your plan is to start with finding the Crone?" Grey prompted.

"The Crone, because she will probably have farther to go, and our team needs time to get in position for Baran," I said. "Maybe I could first stop and visit Baran so I can heal him. I could hide him and then go find the Crone. But . . . if I move Baran first, we will alert Verci and Vigdis that something is going on. If I move the Crone first, it will give me time before they suspect anything."

"Damn," he said.

"What?"

"You are like a ginga-ninja," he said.

I laughed so hard my side ached. "You just called me a red-haired ninja?"

"Yeah, baby. You're sleek, skilled, a fighter, and a ginger," he said.

"Proud of yourself, aren't you?" I asked.

"Oh yeah." He winked at me. "There is a parade on Saturday; maybe Baran will be home by then."

I hoped he was right. I lay down on my bed and laid my hands on my chest. I didn't quite know what to do with them. Where do you put your hands when you might die while you sleep? Grey lay down next to me and wrapped his arm around me.

"I'll hold you all night long. I'll never leave your side," he said.

"Tonight and always."

I looked into his eyes and tried to memorize every feature. I only knew some of the risks of what I was about to do, and if I was going to die on this mission, I wanted his face to be my last waking memory. I took a deep breath. "Could you give me the wolf's bane off the bedside table?" I asked.

He handed me the plant.

"It cures silver poisoning," I said, mostly to myself. "If I could bring that coin back, then I think I can bring this with me."

He nodded.

"I love you, Grey, with every fiber of my being. To the moon and back. Through a sea of forever, I love you," I said.

"I love you, too," he said. "I'll see you later, lover."

I blushed and turned away to stare at the ceiling. I took deep breaths over and over again, trying to calm my nerves, and closed my eyes. Trying to force myself into a dream was difficult, and as the moments dragged on, my body resisted even more. I was so stressed that my body felt rigid.

Grey turned on his phone and started playing a soft acoustic mix. He stood up and walked around the room. I could hear his every move. He lit all the candles in my room and turned out the lights. Finally, he crawled back into bed with me and pulled me into his arms. I rested my head on his chest and listened to his beating heart and the rise and fall of his breaths. He lightly ran his fingers through my hair as I began to relax.

*I opened my eyes down in the tunnels next to the river. I blinked to focus my eyes in the darkness surrounding me. I remembered the dank smell of blood and death down here . . . it was so potent that my eyes stung. I looked around, hoping to see the Crone's fire, but nothing was ever that easy. I was on the south bank of the river, and the river was flowing higher than normal. As I got closer, I realized it was tainted with blood.*

*Panic raked through me. What horrible deed had Vigdis done? How many lives had she stolen to flood the river with blood? What could she gain from so much death?*

*I looked up and saw a ledge above me and recognized the scratches in the stone. This was where I'd sought refuge when the Garm wolves had chased me and I found my mace. I wished I had it with me now. I looked down at my hand to realize I was still holding the wolf's bane . . . it worked. I could bring objects back and forth with me. If only I could bring people. I carefully tucked the flower into my pocket and leaped up onto the ledge. Maybe there was something I was meant to find here. There had to be a reason I woke here of all places in the Realms.*

*I crawled through the small hole into the old burial grave and smelled smoke. I crept silently farther into the cave and spotted a small girl sitting around a tiny flame, trying to stay warm. All the hair on her head had been shaved off. Her face was covered in scars, new cuts, and dried blood. As I looked closer, I saw the arrowhead necklace that Shikoba had given to me. It was her—the girl who saved me in the Bloodrealms and pulled me into the crevice in the rock . . . Jutta.*

*I wanted to rush over and embrace her, but I didn't want to scare her to death. I was invisible to people in the Bloodrealms. I crept into the opening and knocked over a couple rocks to make my presence known. She jumped back and crawled behind one of the burial stones. She held what looked like a human femur as a weapon in her shaking hands.*

*"Get back, demon!" she said. There was a fierceness in her voice even when it waivered.*

*"Do you remember me, Jutta? I gave you that arrowhead necklace once," I said. "I will not hurt you."*

*She barely peeked over the stone, scanning the cave for a sight of me. Her dark eyes were wild with fear. She didn't trust a bodiless voice, and I couldn't blame her.*

*"Are you hurt?" I asked, sitting back against the wall as far from her as I could.*

"Not as much as some," she said.

"Good," I said.

"What are you? Where are you?" she asked.

"I'm a werewolf like you, but you just can't see me right now," I said. "Are you old enough to shift?"

"Um . . ."

"I'll take that as a no." I sighed. "Where are your companions from before? Where are your parents?"

She looked at the bone in her hand and shuddered. "They are all gone."

My heart ached for her. I could only imagine the gruesome things she had been forced to see. "Is that one of them in your hand?" I asked.

She nodded and tears ran down her cheeks.

"I'm glad they are still protecting you, even in death," I said.

She closed her eyes. I wished I'd thought to bring food in my pockets; she looked hungry. I felt around in my pockets anyway and felt a small, round, wrapped disk. I pulled it out and nearly laughed at the irony. A Lifesaver candy rested in my hand.

"Would you like a piece of candy?" I asked.

She nodded but didn't move. I crawled across the tomb with the candy concealed in my invisible hand and placed it on a stone between us and backed away to the wall. As soon as I sat back down, she darted toward it and snatched it before returning to her hiding spot as she unwrapped the tiny candy.

"Jutta, who did this to you?"

She looked around as though someone might be listening. She crept out from behind the rock and dragged her finger in the sand on the ground. I watched her spell V-I-G-D-I-S. She quickly wiped it all away.

"Do you remember me? My name is Ashling. You saved me once in a crack down here."

She nodded. "You're the Crimson Queen," she said.

"I am."

"Will you save us all?" she asked. She was so innocent.

*I took a deep breath. "That's my plan."*

*"She killed my family," Jutta said, staring at the floor where she'd wiped away Vigdis's name. "All of them. I have no one left."*

*I crawled closer to her so only a couple of feet stood between us. "Your heart beats in your chest, sweet Jutta, and the love of your mother and father flows in your blood. They are with you in everything you do. We are never alone."*

*She leaped into my arms and hugged me tight. She somehow knew exactly where I was. I held her close and rubbed her back, wishing with all my heart that I could free her right this instant. The only way to get her out was to take her with me; the risk was terribly high. She would appear to be a little girl traveling alone. Though, that might just be what we needed to survive. No one would see me coming if I had to fight them to protect her.*

*"Jutta, I cannot promise you that we will live through this, but I do promise you I will die trying to save you. I am seeking the Crone. Will you come with me?" I asked.*

*She pulled away and wiped her tears. "I know where she is," Jutta said. "I can take you there." The confidence in her words was shocking. Wherever the Crone was, there was certainly death.*

*"Are you sure?" I said.*

*She picked up the bone again. "I either die alone here in this tomb as I had planned, or I take my chances at life," she said. "And I choose life."*

*"How old are you?"*

*"Eleven sacrifices have come," she said.*

*"Sacrifices?"*

*"Vigdis sacrifices slaves once a year, bleeding them out into the rivers as a warning to all who remain. I just witnessed my eleventh," she said.*

*"We will have to choose you a new birthday when we get out of here," I said. "And I'll buy you a big cake."*

*She smiled at that. "Follow me," she said.*

*She leaped up into the opening above us. She was quick and limber as she climbed up the chimney-like funnel. I leaped up to follow her. We climbed for fifty feet before she pulled herself onto a ledge. I pulled myself up with her and crawled after her in the darkness. I couldn't see where I was going, but the tunnel was so small I knew we wouldn't lose our path. She stopped and I realized where we were. I remembered the smells and the rush of water.*

*"We're in the selection chamber?" I whispered.*

*"Below," she said. "This is a hidden tunnel that feeds into the drainage system."*

*"The Crone has been captured?"*

*"No," she said. "She's gathering bones. She's always here this time of year . . . after the sacrifices, I mean."*

*Jutta slid open a wrought-iron floor grate and slipped through. I followed close behind. She tiptoed forward and stopped, crouching down at the solid metal doorway. The metal was gouged with claw marks. She slowly opened the door, revealing metal spikes covering the other side; a man's hand was still impaled on one of the spikes. I tried to block it from my mind as I peeked inside. I could see the chamber was empty except for piles of bodies that covered the floor. I heard the sound of something being dragged and looked to see the Crone pulling a body at least twice her size into the room with the others.*

*"What is she doing?" I asked.*

*"Preparing to burn them for Old Mother," she said. "We should wait until she's done; we don't want to interrupt the ceremony."*

*Thought I knew in my heart that setting these souls free was equally important to my mission, it didn't make waiting any easier. I wanted to snatch Jutta and the Crone and rush to the cells to get Baran. Then I listened . . . the souls were crying to be free. We needed to give them that.*

*"Should we help?" I asked.*

*She shook her head, scared.*

*We watched as the old woman walked right toward us. Jutta hid behind the door, but I watched. She gently pulled the hand from the spike and placed it into the pile. She walked around the pile in a circle and dragged the head of her staff behind her. As she passed us, I saw the staff was leaving a black powder behind. When she completed her circle, she stopped and raised her staff above her tiny head.*

*"Old Mother Earth, I beg you to receive these souls that were taken out of right. I will you to bring them into your arms and keep them safe. For all are created equal in your love," she said. She slammed her staff down on the ground and ignited a fire. The fire raced around the circle and took into it the bones and bodies of the dead. "Children of Old Mother, I set you free."*

*I closed my eyes and prayed to Old Mother all my hopes for these souls, begging forgiveness that I came much too late to save them, and I prayed she would allow me the strength to save Jutta, the Crone, Baran, and my pack.*

*The flames licked high into the air, but the Crone didn't back up. It was as though she couldn't feel the heat of the flame. Was she dead like Shikoba or trapped in a dream like me? How were the flames not hurting her?*

*Jutta stood and slinked next to the wall; if I didn't know she was there, I wouldn't notice her myself. She had the ability to move so quietly. She crept up right behind the Crone.*

*"Yes, child, what do you two ask of me?" the Crone said.*

*I stared, fully shocked, though I shouldn't have been. She was otherworldly. I walked next to Jutta and tried to find my words.*

*"We seek you," Jutta said for me.*

*I didn't want to call her a crone; the word was so cruel sounding, but I didn't have another name for her. "Do you remember me?" I asked.*

*She looked at the Tree of Life pendant around my neck and smiled. "You're the Crimson Queen," she said. "I know you. What do you wish, my dears? Are you hungry?" Jutta nodded and the old woman smiled. "For you, little one, there is food in my satchel."*

*"I don't know how to ask this . . ." I said, trying to find the right words.*

*She turned and looked at me with her tiny, wrinkled face. "Yes, child, I am the Crone. You need not fear me."*

*"I need you at Carrowmore," I said. "We are here to ask this of you. I can rescue you from this place."*

When she looked at me, I was certain she could see me clearly. She looked at Jutta, who was sitting pretzel style and devouring bread. "Not much of an army," the Crone said.

I laughed. "I don't need an army."

"Ah," she said. "And where would you take me?"

"I know the way out," I said.

"To Carrowmore." She nodded and held her hand out for Jutta. "Come, child, let us be rid of this unholy place."

They followed me through the third doorway to the right. I remembered this door . . . I remembered them all. Grete, Fridrik, and I were carried through this door, and we were all forever changed after that moment.

I thought of Grete and wondered where she was now. Was Selene torturing her, too? The depth of evil in this world was startling. I had grown up so sheltered and naïve. I never knew a world like this could exist.

As I walked through the dark, long hallways, I remembered every step. It was as though I'd never left the Bloodrealms at all. I'd had plenty of time to memorize my surroundings when I was captured in the nets, when I held Fridrik's hand and prayed. Those memories still made my heart hurt.

"I am going to hide the two of you in the labyrinth," I said. "I must seek Baran Killian in the jail cells. My pack is coming to rescue all of you. So while I'm gone, stay hidden and don't make a sound," I said. "Brychan Kahedin, Kane and Shikoba of the Cree, and Dilara Tabakov will come for you."

"You can't leave," Jutta said.

"You'll be safe with the Crone," I said. "You take care of each other."

"But I can help," she said.

I smiled at her. She reminded me of myself at her age . . . so much energy and will. "Until you are old enough to shift, the best place for you is with the Crone," I said. I saw her sadness, and I knew exactly how she felt. I spent my whole life being underestimated and left behind. "When you are old enough, I will be proud to have you by my side."

"Thank you," she said quietly.

*My feet led the way, and my mind felt numb as we approached the endless labyrinth; I got chills just looking at it. It was where I lost Grey, where I was captured . . . so many horrible memories. I would have thought there weren't any good memories in the Bloodrealms, but that would be a lie. Grey and I were married and first made love here. I saved Fridrik. I met Jutta, Dilara, and Conrad; I longed to see Conrad again, and I hoped that Old Mother's fabric had healed his wounds. Despite the terror, there were good memories in this dark place. I had to remember that. Even in the darkest of night, evil did not reign.*

*I studied the enormous walls of the labyrinth, and I had an idea.*

*"Crone, if Jutta and I toss you, can you make it up to the top and pull Jutta up after you? No one will find you lying on the tops of the labyrinth walls. You'll hear and see everything around you, but you'll be out of eyesight and so high no one will smell you."*

*The Crone looked at the walls and sighed.*

*"It's okay. We can find somewhere else," I said, looking around.*

*"Oh child, I can get up there," she said. "It's getting down with these old bones that I don't look forward to."*

*I smiled and chuckled at her. I liked the dryness to her humor. She was real and honest.*

*"Jutta, grab my wrists," I said. We made a basket out of our four arms, and I looked to the Crone for her to get on so we could thrust her up to the top of the wall. The Crone just laughed.*

*"I can manage," she said.*

*She started tapping her staff on a few stones; each one slid out at her command, and she began walking up the wall like a staircase. "Hurry now, Jutta," the Crone said. "The magic only lasts a few moments."*

*I watched as Jutta helped Crone all the way up the enormous wall; each step appeared to be more difficult than the step before for the Crone. I felt bad for making her climb all the way up there, but I knew it was the safest place. The stones all slid back into their original places as the Crone and Jutta passed. When they were finally all the way at the top of the lab-*

*yrinth, I could barely see Jutta peeking over and waving at me. I prayed it wouldn't be the last time I saw her.*

*I began my walk back to the cellblock. Time passed so differently in my dreams. I wasn't sure if it had been days or minutes. I tried to slow my breathing as panic crept in. Would Baran be so horribly injured that I wouldn't be able to heal him? Would he be dead? Or possibly even worse, what if it took days to heal him, and by the time he was ready to move, Brychan, Dilara, Kane, and Shikoba would have gone on without us? What if they left us for dead? Or what if they never made it at all? I shivered at the idea. Without them, I wouldn't know how to get Baran, Jutta, and the Crone out of the Bloodrealms. Without them, both Baran and I would likely die here. I felt certain the Crone would watch over Jutta if I failed, but Baran would surely die.*

*Every corner I turned I knew I was getting closer to the cells. The pungent smell of blood filled my nostrils, making them burn. Centuries of death filled these halls . . . some human and some wolf. The sound of footsteps echoed behind me, and I froze against the wall. My heart was pounding in my ears. There was nowhere to hide, and the only thing on my side was darkness. I didn't dare keep moving; I didn't know the way, and any sound might be my death. I crouched down as low as I could make myself as I waited for the person to come into view. I held my breath as steps grew near. All I had were my wits. I knew they wouldn't be able to see me, but my scent and any sound I made would give me away.*

*Verci walked by me without a care in the world. He didn't sense me at all. He was clean in brand-new leather armor embossed with the Dvergar Bloodmark of three circling wolves. I always thought their mark looked like wolves about to devour prey. I suppose it was meant to strike fear into the hearts of their enemies, but to me it was just honest. They were a merciless pack.*

*He headed away from the cells down a long hall I'd never been before. I slowly stood and began to creep after him. Wherever he was going, I was sure to find Baran.*

# 17
## *Branded*

*I followed Verci for what felt like an eternity. We went through twisting and turning halls and past many open doorways. I kept looking behind me, trying to memorize the path I'd taken. Losing my way could get us all killed, but remembering this path was going to be challenging. I could feel myself losing the path. All the doorways were the same; for all I knew, we were going in circles. When I looked down, I saw claw marks in the stones. Someone fought desperately not to go any farther . . . and lost. I shivered at the idea of being dragged to my death, clawing at the ground to save myself. It made me even more scared to think of where we were going. The person who died this way clearly knew what they were up against, and I didn't have a clue. I stared at the ground as I continued to follow Verci. The claw marks secured my way back to safety.*

*I knelt down and ran my fingers over the deep grooves. It was almost like I could feel their fear. Mesmerized by the claw marks, I almost walked right into Verci's back when he stopped. I held my breath, praying he wouldn't feel my body heat. I cautiously took one step back from him and exhaled.*

*That was too close.*

*I looked around and realized we were in some sort of torture chamber. The room was carved into the stone of the earth and metal beams ran through it. There were chains dangling from the ceiling in front of my face—thankfully, I hadn't touched any of them and alerted Verci of my presence. Whips hung on the walls along with every type of device my father kept in his study. They were all barbaric and horrible tools meant to force information from dying lips, but it was the metal box that I couldn't look away from. It was an iron maiden, and the claw marks led directly to it.*

*I'd never seen one in person before, but I knew what it was. The iron maiden stood about seven feet tall and was intricately marked with the Dvergar Bloodmark. It was filled from top to bottom with foot-long metal spikes, but it was the sight of the bloodstained ground around it that nearly drained the blood from my body. I felt weak just looking at it. Mund had told tales of them; I'd always thought it was fictional, but the blood-soaked stones told a very real story. The iron maiden wasn't a torture device—it was a death sentence.*

*How I wished Mund were with me. He'd protect me. He'd tell me it was going to be okay. I just had to hold his strength in my heart and I'd stand a chance of saving Baran.*

*There wasn't another living soul in that room aside from Verci and me, but I could feel the spirits of the dead surrounding me, trying to pull me down with them. The dead were like that . . . they liked company.*

*Verci moved around the room like a chef in his kitchen, sharpening knives and whistling to himself. It was disturbing how happy he seemed here among all this death. Couldn't he feel the dead? They were all here. Every soul he'd taken was still here. He'd freed none of them. They all came to this room to die, and here they remained. I would truly have to burn the Bloodrealms to the ground to get every bit of blood and bone to save these souls.*

*Liquid dropped on my face and slid down my cheek. As I wiped it away I realized it was blood. I stared at my hand, trying to comprehend what was happening as another drop of warm blood hit my shoulder.*

*I swallowed my fear and looked up into Baran's face suspended high above the room. His eyes were closed but his mouth was open. Blood seeped out of a wound on his chest. His body hung from hooks in the flesh of his back, and his hands were nailed together. I could hear his heart barely beating as another warm droplet of his blood ran down the bridge of my nose. I choked back my fear and closed my eyes as Verci continued to whistle. I was trapped in a nightmare.*

*"Are you ready to play?" Verci called to Baran. "I'm getting quite bored without you."*

*I wanted to lash out and attack Verci, to murder him where he stood. He didn't deserve another breath of Old Mother's air. Verci turned his back on Old Mother long ago. My emotions were fogging my ability to be rational. I had to think this through. Was I strong enough to beat Verci alone? Maybe, if I took advantage of the fact that he couldn't see me. Was I smart enough to rescue Baran? Hell yes I was. I didn't need brute strength right now. I needed cunning. I truly needed Grey, but I couldn't take people with me through my dreams. I'd have to figure it out on my own.*

*It was a strange feeling, being alone. I was so used to my pack surrounding me, supporting me, and guiding me that I felt nervous. I knew I couldn't get Baran down with Verci here; I'd have to wait until he left. It was agony just sitting here while I knew Baran was in so much pain. I hated not having choices. I couldn't even move around this room without bumping into the chains that hung from the ceiling. They were everywhere, and dangling at the ends of many of them were the same hooks that gouged Baran's flesh.*

*I studied the ceiling to see if there was a way to get to him and start healing him now. There were many chains I could climb up to him, but they'd all make so much noise that I'd wake the dead . . . literally.*

*"Wakey, wakey," Verci taunted. Baran didn't move.*

*Verci pushed a lever and Baran lowered down to the floor. I had to scoot back to get out of the way, but luckily the chains rattling and the motor made it easy to move around. As Baran's back came into view, I saw how grotesque his flesh looked. His skin was being stretched by the hooks, and I could see his muscles through the puncture holes. Puss formed under his skin . . . I had to look away.*

*"The legendary Killian Dire Wolves," Verci said as he grabbed a fistful of Baran's hair and yanked his head up to look at him, but Baran's face was sallow and unresponsive. "You're nothing now, Killian. Your kind is nearly extinct. After you're gone, there are just two more of you left to destroy."*

*Verci let go of Baran's hair and his head hung limp again. His long silver hair covered his face. Verci wrapped his arm around Baran's chest, almost hugging him, then he slammed his hammer into Baran's ribs. Baran's body swung back and forth on the chains, dangling only by the delicate flesh on his back. I bit my cheek to stop myself from crying out. I was barely holding my sobbing back, but Baran didn't even move. Was he already dead? My lungs burned from holding my breath, praying I wasn't too late.*

*"Damn it, Killian, this isn't as much fun if you don't cry." He stalked back and forth, coming so close to me that a chain knocked into my face. The cold metal stung, and my eyes watered. "Wake up, damn you."*

*Verci stalked away to the fire and pulled out a red-hot branding iron. "This will wake you up, you pathetic piece of shit."*

*He seared the iron into the side of Baran's stomach. I watched in horror as his flesh burned and sizzled. I had to swallow down my own vomit as I watched the smoke rise into the air and the smell of cooked flesh hit me. My throat burned with stomach acid, but it was nothing compared to the burning wound in Baran's skin.*

*Verci pulled the iron away and threw it across the room. Still steaming, it clattered into the wall. As he studied Baran's wound, a bright smile crept onto Verci's face. I was filled with unnatural rage. I wished with everything I had that I was strong enough to fight Verci, but I knew I wasn't. I'd die, Baran would die, all my people would die. All I could do was pray it would be over soon.*

*"Now you belong to me, Killian, and you have the brand to prove it,"*

*Verci laughed.*

*He walked in front of Baran and backhanded him. The crack was so loud I was certain he must have broken Baran's jawbone, but Baran didn't even make a sound. I couldn't even hear his heartbeat anymore.*

*"Fine . . . just fine." He slammed his hammer so hard into the butcher-block table that the wood snapped and the table broke in two. "Lazy bastard," he muttered as he stormed out of the room.*

*I finally took a deep breath and gagged on the air. I scrambled to my feet and pushed my way through the chains to Baran. How was I going to get him off of the chains? If I started unhooking his flesh, the other hooks would tear through his skin as the balance of his body weight changed. I looked around and saw a heavy metal table that was about the right height. I rushed over through the chains, trying not to let any of them touch me, and started to push on it; the table was so heavy that it barely budged, and the screeching sound of metal on the stone floor echoed off the high ceilings.*

*"Dang it," I muttered.*

*I desperately searched the room. Maybe I could stack things up? I saw a stack of death bricks, used to slowly crush someone to death. I stacked them up under Baran, but they weren't nearly high enough. I started grabbing anything that was flat and began building the platform on top of the bricks underneath him, but the whole platform was unsteady and started to topple. I was running out of time.*

*I growled in frustration as I ran my hand through my hair. I saw a stool across the room, and I knew there was one behind me at the table Verci had broken. They weren't big enough to fully take his weight, but maybe they would be enough.*

*I quickly slid one under his chest and the other under his hips. They were only a few inches lower than how his body hung. Hopefully it was close enough that his skin wouldn't tear off his body as I removed the hooks.*

*I began studying the hooks in his skin. It reminded me of removing fishhooks from the children's skin in Dunmanas Bay; they often injured themselves that way, but these hooks were different. They were enormous and barbed. They weren't meant to be removed, at least not without immense pain. I grabbed a metal cutter off the table and took a deep breath.*

*"I'm sorry, Baran," I whispered and started cutting the hooks.*

*One by one I strategically cut the shafts of the hooks, and as I worked, his body limply slunk down onto the stools. His head and limbs hung unnaturally. As I cut the last hook, his body started sliding off the stools. I grabbed for him, barely keeping him from falling. His limp body was impossible to move, and the weight of him was pushing me down. I stumbled to my knees but kept my arms wrapped around him as he slid down to the floor on top of me. One of the stools fell over. It was so loud I just lay there with my eyes closed, waiting for the Garm to tear us apart, but no one came.*

*I slowly slid out from under his weight and stared at the barbed hook ends that still clung to his flesh. I started to weave the hooks through Baran's inflamed and infected skin. The smell of his flesh made my stomach turn.*

*I was glad he wasn't awake for this. It was torture for me to remove them; I couldn't imagine how it would feel to Baran. He groaned when the last hook slid out of his skin. To me, his groan was the most glorious sound in the world. Even a groan meant life. I spit in my hands and rubbed them all over his back, working my saliva into every wound to numb it.*

*As I rubbed my saliva into the burned flesh on his abdomen, I recognized the symbol, the three circling wolves . . . Dvergar. He would carry that scar for the rest of his life.*

*"I'm here now, Baran," I whispered while I worked. "And this time I'm taking you with me."*

*His eyes flashed open; he looked so very tired. He grabbed my wrist as he pulled my face closer to his. His grip was weak, but there was something in his eyes that scared me. Who was this man? I knew he couldn't see me, but his senses were so good he knew right where I was.*

*When my cheek was touching his lips, he whispered, "Verci's coming. Get out."*

*"I don't hear anything," I said.*

*"You won't. He likes a good surprise," he said. "Now run, and don't ever come back."*

*Tears stung my eyes as he shoved me away. "No," I said. "You get up." I was so angry. How dare he turn me away? Couldn't he see I was here to save him? That I couldn't survive without him?*

*"I am here to die," he said.*

*I shook my head and put my hands on the sides of his face. "You shall never give up, Baran of Killian, for your queen is watching. I will never leave here without you."*

*He hung his head. "I'm spent, ylva. I have nothing left to give."*

*"Old Mother taught us all to give until we have nothing left to give and then dig deep and give some more," I said through clenched teeth, holding back my tears. "So dig deep and get up."*

*He looked up to where he thought my face was, his body torn, broken, and infected, and he laughed. "I should have known you wouldn't give up on me."*

*"Would you have given up on me?"*

*"No." He smiled through gritted teeth as he pushed his body up. "I would have carried you all the way home."*

*As he sat before me, sunken and bent, I still saw the same man who saved my life time and time again. Had it really only been a little over a year since he came into my life? He would always be the same to me. He would always feel like my true father.*

*"We have to get back to the labyrinth. Come on, we have to follow the claw marks," I said. "They will lead the way."*

*Baran lightly grabbed my hand. "He's out there; I can smell him. The only way out is up."*

*I looked up and saw vents; they had to lead somewhere; that was how Jutta and I found the Crone. But I didn't know where these would lead. "Can you climb?" I asked.*

*"For you, I can fly," he said.*

*I wanted desperately to believe him, but looking at his endless wounds filled me with doubt. I knew I wouldn't be strong enough to carry him up the chains. If we didn't make it up, he would die.*

*We each grabbed a chain, and I started to climb. Baran got about ten feet up with one arm dangling to his side. He just kept pulling his body weight up with one arm, wrapping the chain around his wrist as he went and putting most of his weight on his legs as they clung to the chains. I could see him struggling. The higher he climbed, the more I feared he would fall. We were at least forty feet in the air—in his condition, the fall would kill him.*

*"Baran?" I asked.*

*He grunted his response, and I could see his sweat mixing with the dried blood on his brow. This climb should have been nothing for him and yet he struggled. From the flush of his skin, I was certain he had a fever.*

*"Are we going to make it?" I asked.*

*"Hey, you can't ask questions like that after giving me that speech," he grunted.*

*I smiled. "Just trying to make you mad enough to keep climbing."*

*Another grunt.*

*Old Mother, please don't fail us now, I prayed.*

*I climbed farther up, always staying within arm's reach of him. If he started slipping, I didn't think I could catch him, but I'd try. I reached the metal beam in the ceiling first, pulled myself on top of it, and slithered over to Baran's chain. I watched him climb up to me with every agonizing move. As soon as I could reach him, I grabbed him and started pulling him up onto the beam. He was heavy, and his skin was so slick with sweat and blood that he started slipping through my fingers.*

*"Don't you dare drop me," he growled.*

*"I won't," I said through gritted teeth.*

*I gasped for air as I pulled again; I used my body as a counterweight and dangled off the opposite side of the beam as his body slid on. My relief was short lived, as I had to pull my own body weight back up. I closed my eyes and struggled to pull myself back up with him. Exhaustion overtook me, and I rested my face on the cold metal as I regained my strength.*

*"I knew you could do it," he said.*

*"Well, we aren't done yet. We have to get out of sight before Verci comes back."*

*Baran nodded and pointed to the duct above me. "This one," he said.*

*"You first," I said, lying on the beam and watching him.*

*"Fine," he muttered.*

*"Killian, ready or not," Verci called.*

*Baran pulled the vent off and I helped push him up into the stone duct; I climbed up behind him just as Verci walked back into the room. We didn't have time to put the vent back in place. I glanced at the chains, thanking Old Mother they were still.*

*We didn't dare move forward or we'd make noise. We had to wait him out again.*

*Verci stopped abruptly and stared at the hooks on the floor in a pool of Baran's blood. He opened his mouth to scream and black moths filled the room, pure evil flowing out of him by the thousands. I shook with fear. What kind of demon was he? "KILLIAN!" he screamed.*

*Baran reached out and held my hand with one of his and covered my mouth with the other. Suddenly the black moths filled the vent surrounding us. I closed my eyes, trying to pretend it wasn't real. Their wings covered my face as they surged past us. I was so thankful for Baran's hand over my mouth. I wanted to scream. For such tiny creatures, their wings felt like tiny razor blades as they zoomed past us.*

*The silence after the moths was deafening, and Baran removed his hand from my face. I slowed my breathing and kept holding his hand. I liked the comfort of it.*

*Verci stormed out of the room. "Today is your last, Killian!" he screamed.*

*When his screams were so faint that I almost couldn't hear them anymore, I finally gave myself permission to move. Baran slid the vent cover in place to hide our path, and we started crawling into the duct. He was slow and clearly in pain.*

*"Is there enough room in here for you to shift and heal?" I asked.*

*He looked around. I could see the skepticism on his face. He was an enormous wolf.*

*"Maybe if you lie down?" I offered. "You have to heal, or we'll never make it to Brychan in time."*

*"Brychan?"*

*"Yes—Brychan, Dilara, Kane, and Shikoba are meeting us at the labyrinth, where we will also rescue the Crone and Jutta," I said.*

*"Who is Jutta?" he asked.*

*"A little girl who saved my life last time I was in the Realms."*

*"And the Crone?" he said. "You found the real Crone?"*

*"Yes, I did."*

*"Damn," he said. "She must be older than dirt."*

*I laughed.*

*"All right, ylva, I'll try to shift." He looked at me for a moment. "Can you shift in your dreams?"*

*"I always just came to heal you," I said. "I haven't tried."*

*"Thank Old Mother for that," he said. "And thank you, Ashling. I'd be dead twenty times over without you."*

*I wanted to deny it, but I knew he was right. Verci was set on killing Baran. If I hadn't come night after night to heal him, Verci would have succeeded eventually. Though I knew Verci enjoyed dragging it out, he'd eventually lose control and actually kill Baran. But not anymore.*

*"Try," he urged.*

*I closed my eyes and tried to shift, but nothing happened. "I can't," I whispered. "I'm not in physical form so I can't shift."*

*Baran nodded, lay down on his stomach, and closed his eyes. He began to shake. I backed up, giving him space to shift . . . or explode. I'd never seen a wolf shift before who wasn't moving during the transition. This seemed far more violent.*

*What little that was left of Baran's clothing tore apart. I watched his skin stretch as his body enlarged in front of my eyes. In just a moment, he was an enormous werewolf. He nearly filled the entire cavity. It would take some time to heal the wounds he'd received, so I lay down, using his hairy side as my pillow, and closed my eyes to rest. For a moment, at least, we were safe.*

*I knew Baran couldn't answer me as a wolf, but I talked to him anyway.*

*"Baran, I am so sorry it took me this long to save you. I wanted to save you so many times. I'm sorry you had to feel this pain and endure what Verci did to you. It is all my fault. You wouldn't have been in this mess if it weren't for me."*

*I felt so much guilt. It was overwhelming and debilitating. I knew Baran's fight with Verci ranged far deeper than me, but I knew he wouldn't have been caught if he hadn't been protecting me.*

*He turned his giant head and nudged my face. For such a big creature he was gentle and so very loving. Though I knew, even injured, he was a weapon. Baran was a warrior.*

*"I'm glad I'm here now," I said. I breathed in his woody scent and enjoyed the comfort of it. His house in York Harbor still smelled like him, but it was faint. I couldn't wait to get him home. I knew Grey would be eager to see him. "Grey is waiting for you back home. He wanted to be here, but I asked him to protect my body instead. I hope you're not mad."*

*Baran laid his head on my feet as I continued. "Baran, can you keep a secret?"*

*He looked up at me. Even as a wolf, I knew he was giving me that look.*

*"Grey and I got married in the Bloodrealms," I said.*

*Baran nipped me on the arm. "Hey!" I said. "That's not nice. Besides, he's your nephew, you should be happy for us. It was such an intimate ceremony for only Old Mother to see; you would have been proud. We said our vows and held each other safe away from the darkness, even if it was only for one night. And damn it, we survived this horrible place—don't we deserve love?"*

He licked my cheek.

"Thank you, Baran," I whispered.

I hadn't realized how much I wanted to tell him our secret. How much I needed his approval. How much I truly needed him.

He turned and began crawling forward, leading the way down the tunnel. I followed closely behind. I didn't know where we were or how we'd ever get out, but I was with Baran, and that meant I was safe. Every moment he was a wolf, he was healing from his injuries. That knowledge made me feel invincible.

"I love you, Baran," I whispered.

I knew he heard me because he stopped moving for a heartbeat before crawling forward again. I knew he loved me as his daughter, he loved Grey and Willem his nephews, and he was deeply in love with my mother. He was friends with Mund and Dagny and so many more. Saving Baran meant as much to me as all of them. Baran was a symbol of our future. I just had to get him to the Crone and Jutta, and the rest of my pack would be waiting.

We finally came to an opening, and I crept up next to Baran. My body barely fit next to his enormous body; it was tight and uncomfortable, but I liked it. I stuck my head out and closed my eyes and breathed in the fresh air . . . well, as fresh as the air in the Bloodrealms ever got. It still smelled of death and disease, but at least it wasn't so stale and hot as breathing our own air over and over again in the vent. Honestly, Baran smelled like a wet dog in that vent; I was thankful to breathe again.

I looked down at the selection chamber. I'd been in that room far more times than I wanted to remember. The room and balcony were empty. Not a soul seemed to stir.

The fire the Crone had started for the dead was gone, and Old Mother had taken the ash. All that remained was the blackened stone floor. The Crone chose to live in the Bloodrealms to protect these souls. After seeing her magic with the labyrinth, I was certain she had the power to leave at *any time, but her love for these people was much greater than her own self-preservation.*

*"Come on," I whispered, and I let myself drop down into the room like an agile gymnast. It was a bit too much flair considering the circumstances, but I desperately needed to stretch my limbs after being in that vent for so long.*

*From down here I could feel the spray of the waterfall. It felt cool and refreshing. I looked down at my filthy skin and could only imagine what my wild hair was doing. Even in my human form, I probably looked like a wild animal. The Bloodrealms weren't a beauty contest; they were a survival contest.*

*Baran leaped down next to me. His front leg gave out under him, and he groaned as he stood back up.*

*"Are you okay?" I whispered.*

*He nodded his giant wolf head, but I wasn't sure I believed him. I knelt down and touched his leg and paw. The break wasn't fully healed yet, so I massaged it, trying to push all my love into the wound. I wasn't sure if I could heal him in wolf form or only human, but it was worth trying. He was worth everything.*

*"We have to get to the labyrinth. It isn't too far," I said as I finished rubbing the bone back into place. "Let's get the hell out of here."*

*He nuzzled his head under my arm, and I hugged him so tightly. I never wanted to let go, and now I wouldn't have to. He was going to be free again.*

*"Come on." I smiled as I headed to the door where the Crone, Jutta, and I had entered the labyrinth. Baran padded next to me, and I put my hand on his back, working my fingers through his thick fur. I loved the texture of it. He and Grey had coarser fur than mine. There was something about the texture that I loved. I couldn't stop looking at him. It just felt so good to be with him.*

*The sound of heels clicking on the floor ahead of us stopped me in my tracks, and reality closed in. Someone was coming.*

"Baran . . ." I whispered.

I could hear voices from behind us in the selection chamber; it sounded like Vigdis's overgrown guards who had beaten Baran. We couldn't go forward and we couldn't go back. We were trapped in this corridor. This is where we would make our stand. I was so scared my body burned, and I felt like I was being crushed. Old Mother have mercy; I'm so close to saving him, I silently begged.

The heel clicks got louder and louder. Vigdis was coming for us. This time, I wouldn't go unnoticed; I would fight with Baran. I kissed Baran's wet nose and prepared for the evil that came closer and closer in the echoing halls.

I closed my eyes and listened to the cadence of the footsteps. She was tall, but light. There was a soft dragging sound of fabric, like a dress dragging on the stones, but there was something else . . . or someone else. Was it the soft footsteps of someone walking barefoot?

As they rounded the corner and came into view, I found myself staring at Selene in an enormous red Spanish dress and long black gloves with a silver-tipped crop in her hand; in her other hand she held a tiny, delicate silver leash. I lost the ability to breathe as I watched Grete come into view, chained around her neck to the leash. There was a thin line of dried blood around her neck where the collar had damaged her skin, and she had whip marks on her arms. Her clothes were torn and dirty, and she looked only at the ground.

Baran growled at Selene, low and threatening, but not loud enough for the sound to carry to the guards in the selection chamber. Selene stopped and stepped in front of Grete, blocking her from my view. I knew neither of them could see me, but they sure as hell saw Baran.

"Who goes here?" Selene demanded, pulling her crop to the ready. Baran growled and took a step toward her. She didn't move. My heart pounded in my chest so loud that I feared she'd hear it.

Baran was enormous and a warrior, but he was still injured. If she struck him with that silver crop, he'd be human . . . he'd be mortal. I would *have to attack first; she wouldn't see me coming. I could take her out and Baran and I could save Grete, but as soon as we started fighting, the guards would hear. I was running out of choices.*

*"What right do you have to stop me?" she said. Her face was hard as stone as she raised her crop to strike him for his insolence.*

# 18

## *Divine Animal Right*

*My body shook* so violently I thought I might vomit. I felt like a rag doll as I opened my eyes to see Grey kneeling over me and gripping my shoulders so tight, and I could feel his fingernails digging into my flesh. I winced with pain.

"What are you doing? Why did you wake me up? I can't leave Baran. I can't! Let me go back in!" I screamed.

"We can't, we gotta move—*now!*" Grey said.

I felt so disorientated. I could feel fear, but was it his or mine? I looked around—I was no longer in my room. He'd carried me down into the kitchen and laid me down on the floor. We were surrounded by fighting. There was a dead body in the doorway to the living room; from the smell of his blood, I knew he was a Bloodsucker. There was a strong iron scent to their blood because it had mixed with ours. He was a heavyset black man who looked to be in his fifties. I didn't know his face, but there was something familiar about him. I could see another man dead in the living room, and though I couldn't see who it was, I was certain it was another Bloodsucker.

"Where are Rhonda and the others?" I panicked, looking for them.

Rhonda stumbled into the kitchen, barely escaping the blade that came slicing after her and instead split the dead man in the doorway. The man wielding the blade had Rhonda's cheeks and her lips. He was unmistakably her father.

"You little bitch!" he screamed. "You should have been a son. I should have drowned you when you were born!"

"Dad, no! Stop!" she pleaded. Rhonda stood back up and held her sword out in front of her, but I saw the small vibration in her shaking hand.

"No," My voice was barely a whisper.

"We have to run," Grey said.

"Rhonda!" I yelled.

She saw me for the first time and her expression changed; there was a tiny bit of hope in her. Her father raised his sword to chop her down and I screamed. Jamal leaped in and blocked the shot, kicking her father in the chest and knocking him to the ground.

"How many Bloodsuckers are there?" I asked Grey as Jamal and Rhonda joined us.

"Only two left," Grey said, pulling me to my feet. I felt woozy and unstable.

Her father charged at Jamal like a bull, slamming his body into the floor.

"Run!" Rhonda screamed as she ran past me.

The fear in her voice set my legs moving before my mind made a conscious decision. I wished I could feel Rhonda's emotions, but she wasn't a wolf. Fear was the only emotion I could smell on her. I was chasing after Rhonda through the back door, but I didn't know where we were going. My mind was torn between Jamal, Baran, and this new hell.

"Where?" I looked behind to see Grey fighting to save Jamal. My heart stopped.

"Anywhere public; they can't hurt us with enough witnesses," she said. "They can't kill everyone."

I wasn't sure her logic was sound. The look on her father's face made me think he'd burn the entire world to the ground for the chance to kill her. She stopped, looking back and forth, frantic. I heard drums in the distance.

"What day is it?" I demanded.

"Saturday," she said.

"The parade! We just have to get to the parade!" I said. "But we can't leave Grey and Jamal behind—where is Paul?"

"His father killed him, and now my father wants my head," she said. "I'm a traitor."

My heart sank. I'd grown to love them, and Paul died at the hands of his own clan. I wasn't even there to try to protect him. I felt sick with sadness, but now wasn't the time to mourn. This was war, and Rhonda was no more a traitor than I was.

I grabbed her arm and started dragging her with me as I ran. "Do you fight for the people? Do you fight for peace?" She nodded. "Then you're not a traitor—you're on the right side. Now, help me," I said.

"How?"

"We save our pack."

Grey and Jamal were running after us with Rhonda's father and another Bloodsucker coming behind them. The dead man in my house must have been Jamal's father, but this man didn't look anything like Paul. Fathers killing their own children . . . it was something in nature, but it felt utterly unnatural as we ran for our lives.

It didn't matter where we made our stand; he'd never stop hunting his daughter. I looked up at the magnificent, enormous trees that surrounded the road as we ran into town. "We hide in the trees," I said, "and ambush them."

We darted out of sight and scrambled up the trees as quickly as we could. I scraped my hand on the rough bark, but I just licked it to numb the pain and kept climbing. We crouched in the trees and waited.

How had this gotten so messed up? We were running through the city of York Harbor for our lives, and the longer I lingered here, the longer Baran, Brychan, Dilara, Shikoba, Kane, the Crone, Jutta, and Grete were at risk. So many lives were held in the balance of time. Even if Rhonda and I were able to break up the fight, there were no witnesses to protect us. The parade route was still at least four blocks away. We'd have to run that far without them killing any of us. Or we'd have to kill them. I still couldn't see Grey and Jamal. Were they already dead, or had they gone in a different direction?

"Who is the other guy?" I asked.

Rhonda sighed. "Cesario. He is the leader of the South American clan."

Grey and Jamal ran into view below us. Grey looked up at me and quickly looked away. I knew he was trying not to give our position away. Suddenly Rhonda's dad and Cesario stalked into view.

Cesario and Grey circled each other. He was at least a foot taller than Grey and far more muscular. I watched Rhonda's father punch Jamal in the face, knocking him to the ground right below us. Jamal was nearly beaten, and his face was already swelling. Her father looked like a former bodybuilder. His arms rippled with rage as he stood over Jamal. Cesario unsheathed his sword and held the silver blade at Grey's throat. The silver wouldn't poison Grey; he was immune, and he didn't need to shift to heal, but they didn't know that. Did they see Grey as a wolf or a Bloodsucker?

"You're both traitors. The lowest of creation are those who turn their backs on their own kind," her father yelled. "I will kill you first— then I'll bleed out my daughter and that little red bitch."

"You're the traitor," Grey spat. "You knew my father killed my mother, didn't you? All those years you were in my home, and never once did you feel remorse for her."

"Your father kept that little wolf as his pet for a time, but we all knew she had to die eventually. Her kind can't be tamed. She was planning to take you back to her pack. We couldn't abide that," he said.

Cesario swung his sword. Grey ducked and slammed his body into him. They fought out of sight around the trees. It made me anxious not being able to see him.

"You'd kill your own daughter? For pride?" Jamal said. "You're a pathetic bastard."

They didn't have morals or empathy. They didn't protect humans or the earth. These men were just gluttonous for power.

"One more word out of you, boy, and you lose your tongue first," he growled.

Rhonda's eyes were wide. She was afraid of him—her own father. Parents so often failed to realize the immense power they held over their children. He was everything to her. I wasn't sure Rhonda would fight with me. I reached over to her in the tree next to me and lightly touched her shoulder.

I mouthed, "Are you with me?"

She wiped the sweat from her brow and nodded as she linked her fingers with mine, holding my hand. They were right below us now. We leaped from the trees and both landed on her father's back, knocking him to the ground. He grabbed his sword from the ground and sliced the air between us, trying to cut me, to cut anything as he rolled to his knees.

"You little bitch dog!" he screamed at me. "You destroyed my daughter. She wasn't a man, but she was good enough to die for our cause, and now she will die as nothing more than my enemy! I could have at least used her."

"You dare to think your sex makes you superior to us?" I said, my voice loud and unwavering as I watched him scramble back to his feet.

I watched Grey out of the corner of my eye. Cesario held a blade to Grey's neck. Baran and Grey could die in the same moment, and I wouldn't have saved either of them. Baran could already be dead at the hands of Selene. I shook my head, trying to stay in the present.

Rhonda helped Jamal to his feet and they stood beside me. We were all different, in color, sex, even species, but we were one people.

"You are a fool," I said.

He drew his blade, and Cesario prepared to lop off Grey's head. Jamal was slowly closing the distance to Grey. I watched the angle of Rhonda's father's sword and knew his intended target. He wanted Rhonda dead most of all. More than saving his own life, he wanted to take hers.

"One chance to save yourself," I said, circling him like the predator I was. "Drop your silly little knife and back away," I said.

I was breaking his concentration. He was far more hot-tempered and reactive. Grey's father had been so calm and collected, but both wanted me dead.

"You are a disgrace to fathers and to all of humankind," I said. "Rhonda owes you nothing for your lifetime of lies."

"She owes me her life," he said.

I had turned Rhonda, Jamal, and Paul to the side of love, and now they might all die at the hands of their own fathers. We'd already lost Paul.

"Apologize to her!" I yelled.

"I will kill her and purify my lineage," he said.

"You may die, but no gods, yours or mine, will forgive your hate," I said.

"What do you know of faith? You're just an animal. No god would accept you." He said it like a threat, but between his words I heard Old Mother's voice, her love. His words were a toxic lie, a disease that had the power to seep into my bones and poison me with doubt if I let it.

"Faith is in my heart and in the air I breathe and the sunshine on my skin, and no one stands between me and Old Mother's love," I said. "Only poison seeps from your lips. I do not fear you."

Before I could take a breath, he swung his sword at me, but it slammed into Rhonda's shoulder when she leaped into the blade to protect me.

"Uhhhh!" Rhonda cried as her body slumped to the ground.

I shifted into a wolf and attacked him. My teeth tore into his throat. He punched me in the neck. I winced, but his punches only tightened my grip on his neck. I flung my head back and forth until finally his lifeless body slammed to the ground.

I heard Grey and Jamal fighting Cesario as I ran to Rhonda. She fell over her hands and knees with the knife still in her shoulder. From the depth of the blade, it was clear it had cut into her bones; the tip poked out her back. She screamed, clutching at her arm. The blood ran down her arm and chest, coating her leather jacket in darkness. I shifted back into a human, naked to the world. I had to save her.

"Rhonda, just breathe," I said. I wasn't just a warrior . . . I was a healer, and only I could save her.

I heard Cesario gasping for breath as he died, but I kept my eyes on Rhonda. There was so much fear in her eyes. So raw. I looked to Grey as he was taking off his bloodied button-down shirt, exposing his chest. He quickly wrapped the shirt over me. It wasn't modest, but it would do.

Jamal pulled the blade from Rhonda's shoulder. She collapsed to the ground, heaving with pain. I tore her jacket open to see the wound. It was so deep it nearly removed her entire arm. "I need something to cut myself," I said.

"What?" Grey said.

"She needs my blood to heal that wound," I said. We were linked, wolves and Bloodsuckers; the only way to save her was to give her some of myself.

Jamal held out the silver blade toward me, but I was terrified of it. Her wound wouldn't heal on its own, and if I did nothing she'd bleed out here. But the silver blade would poison me and make it impossible to shift and heal. I would carry the scar for the rest of my life. I just had to make sure I didn't cut too deep or I'd be the one to die today, and Baran still needed me. All of my people needed me.

"Grey, cut me," I said.

"No," he said, taking a step away from the blade that Jamal offered.

"It has to be you. If I hold the blade the silver will poison me longer. I won't be strong enough to go back for Baran," I said. "Please."

I held out my palm to him. His eyes were wild with fear, like two emerald hurricanes. He looked from Rhonda to me and back again. She was bleeding profusely and closer to bleeding to death with every beat of her heart that pumped her blood onto the ground around us. I could feel Grey's fear and resistance, but this was the right choice. I could feel it.

"Grey, it can be only you," I repeated.

"What if . . ." his voice trailed off.

"I trust you," I said.

He nodded. His hand shook as he wrapped his fingers around my wrist, but as he took the blade and looked into my eyes, his body calmed. I closed my eyes and I held my breath.

He slowly sliced into my palm and I gasped. Such a simple wound, yet the silver burned through my whole body. I wanted to lick it to numb it. I wanted to shift to heal it, but I couldn't. I dropped to my knees at her side and crushed my bleeding hand as hard as I could, milking my blood out and letting it drip into her open wound.

The pain of the silver blade, the cut, and the horrible violence of squeezing out my own blood made me want to pass out, but with each excruciating drop I watched her wound sizzle and heal. I felt more lightheaded and nauseated as I went. I felt sweat running down my face. Grey held me upright and supported my arm.

Her wound was nearly healed as I lost consciousness.

# 19
## *Lies*

*For a moment, I didn't move. My body felt empty, like every drop of my blood was gone. I closed my eyes and tried to muster any strength I could find. I still felt the silver seeping through my veins. It burned with every beat of my heart and left my head in a foggy maze of confusion.*

*I shook my head. I was back in the Bloodrealms, but I wasn't ready. I wasn't strong enough, but I had to find Baran. I had to find Baran. I had to find Baran.*

*I tried to stand and fell back to the ground. My body was too weak to carry me. I needed to shift and heal, but I couldn't shift in my dreams. I felt terrified and vulnerable. Without my own strength or Baran's protection, my only asset was my invisibility. I shivered.*

*I was still only wearing Grey's shirt. As I curled up in the fetal position, I felt something in my shirt pocket. My eyes flashed open. I carefully pulled it from my pocket and studied a pretty purple flower. It was smashed up and nearly destroyed, but I knew what it was: wolf's bane, the only cure for silver poisoning.*

*Grey had given me my salvation.*

*I plucked one of the delicate petals and put it on my tongue. It tasted terrible, but I could feel it melting into my saliva. I could feel it healing me. One by one, I consumed all the petals until only the stem remained.*

*The burning sensation of the silver in my veins was all but gone. I closed my eyes and concentrated; I needed to shift. My body vibrated, but nothing happened. I tried leaping in the air, commanding my body to obey, but I slammed into the ground still human. I rolled onto all fours, groaning. I needed more time to heal from the poisoning. I simply needed more time.*

*As I stood up and finally looked around, I realized I was standing at the center of the labyrinth—the dead center. The walls were immense stone covered in old blood. The labyrinth walls grew shorter as you got to the outer limits of the labyrinth, but here in the center, they were a hundred feet high. There were eight openings to the labyrinth that surrounded me as I stood in the center of the circle. I knew the winding trails of the labyrinth went on for thousands of miles; without the Crone, I had no way of knowing if I was going in the right direction.*

*I looked at the eight possible paths surrounding me. Next to each opening, carved into the stone walls, was a phase of the moon. It seemed to mark the lunar calendar: Imbolc, Ostara, Beltane, Litha, Lughnasadh, Mabon, Samhain, and Yule, the eight holidays of our people coinciding with the phases of the moon.*

*Four of our holidays were ruled over by the Elder God families; Imbolc by the Vanir, Beltane by the Boru, Lughnasadh by the Killian, and Samhain by the Dvergar. I ran my fingers over the dark crescent moon carved for Samhain. The cold air whistled past me from the tunnel; it was foggy and frightening. I took a step inside the path, and hissing and snarling surrounded me. When I jumped back into the center of the circle, silence surrounded me once again. I stared into the fog, waiting for something to come out after me, but I couldn't see anything.*

*I took a deep breath and walked over to Beltane, the home of my people, the Boru. Would I be safe in Beltane because I was a Boru? I stepped* into the path and swore I could hear my mother's voice calling to me.

"Ashling, my sweet Ashling, help me," she called.

"Mother?" I said, taking several more steps down the path.

I wanted to rush after her voice, but I stepped back out and her voice faded away as though it had never been. I turned and went back to the center of the labyrinth.

I next walked over to Lughnasadh of Grey's pack, the Killian; as I entered, I heard nothing but welcoming silence. No haunting sounds, no fog, no mystery or evil. Not even my mother's voice luring me inside. It seemed calm and inviting.

I stepped back into the center and sat down, looking at the eight options. Could it be one of the other moons that didn't have an Elder God? Was it truly my mother calling for help?

"Oh Mother, how I miss you," I said.

I stared at the hard stone as I tried to decide which way to go. Uaid Dvergar built this evil place. It was his playground, and he was as evil as his son, Verci, and grandson, Adomnan. So there had to be trickery here.

It couldn't be my mother down the Beltane path. She would never beg me to save her; she would tell me to run. I couldn't follow the Killian path; no matter how inviting it seemed, something just didn't feel right about it. I stood up and walked boldly into Samhain, into the path of the Dvergar. If any of these paths would lead me out of the labyrinth, my best bet was to follow it.

The only remaining question was what creatures would try to stop me. I was certain the Dvergar had more evil hidden away in this place . . . not just the Garm and the Draugr, but even more sinister evil waiting to take my life. I suddenly wished for Eamon's Bloodmark on my wrist for protection.

At least I was invisible to everyone in this reality. That was definitely a benefit to traveling in my dreams. I just had to be quiet and I would pass by unnoticed. I prayed Old Mother would protect all my pack while I found my way back to them.

*There was a mossy, wet smell as I walked along the mysterious path. The fog was so thick I couldn't see below my knees. As I walked, the fog swirled around me. There was no way to stop it—the swirls gave away my every move. No matter how slowly I moved, it still reacted. If anyone or anything was watching, they'd know right where I was. I didn't have a choice but to keep moving. The more slowly I moved, the more likely the demons would find me.*

*"Baran, I'm coming," I whispered to myself.*

*The intricacies of the labyrinth were subtle but beautiful. Every stone had been hauled in, shaped, and mudded to create these enormous walls. As I studied them, I wished I had the Crone's staff. Climbing walls sure was a handy power in this place. I wanted to call out to them to see if I was near or even heading in the right direction, but I didn't dare give up my location and presence. Any matter of man or beast could be watching tonight. What day was it, anyway? I had fallen asleep and rescued Baran, but when I awoke, days had passed and it was Saturday. Now that I was asleep again, I didn't have a clue how much time had gone by.*

*I came to a T in the path where I could choose two possible directions, but a monument of eight separate large stones, all over six feet tall, blocked my path in either direction. I had to choose left or right and weave my way through them. Five of the stones were carved with images, and two had runic inscriptions. Despite being surrounded by evil, the stones were quite beautiful. The center stone showed a warrior woman riding a large wolf. The other stones showed other creatures like trolls, sea creatures, and all manner of mythical creatures. I studied the two runic stones, one on each side. I was certain they told me a tale, where to go, or the fate that lay ahead of me, but I had never learned to read runes like this. These were ancient.*

*Left or right?*

*It made no difference, really. I didn't know where either path went. I started to the left. I glanced back at the carving of the woman and the wolf, but they were gone. I looked all around me, waiting for the woman in the stone to jump out and strike me dead, but nothing came. I swallowed down my fear and took a breath as I forced my feet to carry me farther down the path. Everything seemed the same—the same fog, the same smells. Not a single stone out of place. Maybe it was all just my imagination.*

*My nerves were shot. I was scared. Was it my mind playing tricks on me or did I hear something move? As I looked back longingly, the wall closed and the path from where I had come vanished. I walked back to it, expecting it to move again, but it didn't. I touched the stones; they were real, and they didn't move. The labyrinth was changing all around me.*

*Was it taunting me? Pushing me back to the center? Was it Verci playing games with my mind, or was it the labyrinth itself? Was it alive? Both options scared me to death. I just had to wake up and this nightmarish place would be gone, and I'd be free, but I couldn't leave my pack behind. I started walking back down the path the labyrinth had given me.*

*My body ached. I had given all of myself to save Rhonda. I would do it all again to save her, but I had to admit this sucked. Even with the wolf's bane Grey had given me, I was exhausted. I just wanted to lie down and rest, just for a little while.*

*I leaned against the cold stone and sighed.*

*"Grey," I whispered. "My sweet Grey." I missed him. I didn't even get to say good-bye before I passed out back into the Realms, and Baran was waiting for me. They were all waiting for me.*

*Suddenly, I smelled rotted flesh and fresh blood . . . the Garm wolves. Nothing else could smell that foul. The hair on the back of my neck pricked up. I heard the painful sound of claws scratching on stone . . . they were roaming down the path right toward me. How did they get behind me? Wasn't the path blocked? I knew despite their own overpowering stench that they would easily sniff me out. They couldn't see me, but I'd still be dinner. My only chance was to run.*

*I started running as fast as my short legs could carry me. Even though my steps were soft, they heard me. I could hear them running after me. The bastards were never satisfied. Not until every creature in the Realms was dead, and even then I was certain the creatures would kill each other to survive. Garm didn't seem like the type to die out quietly.*

*There were at least three of them behind me, but the echo off the high labyrinth walls made it impossible to know without looking, and I didn't dare turn around. If I tripped, I'd be dead. The path just kept twisting and turning; it never split off. I couldn't outrun them—they were already gaining on me.*

*Why did my mind wake me up in the center of the labyrinth? Did I have a secret death wish? It was bad enough coming to the Bloodrealms, but to get stuck in a bloody labyrinth with no idea how to get out and find my pack?*

*Finally, I saw a split in the trail. If I could just lose some of them, I stood a chance; if I was lucky, I could lose all of them. I ran harder than I'd ever run. Faster than when I ran from Adomnan. I was a machine.*

*My pulse quickened with every step, I wanted desperately to turn off this main path. I wanted safety. I was about thirty feet away, and I could almost taste freedom when the stones started sliding together to close off the path.*

*"No, no, no!" I said. "Not now!"*

*I didn't have any energy to run faster, and with every step I swore I was getting slower and more desperate. I was probably going the same speed, but with every stone that shifted and blocked my path a little more, I grew more and more afraid. It felt as though I was in slow motion. The Garm snapped at my heels, trying to tear my feet out from under me. I could feel their saliva splattering on my skin.*

*The path was covered about four feet high, and more stones closed it off every second. I leaped at it with everything I had left, praying I'd make it to the other side and not slam into it and become dinner. My knee scraped on a stone as I barely skimmed over the top. I crashed into the ground in a heap and sobbed with the pain that ripped through me.*

*I lay there watching the stones continue to shift and close when a Garm wolf tore his way up the wall. His enormous head and claws came into view. He pulled himself onto the ledge of the moving wall and snarled at me.*

*I screamed and looked away. I couldn't outrun him.*

*I heard his pitiful whimper. When I looked back, the dead carcass of the Garm lay lifeless, crushed by stone that had moved to fill the labyrinth wall. I was thankful for the walls. Whatever their plan, they helped me for now. I stood and dusted myself off. I still had a long way to go.*

*As I trudged along, I heard a soft scurrying sound behind me. I couldn't see anything, only fog. There had to be several of them, at least five, but what were they? And what did they want? I closed my eyes, took another step, and quickly turned around. The scurrying stopped. I took another step forward, and they began following me again. Something brushed against my leg and I jumped. It's nothing, I told myself. I started walking more briskly.*

*Suddenly my feet were yanked out from under me, and I fell down on the hard stone. I was completely consumed by the fog—I could barely see. I coughed and sputtered as the wetness of the fog clung to my lungs. The creatures began binding my arms and legs. I saw a glimpse of a tiny distorted face. He couldn't have been more than three feet tall. I pulled hard, freeing my left arm, but they tied it again.*

*"No!" I said. "Stop!"*

*I heard only low mumbles and whispers as they pulled the ropes tight and I was splayed out on the ground. One of them grabbed my wrist. She was almost out of sight, but I could kind of make her out in the fog. She was smaller than the other, maybe two and a half feet tall, with a bulbous nose and long white braided hair. She wore a leather sheath and a pointed leather cap. She studied my wrists; I wasn't marked. I wished for Eamon's Bloodmark to scare these creatures away, but it was no use now.*

*"What are you?" I asked.*

*"Who wants to know?" An angry, strained voice asked from the fog.*

*"I'm . . ." my voice trailed off. Did I dare tell them what I was? "My name is . . ."*

*"That bad of a name?" he asked.*

*"What do you want of me?" I asked. "And can you see me?"*

*"Of course we can see you, silly girl. And you answer my questions first, and I will answer yours."*

*"But I asked you a question first, and you answered with a question. That isn't fair," I said.*

*"She has a point," another squeaky voice said.*

*"Ha. Nothing is fair here," he said.*

*"If you want to know who I am, then I want to know what you are first," I said. I really didn't have anything to bargain with, but I didn't want to sound weak.*

*"She makes demands when she's tied up!" a third squeaky voice said.*

*One of them hit me in the stomach with a tiny mallet of some kind. "Hey! Stop that! That hurts!" I said.*

*"It was meant to," he said.*

*"I take it by your lack of empathy that you're the leader," I said. "Now what manner of creature are you?"*

*The tiny man jumped on my chest and knocked the wind out of me. His dark, beady little eyes stared down at me as he hit me again. I winced from the pain. His long white beard went halfway down his chest and dangled in my face. His nose was wide and made his face look almost like a caricature.*

*"What are you?" I asked again as I bit back the pain.*

*"We are Tomte," he growled. His face was only inches from mine as he smiled.*

*"You are what?"*

*He laughed. "Never heard of the Tomte? Well, you're in for a surprise. We are the echoes of ancient spirits."*

*His tone was a bit sinister. I found myself intimidated by the tiny people. Another came into view. He appeared to be younger; he was rounder, cuter, and his beard was much shorter. He smiled.*

*"We are gift bearers," the young one said. "That means we bring gifts."*

*"Only to the deserving," the female one said. "The undeserving we feed to the Vargr."*

*"What is a Vargr?" I asked.*

*"You'll find out soon enough," the older Tomte said.*

*"So my options are to be eaten or given a gift?" I said.*

*"Not options," the young one said. "We decide."*

*"What do I have to do to not be eaten?" I asked.*

*The old one sat down right on my stomach. "Ooof," I groaned.*

*"Start by answering my questions," he said, hitting me in the head.*

*"Fine," I grumbled. "But stop hitting me."*

*"Who are you?" he asked.*

*"Ashling Boru, the Crimson Queen," I said.*

*He wacked me in the forehead again. "I do not tolerate lies."*

*I ripped my right arm from the rope, scraping my skin off, and grabbed his mallet. "And I don't tolerate being hit," I said. "I am Ashling Boru, daughter of Pørr and Nessa Boru. I am the Crimson Queen, and if you do not stop hitting me, I will break your tiny hammer in half. Now get off of me."*

*He stood and pulled his hammer back, eyeing me with his beady eyes. He wacked me in the knee and laughed. It stung. Such a tiny creature and he still inflicted so much pain.*

*"Stop it," I said. "I demand to know your name."*

*The younger one stepped forward. "They call me Nisse," he said.*

*"Nice to meet you, Nisse," I said as I yanked my other arm free, pulling two other Tomte into view, but they quickly scurried back into the shadows. I could only make out their silhouettes. "And what do they call you?" I asked the older Tomte.*

*He smashed my toe, and the pain vibrated up into my chest. He crossed his arms and stared at me defiantly. Nasty little fellow.*

*"Name," I repeated.*

*"Gudmund," he grumbled.*

*"Well, I guess it is nice to meet you, too, Gudmund," I said, rubbing my toe. "Now, would you kindly let me go?"*

*"Tie her up!" Gudmund yelled, and ropes flew from all around me,*

*yanking me back down to the ground. They had been playing with me. For such tiny creatures, they had a lot of strength and cunning.*

*"Stop it! I command you as your queen!" I said.*

*"You aren't our queen," Gudmund said. "You are a liar, and the Vargr will eat you."*

*My stomach sank. I was going to die. I was going to be eaten alive, and worse yet, I was going to fail my pack.*

*"Please, Nisse, help me!" I said. Nisse only looked at his little pointed shoes.*

*"Only Hyrrokkin can tell if you lie," Gudmund said. "And I think you lie."*

*The sound of a four-legged creature came toward us. I could hear its nails scraping at the stone floor. My breath became shallow as I heard the footsteps slow and walk around me. The creature was enormous, far larger than a dire wolf, but all I could see in the fog was its black, hairy feet and the jagged claws that clicked on the stone as it circled me. It snarled and drooled all over me. Its breath was like rotten fish. It was hungry and waiting for the command from its rider.*

*"Old Mother, save me," I whispered.*

*I heard its rider dismount, and suddenly a woman's face was staring at me. She held small daggers in both hands. She wasn't a wolf, but she wasn't a human either. She didn't smell right. She was larger than any human I had ever seen before—she had to be a giant. I had seen a giant in the Bloodrealms before, but she was different. She wore black armor, and only half of her face showed from behind it. Her hair looked like black glass, but her eyes were as blue as Tegan's.*

*"Gudmund, what do you have here?" she asked. "What have you caught?"*

*"A liar, Hyrrokkin," Gudmund hissed.*

*I stared in wonder. I had heard legend of Hyrrokkin. She was said to have the power to steal souls. She was the protection for the Elder Gods, but she had angered the Dvergar and was killed. But here she stood, and I had no doubt that it was she. Could she see me?*

"A liar?" she repeated. Her daggers turned to snakes before my eyes, writhing and wiggling in her hands as they lashed out to strike me with their teeth.

"I'm not a liar," I said. "I am Ashling Boru."

She put the snakes by her face and they nuzzled her. She leaned down and smelled me, and I tried not to flinch away. Gudmund wacked me again, this time in the shin.

"Damn it, Gudmund, stop that!" I demanded.

"You dare speak to my Tomte in such a way?" she asked. Gudmund sneered.

"Yes, I do," I said, tired of this game. If they were going to eat me, they could very well get on with it. "I am the Crimson Queen, and I demand you make the nasty little man stop hitting me."

He went to hit me again, but she held up her hand; he grumbled as he stopped. "I am sorry to do this," she said, and she stood. "Vargr, sniff out the lies."

The creature put its enormous head on my shoulder and started smelling me as it snarled. I shuddered. The Vargr looked like a wolf but made dire wolves look like puppies. There was a metal plate nailed over its left eye, and its teeth were plated in metal.

I closed my eyes and tried to slow my breathing. It would either eat me or it wouldn't. I couldn't control my fate. I squinted and thought of Grey, Mother, Mund, Tegan, Nia, Baran . . .

My eyes flashed open. I had to save Baran. "I need your help, Hyrrokkin," I said. "I am trying to save Baran of Killian, the Crone, and a little girl named Jutta."

The animal snarled, and its hot breath surrounded me. I gagged. Hyrrokkin lowered her face again to where I could see her. Gudmund and Nisse backed away.

"Jutta?" she asked.

I nodded.

*"You know where Jutta is?" she asked.*

*"That depends—what interest do you have in her?" I said.*

*"Vigdis killed her entire family, and she is the only one of her people left. Every inhabitant in the city of Fenrir was murdered—all except Jutta," she said.*

*"I will not lead you to her to take her life, too," I said.*

*"Noble," she said, smiling.*

*"Can you see me?" I asked.*

*"Every red hair on your head and every scar on your perfect snow-white skin," she said.*

*I gasped. "How?"*

*"With my eyes," she said.*

*"What?" I couldn't understand. Was I no longer invisible?*

*"Because I am not like the other creatures in this world," she said. "Cut her ropes."*

*"What?" Gudmund said.*

*"Do it," she repeated. "This one does not lie, and she is pure of heart."*

*In a moment, I was free and standing before them. At full height, I could no longer see any of the Tomte, but Hyrrokkin and her Vargr towered over me above the fog. I was still unsure of their intent.*

*"What do you want with Jutta?" I demanded as I rubbed my wrists.*

*She laughed. "Willing to die for her, are you?" The Vargr snarled at me as it closed the distance between us, but I stood my ground.*

*"They are all my people," I said.*

*"Good," she said. She mounted the beast and yanked me up with her before I could even scream. "Where to?"*

*"Whose side are you on?" I asked.*

*"The side of the people," she said. "Now, where to?"*

*"The labyrinth opening by the selection chamber," I said, staring down at the giant wolf that I now rode. "Were you really going to let this thing eat me?"*

*"Yes," she said.*

I clung to her back as the stones of the labyrinth quickly flew by. The beast moved at incredible speeds.

"What are the Tomte?"

"They are not that different from you or I, they just happen to be small. You are right, they can be nasty little things, but they give gifts at Yule to all the boys and girls of Fenrir and Stonearch. It is the one time of year that something nice happens to those children," she said. "They may be naughty, but they do good, and the Tomte kill any evil they find." I shuddered as I listened to her. I sure didn't want to see them again, whether they came bearing gifts or not. "As for me, I protect the Tomte and the people of Fenrir and Stonearch as best I can, and I live here in the labyrinth, where even Verci can't find me."

"Didn't the Dvergar make the labyrinth?" I asked.

"Yes, but you can't control a living being," she said. "It moves and shifts and is constantly changing, depending on if it likes you alive or dead."

"So was I on the right path to get out of here?" I asked.

She laughed again. "None of them are the right path. They all lead you to your death if the labyrinth wants you to die."

"Do you want me dead?"

She looked back at me and gave me a slow smile.

# 20
## *Vargr*

*"I knew who you were when I arrived. I didn't want you dead, but I wasn't willing to help you until I knew your character. Just because you are the chosen one doesn't mean that I chose you," she said. "But in case you're wondering, you passed the test. Your heart is strong."*

*"Thank you," I said. I didn't know what else to say. She was right; just because I was queen didn't mean I was worth following. I had to earn that right. The Vargr ran for miles as we continued to talk.*

*"After living here for so long, I've grown a bit cynical," she said.*

*"How long have you lived down here?"*

*"I was banished here a long time ago; my people all think me dead," she said. "I've lived down here for over five centuries."*

*"What is Vargr? Is he a wolf?"*

*"An ancient wolf of gods," she said. "His purpose was to expose liars to the Elder Gods. Old Mother created us all with different purposes."*

*I nodded. I was created to love. That was my true purpose. I had always been that way. I loved the children of Dunmanas Bay, I loved my pack, I loved my friends in Maine, and I loved all those trapped in the*

*Realms. My purpose was to protect them all.*

"*Do you know Conrad?*"

"*Who?*"

"*Ummm . . . Conrad,*" *I said. How could I describe him?* "*A strange little man who lives in a Victorian house on wheels in the city Stonearch.*"

"*Ah, the map keeper. I know him,*" *she said.*

"*Is he well? Have you seen him recently?*"

"*Of recent, he doesn't leave his house. I heard he was flayed for his insolence to the Dvergar. Others say he inflicted the wounds on himself, but everyone agrees he's insane,*" *she said.*

*I knew the wounds she spoke of; Dilara and I had given them to him when he agreed to give me his skin with the tattooed map of the Bloodrealms. With his permission, Dilara had sliced the skin off his back to help us escape. Now we were both back. I hoped to save him this time and that coming back wasn't a disgrace to him after he'd done so much to help me get out. I wanted to show him what life outside the Realms could be. I wanted to show him and Jutta the sunshine.*

*Love was sunshine, pure and warm and inspiring to all.*

*I wondered if Jutta had ever seen the sun or if she had always lived her life in the shadows and cracks of the Realms. It was a hard realization that no matter how bad we had it, someone else might have it worse. Compassion and kindness were the only weapons against pain and suffering.*

*As we neared the edge of the labyrinth, I felt a rush of relief. I held my hand over my pounding heart. I'd have been lost without Hyrrokkin.*

"*Thank you so much,*" *I said.* "*Truly, thank you.*"

"*Don't thank me just yet,*" *she said. Her voice was cold as ice as she pulled daggers from sheathes at her thighs. The snakes began to coil around her arms, and the Vargr snarled.*

*I stared at Hyrrokkin confused—had she brought me all this way to kill me? I nearly leaped off the Vargr when I saw Selene peering around the wall of the labyrinth about fifteen feet away. I looked everywhere, but I didn't see Baran. She must have given him to Vigdis's guard. I knew she couldn't see me, so I slid off the Vargr and patted his butt. I walked quietly toward her. She still had Grete on that damn silver leash. Hatred filled me. I knew Grete was human so the silver was nothing to her, but the leash and collar were torture to any soul.*

*"What business do you have here, Selene?" Hyrrokkin demanded.*

*The sheer size difference between them was hysterical. Selene was taller than me, but Hyrrokkin was a giant riding an enormous beast. They were so different. Hyrrokkin was hard, unfeminine, muscular, and fierce. Selene was beautiful, refined, and demure. Selene looked more like a damsel in distress than the enemy, and Hyrrokkin looked like the enemy more than a friend. Appearances were endlessly deceiving.*

*"I have business all over the Realms," Selene said. "What do you and your pet have to do outside the labyrinth? Should I save you the trouble and call the guard?"*

*Grete cowered behind Selene. As the two women had their argument, I got closer and closer to Grete. She had a fresh wound on her arm from when I last saw her with Baran.*

*"I could crush those measly guards, and you know that, Selene," Hyrrokkin said. "Now, let me pass . . . or you will be treated like one of the guards."*

*"I cannot," Selene said as she readied her silver crop.*

*Did silver work on giants? I didn't think so, but I was sure the nasty snakes that Hyrrokkin held would work on Selene. I wanted Selene to be punished for her crimes. I was standing right next to Selene and she didn't even sense me. I could reach out and strangler her if I wanted and she wouldn't have a clue, but I noticed Grete staring at me. Could she see me or did she sense me?*

*I grabbed the crop from Selene's hand and lightly brushed the silver tips over her cheek, exposing her to the silver's poison. She screamed and grasped at her face where I had marked her.*

*"What manner of evil are you?" Selene screamed at Hyrrokkin. "How did you touch me?"*

*"I didn't," she replied.*

*Selene backed away from me as I lightly ran the silver tips over her shoulders. "No, please! Stop! It burns!" she said.*

*"Where is Baran Killian?" I asked.*

*She nearly leaped out of her skin at the sound of my voice and pushed Grete back. "Who are you?" she asked.*

*I was getting so very tired of having my questions answered with questions. I wacked her shoulder with the crop, and I could see the marks in her flesh welt where the silver tips touched her. "Where is Baran Killian?" I repeated.*

*She grabbed her shoulder. "I won't tell you!" she screamed.*

*I grabbed the leash out of her hand and pushed Selene down. "Tell me where Baran Killian is," I demanded.*

*Hyrrokkin grabbed hold of Grete, and Selene's eyes welled with tears. Was she that materialistic that losing her slave brought her to tears? Or was it just fear I could see?*

*"Give her back to me!" Selene said. "Hyrrokkin, I paid for that slave. She is my property, and you will not feed her to your dog!"*

*Hyrrokkin gave a hearty laugh that echoed off the walls around us, shaking small stones loose to tumble to the ground.*

*"If the Vargr is hungry, it is best for everyone that it feeds."*

*I knew Hyrrokkin wouldn't hurt Grete, but Hyrrokkin played the part of evil so well she even scared me. Poor Grete looked terrified. Grete started pulling away from Hyrrokkin, trying to get back to Selene. I gently grabbed Grete's hand and pulled her close; she fought against me.*

*"I'm not worth killing," she whispered as I unhooked her leash.*

*"I'm not here to kill you," I said. "I'm here to save you."*

*The leash fell to the ground, and I stepped toward Selene. "You are nothing. You are a slave trader. You are lower than the Dvergar," I said.*

*"Who are you?" Selene said.*

*I leaned down next to her face, letting my cheek brush hers as I whispered in her ear, "I am Ashling Boru."*

She shivered and looked away. "Are you dead?" she asked. "Did Hyrrokkin steal your soul?"

I laughed. "No, but I'm here to punish you for your evil. Look at Grete—do you even know her name? Look what you've done to her," I said. "Take a long look, because she is the last person you'll ever see."

"You don't understand a thing about this world. You're only a child," she said.

"A child I may be, but you're a murderer."

Selene wiped the tears from her cheeks. "I've bought slaves for centuries down here. Thousands of them have passed through my fingers," she said. "I gave them a life of service . . . a place of honor."

"Honor? You gave your slaves lives of imprisonment and punishment for being human. Are you proud of that?" I said.

"Yes," she said. "I will die proud of that."

Hyrrokkin circled us on her Vargr; it snarled at Selene. Selene flinched her pretty face away, but she didn't beg or plead. She just chewed on her lip.

"Then you shall die now," I said.

"No!" Grete wailed as she crawled across the stone floor to Selene's side; she threw her body over Selene, protecting her from the Vargr.

"You don't have to protect her, Grete—you're free now," I said.

Selene gently pushed Grete away. "It's okay. Fear not, my pet," Selene said.

"I don't understand," I said. "Why is Grete protecting you? What spell have you put on her?"

"Protection," Selene said with a sick smile. "You don't know what I am, Ashling Boru. You know nothing."

"Then explain it to me."

She looked sad, but she nodded her head. "I am a slaver trader," she said, and the Vargr snarled, dripping drool down her chest. I could smell her fear, but her voice didn't waver. "I admit that I have purchased thousands of slaves from the Dvergar selection chamber in my immortal lifetime, but it is what I did with them that makes me different."

*I shuddered to think. "And what was that?"*

*"I set them free," she said.*

*"Then why does everyone think you're in the slave trade?"*

*"Because I am in the slave trade. I bought thousands of slaves. I paid the highest price for most. To the Dvergar, I am the most loyal of custom-ers," she said. "What they believe and what you believe is that I murdered them when they didn't live up to my expectations."*

*"Even Brychan believes you're a monster," I said.*

*She frowned. "I know. They all do. Well, all except Gwyn."*

*"If you didn't murder or resell them all, and no one has ever seen a marked slave free, where are they?"*

*"I built a city for them in Spain. I hid them all . . . every last one. They have an entire city to do whatever they like; it isn't true freedom, but it is the best salvation I have to offer them," she said.*

*"You want me to believe that you spend a fortune to buy the slaves only to lock them up somewhere else? What kind of freedom is that? And isn't purchasing them and paying into the sick Dvergar lifestyle just continuing the cycle?" I asked. I wanted to believe her, but wasn't she just saying this to save her own life?*

*"If one of my slaves were ever caught out of the Realms by a Dvergar loyalist, they'd be killed on sight and tracked back to me. Yes, by purchasing them, I was paying the Dvergar to continue their evil, but look into their eyes and tell me it isn't worth it to die saving them," Selene said.*

*"What about Grete's wounds?" I demanded.*

*"Do you think Vigdis wouldn't notice if all my slaves were uninjured and clean? I had to do it to protect them. After every mark I made, I cried with them. The only way to save them was to be a part of the darkness. This darkness burrowed into my soul, daring to destroy me at times, but I did what I had to. They experienced pain so I could help them. It started with just one slave. Soon, it became an entire city. I did all I could." Grete wrapped her arms around Selene. "And I didn't have a better way to save them. I was waiting for you . . . we have all been waiting lifetimes for you."*

"*Thank you,*" *Grete whispered. "I'd be dead if you hadn't bought me."* *She looked up at me. "Vigdis didn't have a need for me after Eamon died, and now that Fridrik is gone . . . maybe I should have died, too."*

*I fell to my knees and grabbed Grete's hand. "He's not dead," I said. I felt giddy to tell her of her sweet son. "I took him from the bone cages and carried him out of the Realms myself. He's safe with my mother at the Rock of Cashel. I swear to you, he is safe."*

*Tears streamed down Grete's face, and she broke as only a bereaved mother could. All the deep-rooted sadness rushed out of her, and I could feel relief filling the void. It was the best thing I could have said to anyone in all my life.*

*I heard even Hyrrokkin try to hide her tears.*

*"Selene, what did you do to Baran Killian?" I asked, afraid of the answer I might get. I'd misjudged her, but even still, I didn't know what to expect.*

*"No one can beat a dire wolf," she said. "I tried to hit him with the silver crop to make him human, but he tore it from my hand before I had a chance. He scared me half to death. After I was done screaming, I realized who he was and told him to run. I should have known by his sheer size, but all I was concerned with was protecting Grete. When I heard the guards running toward us, I told them I had screamed because my slave was disobeying me, and they struck her." She shook her head. "I made them stop by saying it was my pleasure and right to punish her, and I dismissed them back to the selection chamber. It's my fault she was hit, but it was the only thing I could think of to give Baran a chance to run."*

*"It's okay. It's all okay. Fridrik is alive," Grete said. "And to save Baran's life, what is one more scar?"*

*Grete, a human woman, was unyieldingly and unfathomably brave. "Grete, you're amazing. So are you, Selene. I'm sorry. I should have asked you the truth," I said.*

*"And I would have lied," she said.*

*"I suppose you would have," I said.*

*"It's weird not being able to see you," she said.*

*"I'm only a dream," I said. "Selene, can you take us to Baran?"*

*Grete helped Selene to her feet. "May as well; my time here is limited. Saying what I just said in these walls is a death sentence. Secrets have a way of traveling here; we must get Grete out while we have the chance."*

*The number of my pack members inside the Bloodrealms was growing by the minute. Kane, Shikoba, Dilara, Brychan, Baran, the Crone, Jutta, Selene, Grete, Hyrrokkin and her Vargr . . . it was unlikely we would get them all out of the Realms unnoticed. I knew Brychan and Dilara were going to lose their minds when I arrived with so many new additions. I couldn't blame them; every time they turned around, I was asking them to do something harder than the time before, but Selene said it best: How could I look into any of their eyes and say it wouldn't be worth dying to save them?*

*I took a deep breath and followed Selene and Grete. Grete walked with the sway of a free woman, and it wasn't because Selene freed her. Grete's soul was hers again because Fridrik lived. Women fractured their hearts when they had children; each child has a piece of her mother's heart, and that piece would always be missing from the mother when her babe was not near. It was the sacrifice of motherhood. I knew my own mother felt it when I was gone, and one day, if I were lucky, I would feel it, too.*

*I imagined the sight of Grey holding our baby in his arms, and my heart swelled with joy. My greatest gift was love, and there was no love like a mother's love. I was born to be a mother.*

*But for today, my greatest gift would be getting these people out of the Realms. Selene led us to a familiar path in the labyrinth. I looked up hoping to see the Crone and Jutta, but suddenly weapons were thrust at us from the surrounding labyrinth walls. I couldn't see the faces of those who dropped them down to us, but I could see their hands. Warriors were coming out of the walls. I shivered with fear.*

*The labyrinth wanted us dead.*

*The Vargr nearly took the head off one of the warriors when I recog-*

nized Brychan's startling blue eyes; even with his skin covered in mud and blood that made him blend into the walls, I knew his eyes.

"Stop, wait!" I said. "It's me . . . Ashling. I'm here."

Brychan lowered his sword and laughed. "Nearly killed you and all your . . ." he paused, staring at Hyrrokkin, "interesting new friends."

I touched the thick goop on his cheek and he laughed.

"We learned a few things from Dagny's friends," he said.

I watched as Kane, Shikoba, and Dilara came out from the darkness. I couldn't help but smile seeing them. We were going home, but where were the others?

"Did you find the Crone and Jutta?" I asked.

"Safely above, where you left them," Brychan said.

"Hyrrokkin!" Dilara said as she climbed up the Vargr to hug her. "Aren't you a sight for sore eyes? Seriously, damn this place after you see sunlight again. It feels like death to return, but now seeing you again, it's all worth it."

"Why would you ever come back here?" Hyrrokkin said.

"To help Ashling save Killian," Dilara said.

"Have you seen Baran?" I asked my pack. "He was supposed to be here," I said as I looked to Selene, hoping we were in the right place. Didn't he make it here on his own? Had Verci found him? I shuddered to imagine going back to the torture chamber, and even if I did, I knew if Verci got hold of Baran again, he wouldn't be so lenient. I stared at her and waited, silently begging that he was okay.

Selene pointed to the top of the labyrinth. "Oh, Lord Killian?" she called, "could you do us the honors?" she said. "I'm not quite sure we can get all the way up there with you."

"He won't be coming down," the Crone said. "You all hurry on up. Guard coming from the east and Garm from the west." She tapped the stones and the steps grew back out of the wall.

"What the . . ." Brychan muttered.

"I know, right?" I whispered. "All I want to know is what else can that *fancy stick of hers do?"*

*Brychan chuckled. "After you," he said as he ushered me, Selene, and Grete to go first. Next, Shikoba walked up with Kane. Brychan then turned to Dilara and Hyrrokkin. "I'd say ladies first, but I don't want to be humiliated today." With a wink and a bow, he went up the stairs.*

*"Charming," Hyrrokkin said. "Who is that horrid creature?"*

*Dilara smiled. "Brychan of Kahedin," she said.*

# 21
## Stonearch

*I knew Dilara liked Brychan, but I was a little surprised she let her guard fall that far. I wondered what happened on their journey into the Realms that made them both so flirty. Had Shikoba put a spell on them to make them fall in love?*

*When I reached the top, the stones were already moving back into the wall. Hyrrokkin and her Vargr were the last to leap up the steps, barely in time before they disappeared completely. I rushed to Baran and hugged his big, hairy neck, burying my face in his silver fur. I hadn't let myself feel it, but I'd thought I'd lost him. My exhaustion was replaced by the pure joy of knowing he was alive. I nuzzled my face back and forth, breathing him in as he rubbed his cheek on my head.*

*"Oh, Baran, praise Old Mother you're safe," I said.*

*I just stood there for what felt like a lifetime, letting his love flow into me. I was truly going to save him.*

*"I love you," I whispered.*

*He nudged my shoulder and I let go. I saw Jutta standing back next to the Crone. I wrapped my arms around her and hugged her.*

"Thank you for protecting the Crone," I whispered in her ear.

She giggled.

I reluctantly let her go as I heard the Garm rushing closer. Even from up here they looked disgusting. It was a pack of almost twenty of them. Their hairless bodies raged after our scents.

"We need to get out of here," I said. "From the look of those Garm coming our way, we better be fast. Those nasty demons are unrelenting. Dilara, Hyrrokkin, and Crone, you have been in the Realms for years. Which way should we go?"

"That way," Jutta said, pointing to the south.

Kane knelt down to her and looked her right in the eye. She reached out and touched his long, dreadlocked hair, playing with the tiny beads and feathers at the ends. "You are our guide, Jutta. Lead the way," he said.

Jutta darted ahead of us and headed south away from the selection chamber. We all followed her in a single line on the top of the labyrinth walls. Only Baran and Hyrrokkin, riding her Vargr, were behind me, so I had a nice view of my pack. Seeing them all together made me realize how strong we were. My pack was fierce. We ran for freedom. I could see for miles when I looked down the treacherous walls to the ground below and far across the span of the labyrinth. I watched as a wall chose to move far off in the distance. It was a living being, Hyrrokkin had said.

Selene's dress snagged on the rough surface and she tripped and fell, sliding off the side of the wall.

"Help me!" she cried as her fingers dug at the stone, trying desperately not to fall. She dangled hundreds of feet above the ground.

Brychan and Kane reached down and pulled her back up on the wall and steadied her on her feet.

"I'm sorry, my lady," Brychan said.

"For what?" she asked. "You saved my life."

"This," he said as he hacked the bottom of her dress off with a knife.

She gasped and stared at him with wide eyes.

"Now you won't trip." He winked.

"You dared to touch me?" she said, appalled.

"Kill each other when we are all out of the Realms safely," I said.

"I agree," Dilara grumbled. She reeked of jealousy, and I almost giggled.

Selene walked over the remains of her beautiful dress and begrudgingly followed Jutta, this time creating much more distance between herself and Brychan. I couldn't blame her for being annoyed; Brychan truly lacked manners sometimes, but it was part of his charm.

I looked back and saw the Garm wolves circling below the wall where we'd climbed up to join the Crone. They started howling and clawing, trying to follow our scent up the wall, but they could only jump so high.

"Run," I said.

Jutta started running at my command, and the others all followed. I could hear the Garm fighting each other, and all the memories and feelings from the night I spent in the burial tomb flooded back. I had been certain those horrible, hairless animals were going to eat me alive. I could only imagine the others all felt the same now as we ran for our lives.

Jutta slipped on a loose rock and fell off the side of the wall and out of sight. "Jutta!" I gasped. Was she broken and dying at the bottom of the wall? I heard her screaming as I dropped to my knees and looked over the edge. She was grasping a vine about thirty-five feet from the ground.

The Garm ran down the path, following the sound of Jutta's cries. They quickly surrounded her from below and started jumping and snapping at her, trying to tear her from where she clung so desperately. She was neither close enough for us to reach her nor far enough down for them to get her, but she couldn't hang on to that vine forever.

"We have to get down there. We have to save her," I said.

"Not you," Hyrrokkin said. She swatted her Vargr and he leaped off the wall. They landed on one of the Garm and crushed it. The Vargr had no trouble with the distance, but the rest of us would likely break our legs.

Dilara grabbed Kane's rope. "Don't drop me," she said to Kane and Brychan as she swung herself down the wall to Jutta. She grabbed Jutta in *her arms. "Fly, little one," she said as she tossed her up the wall. Selene and I caught Jutta's arms and hoisted her back onto the wall. Jutta clung to me. I gently held her in my arms while she cried.*

*Dilara tied the rope around her waist and worked her foot into a small hole in the stone as she steadied herself and began pulling short spears from the pack on her back. Dilara weighed a spear in her hand and flung it down into the skull of a Garm, killing it instantly.*

*Five Garm attacked the Vargr, biting at its flesh, as the other six tried to climb the wall to Dilara. The Vargr was so immense that the Garm went limp as soon as he bit into them. Hyrrokkin swung her morning star–spiked mace and slammed the spikes into the beasts.*

*Howling brought my attention back to the north. Another pack of at least ten Garm raced toward us.*

*"Get back up here," I commanded.*

*"It's not safe," Brychan said.*

*"You guys keep running," Dilara yelled. "I will stay and cover Hyrrokkin and we'll catch up."*

*Not waiting for a response, Dilara turned and continued launching spears down on the Garm that attacked Hyrrokkin and the Vargr. Grete yanked Jutta to her feet and started running again. I felt sick leaving Dilara and Hyrrokkin behind, but if we didn't keep moving, we'd be surrounded.*

*As Baran, Kane, Shikoba, Selene, Grete, the Crone, Jutta, Brychan, and I reached the center of the labyrinth, Jutta took the lead again. Holding Grete's hand, Jutta led us all to the southeast of the selection chamber.*

*"That's the city of Stonearch," Jutta said. "Hurry . . . we can get out through the cities."*

*"And hopefully disappear among the people while we wait for Dilara and Hyrrokkin," Brychan said.*

*If we hid among those people, we would only bring them death. Going through Stonearch was as quick a route as I knew to get out of the Realms; we just had to keep moving through and not give the Garm or Vigdis a reason to search the city for us. By now, it was likely the Garm movements would be noticed, and they would be looking for Baran. I looked back and I could no longer see Dilara hanging from the wall. Had she fallen? I stopped and searched the walls for her; I panicked more with every moment that passed.*

*"Brychan!" I yelled. "She's gone?"*

*He looked out over the labyrinth walls and I knew he knew. His fists balled up at his sides, and his nostrils flared when he breathed. "Keep moving," he said.*

*"But . . ."*

*"Do you want to die, too?" he said. The anger flowed off him in flames. He turned and ran toward where Dilara had been fighting the Garm.*

*"Brychan!" I screamed, but he was gone.*

*Baran nudged me in the back with his big head, and I started running again to catch up with the others and to run from my guilt. Everything I feared was coming true. This one quest would get us all killed.*

*Was I truly ready to die for what I believed in? Would I ever be ready to die? I thought of Grey, Mother, Nia, and the babies I dreamed of having one day; I wasn't ready to give up any of my dreams, my life. We just had to keep running. We had to survive.*

*I skidded to a stop at the end of the wall, and we looked down on the city of Stonearch; it was nothing but smoldering ash. The smell of burning flesh filled the air. We were too late . . . there was no one left to save, and it was my fault Vigdis and Verci were killing all the inhabitants of the Bloodrealms to flush us out of our hiding places. They knew we were here, and all these innocent people had died for it. Everything was burned, leaving nothing more than the city's skeleton.*

*"Are they all dead?" Grete asked in a quiet voice.*

*"No . . . not all," the Crone said. She tapped her staff and the steps appeared.*

*"I will see if I can find life," Shikoba said. She disappeared into thin air like she always did. Kane and Baran went down the stairs first. Grete, Jutta, and the Crone followed them down into the burning city, and Selene*

*and I followed behind.*

"Stay together," I said. I didn't want to lose anyone else. We had already lost too much. "We need to find Conrad."

"Who?" Kane said.

"The man with no skin," Jutta whispered.

"Do you know him?" I asked.

"He used to live over here," she said, weaving through the remains of homes and wolves; bodies littered the ground, half burned and half eaten. I shuddered as I walked over them. I could hear all their screams, all their cries. Every one of them spoke to me. I felt my gag reflex start jittering, and I had to clench my side to stop from vomiting right there.

An entire city of steampunk homes was reduced to nothing more than smoke and char. We turned the corner and I saw Conrad's Victorian home on melted wheels. All the windows were broken out, and the right side was burned. My heart felt as though it might rupture. I might not have killed these people, but someone died from Vigdis's wrath with every move I made. Death followed me.

The air was filled with smoke, ash, and the smell of death. My eyes burned from the stench. I looked around as we walked through the city, hoping to find someone who had survived. Someone who hadn't died because of me.

Shikoba reappeared next to me. "This way," she said. "They are hiding, and they won't come out until they speak with you."

"Who?" I asked.

"The survivors of Stonearch," she said.

I swallowed down the bile that crept into my throat and ran after her. We approached a massive fortress made from remnants of their homes, vehicles, and lives. Cars, doors, metal beams, wheels, entire homes stacked together in a circle to give them somewhere to hide from the attack. The outside was burned, but the metal structures held true. Inside I could see faces hidden in the shadows and the ash. Gloriously beautiful faces. Old Mother spared them, and for that I was endlessly thankful.

"Come out," I urged. I wanted to tell them they were safe now, but we all knew no one was safe in the Realms. "I am Ashling Boru, your queen. You can't see me, but trust my voice . . . I am here."

Conrad hobbled with a makeshift cane onto the hood of a burned car. His arm had been badly burned and his face was black with ash, but I was elated to see him. "I didn't think I'd hear your voice again," he said. "I'm still recovering from my new wounds, you see." He pointed to his leg; the skin had been flayed off his calf.

"What happened to you?" I asked.

"Verci found out I'd given my flesh to you, so he wanted his payment as well . . . pounds of flesh to match what I'd already given. The price I pay to be beautiful," he said with a sigh and smile.

"You're ridiculous," I said. "And I'm so sorry."

"Aye, darling, but I'm alive," he said.

People started crawling out onto all the ledges of their fortress. Some searched for me, but I knew they couldn't see me. So far I counted twenty survivors. How many more hid inside, I still didn't know.

Brychan ran up to me with blood running down his arm where he'd clearly been bitten. I looked behind him, expecting to see Dilara and Hyrrokkin, but no one was there.

"I couldn't find them. They're gone."

I could feel the anguish in his words. The failure he felt. I put my hand on his neck and pulled his forehead against mine. I could feel his sadness. As I took it in, I tried not to drown in it; I tried to give him hope, but I had little to share. I pulled away, and he nodded and fell in line with the others.

"Conrad, we are headed out of the Realms. Do you know which path is safest?" I asked.

"We've already been hit by the Garm wolves and the giants that burned our homes. They both continued on to the north toward the selection chamber, and Verci was with them. I think you keep going into Fenrir," he said.

"Conrad, come with us and help me. It is only a matter of time before Vigdis and Verci kill everyone who still breathes," I said.

"No, my queen," he said. "We are staying to rebuild our city."

"If you don't come with us, you will die," Brychan said.

"This is our city," Conrad said.

"But you're free!" I yelled. "You are so close to salvation—all you have to do is come with us. It is only on the other side of Fenrir, and you will fight your way into the sunshine as free men and women." But they didn't move. They just stared at my pack. I could smell their fear. They were terrified. I was too, but we couldn't just lie down here and let Verci and Vigdis win. Were they too afraid to take the chance to save themselves? Generations of fear filled their fortress. After centuries of living in this hell, they probably no longer knew what freedom even was. Freedom was just a word . . . not even an idea, much less a tangible reality.

"You can't stay here," Selene said. "There is nothing left to rebuild. There is no life for any of you here . . . only death."

"You know plenty about death, don't you, Lady Selene?" Conrad said. "Interesting company you keep, Ashling."

"We don't have time for this game," I yelled. "You either come with us or you stay and die. You decide."

I started walking toward Fenrir when a car exploded in the fortress walls. The gasoline poured out of the tank and spread quickly downhill. Wildfire spread quickly, and screams echoed around us. Conrad had fallen from the heap and landed near me.

"I'm sorry, my queen," he said. "I should have listened."

Baran nudged me to my feet, and I clung to him. I watched as the fortress they'd built to survive was now trapping them inside to burn. Baran ran to the fire and slammed his body into one of the cars. He pushed it open, and people began to rush out toward us. Brychan and Selene helped pull them out to safety.

"Run for Fenrir, and don't look back!" I said to them. I turned to my pack. "Baran, you and Kane lead them!" Kane erupted into a wolf, and he and Baran tore off to the front to lead the people. "Shikoba, stay with Grete, the Crone, and Jutta and protect them." I watched as they reluctant-

*ly started into the flood of the others. Grete turned back to me, terror in her eyes. "Grete, if I am lost, find Fridrik at the Rock of Cashel."*

*She nodded and tears streamed down her face. My heart ached for her. "Thank you," she said, then disappeared into the crowd.*

*Only Brychan, Selene, and I remained. Brychan started pulling apart the fortress to allow more people to escape faster. The smoke was nearly unbearable. It stung my eyes and made my throat tighten. The heat from the flames felt scorching on my skin.*

*There were at least seventy people fleeing from the fire after Baran and Kane.*

*"That's everyone," Brychan said.*

*"Okay, let's move," I said.*

*The smallest cry came from deep inside the fortress. A child's voice. My heart sank. I looked at Selene and she was already running inside. The structure was completely engulfed in flames. As she reached the far corner, I could barely make out her silhouette through all the smoke. She scooped up a small child and turned to run back to us. Suddenly the structure exploded, falling down all around them.*

*"Selene!" I screamed, staring in horror. Where were they? I couldn't see them anymore. I paced back and forth so close to the flames the hair on my arms singed. "Brychan, we have to get in there. We have to save them."*

*"No, we can't see anything," he said.*

*I could hear the child crying and Selene's labored breathing. She was injured. The smoke surged around us, and I could barely see them. I ran to them through the flames and smoke, and Brychan matched my step. Selene was pinned under a metal beam. She was holding a child in her arms.*

*"Ready!" Brychan barked as he gestured to lift the steel off her. As we lifted, my arms shook and my muscles burned with strain. The flames licked my skin, and smoke and ash stung my eyes as the metal burned into my flesh. My eyes welled with tears as the steel slipped from my fingers and slammed back into Selene, and she cried out in pain.*

*I fell to my knees next to her. "I'm so sorry," I said. "I'll try again. We'll get you out somehow."*

The fire chased a trail of dripping gasoline and ignited the remains of Selene's dress. I reached toward her, burning my hands and desperately trying to put it out. She snarled at me.

"You can't save everyone," she growled. "I knew I would die here one day; I'm just glad it is on my terms. Now save this child and all these people." She pushed the little boy away from the flames and into my arms, but I couldn't move. I couldn't leave her to die.

I faltered, but Brychan grabbed my hand and dragged me after him. I was leaving her behind. I watched her struggling to get out from under the steel. I heard her tears as her flesh burned.

"Please, Brychan, we have to save her," I begged.

He only pointed to the fires that were quickly surrounding us. As I finally took in the city, I realized that all these innocent people were still running for their lives, and the fire was winning. If we didn't hurry, we'd be trapped in here to die ourselves. I knew he was right. I knew she was right, but I hated everything about it. Every step I took to my own freedom was a step toward Selene's death.

I felt sick and selfish.

Her screams were horrible. I wanted to rush back to her. I wanted to hold her while she closed her eyes and gave in to the pain. No one should die alone. No one.

We caught up to the others, the old, the children, the wounded; they were all going too slow, and Conrad was among them. The fire was all around us, and the people were slowly running through the doorway into Fenrir. I couldn't truly say if we were going to make it. I looked into the scared eyes of the little boy I carried and almost lost myself in the gray, smoky color. His face was only clean where the tears streamed down his cheeks.

"It's okay," I said to him and to myself. "We're going to make it."

I nested his fingers in my hair, hid his face in my neck, and ran as fast as I could. My hatred for Verci and Vigdis was deeper than anything I'd ever felt . . . deeper than my hate of Adomnan. I wanted vengeance for this.

*I loathed them, and I loathed this place.*

*I tried to block my hate. Hate wasn't going to save me. It was just steal-ing space in my mind when I should be trying to save these people, but the hate was consuming. As I watched Baran and Kane lead the people through the burning Stonearch doorway into the city of Fenrir, I found a bit of hope left inside me. I saw Grete, Jutta, and the Crone cross over, and the people flooded through behind them.*

*"Faster," Brychan barked as the heat of the flames swarmed around us.*

*Suddenly the doorway into Fenrir cracked and an enormous wooden beam slammed into the ground, engulfing the doorway in flames.*

*"Damn it!" Brychan screamed.*

*An old woman wailed and a child tried to run into the burning door-way, but Conrad grabbed her. "Do not fear death, child," he said.*

*There were seven of us left trapped, including Brychan and me, an old woman, Conrad, a little girl, the boy I carried, and a man who had burns all over his body. I should have been happy so many had survived, but I was angry for those trapped with me.*

*"Brychan!" I yelled through the hysteria. "What do we do?"*

*He looked frantic and shook his head. "We could try to throw them over the fire, but I don't think they would clear it. We can't move that beam. It is bigger than the one that trapped Selene. I think this is the end."*

*I looked back to where we'd left Selene behind. I could still hear her crying and groaning. Listening to her die was like watching my own fate. We'd all be dead soon.*

*At least I'd saved Baran. I owed him that. I thought of Grey and wanted to cry. My future was with him, everything I dreamed he was part of, and now I couldn't have any of it. Not a life, not children; I couldn't save my pack or my friends. It was over. Everything I'd fought for was over.*

*Brychan grabbed my shoulders. "Wake up!" he said. "You don't have to die here, just wake up! You'll be home with Grey."*

*What was he saying? I heard the words, but I couldn't understand them. He wanted me to leave them all to die?*

"No," I said.

"It is the only way," he said. "You have saved so many. You can be proud of that, but none of us are worth you dying. You have to live. If you don't live, the people you just saved will still die."

His voice cracked, and his pretty blue eyes were filled with tears. I'd never seen Brychan cry, and I felt as though I couldn't breathe. He carelessly wiped his tears away.

"Tell my family I loved them," he said, nodding. "And Ashling, I am proud to be next to you today. Thank you for trusting me."

"Brychan, I can't leave you."

He gently took the little boy from my invisible arms. "But you must."

# 22
## *Ghosts*

*My throat was so tight that I was choking for air. My whole body shook uncontrollably, and all I could do was stare at him and cry. He pulled his hand away from me and sat down with the others.*

*"Old Mother will claim us as the fires burn our bodies," he said as he wrapped his arms around the old woman. They all put their arms around each other, letting their energy flow through one another. I felt so separated . . . so alone. I wanted to be one of them. "It's time, Ashling. Just wake up."*

*I couldn't stop the tears. "No," I whispered.*

*"Ashling, please," he pleaded. He slid the little boy into the arms of the old woman and stood before me. "You can't die here."*

*"Neither can you," I said.*

*I walked away from him toward the burning doorway. I stood as close to it as I could and screamed. "Baran!" I took a breath and did it again and again.*

*Brychan stood next to me with his hand on my shoulder. "They can't hear you over the fire," he said.*

*I looked up at him so angry and sad. "Maybe he can't hear me, but he can feel me. He's my pack," I said. "He knows. He'll help us. He always helps me."*

*"Damn it, Ashling, save yourself. What is wrong with you? Why can't you just listen to me for once in your life?" I shook my head no, and he hung his head as he wrapped me so tightly in his arms I felt as though I was part of him. "You can choose to die today with me, and I won't fight you anymore. I will hold your hand while we die, but you can choose life, Ashling. You can choose it for your mother, Baran, Grey, and all of your people. You can choose it for yourself."*

*"What kind of queen would I be if I left my people to die?" I asked.*

*"What kind of queen are you if you are dead? Either way you choose, your people die," he said. "That's the bitch-faced truth. We die here either way. Are you going to let them all die, too?"*

*"Damn it, Brychan!" I screamed. "I hate you sometimes."*

*He smiled. "You hate the truth."*

*I rested my forehead on his chest as I cried. I'd known him since I was fourteen. Loathed him sometimes, but through it all, I wanted to be his friend. I couldn't bear the idea of him dying.*

*"Please, Brychan," I whispered.*

*"It's time to wake up, my queen," he said. "Now!"*

*I heard Baran howling on the other side of the fire, and his panic flowed into me. He knew I was trapped. He knew I needed him. Suddenly Shikoba appeared next to me.*

*She looked around and disappeared again.*

*"Maybe they have a plan," I said.*

*"I sure hope so," Brychan said. "I don't really want to die."*

*"You had me convinced," I said.*

*"How else could I save you?" he said. "If they can't help us, you're waking up. Deal?"*

*I nodded.*

*I looked back to Selene. I couldn't hear her anymore, but I felt her spirit around me. I had let her die . . . my fault. The truth of it echoed in my mind.*

Shikoba reappeared. *"Help is on the way,"* she said. *"Get these people to their feet."* With that, she was gone again.

*"You heard the lady; we aren't dying today,"* Brychan yelled. *"Gather your strength—we fight our way out."*

*"Selene,"* I whispered to Brychan.

We both stared back into the smoke. *"I know,"* he said.

A sharp howl pierced the crackling fire, echoing off the high ceilings. *"The Vargr,"* I said.

*"Hyrrokkin?"* Conrad said.

Just then, the Vargr leaped the fire with two riders and quickly closed the distance between us. The giant creature skidded to a stop before us with Hyrrokkin and Dilara riding the beast.

I couldn't find words; staring at them was like staring at ghosts.

*"Did you see Selene? Is she . . ."* I asked.

*"Old Mother already claimed her,"* Dilara said. Shikoba appeared next to me again. *"Thanks for letting us know where to find them,"* Dilara said to Shikoba.

Shikoba nodded. *"If the Vargr pulls from this side and Baran and Kane pull from the other side, we may just be able to move the beam far enough to get the last of us to safety,"* she said.

Brychan gave Dilara a quick hug. *"I'm not losing you again,"* he said.

Hyrrokkin tossed him a chain she carried, and he leaped into the fire and wrapped the chain around the gate hooks. He leaped back out as a wolf, the chain end in his mouth. Patches of his fur were singed off, but he didn't seem to notice the burns and damage to his skin and muscle. Hyrrokkin hooked the chain to the harness of the Vargr.

*"Forward!"* Hyrrokkin yelled. The Vargr walked until the chain was taut and clawed at the ground to pull the beam out of the way, but with all the strength of the Vargr and Baran and Kane on the other side, still the beam didn't move.

Hyrrokkin jumped off the Vargr and started pulling the reins. The *beam creaked and sparks flew out of it as it nudged forward. I watched as the chain dug into Brychan's mouth and blood dripped to the black stone floor. With every foot the beam scraped across the ground, I could see free-dom a little more, but with every moment that passed, the fires closed in tighter around us and everyone clustered closer and closer to me. We were trapped between the flames from the city and the flames that engulfed the doorway.*

*"Old Mother, please," I said. "We want to serve you for another day."*

*Dilara slapped me on the back. "As soon as that opening is big enough, you all start running through it." She was so strong and unwavering; she impressed me, and I felt strangely guilty about my own weakness. As the beam scraped farther, the opening was now about four feet wide. "Now!" she screamed.*

*I watched in wonder as Conrad, the old woman, the little girl, and the burned man ran for their lives. They seemed stronger and fiercer than ever. Dilara scooped up the little gray-eyed boy and ran beside me through the doorway to Fenrir. As we cleared the smoke and ash, I saw Baran and Kane as wolves with blood dripping from their mouths. Even with all the gore, I wanted to celebrate. Far ahead, I could see the Crone and Jutta leading the people into the arena. We weren't safe yet. I feared what evil awaited us in the arena, but it was the only way out.*

*I knew none of them could see me, but Baran ran right next to me. He could feel right where I was, and he wasn't going to leave my side. I was thankful for that. I desperately needed his strength.*

*When I burst into the arena, it was eerily quiet. We were almost out of the Bloodrealms—we just had to climb the spiral staircase to the balcony and three hundred grueling steps through the earth's crust to the surface and we'd be safe with Dagny. I looked up at the stone wolves that had saved my family when we had fought Vigdis and Verci in the Bloodrealms. Their eyes almost seemed to follow me, as though they could see me.*

*"Thank you," I whispered to them.*

*I owed them so much more than I could ever pay; they had saved ev-*

eryone I loved. I never thought I'd find myself running for my life through this horrible place again, but here I was.

"Baran, we're almost there," I said.

"Celebrate later," Dilara complained as she carried the boy. "I didn't come back here to die."

Baran, Dilara, and I were the last on the spiral staircase to the balcony; it was then that I saw her watching us from her throne. She had probably been there the whole time . . . watching . . . waiting. Vigdis's black lace veil covered her expression, but I could feel sickness seething from her. I could almost taste it. She stroked the head of a Garm wolf sitting next to her.

"She's watching us," I whispered. Neither Baran nor Dilara flinched. They stared straight ahead, but I knew they heard me. "Why isn't she attacking us?"

"She can't see you," Dilara said. "Dagny's army is right outside; she isn't going to waste her precious Garm on us. We are nothing without you."

I prayed Dilara was right. We ran out of sight and up the endless stairs into the darkness of night. As I crawled out onto the cold stone under the stars, Dagny pulled me to my feet.

He bowed. "My queen, are you being followed?"

"How did you know it was me?" I said, knowing I was still invisible.

"Your scent, my queen," he said as the rest of my party climbed out to safety.

I wrapped my arms around him and he stood frozen as I hugged him, but soon he embraced me back. I was thrilled to see him, to see stars, to see anything but the Bloodrealms.

"I trust you're pleased with your army?" he said.

I opened my eyes and marveled at all the wolves surrounding us. I didn't know any of them, not even their family scents. There were hundreds of them. He'd kept his word; he had indeed created an army.

*My army.*

Dagny stared at Hyrrokkin riding her Vargr but didn't say a word. She was a legend, a myth, and there she stood in all her glory. Baran padded up *next to me, still as a dire wolf.*

"*My old friend,*" *Dagny said as he hugged Baran. Dagny turned to me.* "*I can never repay you for saving my friend.*"

"*Our war isn't over yet,*" *I said, looking to the broken people we'd saved.* "*We need refuge for these people.*"

"*I will see it done,*" *Dagny said, looking at the near seventy people who had emerged from the Bloodrealms.* "*From the looks of them, they can't travel in their current condition. When they are rested, we will see them to the Steel Wolves of Szabadság.*"

"*Thank you,*" *I said.*

"*Can you bring clothing for our wolf friends?*" *Dilara asked, gesturing toward Baran, Kane, and Brychan.*

"*Gunthar, fetch some clothes,*" *Dagny commanded.* "*People of the Bloodrealms, follow me and I will see you fed.*"

*I watched them all disappear into the shack. They were safe, for now. I turned back to my pack. Baran, Brychan, Dilara, Kane, Shikoba, Hyrrok-kin, Jutta, the Crone, and Grete.*

*Gunthar returned with clothes, and Baran, Kane, and Brychan shifted back into human form. Baran looked around, smelling the air.* "*Ashling?*" *he called. I could hear worry in his voice.*

"*I'm here,*" *I said.*

*Baran rushed over to the sound of my voice and picked me up, hugging me so tight.* "*You did it, Ashling,*" *he said.* "*I never had a doubt.*"

"*I missed you,*" *I said.*

*He set me back on my feet and smiled.* "*I'm always with you, ylva.*"

*I felt whole again. I felt hope again. I turned back to my small pack.*

"*Grete, Fridrik is at the Rock. I would like you to accompany the Crone there. You will both be safe with my family,*" *I said.* "*Jutta, where do you want to be?*"

*She stared at me wide eyed; I always felt she could see me.*

"*You can stay back and rest with these people, or you can go with Grete and the Crone to live with my family in Ireland. The choice is yours,*" *I said gently.*

She still didn't answer. She stared at her toes, and I could smell her fear. I reached out and held her hand. "If you leave the choice up to me, I'd send you with the Crone and Grete to my family. I think you'll love them, and I know you'd love the misty air by the cliffs." She nodded and bit her lower lip. She was trying so hard not to cry as she nodded. "Hyrrokkin, where do you want to be? Would you like to fight with Dagny? Or go with the people to the steel wolves?"

"I am of greatest service to you with Dagny's army, moving the survivors to Szabadság. I will travel with the army to Carrowmore by the Bloodmoon of your birthday," she said. "I will stand with you when you are claimed."

"Thank you, Hyrrokkin. I am proud to have you in our pack," I said as she started riding her Vargr to the shack. "Hyrrokkin, don't give Dagny too much trouble."

She nodded stoically and rode off.

"Kane, Shikoba, Brychan, and Dilara—please protect Jutta, Grete, and the Crone as you travel to the Rock, and notify me immediately when all are safe," I said.

"We shall," Brychan said.

"Baran, my protector, I must wake up now. Travel home safely to Maine; Grey and I will be waiting for you," I said with a sigh. "I will see you soon."

"Ashling, my sweet ylva," Baran said. "You are a force so strong that it could only be love."

I hugged him again and breathed in his musty scent one more time. It was hidden by all the smoke and ash and blood, but it was still there. Still so welcoming.

"Ashling," Brychan said as he held my hand and kissed my cheek. "Thank you for not giving up on me."

"I never will," I said.

He nodded.

"Brychan, keep an eye on Dilara for me, won't you?" I said, smiling and knowing he couldn't see my mischievous grin. He nodded as he watched her talking to the Crone.

"All right," I said sleepily. It seemed strange that I had to wake from my dream to finally get some rest. "Keep each other safe for me."

I knelt down in the grass and closed my eyes to the dream, willing myself to wake up. I wondered where my body would be this time.

# 23
## Homecoming

*I opened my* eyes to see Grey's perfect face. He'd fallen asleep in the most awkward position, with one leg heaped over mine. I gently swept his brown hair out of his face. I could see the fatigue on him. Dark circles lined his eyes. Even asleep, his brow was furrowed. I nuzzled into him, feeling his warmth all around me. I didn't know where we were, but I didn't care. I was with him.

If it wasn't for the obnoxious beeping, I could have lost myself staring at his beautiful face. I glanced around the room. We were lying in a hospital bed; the beeping was my heart rate monitor, and there was an IV in my arm. Why was I here?

He woke suddenly and stared at me with wide, incredulous eyes. He searched my face as though he were uncertain I was real. Was I still in a dream? He grabbed my face and kissed me so passionately everything melted away.

"Ashling, my love," he said between kisses. "It's been six days. I thought I had lost you forever." Grey stopped kissing and looked deep into my eyes; he touched my face and hair as though he were memorizing me. "Please don't go back there."

I smiled and wrapped my arms around him. "I don't have to. We saved Baran!"

His face softened and he smiled. "I know, love. He's here."

"What?"

"He got home before you woke up."

"He's here?" The words came out as a breath.

"Last I checked, he was teaching something to Jamal in the waiting room," he said.

"Where are we?" I asked.

"The York Harbor hospital," he said. "Our home is a bit of a crime scene."

I suddenly remembered the fight with the Bloodsuckers, the brutality, the dead bodies. "Where is Rhonda?" The last I'd seen her I was bleeding myself to save her. I didn't even know if she lived. I'd spent so much time in the Bloodrealms, I'd lost sight of the reality I'd left behind. Was she even alive?

"She's still recovering. Her wounds were substantial, and she's been resting a lot, but you saved her, and every day she is stronger than the day before," he said. "She told me she'd be ready to fight by the time you woke up . . . and I believe her."

"That strong will of hers saved her life," I said.

Rhonda opened the door. "No, your sacrifice and blood saved my life; my stubbornness had little to do with it," she said with a laugh.

"Rhonda . . ." I looked into her face. "I'm sorry for your loss." Rhonda started to argue, but I kept talking. "He may have been an ass and tried to kill us all, but it is still a loss. I'm so sorry."

She nodded solemnly.

"What was your father's name?" I asked

"Jacob," she said quietly.

I nodded.

"Thank you," she said. "And now, you are my family, Ashling.

Sometimes family isn't just blood . . . though I suppose we are that too, now."

I laughed. "I guess so," I said. "And I'm sorry about Paul. He was such a gracious man."

"His presence will always be missed. He was one of my favorites," she said.

"I know I can't take away the pain, but I give free hugs, for what it's worth."

She closed the distance between us and hugged me. I hugged her back as hard as I could, though I still felt weak. We all knew the risk when they joined my pack, but none of us could imagine the pain of her loss.

I looked back to her and Grey. "How did we get here?" I asked. "The last thing I remember was Rhonda nearly dead and me passing out."

"Jamal and I carried you both here," Grey said. "The doctors thought you were in a coma and have been caring for you both for the last few days."

"Why did you bring us here?" I asked.

"Well, both your and Rhonda's blood was all over the ground by Cesario and her father's bodies, and our home was filled with more dead people. Not to mention the trail of blood that followed us. There was no way to hide it from the police, so instead of running, we asked for help," Grey said.

"Officer Gavin has been snooping around," she said. "He's oddly convinced you're evil. What did you do to that guy?"

"Nothing! I swear. He's just too smart for his own good," I muttered.

"Well . . . you do tend to leave a trail of bodies," Grey said. We all laughed.

"Get ready, Ashling, because once he hears you're awake, Officer Gavin will be here to question you like he did me. Man, is he obnoxious," Rhonda said. "Cute, though."

I shook my head. Rhonda was right—Officer Gavin was cute but quite rude when he wanted to be. I wasn't looking forward to what he had to say.

"Grey, I want to see Baran," I said. Grey kissed my forehead and wandered out the door.

After a few moments, Baran hobbled into the room with the tiniest limp to his left leg. "Sweet ylva," he said. I was caught by surprise; his voice overflowed with emotion, and all I could do was stare up into his big eyes. He crushed me into him. "You saved my life, Jutta's life, and so many more. You brought us all together for a greater cause outside ourselves."

"I lost Selene," I whispered in his ear.

"I know," he said. "Not everyone survives war, but I promise you, Old Mother has erased her pain and sorrow."

I knew he was right . . . but he didn't listen to her dying cries.

"Does her family know?" I asked.

"I called them and Gwyn," he said.

"What about her hidden city of free wolves?"

"Her family said they would be informed."

I nodded.

"I feel like I failed her," I said.

"Brychan told me what she'd said before she died. She didn't think you failed, you know that, right?" he said. "She lived a life that nearly got her killed from both sides thousands of times, but she was proud of that life—the good and the bad. You should be proud of her, too. Mourn her, but don't regret; regret will make you lose sight of her grace and sacrifice for all those people."

"She lived her whole life being hated when she was truly rescuing those people," I said. "Do you think she regretted that?"

"Not for a minute," Baran said. "She committed her life to them, as I committed mine to you. I knew I might die when I was taken, but to save you, I'd risk it again."

"You're crazy," I said.

Baran smiled and ran his fingers through his silver hair. "Yeah, but you knew that already." He winked. "Now, let me find a nurse to get you discharged from here; the food is terrible."

I laughed. Baran and Rhonda got up and left the room, leaving me and Grey to have a moment together.

Grey lay down next to me and started wrapping his fingers in my hair. I liked the feeling. It tickled a little, but I just liked being connected to him. It was one part sweet and one part sensual. Although his touch was truly always sensual.

"Have Brychan, Dilara, Kane, Shikoba, the Crone, Grete, and Jutta made it to the Rock yet? Are they safe?" I asked.

"We got the call yesterday. They are all safe at the Rock, and Grete is united with Fridrik. She called, crying, to thank you," Grey said. "And Jutta is with your mother . . . it sounds like they've grown quite fond of one another."

"Good. I'm glad they are safe," I said. I thought for a while about them and about us. "Where are we going to live?"

"I think the police and the cleanup crew that Baran hired are done with the house, so we can probably go home if we want to," he said.

I shuddered to think about it. Would the house even look right when we got there? My sanctuary was now a bad memory. I felt violated that they had attacked us in our own home. It destroyed my naïve sense of safety. I knew it was naïve. Like a little lock on a silly door could protect me from anything. But it made me feel safe, and that's what mattered.

That was all any of us could hope for, that sense of security when surrounded by familiar walls and the love of family and friends; that was true safety.

"Where else do you want to go?" Grey asked.

I shook my head. "I have no idea."

He took my hands. I hadn't even realized they were shaking until his warm touch comforted me. "Let's go home."

Baran walked back in with a nurse and Jamal in tow. "Release my queen," he said to the nurse, winking at me.

"Oh, Miss Ashling, you're awake," the nurse said as she bustled about. She was so gentle as she removed all the needles and wires from me. "You do consistently run a high temperature, though."

"Oh yeah, always been that way," I said, hoping she'd drop it. Wolves had higher body temperatures than humans.

"The doctor will want to talk to you before you leave the hospital," she said.

I rubbed my arm after she removed my IV. "Thank you," I said.

"Mmmmhm," she said, walking out the door.

I found myself enjoying just being awake. I felt like I had finally rested. The most powerful feeling was sleep. There was a hard knock at the door, and I nearly jumped out of bed as Officer Gavin walked in. He looked just as I remembered him—suave, golden, and filled with righteousness to serve and protect.

"Ms. Boru." He nodded. His movements were stiff, and he smelled like he was sweating profusely.

"Should I say, 'Nice to see you, Officer Gavin'?" I asked. "Last time I saw you, you were quite rude."

Baran grunted, and Gavin straightened up even more. I wouldn't have thought it possible. He looked stick straight and no fun at all.

"I do owe you an apology," he said, clearing his throat. "I misjudged the case and didn't realize you were the victim of such terrible crimes."

I let out the breath I'd been holding. "Yes, my friends and I have lived through hell, but finally we can learn to put it behind us," I said.

"I already spoke with Rhonda, Jamal, Grey, and Baran, but do you have anything you'd like to add to their accounts of the attack?" he asked as he pulled out his notebook.

"I was asleep when they broke into the house and awoke to find Paul already dead. We fled the house and ran, trying to make it to the parade for help, but Rhonda and I stopped to try to help Grey and Jamal. That is when Jacob attacked Rhonda and me. I don't remember anything after that," I said. "It's so fuzzy."

I remembered everything in perfect, vivid detail, but Officer Gavin wasn't ready for that kind of tale.

"All right," he said. "Thank you. I believe this case is closed."

"Let me walk you out," Baran said as he ushered the man back out the way he'd come, but the nurse pushed past him with the doctor.

"Hello, Ashling, I am Doctor MacManus," she said. When she leaned in close and listened to my heart and took my vitals, she smelled so strongly of antibacterial soap it made my nose burn. Her blonde hair was pulled up into a bun. "We weren't sure about you for a while there, but I'm glad to see you awake and alert."

"Thank you," I said.

"I'm not sure you should go home so quickly, Ashling. Except for your slight fever," she raised her eyebrow as she looked at me a little too knowingly, "your vitals are all checking out fine, but you've been unconscious for six days after a brutal and nearly fatal attack. We had a difficult time getting your wounds to stop bleeding," she said. I thought of the silver that had poisoned my veins. "I'd recommend staying another night in the hospital so we can keep an eye on you."

I panicked and looked at Baran for help, and his crooked smile made me laugh. The doctor quickly looked at Baran.

"I think this little lady is about ready to be home," Baran said.

The doctor sighed. "I thought you'd say that, Mr. Killian."

I almost snorted. I'd never heard Baran addressed in such an ordinary, formal way.

"You sure know me, don't you, Mac?" Baran said.

She slapped Baran on the back and they both laughed. Were they friends? Was she a wolf? There was no way to tell . . . she smelled like chemicals.

I raised my eyebrow as I studied the two of them. The doctor turned back to me and smiled. "My family resides back home in England."

I knew what she was telling me. Underneath the white lab coat, stethoscope, and the overwhelming chemical smell, she was one of us. "It is nice to meet you, Mac," I said.

She laughed. "Get out of here before I change my mind."

I smiled and jumped out of the hospital bed, holding Grey's hand, and we darted toward the door with Rhonda, Jamal, and Baran behind us. Freedom never smelled quite so sweet.

As we walked outside, I saw the snow on the ground. Fall had passed, and the cold winter was upon us. We piled into Baran's Land Rover; Jamal hopped up front and Grey, Rhonda, and I sat in the back. The drive home was oddly quiet, and the silence made me feel itchy. "Baran, have you been home since . . ." my voice trailed off. Since he'd been taken, tortured, and nearly died . . . since people had died in his house . . . since everything had changed.

"Once," he said. "It looks the same, but it didn't smell right. You guys weren't there."

That was my fear, that his scent had been fading for so long. It was hard for me to navigate the world without him. Baran had become a part of me. I'd done everything in my power to save him, and here he sat, in the flesh.

"I missed you, Baran," I said.

"Oh, ylva, I missed you. Your beautiful face is a homecoming," Baran said.

"What about my beautiful face?" Grey asked. He almost laughed at his own joke. He tried so hard to hide his own amusement, but his mischievous grin was all over his face. He reminded me so much of the rebellious boy I'd met so long ago.

"Nah, you're a troublemaker." Baran chuckled.

I winked at Grey and smiled like a fool in love. He was still that boy, but he was also a man. My man.

Baran parked in the driveway of his simple home. I didn't know what this moment might feel like, but as I faced my fear, it still felt like home to me. This was where we belonged.

As we walked to the door, I reached out and held Rhonda's hand. I knew she was strong, but I wanted her to know she wasn't alone. The five of us walked into the room where we lost Paul. It looked exactly the same . . . all the damage had been fixed as though nothing had happened here. But Baran was right—it smelled different.

I looked around the living room and it was like I could still see all of them, lying there dead. I knew where both of them had been. I remembered their faces, one stranger and one friend.

Rhonda stared at the floor and no one said anything. I closed my eyes and still held her hand tightly. "Old Mother, please give us the quiet of the earth, the shining of the stars, and an infinite, deep peace as we learn to live once again," I said.

"Infinite peace," Rhonda said.

Grey picked up his guitar from the sofa and began strumming. It was sad but peaceful. It was his way of saying good-bye. We all listened for a while, letting the music wash over us.

"I'm gonna crash," Jamal said and disappeared down the hall.

"Rhonda, did I miss Paul's funeral?" I asked.

Rhonda nodded and tears glistened in her eyes. She opened her mouth like she might say something, but she closed her mouth again and just stared out the window. I hated that I'd slept through their mourning. I wasn't there to protect them, and I wasn't even there to mourn with them.

"Rhonda, do you bury your dead?"

"Yes. Paul is at the cemetery," she said, staring off into the clouds. Finally she looked at me and continued. "Would you like to visit him?"

"I really would," I said.

"I will take you to him," she said.

Rhonda and I went out to my car, and I let her drive. We drove in silence across town to the old cemetery behind the church. I didn't truly know Paul, but I'd heard him laugh, I'd shared food with him . . . he was one of us. I felt his loss but not as deeply as Rhonda. I could see the toll it took on her. She pulled in front of the cemetery, and I stared at the enormous place before us. There were headstones as far as I could see. She parked the car and we walked slowly through the rows of markers, each one with a different name. There were families, children, and couples for generations. There was something immensely sad about the endless number of dead here.

She finally stopped at a patch of dirt. There was no headstone marking Paul's place, no grass growing over the ground where he was buried. It seemed so impersonal and forgotten. I wanted to see his name, to touch his stone and try to feel his energy.

"Why doesn't he have a headstone?" I asked.

"They don't put them in for several months, until the earth settles," she said.

It was as though they had to wait to see if the earth accepted his body. Their way wasn't that different from our way; we burned our dead and gave them back to the wind and Old Mother. What was different was that Bloodsuckers—humans—seemed to only mourn their dead in one place. We celebrated our loved ones in nature, in the wind, in the sun, everywhere. Their way seemed sad to me, but my traditions weren't better than theirs, just different.

We sat down in the grass. I laid my hands in the dirt of his grave, feeling the texture between my fingers. "Paul, I shall think of you all my days. You are one of us. I am sorry I wasn't there to protect you."

"He knew the life," Rhonda said. "I will miss him very much, but he knew what we were born to do, and he knew what he was doing when we pledged our lives to your pack. A warrior's life isn't a safe life."

"But I feel responsible," I said.

She laughed, "Of course you do. You punish yourself for crimes that are not yours. You didn't take Paul's life, my father and his father did. So don't mourn and feel guilty. Love him as you did before."

She was so wise, far beyond her years. I hugged her tightly and prayed to Old Mother. "Old Mother, Paul is one of your children, one of our pack, and my friend. Please take his soul with you," I said.

"And show him a damn good time," Rhonda added.

I laughed. "Amen to that."

# 24
## *Starry Sky*

*Weeks passed, and* it was already past Yule; my days were filled with the gloriousness of adolescence, but my nights were filled with worry. I needed to find the Mother before my eighteenth birthday; I only had four more months, and I was filled with frustration that I hadn't figured it out yet. Who was she? Did she know I was seeking her? Did she know I even existed?

In order for me to be claimed under the Bloodmoon at Carrowmore, I needed the triple goddess: the Crone, the Mother, and the Maiden . . . me. Without the Mother, it wouldn't work. I needed both of them with me or the prophecy wouldn't be fulfilled. All the death and fear and fighting would be for nothing. I scanned Calista's journal yet again, but I didn't find anything new. I had been reading this book every night over and over again, but the words never changed.

Grey walked into my room. "Still at it?" he asked, yawning. I glanced at the clock; it was after midnight.

I stared at the journal, hating everything it stood for. My entire life changed because of one little journal, one silly prophecy. I yearned to still be on the coast of Ireland, still a naïve child leaning into the winds over the cliffs of Dunmanas Bay. I missed the simplicity of my life there, but it was like this damned journal was taunting me.

"Ahhhhh!" I screamed as I shoved it away. "Why am I so stupid?"

"You aren't stupid," Grey said. "Don't say that."

I stared at him with anger, letting my eyes tear into him. What did he know, anyway? Did he think he had the answers I couldn't find? "Whatever," I said. "Thanks for pointing that out."

"Why are you mad at me?" he said. "I love you. I'm here. Let me help you."

I leaned forward into my hands and crumbled under his grace. Through my bitterness and anger, he still loved me. He saw me through my pain. I closed my eyes and let my frustration flow through me so I could see it all and accept it. I was failing myself and my people.

"Baby, show me where it hurts," he said with a smirk.

I smiled through my anger and pointed to my heart. He bent down and kissed my chest. My skin tingled with every breath he took as the air swirled over my skin.

"You will never be alone because my love surrounds you," he said. "We can figure this out together."

I leaned my forehead against his cheek. "Oh, Grey, you are my center, my love." I shook my head. "I'm sorry. I'm just so scared to fail."

"We all fail sometimes."

"Not this time," I said. "I can't fail."

He smiled like he knew I would say that. "You won't. We still have time if we work together."

"All right," I said, grabbing Calista's journal. "Let's see if there is anything I've missed. I've looked through this a hundred times, but never with you."

"Perfect. But first, let's make a late night snack," he said. His smile was all mischief and sex appeal.

"What kind of snack?" I asked suspiciously.

He grabbed my hand, pulling me into his arms and pressing our bodies tightly together. "I think something with rosemary would be nice." He kissed my neck. "It is an aphrodisiac."

I giggled and squirmed in his arms. My body ached for his touch. I leaned in and nuzzled his neck, loving him more deeply with each delicious breath.

I tried to reconnect with my logical brain, but I was so distracted by his touch, his hands roaming over my body, and the naughty ideas in my head. "What are we putting the rosemary on?" I asked.

"Your body," he said. The pure wickedness in his words was enticing.

"I thought you said we were going to make a late night snack?"

"You are my snack," he said, licking and nibbling my ear.

"Grey . . ." I murmured.

"Okay, okay," he said. "Food first . . . dessert later."

I laughed. "That I can't argue with. Now, sir, to the kitchen!"

He pulled me down the spiral stairs and into the kitchen. He gently picked me up by my waist, set me on the counter, and began flipping through a cookbook. I watched his cute mannerisms, and he'd flip the pages and stop to read and then flip again. He finally stopped on a page and tapped the picture, smiling.

"This, my love, this we eat," he said.

I glanced down at the title, "Rosemary Chicken?" I asked.

"An aphrodisiac." He smiled.

"Well then, let's cook."

"Can you get some rosemary from Baran's herb garden?" he asked.

"Sure," I said. I wandered out the patio door to pick some herbs. I walked back in to find him smearing olive oil over the chicken thighs. I handed him the rosemary and asked, "Is everyone asleep?"

He nodded. "The kitchen is all ours tonight."

I liked the sound of that. Our movements around the kitchen were like a choreographed dance as we prepared the chicken and marinade. Even when we didn't speak, we found a perfect rhythm together, matching each other's moves and mood. It was so romantic cooking with Grey. We'd never done it before; it made me feel closer to him, and he was right—just the smell of the rosemary made me want him that much more.

The chicken was golden, and the aroma filled the house. Grey pulled it out of the oven, sliced off a piece, and fed it to me. As the moist meat hit my tongue, it was like a sensual flavor explosion.

"Mmmm," I moaned. I opened my eyes and picked up a slice of the meat, and he opened his mouth eagerly. I placed the chicken on his tongue, and he licked my finger.

He looked me right in the eye—so bold. "That is good," he said.

"Yes, it is."

We devoured the chicken until all that was left were the bones. I licked my lips and fingers. Grey grabbed my hand and licked the salty oil off my thumb.

"To bed with you, my wife."

"Oh, you think so?" I asked, playing with him.

"Only if you want to have your way with me." He smiled wickedly. "Do you want to have your way with me, Ashling?"

"Every damn day of your life." I laughed.

I headed back up to my room and he followed behind. I was almost surprised he didn't race me up there, but I could smell his need . . . I knew he wanted me just as I desired him.

I lay down on my bed and looked up into his green eyes, anticipating his touch, his body over mine, the warmth of his skin.

"Make love to me," I whispered.

"Every damn day of your life," Grey said as he pulled his shirt over his head and straddled me. His bare chest rubbed against my skin, making me moan. He lightly rubbed against me, teasing me, until I couldn't take it any longer.

"I surrender," I said, gasping.

"You do?" he asked, pulling away.

"Nope." I smiled as I flipped him onto his back. "It's my turn."

I covered him in kisses and lost myself to the touch of his skin. For at least a little while, we could just be two silly kids in love.

I collapsed onto his chest, panting for breath as our bodies melded into one sweaty, glistening mass of tangled limbs. I loved breathing him in when his body was warm from exertion. His scent was always so much stronger, like a sensual haze of deliciousness. His hands were tangled in my sweaty hair, and my head rose and fell with his every breath. I could feel him falling asleep, and the slow, steady beat of his heart lulled me to sleep as well.

I woke the next morning to Grey mumbling in his sleep. I couldn't quite make out what he was saying, but the rough sound of his voice was mesmerizing. I lay there watching him sleep and studying his movements and handsome face. His hair was messier than usual, and his muscular chest was so very enticing, but I didn't want to wake him. I lightly ran my fingers over his chest in lazy circles.

I knew as soon as he woke up and rejoined civilization that our stolen moments would be gone. I would have to thrive on the memory of the night before. Only hard work and war awaited me downstairs . . . well, that and bacon, by the smells wafting up the spiral staircase. Bacon was a human food I had learned to love while in York Harbor; as I understood it, everyone loved it. The idea of eating made my stomach growl with anticipation. After all the energy we'd spent the night before, it was a wonder I'd lasted this long. I was starving. I kissed Grey's earlobe and lightly nibbled the fleshy skin. Grey wrapped me in a hug and pulled me on top of him.

"Mmm, baby," he said. "If you keep that up, we won't be getting out of this bed anytime soon."

I giggled.

"I feel like I should thank you for last night," he said as he kissed my forehead. "You're quite good at that."

"So are you," I said.

"So should we tackle the mysteries of Old Mother today?" he asked, yawning.

"After a shower and breakfast, I think."

He nodded, scooping me up in his arms like I weighed nothing more than a feather. "Good idea," he said as he carried me into my bathroom. He set me down and turned on the hot water.

We stepped inside and took turns washing each other in the hot water. I put my face right in the stream of water and let it rush over me. I wanted to start the day without useless worry and only with an open mind and heart. When I opened my eyes, Grey was staring at me.

"What are you thinking?" I said.

"Just how much I love you," he said. "And how grateful I will always be that you came back to me. And how hot your backside looks with the water rushing over it." He winked and swatted me on the bottom.

"Hey!" I smiled.

He chuckled as he washed his hair. I liked the way his muscles flexed as he moved.

His eyes suddenly opened. "Maybe we need to read each other's book instead of our own—you read my love spell book and I'll read your journal at the same time. They were both written by Calista," he said. "I can't believe we've never tried that."

"Oh, heck yes," I said, jumping out of the shower.

"Hey, get back here, there is still soap on your back!" he called.

"No time," I said, wiping it off with a towel. "Hurry up!"

I heard him laughing as I leaped onto my bed wrapped only in a towel. I flipped open his spell book and began reading all the lines, devouring the content. Grey went downstairs and brought up a plate of bacon.

"It's Baran's 'welcome home' bacon," he said. I laughed. He sat next to me with Calista's journal and popped a piece in his mouth.

Hours slipped by and I found nothing of use. The love spell book was beautiful. It even spoke of rosemary bouquets and of our love, but nowhere did it give me any indication of where to find Old Mother.

"Blahhhh," I whined, flopping back on the bed into Grey's arms. I stared up into his handsome face, wishing he could help me. "This is no help at all."

"Neither is this," Grey said, dropping Calista's journal next to the love spell book and the empty plate.

"It was worth a try." I halfheartedly smiled as I stared at the two books that left more questions than answers. Where was the rest of the story? How did this all end?

"We aren't giving up," Grey said.

"We aren't?"

"No way."

I shook my head and lay back down on his chest. I stared at a dark splotch on the edges of the pages of the journal. It looked like a weird ink stain. I looked at the love spell book and saw ink stains on the side of those pages, too.

I closed the journal and studied the stain. One part looked like half of the Tree of Life; the rest just looked smeared. I set it back down and picked up the book of love spells, closing it; upside down, it also looked like the tree of life symbol. I jolted up.

"What if . . ." I said.

I opened both covers and set the pages next to each other, staring at the edges of the page. I didn't see anything. I flipped one book around and did it again and suddenly I saw the Tree of Life staring back at me, half on each book. As I looked down at the stained pages, I realized it was a message in Greek.

I read aloud the words Calista had written so carefully on the edges of the two books. This secret she gave only to Grey and me when we were together. "You will seek the Mother, and her eyes are like starry skies."

"What does that mean?" Grey asked.

"I don't know," I said.

"It's a clue, though—that's more than we had before."

"It's a riddle," I said, sulking. "I hate riddles."

"Well then, why don't we go do something else for a while and clear our minds?" he suggested.

"I think first I shall put on some clothes," I said, looking down at my towel.

"Darn," he said. "If you must."

I dropped my towel and stood before my husband, naked and exposed. He devoured me with his eyes from the tip of my head all the way down my pale skin to my toes. I shivered from his uninhibited appreciation of my body. I felt bold and beautiful and exquisite in my own skin.

"Tease." He winked as I started to get dressed. "I'll meet you downstairs." He walked over to the door, opening it. "Every bit of you is as beautiful as your heart."

I blushed. "I love you."

"I love you, too," he said before disappearing.

I listened to him descend the stairs, leaving me alone to clear my very distracted mind. It was so easy to forget everything when I was with Grey. Our love was so powerful it could move mountains, but we also had a duty to our people and Old Mother, whoever she was.

Somehow I'd find her in the stars.

I pulled on a blue tight-fitting dress and my favorite brown boots and headed downstairs to join the others. As I walked into the kitchen, Baran handed me a sandwich.

"Welcome home," he said. "I'm glad we are all back together. Even you kids," he said, pointing to Rhonda and Jamal. "Never thought I'd have your kind hanging out in my house."

"Never thought I'd be breaking bread with your kind," Jamal said.

"And here we all are, suddenly all realizing we all love food," I said.

"Who knew food could bring people together?" Grey said.

"Everyone," Jamal said.

We all laughed and devoured lunch together. It was the perfect meld of jovial banter and deep discussion. It actually made me miss Mund terribly. He was right where I needed him to be, but it didn't make me miss him or Mother or Nia any less. I found my mind wandering to them all the time.

"Ashling found a clue," Grey said.

"Really?" Baran asked.

"Grey helped. It was a clue to find the Mother," I said. "It was hidden and could only be found by putting the journal and the spell book together."

"What was it?" Baran asked.

"The Tree of Life with the words, 'You will seek the Mother, and her eyes are like starry skies.'"

Baran twirled his mustache. "Hmm. That's all it said?"

"Yeah," I mumbled.

"Starry skies," he repeated.

"Maybe she's already dead?" Jamal asked.

"Or maybe she lives somewhere where she can enjoy the stars. Maybe somewhere up high?" Rhonda said.

Grey shook his head. "It doesn't feel right. We're missing something."

Baran ran his hands through his long silver hair as he hummed.

"What song is that?" I asked.

"Some Celtic tune," he said. "They all linger in my mind after all these centuries, but I never remember which is which. This one just came to mind when I was thinking of stars."

"Baran, do you think Old Mother is real?" I asked.

I felt guilty saying it out loud, but sometimes I truly wondered if she existed at all or if she were even still alive to care about us. Maybe she had died long ago, and we all fought a useless battle.

"Ylva," he said. "Just because you can't see the wind doesn't mean you can't feel its power."

The wind. I missed the wind. I sighed thinking of the feeling of the wind in my face as I leaned into it, letting it suspend me above the jagged rocks of the Irish cliffs. The power of the wind was immeasurable, as was the love of Old Mother. I knew Baran was right. I just found it so hard not to struggle against my faith in times of darkness.

"I know," I said. "I'm just frustrated. Months are floating by and here I sit, no closer to the Mother than I was before."

"Starry skies," Grey said. "Her eyes are like starry skies." He paced back and forth, repeating it over and over again. He moved in such a way that it was almost hypnotic. Suddenly he stopped and smiled so big that his eyes twinkled. "We looked into her eyes, blind with cataracts, and it looked as though there was a starry galaxy in them."

"Grey, you're a genius," I said, kissing him right on the lips.

# 25

## *The Mother*

*I felt excited.* I felt like all my worry was for nothing because finally the truth had revealed itself to me. I ran out the door with Grey and Baran right behind me. I looked back at them both smiling like children. I almost had to laugh at them as we jumped into my red Ford Mustang.

"Are you boys coming with me?" I teased.

"I go where you go, cutie," Grey said. I smiled.

"I'm not missing out on meeting Old Mother, whoever she is," Baran said. "I've waited my whole life for this moment."

"Buckle your seatbelts," I said as I waved to Rhonda and Jamal and backed out of the driveway. "We'll be back tonight!" I shouted out the window.

I sped down the residential street for the highway to the Bar Harbor bookstore. All this time she'd been right there. She was so close I could have touched her and I'd never known it. But what if we were wrong? What if she wasn't the Mother? I had to shake my nerves away. I tightened my grip on the steering wheel and prayed.

*Old Mother, please lead us to you, to your love and salvation. Please reveal yourself to us and let yourself be known to us.*

The drive was excruciating. Every time I'd speed, Baran would clear his throat and I'd slow back down. I tried to concentrate on the road as beautiful snowflakes gently fell from the sky around my car. So many thoughts milled through my mind; most of them had to do with my feeling inferior. Were her children meant to meet her in life? I had questioned my faith so many times, and I had been tested. I felt afraid she would reject me for my failures.

"Can someone talk about something? Anything?" Grey asked.

I heard Baran laugh from the backseat. It was disturbingly quiet in the car, and we still had a way to go.

"Baran," I said. "I found your book."

He was silent.

"I cried on it," I said. "I saw what you wrote."

He squeezed my shoulder. "I'm sorry I wasn't there for you," he said. "I left that note in case I died when we went into the Bloodrealms. I made my peace with death long ago, and dying to save you was something I was fully willing to do."

"What did it mean?" I asked.

He cleared his throat. I kind of wished I'd asked him this when Grey wasn't in the car, but Grey was my partner; I'd never have kept the secret from him anyway. And Baran was Grey's family, so I was certain he'd tell Grey if he asked. Still, I wasn't sure I was ready for the answer. I looked into my rearview mirror and saw tears flowing down Baran's cheeks.

"Baran? What's wrong?"

"Ashling, you're the daughter I have always wanted. From the moment I saw your stubborn little face, I knew I loved you. I was hired to protect you, but you're family now, and it broke my heart to think I might have to leave you behind," he said.

"I love you, too, Baran," I said with a smile. It felt wonderful to be accepted and loved and supported. He didn't have to, he chose to. There was something so powerful about choice.

"If you play their games, by their rules, you will certainly fail. None of them play fair," he said. "Your will and rebellion are the reason you'll live."

"Why can't Grey claim me?" I asked. "You said not to let them claim me."

I held my breath, waiting for his answer. I prayed for Old Mother to help me; I wasn't ready for this.

"You choose, Ashling. Only you. Not me, not your father, not even Grey. You choose. Don't let them claim you," he said.

"So I can pick Grey?" I asked.

"If you want him and he wants you, no one can stop you."

I closed my eyes for a second and felt so thankful. "I thought you meant Grey couldn't claim me," I said.

"He can't," Baran replied. "Not without your permission. That's what I was trying to tell you. Vigdis and Verci can't claim you unless you agree. No one can."

"So that's it then?" I asked.

"Just a giant piss-off to the rules," he said. "It is your life, ylva—live it."

It finally all made sense. He wasn't trying to keep me away from Grey. He was showing me what freedom looked like.

"I thought I was going to have to kick my own uncle's ass," Grey said.

"Go ahead and try," Baran said. "You might be a dire wolf, but you're still a pup. Even crippled I could still take you out."

They both laughed, but soon silence settled over us again as we entered Bar Harbor. I practically vibrated with anxiety as I pulled in front of the small bookstore. We were either right and about to meet our creator, or about to be very embarrassed and back to square one. I swallowed hard, trying to prepare myself.

"Are you ready?" I whispered.

"No," Baran said. "But I'll never be ready. For all my days, I could sit and wait and never feel ready for this moment."

"This moment is ours," I said as I boldly got out of the car. I heard the car doors shut and them following me only a few steps behind as I opened the bookstore door with the Tree of Life carved into it.

I smelled her as soon as we entered. Her scent was so familiar. She actually smelled like the wind. Did the wind even have a scent? Maybe I was just hoping too hard that we were right. I walked slowly to the counter and saw her, hunched back, blind white eyes with starry constellations in them. She was so simple and yet so happy.

"You're back, Ashling of Boru and Grey of Killian, but you bring a friend with you," she said, reaching out her hand.

Baran put his hand in hers; she rubbed his wrist. "Ahh, Baran of Killian. I should have known, but your scent is marked yet by the Bloodrealms." She smiled and let go of his hand and gave it a soft motherly pat. "What do you seek today, my Crimson Queen?"

"You," I said.

"I am at your service."

"May I see your Bloodmark?" I asked.

It felt intrusive and bold to ask to see her mark. What right did I have to ask such things of the Mother, or anyone for that matter? A Bloodmark was personal. It was your family lineage, your partner. It told your life in symbols. She held out her wrists—she held no mark. I held my breath as she turned and lifted her white hair, revealing her neck. There, faded and blurred, was the Tree of Life. The symbol of Old Mother Earth.

"Is it you?" I said. "All this time . . . was it you?"

She took my hands and held them. Her hands were soft and warm, like a blanket. She had the touch and comfort that only a mother could.

"Whom do you seek?" she asked.

I bit my lip. I couldn't say the words. I was too scared, too overwhelmed. I wanted to rush out the door and never look back. Grey and Baran each put a hand on my shoulder, and I felt their energy flow into me. It was strong and violent and so very masculine, but I fed on their strength. Tears came to my eyes but didn't pour out. I needed her to say it. I needed to hear the words.

"Caoimhe, are you Old Mother?" I asked. My voice was strained and weak.

A huge smile spread across her face. "Ah! You have found what you seek," she said.

"Why are you here? In a bookstore?" I asked. I was in shock. I had so many questions. "Why aren't you somewhere amazing and beautiful? Why don't you live in the stars? How long have you even lived here?"

"I have been all places and am all things," she said. "I like it best among my children as one of them, helping them carry their struggles. My energy is everywhere, but I've only been here at this bookstore in physical form for a little over a year."

"Where were you before this?" Grey asked.

"I spent sixteen years in Dunmanas Bay, Ireland, nine months in Cashel, Ireland, and before that I spent most of my time traveling around, keeping an eye on all my children," she said.

Her words hit me like a garbage truck. I felt like I couldn't breathe, much less speak. She had been all the places I'd lived. She had walked with me on my entire journey. She'd been there all along, I just hadn't seen her.

"Have you been following me?" I asked.

"I created the most precious gift to all living creatures. I created love. Something as powerful as love needs to be protected."

"Me?" I said.

"Of course," she said. "You are the embodiment of love, and you alone have the power to spread it over the earth. I knew when I created you that many dark souls would try to take you from us. That's why

I've followed you around since you were still thriving in your mother's womb. It is my duty to love and protect my children, and you are one of them."

"All this time you were here. I visited you. Why did you never reveal yourself to me?" I asked. I felt hurt by her secrecy. She knew I was looking for the Triple Goddess—why wouldn't she just tell me who she was?

She stared right at me with her cataractous eyes like starry storms and said, "It is not for a god to reveal herself, to intrude on life; it is up to her people to invite her into their lives."

"Will you stand with me at Carrowmore under the Bloodmoon when I am to be claimed?" I unconsciously looked to Grey when I said it. I knew he would claim me on my eighteenth birthday. He was my husband, my love, my best friend. I looked back into Caoimhe's cloudy eyes and waited for her answer. Normally, I'd have prayed to Old Mother for what I needed, but this conversation in itself was a prayer—I was talking to a god.

"Oh, my sweet child, I have been with you from your first step, and I will be by your side for all your days," she said. "And I will be by your side at Carrowmore."

"Thank you," I gasped as I pulled her into a hug. I wasn't sure I was allowed to touch Old Mother, our creator, but I was so grateful I couldn't stop myself.

I had waited so long to find her. I prayed to her so often I had felt like I knew her, and yet here she stood before me in the flesh, a sweet grandmotherly woman who was hugging me back. Her love flowed into me so fast and full that I felt faint, but I clung to her and let her heal me. Still, I had so many unanswered questions.

"Why haven't you stopped the Dvergar? They have destroyed humans and wolves and your earth. Why have you not done something?" I asked.

"It isn't that simple," she said sadly. "The Dvergar abandoned me; I couldn't lead them to the right path even when they saw it."

"Why didn't you just kill them?" Grey asked the question I was sure all of our people wanted to know.

"Their disease was fast spreading, and it caused all my children to hide in fear. I work through you, I am part of you, but fear separates you from me. I needed hope to restore the balance and love to stop evil," she said. "I needed you, Ashling. I needed a leader who could bring my people back to me, to a world where love was the rule. You are the only one who can give hope back to our people, and you do it in my name."

We were quiet for a while, but it wasn't awkward or uncomfortable. It was calming, like meditation or a light sleep. It almost felt like she gave off a soothing vibrational energy.

"How is my mom?" Grey asked.

My breath caught. I knew Grey mourned his mother still. I'd felt it in him so many times.

"She follows you," Old Mother said. "And sometimes I know you think you see her. When this happens, I shall tell you, it is truly her." Grey's green eyes glistened as he listened to Old Mother speak. I reached over and held his hand.

"Thank you," he whispered.

"And for you, Baran of Killian, your father is a bit more pushy," she said with a laugh. "He wants you to take back the Killian lands. And I have to say, I agree; it is high time the Killians were guarding the Scottish once again. You are, in fact, my favorite heathens."

Baran let out a deep belly laugh. "I will see it done," he said.

"Will you travel to the Rock until my eighteenth birthday?" I asked.

She nodded and started milling about collecting books, both old and new, into her bag. "Can't leave home without a good book," she said with a wink.

# 26
## *Racing*

"*It has been* a long time since I saw the Crone," Old Mother said. "Centuries pass in the blink of an eye. We have been together so long, sometimes I barely remember the beginning."

"Has she . . . always been that old?" Grey asked.

I bit my lip, trying not to laugh.

Old Mother smiled. "Well, she is a crone."

I didn't know if that was a yes or a no, but I liked her wit. It was surreal watching her, knowing who she truly was. I'd prayed to her my entire life, and now I knew my prayers had been heard. She may not have granted all the silly things I wished for, but she kept me safe.

"Okay then," she said as she bent to pick up her bag. "I'm ready."

"I'll get that," Baran said, taking the bag.

We walked out the door and back onto the street. As Old Mother closed the door behind us, the Tree of Life carving disappeared. I blinked over and over, but it was truly gone. I reached out and touched the door where the symbol had been and it just felt like a smooth wooden door.

"How did . . ." I said. Old Mother smiled. "Never mind." If Old Mother could create everything that is, was, and would be, should it be a surprise that she could make a simple woodcarving disappear?

"You'll know how to find me now next time, won't you, dear?" she said. "Just look for the Tree of Life. Do you think it would be okay if I drive?"

My mouth fell open and I just stared into her blind eyes. She chuckled as she climbed in the backseat of my car, and I had to laugh with her. There was something so quirky about her. She had a dry sense of humor that I quite appreciated.

"Hurry along, then," she said. "No time to waste. I smell them on the wind."

"Who?" Baran asked as he smelled the air.

"Verci and some of his beasts," she said. "I'd speed a bit if I were you."

"If you insist," I said as I turned the ignition and sped away from the bookstore, back home to York Harbor. "Call Rhonda; let her know we might have unexpected guests," I said to Grey.

"Why don't we just go straight to the airport?" Grey asked.

"I could drop you and Baran off to escort Old Mother to the Rock," I said.

"I go where you go, Ashling. That's a thing," he said firmly.

"We can't leave you with just Rhonda and Jamal for protection, Ashling," Baran said.

"And I can't send Old Mother to the Rock without protection," I said.

"Call Rhonda; have them meet us at the airport," Baran said. "We all go."

"I don't think we can leave these people unprotected," I said.

Grey nodded. "I agree with Ashling."

I grabbed the phone and dialed.

"Hello?" Rhonda said.

"Rhonda, you and Jamal have a choice: Do you want to come to the Rock with us, or do you want to stay in Maine with the people?"

"I think our duty has always been to these people, so we shall stay if you feel you are safe," she said.

I looked at Baran, Grey, and Old Mother. "Safe as I will ever be," I said.

"Then we have our orders," she said.

"Verci and some of the Garm wolves were in Bar Harbor. Do you want us to stay until they pass?" I asked.

"The best course of action will be to get you and the Mother safely to the Rock as soon as possible. We will stand guard and protect the people," she said.

She suddenly sounded so mature and soldierly. I believed every word she said. That girl could lead me into war and I would follow her.

"Thank you, Rhonda."

"Don't you die on me," she said.

I knew that was her way of showing she cared for me. She never was very fluffy with her compliments. "I won't. You either."

She hung up. The silence was so final. I handed the phone back to Grey and turned the car toward the New York airport. Grey called the airport to secure flights, and Baran called Mund to tell them our plans. I wasn't really listening to any of it. I was concentrating on the hum from the tires—something wasn't right about it. There was another sound. It was rhythmic but organic.

"Shhh," I said, trying to listen harder, concentrating on that one sound. "Someone is following us."

"Garm wolves," Baran said. "I recognize the stench of their rotted flesh."

"Is Verci with them?" Grey asked.

"I don't think so," Baran said. "I can't smell him."

Suddenly, two enormous Garm wolves leaped onto my moving car. I heard the metal crinkle and dent with their weight. The sound of their snarls brought me right back to the Realms, but now Verci had brought his evil into the human world. I loathed those disgusting beasts. They started clawing at the roof, trying to tear their way through the metal. With each earsplitting scratch I shuddered, and they got that much closer to their dinner. "Bastards!" I said as I floored it.

"When they rip off the roof, prepare to fight, Grey," Baran said. "I need you at my back."

Every moment I dared to think it was okay to breathe, I was pushed back down, attacked, bullied, and I was damn tired of it. I wasn't about to lose Grey and Baran after everything we'd been through. I swerved the car left and right, trying to knock the beasts off, but their claws punctured the steel and they clung on.

My heart was in my throat. "Old Mother, I'm sorry we've endangered you."

"I might be old and blind, but I've had to fight for my life a few times," she said. "Besides, I was in just as much danger in that bookstore."

I looked up to see the claws of one of the Garm; one had finally pierced the metal. I, for one, would have preferred to be in the bookstore instead of racing down the road with Garm wolves clawing their way through the roof on my car. It was only a matter of time before we were eaten alive at eighty miles an hour.

I saw something moving swiftly through the dark. It was just a blur, but something was running right at us. "Brace yourselves!" I yelled.

"Rahh!" Rhonda screamed as she came running right at my car and leaped at us, slamming her knife into one of the beasts.

I nearly crashed my car I was so terrified. Suddenly Jamal dropped from a tree overhead, and I heard a sword cut into the other Garm. They snarled and fought against Rhonda and Jamal. In all the fighting, they lost their grip on the car and all four of them tumbled to the road.

"Keep driving," Baran said.

I nodded and sped away. I felt guilty leaving them behind, but after seeing Rhonda leap onto a moving car, I couldn't possibly see her as weak. Besides, there were only two Garm wolves, and they had injured both. "Are they going to live?"

"That girl kills things in her sleep," Baran said.

He was probably right.

We didn't talk the rest of the way to the airport. I think everyone was listening just like I was. I didn't want more surprises. I'd had enough for one lifetime. I wanted some good old-fashioned peace.

"Think there is anything else out here tonight waiting to kill us?" Grey asked as we turned the corner to the airport.

"Many eyes are out tonight," Old Mother said.

"That isn't very reassuring," Grey muttered.

I had to agree with him. I remembered when I first traveled to the Rock with Mother, Mund, and Tegan, and when Mother and I traveled to Wales. Every time I traveled, all manner of creatures seemed to know it. At this point, I should have been used to being tracked, followed, attacked, and watched, but I still hated it all.

I pulled up to valet parking at the airport, and I handed my keys to the attendant. "I will have to report that it was brought in looking like that," he said, staring at all the damage.

"Sure thing, kid," Baran said.

With that, we left my mutilated car behind. Mund was going to die when he saw it, but that was the least of my problems. We walked quickly through the airport to the ominous-looking security gate.

"We don't have a passport for Old Mother," I whispered. "We don't even have ours."

"Got it covered," Baran said. He waved to a skinny man with glasses. The man nodded and ushered us forward to his line. We walked around all the people waiting. "Hi, Mike, good to see you."

"You too, Killian. What do you need?" he said.

"We need to be on the next flight to Ireland," Baran said.

He nodded and shuffled papers as he pushed his glasses back up his nose. "Everything is in order." He handed a stack of papers back to

Baran and gestured for us to walk through.

My heart was pounding as I walked by him. I was waiting for someone, anyone, to know our secret. Did anyone even know their creator walked in their presence? I glanced at Old Mother and shook my head. It was unreal. We each took our turn walking through the metal detector before we were passed on to our gate.

"How did you get us through?" I asked Baran. "Who was he?"

"Head of security at the New York airport, but more important, head of security of the German royal pack," Baran said. "Good to have friends in the right places."

"He looks like a nerd," Grey said.

"Well, that nerd could have taken all our heads off," Baran said. "Never underestimate people—especially wolves."

When we landed hours later in Ireland, there stood Mund, Quinn, Brychan, Kane, and Dilara, and right behind them stood Mother, beaming with happiness. I ran over to her and nearly crushed her in a hug. She smelled like home.

"Mother," I said.

*"M'eudail."*

"I missed you," I said.

She lightly rubbed my back as she held me tight, and she began to hum. I melted into her. There was nothing more comforting and beautiful than my mother's love.

"Welcome home," Mund said.

"We've been waiting," Brychan said. "What took you so long?"

I pulled away and wiped my eyes. "Mother, may I introduce Old Mother Earth, our creator."

There was a collective gasp as they stared at her. She was old, blind, and bent, but could they feel her love and see who she really was inside her worn body?

Mother bowed low to her, and the others followed suit. "Old

Mother," she whispered. "Welcome to the Boru Kingdom . . . we are your servants, now and forever."

"Oh dear, you can stand," Old Mother said. "I'm here to serve you. Now, now, give me a hug."

Mother leaned down and hugged Old Mother Earth. My mother gasped as Old Mother's energy and love flowed into her. It was shocking. To feel a love that pure and beautiful and free was nearly addicting.

Old Mother whispered into her hear, "You don't need forgiveness, child; you're loved."

I didn't know what they were talking about, but Old Mother must have felt my mother's pain or heard her thoughts because she seemed to know what my mother needed to hear.

Mother nodded and wiped the wetness from her cheeks. "Let's get us all back to the Rock safe and sound."

My pack made a formation around Mother, Old Mother, and me as we walked through the airport. People turned and looked at us as we passed. There was nothing inconspicuous about us. The three of us were literally surrounded by warriors, and good-looking ones at that. Humans always noticed when wolves moved in packs, even when we walked on two feet.

We exited the airport into the crisp air, piled into three Humvees, and took off for Cashel. The airport security split us up so Mother, Old Mother, and I all rode in separate vehicles. I rode with Baran and Grey. We passed the familiar limestone and sheep and endless green, and it all looked so beautiful, but the closer we got to the Rock the more scared I felt. Something was wrong. Something was coming, like it was racing us to the castle . . . I could feel it.

"You have to drive faster. Someone is following us again," I said.

"I know," Baran said. "I can smell him . . . even the subtlest waft of his scent I would know anywhere."

"Who is it?" Grey asked.

Baran cleared his throat. "Verci."

# 27
## *Watched*

"*I will call* Mund and Brychan," Grey said. "Tell them who's coming to dinner."

The way Grey spoke put a chill in the air. Verci was coming, and he was coming for all of us. Not just me. He had a vengeance in him.

Grey called and warned Mund and Brychan as we sped through the countryside into the city of Cashel. Every time I returned here, the memories flooded me, all of them, the good and the bad . . . mostly the bad.

I could see the Rock looming high above us, and it was the most welcoming sight. I hoped my army had made it there already. It was only January, but I would need Dagny and Hyrrokkin and the steel wolves. I needed an army to protect my people. The Bloodmoon of my eighteenth birthday was only four months away and then the claiming ceremony would begin and all of this would end.

"Baran," I whispered. "Will he ever stop hunting us?"

"Not until we kill him," Baran said.

I nodded. I knew the answer before I even asked the question.

Verci was twisted and broken and evil. Nothing would stop him from what he wanted.

We finally raced through the gates of the Rock and skidded to a stop. Before we were even out of the car, the guard had surrounded us, but there was no sign of Dagny. Old Mother help us if Verci brought the Garm. Without Dagny's army and the steel wolves, I wasn't sure how long the Rock could stand before we'd be taken over.

"Inside. Now!" Flin yelled.

Mother, Old Mother, and I were rushed inside the fortress, down into the bowels of the Rock, and through the stone archway to the informal dining hall. I saw Tegan with Nia on her hip, standing next to the eight-foot hearth and stoking the fire.

"Tegan!" I yelled, rushing over to them.

It had been months since I'd seen them last. I felt like I'd sent them away a lifetime ago. Tegan looked exactly the same with her beautiful long brown hair and startling blue eyes, but Nia had grown. She looked so different from the last time I'd seen her. My little angel; it seemed like every time I turned around she got bigger.

"She's so grown up," I said.

"I know," Tegan said, brushing the wild hair out of Nia's face. "She's growing up too fast, but then again, so did you."

"Oh, I'm the same," I said.

"No, you aren't," Tegan said. "You're not a child anymore."

"What do you mean?"

"I see it in your eyes," she said with a knowing smile. I felt the blood rush to my face.

"Is that you?" Grey asked, staring at the little red wolf in our family's portrait.

Mund laughed and messed up my hair. "Oh yeah. That's our little Ashling."

Grey smirked and his eyes twinkled with delight as he looked from the painting to me. "Oh, don't you start, too," I complained.

"Baby, you're adorable," he said.

"Mmhmm."

"All right, all right. It's a little funny. But you're still cute," he said. I rolled my eyes.

Old Mother sat down next to the fire and warmed herself. "These aching bones," she said. "It is far more fun living with you all, but it is very hard on the body."

"Are you well, Old Mother?" I asked.

The room became eerily quiet. I turned and looked at all their shocked faces as they stared at their creator, a sweet elderly woman sitting on the ground, warming herself by the fire.

"May I introduce you all to Old Mother Earth," I said, bowing to her. "She has come to join the battle."

Everyone stared at her in wonder.

"My lady," Mund bowed. "I have seen you before."

"Yes, my dear Redmund, you have," Old Mother said.

"You sold us the lamb in Dunmanas Bay," he said.

"And such a succulent meat!" she said. "I watch over all of my children."

Tegan, Gwyn, and Cara sat on the floor in front of her just to be near her. Quinn, Flin, and Channing just stared. She loved everyone openly; I could see it on her face.

I turned to Brychan. "I need your phone. I have to call Rhonda."

He nodded and handed his phone to me. I dialed the number for Baran's house and tapped my fingers on my collarbone as I waited for them to pick up. "Oh, please pick up," I said.

"Hello?" Rhonda said.

"Thank goodness!" I said.

"We killed the beasts. The city is safe for now," she said.

"Thank you, Rhonda."

"I will tell you, those foul creatures' blood leaves a stench on my skin," she complained. "Ah well, glad you traveled safely. I'll tell Jamal."

"I miss you already," I said. All I heard was the dial tone. She was always so fast at hanging up. I breathed a sigh of relief that they were well; that meant my human friends were also safe. I was so thankful for them.

"Down to business," Baran interrupted. "Flin, Mund, take me to Pørr. A war is about to rain down on us, and we better be ready for whatever is coming."

"Once you find Father, bring everyone to the throne room," I said. "This is my war."

Minutes later, all of us—Brychan, Dilara, Father, Flin, Felan, Mund, Quinn, Kane, Channing, Shikoba, Willem, Khepri, Baran, Grey, and I—entered the throne room. There was a tension among the group. This was the first time most of us had been together since we fought Vigdis and Verci in the Bloodrealms, and we were all nervous. Yet each one of us was a leader.

Suddenly the doors creaked open, and Old Mother, Mother Rhea, Lady Faye, the Crone, and my mother all walked into the room, a counsel of women. I was in awe watching them. Mother nodded to me, and I smiled as I took the floor, knowing I had her full support.

"Father, is the castle secure?" I asked.

"Locked tight and ready for war," he said.

"Why are Dagny and my army not here to protect my people?" I asked.

"We have heard no word from them in over a week," Flin said. "We sent scouts yesterday."

"When were they due to arrive?" Baran said.

Flin glared at Baran. He was still ruffled from the last time they'd seen each other. Baran had basically told Flin to shove it, so I'm sure my eldest brother was still feeling a bit put out about it.

"Well?" I asked.

Flin's nostrils flared. "Yesterday morning."

"Send for the steel wolves. We will need their strength by our side,"

I said. "I doubt Verci comes to our doorstep with only a handful of the Garm."

Kane nodded.

"As soon as the scouts return, I want everyone who is in this room right now to come back here for the report. Do I make myself clear?" I said.

Flin glared at me this time, but I didn't care. It was time he started respecting everyone in my pack. I would not tolerate disease growing inside my people. If we were going to survive, we would have to do it together.

"Verci chased us into the city," Grey said. "We need to be prepared to fight."

I loved the authority in his voice. He was right there by my side fighting with me, and I loved it.

"What makes you think you're in charge?" Flin leaped into a wolf and landed only a few feet in front of Grey and me. Flin bared his teeth and snarled at Grey, challenging him.

Grey shifted into a wolf and Flin attacked, knocking Grey to the ground. Grey was twice Flin's size, but Flin caught him off guard. Grey wrestled Flin and landed on his back, biting Flin's neck.

"Stop this right now!" I yelled.

Mother Rhea walked over and snapped her fingers in front of their snarling faces. "You dare to disgrace Old Mother Earth? Do you not see your creator right there?" she said, pointing to her. Mother Rhea shook her head and removed a cape, revealing several more underneath.

"Why are you wearing so many cloaks?" I asked.

"Because otherwise everyone would be naked all the time," she said as she handed Grey a cloak to clothe himself. I laughed heartily. She had a point. "Too much wolf fighting means too much nudity."

Grey shifted back to a human and wrapped himself in the cloak like a toga. Even though it was a little silly, I couldn't deny it was a good look on him. Mother Rhea held out a cape to Flin, who reluctantly shifted back as well.

"Stop acting like barbarians," I said to both of them. I was deeply annoyed. Facing Flin, I said, "Grey is right; Verci is the threat we need to prepare for. We don't need to be fighting our own."

Father walked over and pushed Flin back into the group. "Mund, ready the guard. Kane, summon the steel wolves, by order of the Crimson Queen. Felan, you're in charge of the scouts. Does anyone else want something to do?" Father asked. No one spoke. "Good. Then be gone."

Everyone filed out except for Baran, Grey, Father, and I. "Thank you, Father," I said.

"You will have to learn to rule them, even Flin," he said. "Killian, let's talk strategies to protect the castle." He stood and looked at me. "We'll report back." He smiled and nodded. Father and Baran walked off.

I couldn't help but feel happy, despite everything. "I think my father and I have a promising future," I said.

Grey nodded with understanding. Like Grey, I had also never seen eye to eye with my father. Even though Grey's father was dead, and he could have easily killed Grey and me for loving each other, I knew Grey wished he could have had the chance at a real relationship with him. Part of Grey surely wondered: if his father had lived long enough, would he have seen reason like Rhonda, Jamal, and Paul had?

"I need some fresh air," Grey said. "Walk with me?"

I nodded. Grey wrapped his fingers with mine as we walked.

We climbed up to the tower that overlooked the city. At the top, I looked out across our land all around the edges of the castle. Had Verci reached the city yet? I felt like he was lurking in every shadow, but it was likely just my imagination torturing me.

Grey leaned against the wall, staring out over the city. "We made it this far," he said.

"Pretty amazing, really," I said.

"Nah," he said, grabbing my waist and pulling me back into him. "I knew we would. Just figured I'd have a few more scars by now . . .

physical ones, I mean."

"Grey, that's not funny."

He laughed anyway.

"He's out there, you know," I said.

"Yep. He's right there. Standing on that hill, watching us," Grey said, pointing. "I could recognize that ugly bastard any day."

I looked out to where Grey pointed. It felt like Verci was right in front of me and not across the entire city, but there he was. Seeing him watching us made me want to vomit. His bald head and bare chest shined in the light.

"What do you think he's up to?" I asked.

"Got me," Grey said. "But when he comes looking for trouble, he'll find it."

"He was looking for Willem. I heard him when I was escaping the Realms with Dilara. He thinks Willem belongs to him."

"Are you sure it's Willem?" Grey asked.

"I don't know," I said. "That's what we have to figure out. It could be you?"

"Maybe it's you, Ashling," Grey said. "Maybe you should let me protect you for a change."

"You said your vows to me, Grey Killian. We protect each other," I said firmly.

He nuzzled my neck. "I know . . . you've got my back," he said.

"Never doubt," I said.

"Let's go get some rest," Grey said.

Grey and I walked back to my room, and I shut the door behind us. Closing him in my room, I stared at him like a starving animal. I desperately wanted his touch.

"You're going to get in trouble for having a boy in your bedroom," he teased.

"My life. My rules," I said, pulling him into my bed. "My husband."

# 28
## *Army*

*I woke in* the middle of the night to banging at my door. "Ashling!" Felan yelled. "The scouts are here!"

I leaped out of bed in my short silk nightgown and pulled on a white robe as I ran out the door with Grey a step behind. I glanced back at him and he was wearing a matching robe. Nothing said guilty like showing up together in nothing but robes . . . not that I cared anymore.

We burst into the throne room as everyone else was pouring in. One scout stood before me. His soaked clothes were nearly torn off, and he was covered in blood that I was sure didn't all belong to him. He was shivering from the cold, but he stood tall before us.

"Report," Flin said.

I walked between Flin and the scout, took off my robe, and wrapped it around his shoulders. "Build a fire," I said. He stared at me. I'd never seen him before, and I could only imagine that my wild hair was quite the sight. Not to mention I was now only wearing my tiny nightgown. But I couldn't let the poor man freeze after all he'd been through.

Felan went to the fireplace and stoked the embers as he tossed a few more logs in the dying fire. Soon the room filled with radiant warmth.

"Please," I said to the scout.

He nodded. "Dagny's army will be here by sunrise," he said.

"Weren't there two of you?" I asked.

"Yes, my queen," he said. "We were attacked by Verci on the hill. We didn't know he was there, and he caught us by surprise. He killed Jack."

I felt blind with fury. Verci and Vigdis had to die, and they were going to die at my hands. I was filled with rage. My hands shook as I tried to stop myself from shifting.

"He will be punished for his crimes," I said.

He had to be, or there was no justice in the world. Verci needed to be exterminated from the earth. He was the bringer of the plagues, a disease on the earth, a murderer.

"Was Vigdis with Verci's army?" Grey asked.

"No, sir," he replied. "We saw no sign of her."

Why had Verci and Vigdis separated? What horror had they planned for us now? I half-expected someone to burst into the room saying her army came to attack us from the north, cutting us off completely.

"Do you have any other news?" Baran asked.

"No, sir," the scout said.

"Then go find food and rest," Mother said.

Everyone turned to leave. "We have another matter to deal with," I said. They all turned back to me. A look of confusion was on all their tired faces. "When I was trapped in the Bloodrealms with Dilara, we overheard Verci speaking about a son he wanted to claim, someone Verci considers his property. Two men are possibilities. Brenna's eldest son, Willem," I said, looking at Willem. Khepri gasped and grabbed his arm. "And Brenna's youngest son, Grey," I said.

Whispers filled the room. I could smell the fear and tension in the room. I could plainly see it on their faces. None of them were good at hiding their fear when they were under such stress.

"Why would he want either of them?" Channing asked.

"Because I am his son," Willem said.

The entire room went silent. I thought it was common knowledge, but from all their reactions, Willem's paternal parentage was one of the best-kept secrets in the kingdom. Willem stood tall and didn't bend to the stares.

"More importantly," Baran said as he walked over to Willem, "He is my nephew and a Killian."

No one dared disagree with Baran. Even with a crippled leg, Baran would still tear their faces off before they had a chance to shift. I wasn't really concerned about a fight right now. I was hoping they could get past their fear and help me protect them.

"Is there no way to know if he wants to claim Willem as his son, his heir, and property or if he is after Grey for some reason? Or does he have any other children that I don't know about?" I said.

"Why would he want Grey?" Flin said. "Grey, are you Verci's son, too? Because I was told you're a Bloodsucker."

The malice in Flin's words was clear. He hated Grey, and he didn't bother to hide it. He hated Baran and Willem as well. Something about the Killian pack made Flin a bitter man.

"Flin Boru," Mother said. "You will address all of our guests with the proper etiquette and respect of our house. I will not have a son of mine disgracing our name."

Flin scowled.

"Because my mother, Brenna, was raped by Verci before she was claimed, he has claimed her by the old laws," Grey said. "Therefore, he could argue that I am his kin as well. But I am not, and will never be, a blood relation to Verci Dvergar. I am the son of Robert Donavan and Brenna Killian. I am the brother of Willem Killian and the nephew of

Baran Killian. I am the one to claim Ashling; she stole my heart and willingly gave hers to me. So if you don't have any other ludicrous questions, can we please move on to solutions?"

I liked the way he spoke, the tone of his voice and cadence of his words.

"Solution-minded people are far more useful than people who spurt out random, bigoted allegations," Brychan said, staring right at Flin. "If I am supposed to protect your ass, it would be great if you could stop insulting my friends. I've never been known for being a cool-headed guy, so you don't want to piss me off, Flin."

"Though I adore the sentiment," I said to Brychan, "I'm also not interested in fights among my pack members."

"Should we put a guard by Grey and Willem?" Dilara asked.

"I'm more inclined to think he would want to claim his biological son than Grey," Father said. "Though I do not think either of them needs a guard; both are exceptional fighters and have proven their worth. For now, I say we proceed with caution, but as is. Do you agree, Ashling?"

I nodded.

"Then it is settled," Mother said. "Since we are all up, why don't we make a bit of food and hot tea with honey?"

Mother led the way to the kitchens. It wasn't typical for wolves of their status to be in the kitchens other than on holidays, but they all followed her regardless.

"Would you like some tea?" Grey asked.

"Let's watch the sun come up from the tower," I said.

"You want to keep an eye on Verci don't you?"

"I want to know what he's up to," I said.

"Do the specifics matter? He wants us all dead, except probably Willem," he said.

"Specifics do matter. I don't want a single one of my pack to die, so knowing his next step before he takes it would make it easier to keep them all safe."

"Well then, I will grab the tea and meet you up there."

He bowed, a ridiculously bad bow at that. He had no formal training in etiquette, and it showed. But the mocking way he did it made
it even funnier.

"I'll bring the blankets," I said.

I climbed up to the tower and sat down, buried in wool blankets
as the night mist coated everything in a chill. In the darkness and mist
I couldn't see Verci, but he was downwind, and I could certainly smell
him. Grey sat down next to me and handed me a steaming cup of tea
as he nestled in under the blankets.

"Do you think he will attack soon?" Grey asked.

"I don't know," I said. "I wonder if he isn't just messing with our
heads."

Brychan and Dilara came up and sat next to us. Brychan put his
arm around Dilara's shoulders and I saw her tense a little. I wondered if
it was because I was there. She didn't have a reason to worry, though—
Brychan and I were much better as friends, and I thought Dilara and
Brychan would make each other happy.

"What's the freak up to tonight?" Brychan asked.

"Who knows," Grey said. "But he reeks."

Brychan laughed. "I like you, man."

I rolled my eyes at the very strange way they interacted. In fairness,
women were often strange creatures as well. I still liked children the
best. They were pure, innocent, and honest. I'd always devoted my life
to protecting children and I was sure I always would. I hoped someday
I would know the beauty of having my own children.

"What do you think he's waiting for?" Dilara asked.

"An army," Grey said.

"An army of what?" I said.

"Exactly," Grey said.

Verci's army had arrived. Our scouts counted at least a thousand Garm wolves hidden in the Irish landscape. I became obsessed with watching Verci. For several nights, I would fall asleep watching him, and every morning I'd wake up wrapped in Grey's strong arms in my bed. I was afraid that if I didn't watch him, Verci would attack and I would miss my chance for an advance warning.

We smuggled more and more of our pack into the city. Channing's family was here, as was Brychan's and so many more. Verci didn't seem to notice, but that was what scared me more. He wanted us to think he didn't see our every move, but he did.

A couple of weeks later the sky opened up, and spring finally came with the rain; only two months stood between me and my claiming. Still Verci hadn't attacked. I was in the tower, and I shivered from the dampness in my clothes. The wind made the rain misty, but I could still see him. He stood perched like a gargoyle on the hill, day in and day out. The rain poured down over his bare chest and shaved head, but he still just stood there, watching me.

It was so creepy.

I smelled Mund before I saw him. "Why is he just watching us?" I asked. "Why doesn't he just attack? It has been weeks."

My eyes were bloodshot, and I hadn't showered in days. Verci's constant presence was wearing my sanity thin. I was exhausted.

"Whatever he is waiting for is far worse than your most devastating nightmare," Mund said. "He wants us to see him. He wants to build fear in our hearts."

"Are you afraid?" I asked as he put a wool blanket around my shoulders.

He looked back at Verci for a while before he answered. "That bastard means to kill us all—every man, woman, and child. I'm not scared to die, but I'm scared to fail at protecting my family," Mund said.

"I'm scared, too," I said. "I know it doesn't matter if I want this or if I'm ready, because his evil will force us. I hate that. I hate that I can't control this and stop him."

"Control is a figment of our imaginations," Mund said.

I nodded. "I suppose so."

"He's going to attack us soon. I feel it . . . it's like a shift in vibra-tion," he said.

"We need to move these people," I said, pointing to the humans who had no idea of the war that that was about to rage around them. They went about their days, worrying about silly things and laughing with their friends. Little did they know that their city was about to be taken over and their lives stolen. "We are their protectors. It is our duty."

"We can't bring them all in here," he said. "They would find out about us."

I started laughing at the irony. "Mund, you're so silly. Don't you think they'll find out about this other world when the Garm and what-ever other evil Verci brings starts killing their children?"

He sighed. "You're right, but there is nothing we can do."

"Yes, there is," I said. "We move the people into the castle. We fight for them. It is our divine purpose."

"There aren't supplies for all those people. We can't sustain them," he said.

"And we can't sit back and watch them die," I said.

He nodded and sighed. "Yeah, you're right, but the others aren't going to like it."

"But I will have you to help me convince them," I said. He smiled. He'd always been my ally, and I would need him more than ever now.

"Come on, queen. Let's take a break from watching this asshole," he said.

As we descended the tower, we passed Quinn. "Gather everyone in the throne room," I said. "I have new instructions."

Quinn looked at Mund and me. "Of course," he said as he ran off. I could feel the apprehension in him. He didn't want to hear what we had to say. None of them would. With every day that passed, my pack became more and more scared. Verci was eating away at their sanity one day at a time. It was like emotional terrorism. I felt the weight of it, and I could feel it in my pack as well.

What worried me more were the attacks around the world. I knew the warpath Vigdis raged on, I heard it every night on the news. More wolf attacks. Humans dying everyday as Vigdis exterminated our allies. The strangest part was that she wasn't headed this way. I'd been mapping her route, and it didn't seem she was headed to Ireland anytime soon. She was searching for something else.

I stood in the shadows by the curtains and watched as everyone slowly entered the throne room. The tension had been growing thicker for days. They were milling about nervously and whispering to one another. I saw Old Mother, the Crone, Lady Faye, Mother Rhea, and my mother talking among themselves. They were the calmest of all my guests, as I would expect them to be. There was something about them, a collective of mothers, that was infallibly protective. Grey easily found me in the shadows and hid next to me.

"What's the plan?" he asked.

"I'm about to make everyone angry," I said.

"Oh, well, that sounds right up my alley," he said.

"Will you stand by me?"

"Always, my love," he said.

I walked out of the shadows with Grey by my side. The whispers all stopped as they stared at us.

"We all know Verci has been watching us for weeks. You've all seen him and fear him. Whatever he's waiting for will rain down a hell upon us that we have never faced before. We stand together as a pack of equals. I am your queen, but I am your equal in battle. I will stand with you and fight with you. That day isn't upon us yet. But it is coming."

Murmurs erupted around the room, and the fear that poured out of them nearly dropped me to my knees with nausea. Grey squeezed my hand. I closed my eyes and took a deep breath.

"What are we?" I asked.

"Wolves!" Baran yelled.

I smiled, feeling Baran's energy. "We were born to fight. We were born to be one pack. But most of all, we were born to protect. We protect each other and we protect our humans. We stand before our creator herself, Old Mother, who stands with us in this room as our greatest challenge approaches," I yelled. "The winds have changed and war is coming. It is time we move the humans inside our walls."

Argument and fear erupted. I understood their fear. I asked far too much of everyone, but together it was something we could achieve.

"We must protect them," I said. "It is our duty. It is in our blood," I reminded them. "There are choices in life that we must make. Do we protect the innocent, or do we stand back and watch them die? I, for one, will protect them. So what are you?"

"Wolves," Mund said.

"Goddamn wolves," Brychan said.

"This she-wolf has your back," Dilara said.

"We can't save them. They are already dead to us," Flin yelled. "We don't have the supplies or the wolves to protect them. You aren't queen yet, and you will not lead us all to starvation and demise," he said.

The threat in my brother's words cut deep. There was a rift in my pack, and arguments sprang up all over the room.

"Silence!" Father yelled. Everyone quieted, even Flin. Father walked right up to him and got so close their noses nearly touched. "You dare to question our queen?" he roared.

"Yes, my king. She has not been crowned at Carrowmore. My allegiance is yours, Father," Flin said.

Father nodded and walked toward Grey and me. Baran, Brychan, and Dilara closed the distance and stood behind me. They were ready to protect me no matter what Father said. I swallowed hard and stared into my father's eyes. I couldn't read him; I didn't know what he was about to say. Would he betray me now?

After all the years of his rejection, I would have thought I'd be prepared for it. But I wasn't. I didn't want to feel his bitter betrayal again. I wanted to plead with him to support me, but begging would only make me look weaker to my pack. I stood up straight and held Grey's hand.

"Some of you may see Ashling as the Crimson Queen, and your allegiance is to her. Some of you may see her as a child of seventeen that will be claimed by a great man and then become the Crimson Queen, so until that day, your allegiance is to me, King Pørr Boru of the Rock." His voice echoed in the hall. "As you follow me as your king, you best fall in line. I follow Ashling Boru, the Crimson Queen."

Flin's mouth fell open; he stared at our father, who stood before all of our people, pledging his allegiance to me. I felt invincible, taller than the highest mountain. My father finally, truly believed in me . . . if he could believe in me, I was unstoppable.

"Anyone who questions the Crimson Queen will cower at my feet," he said. He turned to me and bowed. "My queen, what is your plan? We serve you."

I cleared my throat. "We have to move all the innocents into the castle. If we ask them to bring provisions, it may help sustain us longer, but I will not stand by and watch them die while we hide." I shivered thinking of all the dead in Mycenae. "Mund, Brychan, Dilara, and Kane, please form the teams that will go out and collect our people."

"Let's do this," Brychan said. He was always cocky and ready for a fight. It was both helpful to me and somewhat annoying.

"Mother, please begin the preparations for our guests," I said.

"With pleasure," she said.

I gestured to Grete, who had followed Mother, Mother Rhea, the Crone, and Old Mother into the throne room. "Grete, can you join me, please?"

Grete reluctantly handed Fridrik to Gwyn and came over to Grey and me. It was the first time I'd truly spoken to her since I'd returned to the Rock. She looked happier and healthier than when I last saw her. I was certain it had less to do with her diet than it did with being reunited with her baby. The connection of a mother and child was deeper and more important than any other connection in the world.

"I never got to truly thank you for what you did," Grete said. "You saved me, you saved Fridrik, and you brought us both back together. I can never repay you."

Hearing her words was humbling. I second-guessed so many of the choices I'd made, but saving my people was never a choice.

"Grete, you are welcome, but you owe me nothing more than to be a great mother. That is your duty in life. When you carry a babe in your womb and in your heart, they become your reason to live," I said. "But you don't need me to tell you that."

She smiled.

"What do you ask of me?" she said.

"Grete, you're human. We are not," I said. "When these people flood into the castle for protection, they will look to you for reassurance."

"I'm not a leader," she said, taking a subconscious step back.

"You're a mother, and you are one of us," I said. "They are our children."

"But I don't know how."

"Just love them," I said.

"I shall try," she said. She bowed and quickly darted out of the throne room. Everyone else filed out as well to begin their tasks.

Grey and I sat alone in the echoes of the chamber. I walked over to Calista's sarcophagus and put my hand on the carving of her likeness. "I hope you knew what you were doing when you picked me," I said.

"I did," Old Mother said from behind us.

Grey just about jumped out of his skin, but I'd smelled her. My sense of smell was far stronger than anyone else's in the pack. Baran always said it was because I was a ginger. What he truly meant was I was the one with the crimson hair that the prophecy spoke of, but frankly, I liked the way he said it best.

"May I speak with Ashling alone?" Old Mother asked.

I heard Grey bow and leave, but I didn't look up. I was lost in the intricacies of the carving of Calista's face. "Was she truly this beautiful?" I asked.

"Even more so," Old Mother said.

"She died for love," I said.

"And truth," Old Mother said.

"Was it worth it?" I asked.

"Death isn't final," she said. "Calista is united with Ragnall. Their spirits walk together all around us, even here."

I looked around the room expecting to see them, but we were alone. I couldn't see the dead and I could only hear them before they were burned and set free. Did my deceased ancestors surround me?

"Yes, they are all here. The Vanir, the Boru, even the Kahedin, Kingery, Syalla—they have all come," she said.

"Why are they here?"

"They have all come to protect and witness the Crimson Queen in her claiming," she said.

"Old Mother, am I making the right choices?" I asked.

"Are you following your heart and speaking the truth?"

"Yes."

"Then you are exactly where you should be."

"But it is so dark here," I said.

I felt surrounded by darkness, despair, anger, and fear that all the evil in the world was closing in on me. Even in the presence of my creator, I found myself struggling for faith.

"The darkness always comes before salvation."

"I hate that."

She laughed. "But your faith will lead you through the darkness," she said. "Have you chosen who will claim you at the ceremony?"

"Grey."

She nodded. "As you will."

"Do you disagree with my choice?" I asked.

"It is not for me to choose for you."

"I love him," I said.

"I can see that, and I am blind," she said.

# 29
## A Mother's Stand

*"How do you* expect us to convince the humans to come into the castle?" Brychan asked as we walked in the courtyard with Grey and Felan. The spring air smelled fresh. "I mean, I can force them in, but somehow I imagine you want us to do it more gracefully."

I smiled at him. "Brychan Kahedin, don't you hurt a hair on their heads. They are our guests."

"You know I wouldn't," he grumbled. "So what do you want me to say?"

"Don't start with the truth," Grey said.

"Felan, can you make all the weather channels say a storm is coming?" I asked. Felan was a development genius in his spare time and quite the hacker, though I knew he didn't really want anyone else to know of his nerd status.

He looked around nervously but nodded.

"Tell the people that due to the storm, the safest place is in the shelter under the Rock. Ask them to bring food, water, and blankets," I said.

"Not a bad plan," Mund said as he messed up my hair. I stuck out my tongue at him.

I watched from the courtyards as the teams went out to try to get the humans into safety. Mother, Mother Rhea, Old Mother, Lady Faye, and the Crone joined me.

"Mother, are we ready for all these people?" I asked.

"It will be tight. Many of the royals have agreed to bunk together to make more room. Many of the humans will be forced to sleep in the throne room and great hall, but we'll make room." She smiled at me. "I so love caring for people."

Everyone knew that about my mother. She was the most caring soul on earth. She took in all the broken souls and mended them. Mother didn't care about someone's status or wealth; she loved them all just the same.

Quinn ran up to us, gasping for breath. "They're here! They're here!"

"The humans?" Grey asked.

"No. Dagny's army," Quinn said.

Hyrrokkin rode into the courtyard on her Vargr with Dagny running beside her. Though I was certain the Vargr wasn't running at full speed, Dagny kept up despite being in his human form.

"I'm surprised to see you on two legs," Baran said.

Dagny chuckled. "I can't come before all the wisest women in the world naked, now can I?" he said as he bowed. "The world is run by our women."

Flin scoffed. I wanted to walk over and punch him right in the nose, but he wasn't really worth it. He'd either accept his new place in the world as an equal or he would get smacked by one of these women.

Mother gave Flin a dirty look and he quieted. "Welcome to the Rock, Dagny." Mother looked at Hyrrokkin and smiled. "Before you comes a great legend . . . I welcome you, Hyrrokkin, to our home."

Hyrrokkin leaped off her Vargr and stood several feet taller than my mother. "It is I who am honored."

"We saw Verci standing on the north face," Dagny said.

"Why didn't you just kill Verci on your way into the city? You have an entire army at your back. You have a bloody Vargr. And yet he still stands," Flin said.

"Clearly you've never been to war, little boy," Dagny replied. "For one, your pack are outside the gates gathering humans, so attacking now puts them all at great risk; attacking before we join our forces with the forces at the Rock puts us at a great disadvantage. We raced into the city when my scouts spotted an army of Garm wolves bigger than I've ever seen coming from the north. I sent most of my force to the northern edge of the city to protect your pack and the humans as the Garm flock to the walls."

Flin sulked into the background yet again. Darkness loomed over his heart. He seemed to only see the doom and not the hope that our people were building. I worried for him. Had he lost all hope?

"I will send our guard out to surround the castle to cover everyone." I motioned to Tegan, who was talking with Gwyn. "Tegan, send for the archers. Silver-tipped arrows to kill the Garm," I said.

She nodded, trying to hide her frown. Mund was out gathering humans. We were all in danger until the gates to the castle were closed again. With half of our army and pack outside the walls, we were the most vulnerable we'd ever been.

"We've summoned the steel wolves as well," I said.

"Good," Hyrrokkin said. "By the look of the Garm army, we'll need them at our back."

I tried to stop my fear from overtaking me. This would be the greatest test of my leadership. I looked to my father and hoped he had something fierce to say. The vein in his forehead bulged as he paced back and forth. No good would come from idle hands. "I'm going to the tower to watch," I said to him.

"I'll join you. I could use the fresh air," Father said. "Dagny, Hyrrokkin, help yourself to our fare."

Father held out his arm. I tucked mine underneath his and he escorted me up to the tower. It was oddly formal and he was endlessly quiet. As we looked out over the kingdom, he sighed.

"These lands and these people have been mine to protect for centuries. I never thought a day would come that I feared losing our throne," he said.

He was so vulnerable and sincere. I connected to him on a level I had never before. Seeing him without his kingly armor was endearing.

"Father, I won't let you down," I said.

He looked at me for the first time and smiled. I wasn't sure I'd ever seen him smile before. "I know. I won't let you down either."

"I love you, Father," I said. I even surprised myself as the words escaped my lips, but I knew they were true.

He nodded and turned away to leave, but not before I caught a slight mist in his eye. "I love you, too, Ashling," he said. He disappeared back into the stairwell.

These were words I had waited nearly eighteen years to hear, and never in my life could they have meant more to me than in that moment. I truly always loved him, even when I hated him. The acknowledgment of the love we shared was as overwhelming as it was glorious.

"Thank you," I whispered.


Dagny's army was like a wall around my pack and the humans. Home by home, the humans were directed to the castle. Some of them ran in a panic while they clutched bags of food to their chests. Others were sick or old and slowed the procession.

I sat diligently for two hours and agonizingly watched every single person run through the gates. Finally, Dagny's army flooded into the walls as my guard closed the gates behind them. The archers stood guard as they all filed into the underground fortress, finally safe. I let out a breath so deep that I felt like I was breathing for the first time.

Grey, Brychan, Dilara, Mund, Tegan, Quinn, and Gwyn joined me in the tower. Grey wrapped his arms around me.

"The Garm have united with Verci," Mund said. "It is only a matter of time now."

I shuddered as I stared at Verci on the hill. He was still sitting there, the smug bastard that he was. He wanted us to know what he'd brought to kill us all in our sleep. If he'd wanted to hide the Garm from us, he would have. I had no doubt that this was all part of the show.

"Come on," Brychan said as he leaped up onto the roof. "Let's watch something hopeful for once," he called down to us.

I jumped up after him; one by one, the rest followed us onto the flat roof of the tower. We all lay down and looked up at the rising stars. I felt like we were a pile of naughty kids hanging out on the roof and stealing a moment of youth and peace. Dilara lay down next to Brychan and he put his arm around her. I couldn't help but smile. I was so proud of them for allowing their hearts to open after all the pain they had both lived through. They deserved a chance at love once again.

A shooting star whizzed through the sky and I made a wish. *Please let us survive the night*, I thought. I glanced to where Verci was always standing, but I couldn't see him through the night mist and the darkness.

Grey pulled me onto his chest, and I let his heartbeat soothe me. Even when death awaited us, his love still surrounded me in hope. Our love was powerful and indulgent. I started to doze to the sound of his heart and the rise and fall of his chest as he breathed.

Sickening howls pierced the evening. The hair on my body stood on end. I knew what it was, but I crawled to the edge of the roof and looked down in horror.

The Garm rushed over the hill toward the city. Their backs were engulfed in flames as they leaped over and through the houses. I watched as the city burst into flames and a thousand flaming Garm rushed toward the castle.

Brychan jumped to his feet and slid down the steep roof, leaping down to the tower. "Hurry!" he yelled.

We all rushed down the roof after him. I slipped and cut my palm; ignoring the pain, I slid down off the roof. We had to warn the others and organize the warriors to defend the castle. My worst nightmare had finally come true.

"My baby!" Tegan screamed.

Tegan started running toward the opposite staircase. She was headed to the living quarters, and Brychan was headed to the war room. Mund looked sick as Tegan disappeared into the stairwell.

"Stay with Tegan," Mund begged me. "Please."

I nodded and ran after her as fast as I could to catch up, but she was quick. I could hear her on the steps far ahead of me. I hopped onto the metal railing and slid down. I leaped off the bottom of the stairs and tore after Tegan through the chaos into the Boru quarters.

The sound of the Garm howling and snarling echoed through the underground tomb; they were inside. Humans and wolves alike were screaming in terror. Tegan and I rushed into her room to find Grete holding Nia, Fridrik, and Jutta on the bed, rocking back and forth and trying to soothe them as they cried.

Nia saw Tegan and wailed louder as she reached for her mother. Tegan scooped her up and fell to her knees crying, clutching her baby to her chest as she let all her fear pour out of her. The rush of her emotions was overwhelming.

"My sweet baby girl," Tegan murmured into Nia's soft curls.

My heart ached for Tegan and Grete. I knew I couldn't fully understand the depth of their love and fear since I wasn't a mother, but I could see enough to know this was their true nightmare.

Jutta rushed to me and wrapped her arms around my body. She was scared, as was I.

"I'm going to lock you guys in here and find out what the plan is," I said.

"No, please," Tegan said. "You can't leave us. We need you to help protect our children."

Grete's eyes welled up with tears. "I can't protect Fridrik without you," she said.

"Okay . . . you're right, we must stay together," I agreed. If I wasn't able to get back to them, Tegan would be left alone to protect Grete and the children. "Tegan, help me block the door."

I slid the metal bar over the slats. I chewed my lip knowing that it wouldn't stop the Garm for long. She handed Nia to Grete and we started pushing all the furniture in front of the door. We stacked it and covered the door as best we could.

We could hear fighting all around the castle. It sounded as though the Garm were trying to claw their way through the outer stones and through the dirt to devour us. I could hear my pack rushing around and arrows flying, but I had no way to know if we would be able to keep the beasts out.

Fridrik and Nia didn't seem to notice the chaos outside our room. The noise was so constant it almost disappeared; the children started giggling at each other, thankfully oblivious. It was a surreal sound in the middle of war, but nothing is as innocent and lovely as children's laughter.

Screams pierced our peace, and I knew the Garm were close. I wanted to run out of the room and find Grey and Mother. I wanted to bring every last human to safety. I wanted to fight. I looked to Tegan and she bit her lips and shook her head no. She knew what I was thinking, but I didn't have a choice. They needed me.

I closed my eyes and let Grey's emotions flow into me. No fear, only anger. I could feel him rage and fight, but there was no pain. I sighed with relief. I hoped he wasn't alone. I heard a small pack of Garm enter the Boru quarters. I could hear the sound of their nails on the cobblestone floor.

"They're coming," I whispered.

"Maybe they will pass us by," Jutta said.

I sniffed the air; our scents were warm and pungent from stress. There was no way those animals wouldn't track us here. We sat on the bed and held on to each other. Grete cried and Tegan sang to the babes. Jutta just stared at me.

"They are going to kill us, aren't they?" she said.

"They will try," I said. There was no use lying to her. She deserved to know the truth. "But we are going to fight them. We aren't going to lie down and die. We are women, and we are warriors."

Jutta looked at me with her wide eyes. "I am a warrior, but I can't shift yet."

"I know, Jutta, but your job in this is equally important. When the time comes, your job is to hold Nia and take her, Grete, and Fridrik out of the room. Tegan and I will distract and fight whatever Garm wolves come in here while you and Grete run with the babes," I said. "Do you understand?"

She nodded.

I could feel her sadness and fear. I wished I could ease her pain and worry, but I couldn't stop her fear any more than I could stop my own.

We sat quietly as the beasts clawed at our door. The wood was stripped away with my sanity as the creatures tried to get through. They wanted our flesh. I held my friends tighter, wishing I could truly protect them. I heard the wood splinter and crack, and a claw broke through a small spot at the top of the door. Grete let out a scream. She covered her mouth with her hand, trying to muffle her fear. It would only be a matter of time before they ripped the door down and broke through the furniture. There was no way out.

I started pacing back and forth. I only had minutes to save them. The dresser fell to the floor with a clatter, and one of the disgusting, hairless Garm pushed its head and front leg through the hole. It snarled and snapped and stared at us with its beady eyes. Its foaming saliva was splattering all over the room. It tried to pull itself through, but the hole was much too small. Jutta whimpered.

"We are going to die!" Grete said.

"I'm sorry," I said. "I failed you."

I put my forehead on the cold stone wall and rallied my strength. I would fight as long as I could to protect the others. Maybe Grete and Jutta could save the babies. I just had to fight.

I was born to protect. I was born for this moment.

I sighed as I pushed my hand against the stone wall to stand. Suddenly, the stones began moving. I lifted my hand and saw a small, red stone moving with the others. I stared in wonder; the Boru tunnels were real. The bedtime stories Mother told were true; she had said every Boru bedchamber and the throne room had a single red stone, and if I put my hand on the stone, the path to safety would appear. I gasped as the stones revealed a hidden stairwell going deep into the earth.

"How?" Jutta asked. She looked hopeful and in awe.

I stared at the cut on my palm. "My blood," I said. "Only a Boru can open the secret passages. I didn't know they were real."

"Where does it go?" Tegan asked.

"The stories say they all lead into the labyrinth," I said. "Good time to find out," I muttered as the Garm were nearly through the door.

I grabbed the oil lamp from the table and chucked it at the stack of furniture as the Garm tried to claw their way into the room. It ignited in flames immediately, burning the Garm wolves at the door.

"What are you doing?" Grete asked, panicked.

"Burning the bastards," I said. They howled as the flame burned their rotting flesh, but it didn't stop them. "Now run!"

Tegan grabbed Nia and ran down the stairs with Grete, Fridrik, and Jutta following closely behind. I stepped down and scraped my hand on the stones, reopening my wound, and the stones began to close.

A burning Garm tore across the room, snapping and snarling at me; the stones closed just in time as his jaws opened to rip into my face.

"Praise Old Mother," I said. Suddenly, I worried about Old Mother, the Crone, and my mother. They were somewhere in the castle. I prayed they were all safe. I wished I had some way to know they were okay, but I'd have to lay down and fall asleep, and that was far too dangerous for the people I was with.

I rushed after Tegan, Jutta, and Grete down the dark, winding stairs. "I'm scared," Jutta whispered as she grabbed my hand.

"You led me through the dark in the Realms; this time it's my turn to protect you," I said.

We rushed down the stairs through the pitch black. I knew it would lead us to the labyrinth; I could smell it. These were the very tunnels Baran and I had escaped from when I was sixteen, but I didn't know where in the labyrinth this tunnel would take us. Nor did I know if we should head back into the castle or run out the tunnels and hope Verci didn't know where they let out. Both options might get us killed, but so would sitting still. We didn't really have a choice. I forced my feet forward into the unknown.

We rushed into the labyrinth and I thought of Baran. He led me through here with ease nearly two years ago on his motorcycle, and he was a Killian. Father must have opened the tunnels for our escape. "This way," I said, deciding to lead us out of the tunnels the way Baran and I had once traveled together. We walked on for an hour, but the way the labyrinth was built and lit, it seemed as though you weren't moving at all. The stones were perfectly placed so it repeated over and over again. It was a trick of the mind, but I knew the secrets of the Boru.

"We aren't getting anywhere," Tegan said. "It's a loop."

"I know the way," I reassured her. "It is meant to confuse you into giving up."

"The Boru are trickier than I ever knew," she said.

I laughed. "The Boru are brilliant," I said.

"Yes, they are," Tegan agreed. "Do you think they are safe?"

We could still hear the echoing of the battle that raged above us, and dust sprinkled down over us as they fought. The war wasn't over.

"Mund, Brychan, Dilara, Father, Kane—they are all up there fighting together, with the strength of the Boru and Dagny's army," I said. "They fight for all of us."

Something crashed directly above us. The ground shook under our feet and knocked us to the floor. It felt like an earthquake. Grete fell with a grunt, and I could see from the angle of her leg that she'd likely sprained her ankle, but she never let Fridrik from the safety of her arms. Dust and debris fell from the ceiling on our heads and made it impossible to see in the tunnel. I shuddered. Again and again we heard something crash above us, and the aftershock vibrated my bones. Were they bombing us?

I put my body over Jutta's head to protect her from the falling stones. Tegan and Grete did the same for their children. A stone slammed into my back, and I groaned with pain. I felt my skin tear open and warm blood seep down my side. It was just a flesh wound, but it bled like a stuck pig.

In all the chaos I could feel everyone in my pack—pain, fear, and anger—but I couldn't tell who was feeling what, where anyone was, or if they were safe. I couldn't feel Grey. I told myself he was in the mix somewhere, but it made me so nervous that I couldn't single out his feelings. I prayed Old Mother could keep him safe . . . keep them all safe.

Suddenly the ceiling gave and the stones began showering down around us.

"Quickly, to the walls!" I screamed. We ran to the edges of the tunnel, where the gentle curve of the wall gave us slight protection, though not enough. The boulders fell all around, slamming into the stone. I smelled their fear and it fueled mine. Whatever was up there, Verci had summoned it from hell itself.

I knew Verci would stop at nothing to kill us all. I could smell it on him for weeks; he just stood there watching us, and every day that passed the sour smell to his blood deepened.

I looked up into the dust that filled the air, trying to see what evil pursued us. Through the jagged rock a Cerberus pushed its enormous three heads down into the tunnels. The creature was at least five times the size of Hyrrokkin's Vargr. It snapped and snarled at us, and all three of the beast's heads tried to snag us like little morsels of food. Its necks were so long it could nearly reach us twenty feet below. Two of the heads started fighting each other while the other snapped again at Grete. She screamed, crawled out of the grasp of the creatures' stained teeth, and started hobbling down the tunnel with Fridrik in her arms. I shoved Jutta toward Tegan and ran after them.

The animal was too large to get through the hole for a few minutes. Hopefully it would be enough time to get away. I heard something fall to the ground behind us. It sounded much smaller than the Cerberus. I glanced back to see what beast pursued us: Verci stood under the Cerberus and smiled at me as the creature tore its way through the rock.

"Do you like my pet, your highness?" Verci sneered at me. "I brought him just for you. Oh, don't run. I have waited to bleed you out for years. I will bathe in your blood at Carrowmore and claim your power for my own!"

I shivered as I ran after the others, catching Jutta as she tripped and pushing her back to her feet. We didn't have time for mistakes. Verci himself was right behind us. He opened his mouth and filled the tunnel with black moths. They flew after us like a thick, foggy plague. I could barely make out Verci's bald head through the cloud of moths.

"What is he?" Tegan asked.

"A demon," I said. "If we can't outrun him, we send the babes on with Grete and Jutta and we fight. Can you do it?"

Tegan's tears came in the blink of the eye, and she clutched Nia to her chest as she ran. I could feel the energy rolling off her. She was saying good-bye. My heart broke for her. I didn't want to separate them, but if Nia and Fridrik were to have a chance, I needed her by my side.

"I can fight," Jutta said as we ran. Her will was far greater than that of most men.

"Your time may come yet, sweet Jutta," I said. "If Verci gets past us, you will be the last line of defense for Grete and the babes. So then, Jutta, you fight with all your heart."

She nodded as we ran.

"Take Nia," I said.

Tegan bawled so hard that she nearly fell to the ground as Jutta took Nia from Tegan's arms. I wanted to vomit. I had witnessed the unholy desecration of a child being forced from his mother once before when Fridrik was ripped from Grete's arms in the selection chamber. My own mother flashed through my mind; whenever I was forced from her side, haunting sadness would fill her as I'd leave. It was unbearable. And now I'd asked the worst thing I could of Tegan. I'd asked Tegan to let Nia go so that Nia might live.

"Keep running, and no matter what you hear, you never look back," I said to Jutta and Grete. They turned and ran as fast as they could.

Tegan wiped the tears from her face and looked up at me. "Let's kill him," she said.

# 30

## *Vercingetorix*

*"I've spent my* entire life running. It's time to fight," I said, closing my eyes. I panted for breath, trying to calm my nerves; in and out, in and out, over and over again as Verci's odor permeated the tunnel. "It's time to end Verci's reign."

Verci's footsteps echoed off the tunnel walls as he grew nearer and nearer. "He's coming," I whispered.

Tegan let out a breath. Terror filled my heart with every step Verci took. I didn't want to fight him. Verci was more evil than Adomnan or Æsileif. I'd seen what he had done to Baran. He was ruthless.

"I love you, Tegan," I said.

"I love you, too." She smiled for a moment before her face turned back into that of a malicious killer, the face of a mother protecting her young. It was her divine right to protect her baby.

"We protect Nia, Fridrik, and Jutta. We protect life," I said.

Her nostrils flared as she breathed, and the anger that rolled off her fueled my own rage. It was time to end this . . . one way or the other.

Verci walked into view. I wanted to run, but I stood my ground. I knew why we were standing there in front of the most merciless killer of our kind. It was worth my life to die to protect Nia, Fridrik, Jutta, and Grete. If I could save one soul, I would have fulfilled my purpose on earth, but it didn't make staring into the face of this murderer any easier.

"Finally, my lambs have stopped running. I do love a good chase, but I was getting a bit bored," he said. "Lady Tegan, how lovely to see your face."

"Vercingetorix Dvergar, I hoped to never see yours again," she said.

"Ahh, but I have seen you many times," he sneered. "Now come here, my sweet one, and die with grace. I promise to be gentle." He turned and stared right into my soul. I shuddered at the intensity of his eyes. "You, my Crimson Queen, I will take alive, for you must die on the Bloodmoon for me to gain your power. So come and be a good pet until then. If you want, I could keep Tegan alive for you until the ceremony, and she could stand witness to your death as my gift to you."

"I'm not playing your little games, Verci," I said, remembering Baran in Verci's torture chamber.

"I don't play games, child," he said.

"We are not going to just lie down and let you kill us," Tegan said.

"Lady Tegan, if you prefer, I could keep you alive for years, torturing and nurturing you in the Realms. You might like my company." He gave her a terrifying smile.

"Oh, Verci, but we mean to kill you," I said.

He laughed, head thrown back in delirium. It made me hate him that much more. I loathed him, everything about him. Rage flowed through my veins as I tried to see my opponent the way Mund would, but all I saw was a crazy man.

"Do you really think two little flowers such as yourselves could ever hurt me?" He turned his head to the side as he studied us. There was even something creepy about the way his head moved.

I didn't want to hear him speak anymore. I wanted to fight. But the longer he gave his narcissistic monologue, the farther Grete and Jutta could get away from him. I took a deep breath, calming my anger. I had to keep him interested but not so angry he'd attack.

"Verci, what is your plan? Kill Tegan, bleed me out on my birthday, and then what, destroy the entire world?" I said. "I mean really, aren't you just Vigdis's pet?"

The smile on his face transformed into an expression that I was far too familiar with from his nephew—Adomnan had looked just like him. The same quiet rage, furrowed brow, and sick look in his eyes. *I killed Adomnan,* I reminded myself, and I could kill Verci, too. Fear was my enemy as much as Verci was. Fear ruined our ability to be objective and see what was truly happening before us. Tegan looked at me; for the first time there was doubt in her eyes. But I nodded to her, and she steeled her face once again.

"Don't you just do everything Vigdis tells you to?" I asked, poking and prodding at his pride.

"Listen, you little bitch," he said, "no one owns Vercingetorix."

I smiled, batting my eyes. "Sure looks like you're on a leash."

His mouth opened, baring his sharp teeth as he screamed. A black fog of moths rolled out of his mouth. They swirled across the ground and around our legs like little black hands trying to pull us down. I bit back my fear.

"Verci, it is okay to admit you are just a watchdog," I said. "Besides, do you truly believe that Vigdis would let you claim me, dead or alive? Do you really think she'd let you have all my power?"

He paced back and forth, making the fog churn around his every move. He jumped and was suddenly right in front of us. Only five feet separated him from us, and we all knew that wasn't enough room to run.

"No more of your poisonous words," he said. "It is time for you to decide if she lives or dies." He grabbed at Tegan; she shifted into a wolf so fast that I barely saw the blur. She bit into his left hand, ripping off his pinky and ring finger. I heard them crunching and cracking as she chewed the bones.

He screamed and backhanded her into the wall. She whimpered on impact but leaped back up and was back at my side. I could see a small gash on the side of her face, but it was healing before my eyes.

"Didn't your mother ever teach you not to hit girls?" I said. I shifted into a wolf and launched into his stomach, tearing away at muscle and flesh. His blood was sour and bitter on my tongue. I spat his flesh out on the ground, nearly gagging on the rancid taste. I would take him apart bit by bit if I had to. We snarled at him, baring our teeth.

He laughed looking at his bloody wounds. He tore his necklace of eyeballs off and sent them scattering down the tunnel. His body ripped and erupted as he shifted into a large black wolf without even moving. I had never seen someone do that before. The way his flesh ripped and sloughed off made me want to vomit, and he was missing two claws on his front left foot. He growled so fiercely it filled the tunnel with echoes; the sound reverberated from every corner and surrounded us. My hair stood on end as I stared into the evil eyes of a wolf twice our size.

We attacked.

My veins were filled with hate as I bit into his cheek. He turned on me and charged, dragging me as I still clung to his face. He slammed into my side and I fell to the ground. His head felt like a sledgehammer, and I gasped for breath. My ribs felt broken. I could barely see through the moths that continued to swarm around us. They seemed to ignore Verci, as if they knew they were to do his bidding.

I heard the tendons pop as Tegan bit Verci's paw. He turned on her and clawed her face. She howled in despair and fell into the black fog. I couldn't see her, but I could feel her pain and fear. I knew where she fell, and he was pursuing her. I desperately pulled myself back to my feet and jumped on his back, tearing with my teeth at the muscles that bulged there. I had to save Tegan. Nia needed her.

I saw Nia's sweet face in my mind and tore through the muscle as fast as I could. The disgusting sounds filled my ears, but I didn't care. I had to win. I had to save her.

Verci howled and slammed my body into the walls. I whimpered and moaned, but I clamped down harder and held on for dear life. Finally he hit me so hard I cried out and let go of his back. I fell down into the dark fog. I lay there in the darkness as though I'd fallen into a nightmare. I wished for the strength to continue. I had to die fighting or he'd kill me at Carrowmore and destroy the world and everything I loved.

I could hear him licking his wounds and growling. He was about ten feet away. He would finish us soon.

I opened my eyes as Tegan crawled over to me. Her glowing, brilliant blue eyes were filled with terror. Her face was still damaged. I knew what she wanted. She wanted to run. I nodded my head and we both leaped up and started to run away from him as fast as we could.

My claws tore at the stone as we ran for our bloody lives. I heard him begin to run after us. He was huge—it wouldn't take him long to catch us. My heart pounded so loud that my ears rang, but it still didn't drown out the sound of Verci chasing after us.

Verci was so close I could feel his hot breath. The tunnel split ahead and I desperately tried to remember which one was the right path. In all the fighting I'd lost track of where I was.

Suddenly Verci jumped on my back and bit me in the neck. I felt his teeth sink into my flesh, piercing and tearing away at my muscle. He was biting hard enough to drop me to the ground but not enough to kill me. I wasn't sure if I was glad he hadn't killed me or not. Tegan bit into his exposed neck. With a snap of Verci's head, he flung her into the wall. I heard bones crack with the impact. Her body slumped to the ground and she didn't move anymore. I couldn't feel her emotions, but I knew she was alive, for now.

I'd failed her. I'd failed Mund, and to my horrible shame, I'd failed

Nia. I could feel Verci's satisfaction when Tegan didn't get back up. Verci still held me in his jaws and dangled me over the ground like a limp baby kitten in its mother's mouth. He started carrying me back down the tunnel. I squirmed and fought, but it was no use; his jaws were locked. All I could do was stare at Tegan's unmoving body.

I felt lower than I'd ever felt before. Not only had I failed Tegan, I'd also let our greatest enemy capture me. I was disgraced. My only redemption was the fact that Nia, Jutta, Grete, and Fridrik were safe. At least I'd done one thing right before I submitted. I howled, mourning Tegan. I wanted so desperately to go back and see if she was okay. My sad song filled the tunnel and vibrated off the stones. I knew I wouldn't die today, but I was as good as dead. Verci and Vigdis would claim me now.

A hideous snarl came from ahead of us in the tunnel. Was the Cerberus coming to finish off Tegan? Or had the Garm wolves finally broken through the castle and killed everyone on their way to the labyrinth? I braced myself for whatever evil creature came charging toward us.

Suddenly a scent hit me and sent shivers over my body. A giant silver and black wolf leaped onto Verci and tore the flesh from his neck. Baran.

Verci growled and dropped me. I lay on my side and forced my front paws to drag me out of the way of the fight. My neck throbbed, and with every beat of my heart it felt like flames igniting my neck and face.

Baran bit into Verci's head. As Verci pulled away, his entire ear ripped off and dangled in Baran's mouth. Blood ran down Verci's body, coating his fur and the stones. Verci let out a pained howl.

The sourness of Verci's blood burned my nostrils and churned my stomach, but Baran was winning. Every fiber in my body celebrated as I waited for my body to heal enough to move so I could help him win.

Suddenly Verci had Baran's neck in his mouth and I howled. I heard Baran's neck crushing in Verci's jaw. Baran was struggling to breathe. I could feel his panic, and I knew it wasn't for himself—it was for me. I'd saved him once; I would do it again.

I forced myself to limp into the fight. Every excruciating step sent pain through my body and made me dizzy. It was like everything was in slow motion and I couldn't get to Baran fast enough. I wanted to lay down and die, but my will was stronger than my pain.

Verci shook Baran back and forth. Though Baran was larger, Verci's jaws were like iron, and Baran dangled helplessly.

Baran whimpered and I attacked.

I bit into Verci's nose; I felt the cartilage crack and tear off, and my teeth sank into the bone, cracking the bridge of his mouth in two. I kept biting down with all the strength I had left until finally he dropped Baran; even then, I didn't relent. I came after him again. He looked like a skinless beast with one ear. I tore into his neck, trying to rip his throat out. I yanked and I heard something pop, but he bit me in the back and I let go.

Rage filled me, mixing with the pain like napalm. I was just as likely to win as pass out from the adrenaline rush that flowed through me.

I felt the flesh on my shoulder tear. I saw what looked like red ribbons blowing in the breeze. I gagged down stomach acid and mustered all my power to fling him off of me. I lunged at him again, this time catching his throat. I yanked and pulled back up, snapping my head back and forth. He howled and tried to break my jaw loose, but I wasn't going to lose. I would protect Baran.

I heard his blood gurgling out of his air pipe as his throat finally ripped free of his body. Verci fell to the ground in an enormous heap of blood and bones. Blood ran like a river of crimson down my front leg as I hobbled back to Baran's side.

He still lay where Verci had dropped him, but as a human. His eyes were glassy, but I could hear the faint beat of his heart. I shifted back into a human, grabbed pieces of ripped fabric, and pulled a piece over

Baran to cover him and keep him warm.

"Baran, wake up," I said. "It's over now."

Baran looked at me, but he didn't speak, he just smiled. I heard voices coming from the way the girls had run. I looked back to see Mund, Brychan, Dilara, and Mother running toward us. Mund and Dilara stopped at Tegan, but Brychan and Mother ran over to Baran and me.

Mother dropped to her knees and crushed me in her arms; she grabbed Baran's hand. Brychan touched my shoulder—it still bled, and four distinct claw marks were scarred into my flesh. Mother's eyes glistened as she looked into Baran's eyes. Baran reached up and caressed the side of her face, and she began to sob. I put my hand over my mouth and stared at them.

"I love you, Baran Killian," she whispered.

He watched her, but I could see he struggled to breathe. The wounds on his neck were deep, and every time he breathed, blood squirted out. We'd walked through the hells of the Bloodrealms together and escaped—Baran couldn't die here, not like this. I needed him. He was mine.

I looked at my mother. Tears ran down her face, and she began to shake in uncontrollable sobs. She loved him more than I'd ever known. She'd hid it from everyone, most of all herself, but now I could feel her love mixing with her sorrow. She was consumed in the purest, most awful pain, which could only come from centuries of unrequited love. Mother rocked back and forth and said a Celtic prayer to Old Mother.

My eyes burned with my own tears. I laid my hands on Baran's neck to heal him as I had in my dreams, massaging his skin and mumbling my prayers, but more blood seeped out every time I rubbed his damaged flesh. Why couldn't I heal him here, like this? Why wasn't it working? Why would I have the divine power to save him in my dreams and not in the flesh? I felt sick and weak. I pulled my hands away and stared at them as they shook. Baran's precious blood coated my hands. I clenched my hands into fists trying to hide his blood, to hide the truth.

"You're going to be okay, Baran," I said.

He smiled but his face didn't look right. He was dying. I could smell it on him.

"Please, don't leave me. You have to stay," I sobbed.

"I can't, ylva." He breathed heavily. "This is my end. But I'm glad—" he reached up and ran his fingers through my mother's hair, "I got to see you," he said. It was such a gentle, intimate touch.

"I've lost you so many times," Mother cried as she clung to him.

"I will always be in the wind," he said.

"Baran, we can't go on without you," I said. "We need you. Shift, damn it!"

"I will be here always. You'll feel me," he said. Blood seeped from his mouth as he coughed.

"Baran, don't do this," I sobbed.

"I will be right here, sweet Ashling," he said. He wove my hand with my mother's and covered them both with his. "Even in death, I am yours," he said.

Mother sobbed so hard her body shook as she slumped over him. I gasped for air as I cried, gagging on my tears and saliva. Baran's breathing slowed, and his heartbeat grew sparser and less rhythmic. Finally, his heartbeat stopped—the strongest wolf I would ever know was gone.

# 31
## *War for the Rock*

*I looked up* at Brychan with very little energy or will to survive. I blinked back my tears and said, "Report?"

He wiped the tears from his eyes and nodded. "The castle is secure for now. The steel wolves arrived in time to help us eliminate the Garm army before they made it into the castle residence. We lost many in the battle. Quinn is taking a head count, and Old Mother is healing the wounded."

"Were the humans hurt?" I asked.

"Many chose to fight with us," Brychan said.

I knew many had died. I could see the haunted reflection in his eyes. Death surrounded us. I looked at Baran as my mother held him close; his soul was waiting to be set free. Every time I looked at Grey, I'd see a piece of Baran in him.

I looked from Brychan to Mund and back again. "Where's Grey?" Neither of them would look me in the eye. "Where is Grey?" I repeated.

Panic raked through me, stealing whatever strength I had left. I felt hollow. I laid my face on the cold stones and tried to find Grey with my mind. I couldn't smell him, I couldn't hear him, but I could feel him. It was faint, as though he were unconscious, but he breathed.

I looked back to Brychan and grabbed his hand, pulling his face only inches from mine. "Where is he?"

"I don't know," he said, shaking his head. "We were searching for you. When I heard you howl, just the faintest sound in all the chaos, we rushed down here. Kane is still searching for Grey."

My nostrils flared as I breathed slow, uneven breaths.

"Find him," I said. Brychan and Dilara ran off down the hall. When I finally had the strength, I looked to Mund. "Is she okay?" I asked.

"Yeah. Her ribs are still healing; they must have nearly shattered," Mund said. He held Tegan's wolf body in his arms and caressed her fur. "Nia, Jutta, Grete, and Fridrik are with Mother Rhea, Lady Faye, and the Crone," he said.

I heard Mother's breath rush out. Mund carried Tegan over to me and Mother and laid her furry head in Mother's lap. The three of us rested our heads together with Tegan in the center. I prayed she would wake healed and healthy.

Mund touched my shoulder and I flinched. I looked down at the wound; it was healed and the blood had stopped, but the flesh was angry with the new scar that ran down my shoulder.

"I'm sorry," he said.

I nodded.

"No, Ash," he said as he looked into my eyes. There was so much pain in his brown eyes. "I am so sorry about Baran; I feel lost without him too, but I know how much you loved him," he said. "We will find Grey."

"He's alive," I said. "I can feel him breathe."

Mother looked at me with wide eyes, but Mund answered for me. "Grey and Ashling can feel each other's physical bodies," he said.

"That's possible?" Mother asked.

"With her, I stopped questioning," he muttered.

Tegan's eyes finally opened and she looked around the room, disorientated. Mund leaned down and kissed her wolf nose; Tegan responded with a lick. She nudged his hand.

"Nia is safe," Mund said.

Tegan tried to stand and she winced. Hopefully her pain would heal quickly in her wolf form. Mund scooped her back up in his arms to carry her to her baby. I smiled at them as he walked away. I did do something right. I protected Tegan, Nia, Jutta, Grete, and Fridrik.

I looked down at Baran. Even in death he seemed so strong. I couldn't leave him here for someone else to collect. He deserved a proper werewolf funeral. I knelt down and pulled Baran's body into my arms. He was at least twice my size in height and weight, but I cradled him and rose to my feet, wobbling from the strain of his weight. Mother helped me.

"This is where we first met," I said to Baran's body. "Do you remember? I was so scared of you then." I smiled, remembering all my feelings that fateful day. I was certain the tall dark stranger who kidnapped me was going to kill me and yet here he was in my arms as I carried him to his funeral to set his soul free.

"I asked him to come," Mother said. "If I couldn't be with you to protect you, he was the only other person I trusted. Every night he'd call me after you fell asleep and tell me about your day."

"He never told me that," I said.

Mother smiled. "It was our secret."

We headed up the stairs into the moonlight of the courtyard, safe inside the walls of the Rock. The moon shone down on the castle with an eerie orange glow. The Bloodmoon was near, and the light was tinted red. I carefully lay Baran down in the grass where a sliver of moonlight hit the ground.

"I will always love you," I said to Baran.

Mother and I sat there next to him. I felt weird hanging out with a dead body, but I could still feel Baran's presence so I could almost pretend everything was okay. We waited for Mund to find Grey and Willem so we could properly mourn Baran together. That's what families did. They celebrated together and they mourned together.

I studied the walls that surrounded us as I took in the damage. The south wall had been broken halfway down, and only fires burned to keep our enemies out. Dead bodies of Garm wolves were being piled to burn as my people slowly uncovered bodies of our packs and our humans. I watched as each lost soul was placed in the grass near Baran.

Each one was a son or daughter, a husband or wife, a mother or father. My heart filled with sadness. Soon all their loved ones would know the loss.

Kane, Brychan, Dilara, and Willem ran up to us. Willem was nearly out of breath and severely injured. His left hand was missing, though the wound was now fully healed. I was so shocked I couldn't look away. I just stared at the stump that used to be his hand.

"He's missing," he said.

"Who?" I asked.

I knew damn well to whom Willem was referring, but I couldn't bear the idea of facing it. I didn't want to know; maybe, just maybe, I was wrong and Grey wasn't missing. Maybe it was someone else, anyone else.

"Grey," Willem whispered.

I closed my eyes. "What happened?" I asked quietly.

"Grey and I were fighting to keep the front stairs protected so the Garm couldn't get down into the living quarters," Willem said. "I was knocked down by four Garm and I couldn't get back up." He shook his head back and forth as though he were trying to forget what had happened. "Grey saved my life."

"And where is he now?" My voice was as calm as ice. Unwavering.

"Vigdis took him," he said. "I'm so sorry. I tried to get to him, but they disappeared."

"Vigdis?" I repeated. "She wasn't with the army."

"It was her," he said. "I'm certain."

"How did she just walk into my castle without notice and then walk right back out with Grey?" I ground my teeth.

"I don't know," he said. "It was just Grey and me protecting the stairs from an endless flood of Garm when suddenly she appeared behind us. I rushed to fight with him but one of the Garm ripped off my paw. When I looked back I could hear her laughing, but they were both gone."

"That doesn't make any sense," I said.

"I know," Willem said.

I nodded. "Kane, report?" I said, trying to close out my pain and show strength for my people, but I knew I was a fraud.

"One-hundred-five injured, twenty-nine dead, and one missing," Kane said. "The castle is secure except for the south wall, but if we keep the fires burning it will keep the evil out." There was sympathy in his eyes as he watched me. I wasn't ready for sympathy.

"Who did we lose?" Mother asked.

"Baran Killian, the Flattery boys, Jacob of the guard, some of the Kingery, and many humans," he said. "And Grey Killian is missing."

I closed my eyes and took a deep breath, channeling any strength I had left. There had to be some piece of me that hadn't given up yet. I thought of Baran and it was almost like he was hugging me and filling me with his strength.

"It is time to mourn our dead. They should not have to wait all night," I said.

"What about Verci's body?" Brychan asked. The bitterness in his words sank into me like talons in my flesh. I hated Verci more than anyone and yet I wanted to set him free, too.

"We burn him," I said as I watched Old Mother and the Crone cross the courtyard to me.

"Why?" Willem asked.

"The Dvergars abandoned Old Mother and it destroyed their hearts. The only way to ensure their spirits won't haunt us is to give them back," I said.

"Even the broken need to come back home," Old Mother said.

Kane gave the orders for funeral pyres to be built around us in the courtyard and returned to where we sat with Baran.

"I heard you fought Verci," Kane said. He stared at the scar on the once-porcelain skin of my shoulder.

"I did," I replied. "And now he's dead."

Kane placed his hand on my scarred shoulder and his forehead on mine. "I want you to picture Verci's face and Adomnan's face . . . see them on fire, burning, smoldering, reduced to ash. Watch them blow away with the breeze." I could see it as though he controlled my mind. They stood on the rocky cliffs of Dunmanas Bay, their bodies burning in the wind. With his words, they disappeared, and all I saw was Kane. My heart felt lighter and only hope remained. What type of witchcraft was this? I felt as though he had walked through my heart. "Their souls cannot haunt you if you choose to set them free."

I didn't know what to say. Had he really set my demons free? Or had they always just been a figment of my imagination? Kane walked away to oversee the pyres being built. It was a circle with nineteen pyres, one for each of my dead wolves. Holes were being dug in the cemetery of the Rock for the ten dead humans.

The humans filled the courtyard and surrounded my pack. Even after fighting side by side with us, they watched us with curiosity, concern, and wonder. Humans were truly inspiring creatures. Old Mother was right to love them as she did and to create us to protect them. They had strength in them far greater than what resided inside of us.

I closed my eyes and concentrated on Grey. He was somewhere out there, alone. I could feel his heartbeat, but it was slow as though he'd been drugged. I tried to feel his body; there didn't seem to be any dismemberment or grotesque wounds, but I couldn't tell where he was.

Maybe I could find him in my dreams like I did with Baran.

We would be together soon.

"The pyres are prepared," Mund said.

All my dead had been placed on their rightful spots around the circle; even Verci was given a spot. Only Baran's body was left to be moved. I reached my hands under him to lift him, and Father slid his arms under Baran, too. I looked up into his face, and his eyes glistened with tears.

"Let me honor him," he said. "Please."

I nodded and watched my father carry Baran to his place in the circle. As he gently placed Baran to rest, I saw a single tear escape my father's eyes. I had no idea what Baran meant to my father and I would likely never know, but jealousy was no match for love, and his tears betrayed the pride he once clung to. I grabbed four unlit torches from the bin. I walked over to Jacob's mother and handed her a torch.

"Thank you, my queen," she said.

I continued around the circle and handed a torch to the Flattery boys' mother. Tears rolled down her cheeks, and I had no words of comfort for her. Her blue eyes were rimmed in red from all the tears she had shed. She bowed her head to me, and I bowed back. I continued on and handed a torch to Channing's father, Lord Bjorn Kingery. He nodded, and I finished my way around the circle and stopped in front of my mother. I reached the final torch out to her, and she reluctantly took it in her shaking hands.

I nodded to the Crone; she raised her staff above her head. "Today you will be the wind." The torches burst into flame, sending orange embers into the night sky. I found myself oddly mesmerized by the way the embers matched the color of the moon.

"Today, my daughters and sons, I take you back," Old Mother said. "Today, you are free."

My mother, Lord Bjorn Kingery, the Flattery boys' mother, and Jacob's mother all walked to the platforms where their loved ones rested and lit the fires below. The flames raced around the circle and engulfed all the bodies of the dead. I watched as Baran's body lit on fire and his hair began to curl as it burned. Before long, he was overtaken by the flame and I could no longer make him out.

I watched as Old Mother herself controlled the flames and the wind; she danced them together to claim her children. She controlled all the elements, and with her will, they obeyed.

My pack began dancing around the fires, and the humans joined in the celebration as well. I couldn't celebrate. I just stared at the fire where Baran had been. How could someone so strong and so much a part of my life be gone just like that? In the blink of an eye I felt like an orphan.

Without Baran or Grey, I was truly lost in this world. Even Mother found a smile among her tears as she danced and sang under the moon, but I had nothing left to give.

I stood quietly and disappeared into the shadows of the castle and down into the Rock. I wandered through the damaged hallways, barely even seeing any of it on my way to my room, Calista's room. I lay down on the bed and waited for my dreams or death to take me. I closed my eyes in the darkness of my room, and the chill of the night made it feel damp and unwelcoming. It felt so empty without Grey in it. I rolled over and smelled the pillow where he'd slept. As I breathed in his thick, delicious scent, my mind began to weave into sleep. I begged my dreams to take me to him . . . to my love.

*I opened my eyes and I was standing on the cliffs of Scotland. I looked down the steep cliff to the ocean below as the angry water churned. I felt like it was trying to tell me something. Something important.*

*The sunset was pink and orange and the air was cold. I turned around and found myself staring at the ruins of Dunnottar Castle. It was known to be one of the Dvergar hiding places after the Killians were murdered. I searched the broken windows for a glimpse of someone, anyone, but nothing moved. I felt like needles were pricking my skin . . . someone was watching me.*

*Was it Grey? Waiting for me to find him? I smelled the warm air, and the faintest smell of Grey filled me. I started to run to the castle to find him. My heart was pounding in my chest as I ran through long grass and over boulders.*

*Suddenly I saw Draugr dropping from the ruins like bats. I looked over the hills—thousands of Draugr moved toward the castle like a sea of rotten flesh. I had to get to Grey. I had to save him.*

Suddenly I was shaken awake. I opened my eyes to see Brychan kneeling above me as he clutched my shoulders. "I thought you'd try this," he said. "Can't you see it's a trap?"

"I'm going in to save him," I insisted.

"I can't let you," he said.

"Let. Me. Go!" I screamed.

Mother, Father, Mund, Kane, Dilara, and Old Mother ran into my room. They all stopped as they stared at Brychan nearly crushing my shoulders as he held me above my bed.

"Vigdis has an army, at least ten thousand Draugr," I said. "You have to let me save Grey."

"I will not let you go," he said.

"What is the meaning of this?" Mother demanded.

"She is trying to go through her dreams to get to Grey," Brychan said, betraying me. "I am certain it is a trap."

"I agree," Old Mother intervened. "If you enter the dream world to find Grey again, Vigdis will find you instead. I feel her waiting for you to return."

"I can't just leave him," I said. "I love him."

"She won't kill him; he is the only bargain she has left to offer," Dilara said.

"But he's my husband! We promised in life and in death!" I yelled. "I have to save him."

Mother gasped and I could feel Father's eyes burning a hole in my skin. I had revealed our secrets. Our marriage. Our love. Our connection. All bared for them all to see.

"You're married?" Mother whispered.

"Without our blessing or consent?" Father fumed.

"They had both," Old Mother Earth said. "I stood witness to their pure love."

"My baby gave her vows?" Mother said as she hugged me tight. "I wish I had been there."

"I wish that, too," I said. "We thought we were going to die in the Bloodrealms so we wanted to give our souls to each other."

"That's beautiful," Mother said. "I'm so proud of you for following your heart."

Relief washed over me. "Thank you, Mother," I said.

Father sighed. "You certainly do everything according to your rules, don't you?"

Brychan laughed. "About time you accept that one, Pørr."

"I don't really have a choice. She is no longer mine; she belongs to Grey and the Killian pack now," he said.

"Vigdis will want Ashling in return for Grey's life," Mother said. There was a deep sadness in her words. She'd lived her whole life without Baran. She'd sacrificed her happiness to save the man she loved and then lost him anyway. I knew she would stand by my side to save Grey; she knew all too well the loss I would feel.

"I'm sorry for your loss; Grey was a good man," Kane whispered as he left the room. I stared after him; had he truly given up hope for Grey? *For the greater good,* I could almost hear Flin say.

Dilara and Brychan bowed and left me to my thoughts.

I shuddered to think of Grey dying, of choosing his death for him. It was my life or Grey's. Vigdis would kill him if I didn't give my soul to her, I was certain of that. She might even kill him to punish me for killing her daughter, to take away my hope so I would willingly surrender to her.

I just wanted to go to him in my dreams, curl up next to him, and feel his warmth. I wanted to tell him I was sorry that I couldn't stay with him and share the life I had promised. I already knew in my heart I would sacrifice myself for him. I just wasn't sure I was ready to be murdered in front of all my friends and family or to hear my mother cry as I died. My heart felt heavy.

"We have two weeks to prepare to safely move Ashling to Carrowmore. If Vigdis has an army of Draugr, we will need all our strength. We will ready the armies," Father said. "And now you have to decide who will claim you."

He didn't say it, but I knew. I could feel the vibrations in all of them. Grey was already dead to them. I closed my eyes, scrunching up my face as I breathed.

Father walked over, side-hugged me, and whispered, "Even though you are a Killian now, you'll always be my baby girl." With a quick squeeze, he stalked out of my room, leaving me to swim in his words. Finally he knew how to show love. I watched as everyone followed him out of my room, leaving me alone with Mund.

"You okay?" Mund asked before he left.

"No," I said half-laughing.

"Me either," he said. "It just doesn't feel right being in a world without Baran."

I stared at my hands and bit my lip to stop myself from crying. "I still feel Baran," I said. "He's here. Can you feel him?"

Mund closed his eyes and I watched him. His face was so familiar to me. All my life he was always there. He always chose me. Even when I was a wild animal child with crazy red hair, he still liked me.

Mund's chocolate-brown eyes looked into me, and I felt a sadness so deep I felt I might drown in it. "I can't feel Baran," he said. "I'm not strong like you."

I reached out and squeezed his hand. "Well, he's still here, just like he promised."

He smiled and nodded, looking around the room. "Can you see him?"

"No, but I feel him. I feel his love, his energy. The same way we could feel him before, just now I can't smell him," I said. "I miss the way he smelled."

"We'll always remember that," he said.

"I'll always remember a lot of things that happened," I said.

"Tegan told me about the fight with Verci." He paused to clear his throat. "Thank you for protecting my wife and my baby," Mund whispered. "Those girls are my whole world, so thank you for fighting for them. I can never truly repay you."

Every moment of the fight flashed back through my mind . . . every terrifying second. I shuddered. It was still worth it to end Verci's evil reign. "I know what they mean to you, because I know what Grey means to me. And I love them too, so much, Mund. You are all my family. Without all of you, I would feel like a ghost, like a soul without a body."

"You must be utterly lost without Grey by your side."

"He stole my heart," I said.

"And you stole his," he replied. "Just remember that you are bound to each other. Neither of you can live without the other."

"Thanks, Mund."

"I'm going to go hold my girls while they sleep," he said. "Get some rest, Ash. You're going to need your energy in the next few days."

He leaned forward and kissed my forehead, and I breathed in his scent. Memorizing it. I was going to die in two weeks, and I wanted to remember everything. So when it hurt I could just picture all of them and all my memories until I was no longer of this earth.

"Don't go to Grey in your dreams, now," he said. "It's just what she wants."

"I know. I won't . . . goodnight, Mund," I said.

I sat alone in my room again. There wasn't even a familiar sound to keep me company. The secret door that led to Baran and Grey's room . . . my protectors, my dire wolves. No one was there to save me now. They both were sacrificed for loving me. Vigdis had promised she'd take everything from us. At least there was one thing I could count on . . . the depth of Vigdis's hatred.

I flopped back on my pillows and stared at the ceiling, wishing the answers were hidden there. I knew Father was planning ways to keep me alive so I could make my choice at Carrowmore, but I couldn't sleep. I was a queen, and a queen should have a plan.

The next morning I woke to horns echoing throughout the castle. A warning. I leaped out of bed in only my T-shirt and underwear and ran to the foyer of the royal chambers. I spotted Mund and ran after him up the stairs.

"What has happened?" I asked as we jumped the stairs two at a time.

"Attack on the southern wall," Mund said.

We burst out into the chaos of the courtyard. "Brychan!" Mund yelled. We spotted Brychan running through the courtyard toward us.

"It's a half dozen giants," Brychan said. "Ugly bastards."

We raced after Brychan onto the rampart walls around the castle and looked down on the giants as they slammed their mallets into the stone walls. The impact made my teeth chatter. I recognized one; he'd tried to capture me in the Realms before Grey saved me on the motorcycle.

"Where's Vigdis?" I said, searching the darkness.

"No one has seen her," Brychan said.

"Then why do you suppose they are here?" Mund asked.

Dilara suddenly slid down the roof above and dropped down onto the wall with us. "Could be a diversion," she said. "But I've searched all the walls; I don't see anyone besides these cumbersome brutes. Kane,

Quinn, and Willem are securing the labyrinth."

"Give the orders," Mund said. "Destroy them before they destroy the castle. Burn them out, protect us."

Dilara nodded and leapt back up on the roof, giving orders as she went.

"Do you think she's going to chip away at us one day at a time?" I asked Mund as we walked back into the castle.

He shook his head. "I don't know, Ashling, but I am going to protect you."

I stopped on the stairs and looked up into his exhausted face. "Get some rest, Mund; you're starting to look your age."

He smiled and messed up my hair and wandered away back to his room. I stared after him. Wishing I knew how to tell them all goodbye. I heard the sounds of fighting and the vibrations of the giants falling. We were winning, but nothing felt like winning anymore.

I wandered through the castle, watching every beautiful face I passed. My humans and wolves were living together in peace and harmony even in the middle of a war. That was something to be proud of. They all smiled at me, but it was a sad smile. They all knew what I'd lost. The rumors had spread through the castle. Grey was gone, and they all expected me to let him die so they could live.

# 32
## *Faith*

*A week went* by in slow motion. I barely spoke to any of them. And they didn't seek me out either. Not even Mother. Did they know the depth of my agony? Could they feel my sorrow pouring out over the earth? I found myself alone even when I was in a room full of my pack. I felt so numb.

I didn't want to die. There was so much left I wanted to do on this earth. There were so many things I wanted to see, but without Grey, all my dreams seemed hollow.

The moon was nearly red now. I sat on the roof of the tower, watching it burn in the sky. When the sun rose this morning, only six days would remain before my birthday.

I felt a sadness inside of me that I'd never felt before. It was so dark that I felt it consuming me. I knew who I was. I was wild and free spirited; I wasn't this ghost of a person I'd let myself become. But I didn't know how to find myself again. I felt so far away from everything and everyone, even (or especially) from myself. I stood up and slid down the roof onto the rampart walls.

I needed to talk to Old Mother. I needed answers. I looked down on the courtyard and spotted her drinking coffee in the early morning light. It seemed strange that she would engage in such a normal human activity, but then she was always surprising me.

I walked down the stairs and across the yard to her. Her back was to me, and she didn't turn around as she sipped her coffee.

"Ashling Killian," she said. "Why don't you sit with me and watch the sun rise?"

I'd never been called by the Killian surname before, except for when Grey used it. I liked the sound of it. I half-smiled and sat down next to her.

"Can you see the sunrise?" I asked, looking into her blind cataract eyes.

"There is more to seeing than just using your eyes," she said. "I've watched you all of your life."

I thought of all the times I'd felt so rejected and alone in Dunmanas Bay. I thought of being sent away by my father, my fear of Baran, being chased and stalked by Adomnan, being kidnapped, being whipped and beaten, being trapped in the Bloodrealms. I thought of all the lives I'd seen lost, of all the times I was terrified and so desperately needed help. I remembered watching Baran die. All of these horrible things had happened and my faith felt destroyed, yet here she sat before me, Old Mother Earth, my creator.

"But why weren't you there? I cried for you. I prayed. I begged. And still you did not come," I blurted out. "Why did you abandon me?"

"I have been with you every step of the way. I heard your every thought and cried with you. I was there when you fought Adomnan. I was there when you hid in the burial graves. I was there when you said your vows with Grey. You were never alone," she said. Tears rushed down my face as I felt the truth of her words vibrate through me and yet I still didn't understand. "There is always a plan."

"I was beaten nearly to death. Nearly raped. I was attacked over and over again. Tested and retested. And you never protected me," I said. "You never came."

"I chose your mother to raise you for I knew she would show you faith. I led Baran to you to protect you and love you, for I could feel you yearn for a father. I led you to Grey for I felt your heart was ready to fall so deeply in love that you would finally find the peace you've always sought, and I knew he was the right man for you. I asked Shikoba to watch over you. I brought Dilara to find you in the Realms. Everyone who surrounds you is a person I led to you and then they choose to stay," she said. "I work through all of you, and I held you while you cried. I was there Ashling. I never left your side."

"But I feel so alone . . . so broken," I whispered.

"You never have to doubt in your faith. For I walk with you. I carry you when you fall, I hold you when you're sad, and I rejoice with you when your heart is filled with love. Just quiet your mind, calm your breathing, and you will hear me. I am all mothers, and I am inside of you," she said. "And when the wind blows, you will feel my love."

I leaned into her as she wrapped her arm around me, pulling me close. "Why me?" I asked.

"Oh, sweet child," she said. "Every one of my children has a purpose, a battle they fight that you know nothing about. Struggles that they alone must overcome. When I looked down upon my children, human and wolves alike, I knew they were lost and broken; they needed to find their way back home, but I could not force them. I needed someone to give them hope, to show them that love still exists. I knew bringing you would allow light to open their hearts and they would be able to be free once again, because you showed them how.

"Just as I brought Baran and Grey to you, I brought you to all the world. You are all an interconnected web, and each of you must give love to the world," she said. "Your castle is filled with wolves and humans from all over the world, and every one of them chose you to lead them. I may have led them to you, but they chose you, and you chose to lead."

"What if I fail?" I said. "What if Vigdis kills me?"

"You are pure love," she said. "She can't consume love."

I stared at her, trying to decipher her words. I knew Vigdis planned to claim me and drink my blood at Carrowmore, but something in Old Mother's voice led me to believe that it wouldn't end as Vigdis was expecting.

"Would Vigdis die if she drank my blood?" I asked.

"Certainly," Old Mother said. "You are a pure love so powerful that your blood would destroy hate, and all that is left of Vigdis is hate."

I smiled. I finally knew the answer. I wasn't abandoning my people by sacrificing myself to save Grey. I would still be saving them. Vigdis's reign would end. Even in death I could protect my people.

"Old Mother?" I said.

"Yes, sweet one?"

"Do you think Baran is okay?" I asked.

She smiled. "You already know the answer. Now come, let's break our fast."

She stood and we walked quietly into the castle. We wandered down to the dining hall filled with my people. She led me to a table where Lady Faye, Mother Rhea, the Crone, Mother, Flin, and Quinn sat.

My mother reached up and held my hand, and I took the seat next to her on the bench. "It is good to see you," she said.

"Have you decided which of these young chaps will claim you at the ceremony?" Mother Rhea asked.

I could feel the tension at the table, and Mother squeezed my hand tightly. In the last week, they had all behaved as though Grey were already dead, but he wasn't dead. I could feel him, and none of them could know my plan. My sacrifice.

"Channing Kingery would be a fine choice," Lady Faye offered.

"Or Lord Brychan," the Crone added. "He's a fierce one."

Brychan's heart was already spoken for. I looked across the room to where Brychan sat with Dilara. They were so in love. I was happy for them.

"You could always look to one of the other packs," Mother Rhea said. "There are a lot of new faces in the castle these days to consider for the honor."

"I will decide," I said.

Mother picked up on my tone and changed the subject. "Have you tried the dried buffalo that Kane and Shikoba brought?"

"Buffalo?" I said.

"It is quite delicious," Mother continued. "I quite like the flavor of bison pemmican that the Cree make."

Mother handed a plate to me with a smile. "Thank you," I said.

I heard them all talking around me, but I wasn't listening as I tasted the meat and remembered my short stay with Kane and Shikoba in Canada. The thinly sliced meat was almost brittle on my tongue but satisfying. I devoured the entire plate of buffalo as Mother slid a plate piled with blackberries in front of me.

I hadn't realized I was even hungry. The Crone slid a crust of bread toward me as she wandered off to fill her cup. I was thankful for the food and the energy it would give me.

Fully satisfied, I sighed and stood. "I think I shall retire."

I turned to leave, but Mother Rhea reached out and gently touched my arm. "It was always you, dear," Mother Rhea said. "I knew when you were born at Carrowmore that you would change the world."

I smiled at her. There was so much kindness in her tone, yet I knew she was trying to guide me to another man's arms for the safety of our people. She didn't think I could save Grey.

"Any of those boys would be a good choice in a mate," Lady Faye added.

"I'm already married," I said.

"You mean *widowed*," Flin muttered.

# 33
## Mirror

*I turned and* walked out of the room as fast as I could before I exploded on Flin. I loathed him. He was always so judgmental and mean. He lacked all the grace of the world and yet still I loved the idiot. He was still my brother.

I walked to the library and closed my eyes, smelling the old, musty smell of books. It had all begun in this fateful room two years ago now. I looked up at that silly little window I had escaped through. The bars had been replaced to secure the fortress. No one was getting in or out.

*That's what they thought last time,* I thought with a smile.

I climbed up the ladder to the highest rows of books and ran my fingers over their spines. Each one had a story. Some were fiction, but I knew that the legends and myths were all true. Not one story in here was truly made up.

I grabbed a book about demons, put my feet on the outer edges of the ladder, and slid all the way down to the bottom. I walked across the room to the table and chairs at the center and sat down to read.

As I flipped through the pages, I came to all the loathsome crea-

332 · *Aurora Whittet*

tures I'd come to know; the Garm, the Draugr, and so many horrors I had yet to meet like the Skoll, Lindworms, and Romulus. Hopefully they were all extinct.

I laid my head back against the wood chair and closed my eyes. I needed rest. I needed a miracle.

I awoke to the sound of footsteps as Father walked into the library with Brychan, Mund, Dilara, and Dagny in tow. I glanced at the tiny window; the sun had begun to rise once again. Another day had slipped past.

"We have a plan," Father announced.

"Oh?" I said.

They sat down around the table with me. "We will send the steel wolves out first to create the perimeter. Then you and the royal family, including Old Mother and the Crone, will exit the castle. Dagny's army will take the back. We are nearly five thousand strong, and we will escort you on the eve of your birthday to Carrowmore."

"Who will remain to protect the humans?" I asked.

"We need every man and woman capable of fighting with us to protect you," Father said. "It is of the utmost importance that you are safe."

I smiled at them. "It is of the utmost importance that our humans are safe," I said. "That is our purpose, after all."

"Ashling, ensuring your protection means that they will be safe," Brychan said.

"No," I said.

"I told you she wouldn't agree," Mund said.

I stood before them. "I appreciate your concern and love, but I have already made my decisions," I said. "Father, Mother, Mund, Brychan, Dilara, Channing, Willem, Khepri, Old Mother, and the Crone shall accompany me to Carrowmore. And I shall leave Dagny in charge of protecting all the lives left within the castle walls."

Father stood to object, and I held up my hand to silence him.

"I know that you all fear for my life, and you want to keep me safe, like a stained-glass window. But we can never endanger our people for our own salvation," I said. "I believe we can move swiftly with our small pack. Leaving our army to protect the castle is the right choice."

"Are you sure?" Mund asked.

"Completely," I said. "It seems a new day has dawned and I have yet to rest."

I walked into my room. Leaving my door open, I flopped down on my bed and Grey's scent surrounded me. Oh, how I missed his touch. It wasn't long now. Only four days left.

I heard a light knock at my door and my mother's smell filled my room. I smiled at her scent. I wondered if she had sensed my choice yet. That I was going to sacrifice my life in exchange for Grey's.

"Hi, Mother," I said.

"May I join you?" she asked.

"I'd love that." More than she'd ever know.

She lay down on the bed with me and started to absentmindedly play with my curls like she did when I was a little girl. I wasn't sure she even knew she did it.

"I'm sorry I missed your wedding," she said with a sigh. "I would have liked to have been there."

I smiled and leaned over to kiss her cheek. "You were there; your love follows me everywhere I go," I said. "But I'm sorry, too; we truly thought we were going to die down there. We wanted to die knowing our souls could be together for all eternity."

"I would have done the same thing," she said. "I always liked that boy."

"Me too," I giggled.

"Oh, I could tell," she said. "The two of you watched each other's every move. It almost seemed as if you were connected; if one moved, the other would follow. A beautiful dance, really."

"Mother," I said. "Do you think he's okay?"

She sighed. "Well, I know Vigdis won't kill him. She needs him. But I fear she might hurt him."

I closed my eyes, trying to feel him. His heartbeats were slow; he was still unconscious. "It feels as though she's drugged him," I said. "He feels like he's lost in dreams."

"Well, the longer he's asleep, the safer he will be," she said.

I nodded. "Mother?"

"Yes, *m'eudail?*"

"I love you," I said, burying my face in her hair. My voice tightened as I spoke. "Thank you for wanting me when no one else did."

"Oh, my sweet, I grew you in my tummy and carried you long after you were born. My heart beats in your chest now. I love you, Ashling, with all my heart," she said.

"Why does it hurt so much to be away from you?"

She hugged me tight. "Because you are not only my baby, but you are my best friend," she said.

She was right. Everything I learned about life and love and nature and faith came from her. My love of art and books and adventure were all pieces of my mother that she had freely given to me. Even when she was annoyingly being a mom, she was still the one person in the world who was always there, always ready to listen and put me back together while I cried, and she was there laughing with me through all my memories. I had nearly eighteen glorious years with her, and I could live to a thousand years old and it would still never be enough time with her. Her love was too big, too irreplaceable, and just simply beautiful.

"I know what you're planning," she said.

"What?" I said.

"I feel it," she said.

"I'm sorry," I said quietly. "I can't let him die."

"There has to be another way," she said.

"Even if someone else claimed me, it wouldn't stop Vigdis. There would still be war, and until she died, we would live in fear. Vigdis has an army of Draugr nearly twice the size of our army. We can't beat her. My only choice is to give her what she wants," I said.

"But then she will rule the world," Mother said.

I shook my head. "No. She will certainly take my life, but drinking my blood will end hers," I said. "So my sacrifice will save everyone I love."

"I can't lose you," she said. "I already lost Baran."

"I'm sorry, Mother, but I can't lose Grey, I can't lose you. This is my purpose."

I saw it in her eyes, the understanding. She'd lost Baran; she knew the pain I faced. She held me in her arms, and I could feel her warm tears as they splashed on my cheek as she cried. "Oh, my baby. My sweet baby."

"I'm sorry I can't stay with you," I whispered.

"You will still be here. I know where to find you if we lose," she said. "You'll be with Baran."

"Can you feel Baran, Mother?"

"Yes I can. In every breath I take. I know I'll still feel you, too," she said. "Grey would also die for you, you know."

"I know," I said. "He loves me."

"That he does," she said.

"Mom, I'm scared," I said. "Vigdis is going to hurt me."

"She will try, love," she said. I clung to her. "I'm scared, too, but do you know what Vigdis can never do?"

I shook my head.

"She can never steal our love," she said. "She doesn't know what it is; she cannot grasp it. So she can never take it from us."

"If she kills me, will you sing, so the last thing I hear in this world is your voice?" I asked.

She wept and gagged on her tears. "I would do anything for you," she said.

"Take care of Grey," I said. "And everyone."

"I will," she whispered.

"And don't tell anyone my plan, please," I said. "It is hard enough knowing I'm going to die, but to have everyone try to talk me out of it is more than I can take."

"I promise," she said.

"Mother?"

"Yes, Ashling?"

"Will you stay with me tonight?" I asked. "I don't really want to be alone."

"I will be with you forever."


I woke the next morning still wrapped in my mother's arms. I watched her angelic face as she continued to sleep. She was truly beautiful, inside and out. I felt thankful and stronger knowing she knew. I needed her to understand. I couldn't bear the idea of leaving her behind without telling her I loved her.

I slid Calista's ring off my finger and slid it onto hers, back where it belonged. I didn't want Vigdis to have it. Mother had given it to me when Baran had taken me to America. Now it was back on Mother's elegant fingers. The dark, intricate patina of the metal was beautiful on her skin. Mother woke and looked at her hand. Her eyes filled with tears, but she blinked them back.

"I remember Calista," she said. "I was so young then, but I remember her."

"Do you think I have lived up to her expectations?" I asked.

"No," she said. "You are far better than anyone could ever have known."

"Well that's because you're my mom."

"You better believe it," she said with a laugh. "Come on, let's break our fast before they send a search party after us."

"Okay." I yawned and stretched.

Mother slid off the bed and walked over to the closet, opening the door to reveal a giant mirror. I watched her study her reflection.

"Are you okay?" I asked.

"I haven't looked in a mirror in eighteen years," she said. "Not since I was pregnant with you."

"Why?"

She turned and smiled at me. "A silly wives' tale," she said as suddenly a hand plunged out of the glass and started strangling my mother.

I leaped off the bed and ran toward her to see Vigdis on the other side of the glass. She laughed and my hair stood on end.

"Help!" I screamed.

I grabbed Mother and tried to pull her back away from the mirror, but Vigdis's grip was like iron on Mother's throat. Mother's face was losing color; she was gasping for air as Vigdis tried to pull her into the mirror.

"Someone help me!" I yelled.

Mother's arms disappeared into the mirror, and the glass pooled around her face as Vigdis pulled. My mother was disappearing before my eyes. Panic raked through me. No one was coming to help. I looked around my room and saw a letter opener on the table. I grabbed it and ran to the mirror as only my mother's feet were still in this world.

I stabbed the silver letter opener into the glass where Vigdis stood. Vigdis hissed and screamed, and Mother tumbled back onto the floor next to me as the mirror shattered.

Vigdis screeched as she disappeared.

I fell to my knees next to Mother. She was pale and motionless. She wasn't breathing. "Not you, too," I said as I pounded on her chest, trying to restart her heart.

Mund and Tegan rushed into the room with Father close behind. Tegan gently pushed me aside and began compressions. I lay down on the floor next to Mother and wrapped my fingers with hers. Her eyes opened. She wheezed with every breath, but I was relieved.

"Mother," I said, pulling her into my arms.

"What happened?" Father asked, looking at the broken mirror all around us.

"Vigdis," Mother moaned.

Mund stared at me. "Through the mirror?" he said. I nodded. Mund ran out of the room, and I could hear him yelling orders to destroy all the mirrors. His voice faded as Father knelt down and scooped Mother into his arms. The worry on his face aged him, but it was beautiful, too. He really did love her.

"My lady," he said. "I shall make you some gingerroot tea to soothe your throat."

Tegan's eyes were wide with fear. I pulled her into my arms and held her until she stopped shaking. Nowhere was safe until Vigdis was dead. Her evil could reach me in my dreams, through mirrors, through paintings, and through attacks on our castle. Not one of my people was safe until I killed Vigdis.

"I never got to truly thank you for what you did, Ashling," Tegan said. "I could never have protected Nia the way you protected us."

"Tegan, you fought with me against Verci, and you just saved my mother—you are a badass," I said. "I was honored to fight with you."

She laughed. "I think I'm a better mother than a fighter."

"That I can agree with," I said. "You are truly a wonderful mother."

"You will be one day, too." She smiled at me. I tried to hide my sadness, but she saw it. "I'm sorry. I shouldn't have said that."

"Don't worry," I said. "I am just freaked out after the attack."

She knew I was lying. I could see it on her face, but she smiled anyway. "I love you, Ashie," Tegan said.

"I love you, too."

I watched her walk away, and when she glanced back at me, I knew she knew. I quickly looked away. I couldn't take the tears in her eyes. I couldn't handle that today. I abruptly stood and turned to go outside when something glimmered on my dresser. I walked closer and saw

Brychan's beautiful sapphire ring. He'd given it to me when I was four-teen, his promise of betrothal. I picked it up and held it in my hand, studying the blue stone.

I quickly shoved it in my pocket and went out of the castle and into the sunshine of the courtyard into the summer air. I walked out into the old, overgrown cemetery and ran my fingers over the old carved stones. On some, the names had been lost to erosion long ago and yet the stones stood telling the tales of the human lives that had come and gone at the Rock . . . our humans.

I felt safe with the dead. There was something so welcoming about cemeteries. I often wondered if the spirits were happy to have com-pany. I slid my back down a Celtic cross and nestled into the weeds. I breathed in the world around me and let nature purify my heart. I would let my faith rule the day.

# 34

## Cemetary

*I heard two* sets of footsteps through the grass, and I knew from their scents whose they were. I smiled as I thought of the love they were still trying to hide. I looked up at Brychan and Dilara as they approached and smiled. Their hands were nearly touching, as though they were grasping the other just moments before.

"It's okay, you know," I said. "I know you like each other."

They both looked truly surprised, and I couldn't help but laugh.

"Really?" I said.

"I . . . ah," Brychan said. For the first time I'd ever seen, Dilara seemed to blush a little.

"I'm happy for you," I said. "I kind of saw it back in Maine."

"What?" Dilara said. "No way. We weren't a thing then," she insisted.

I smiled. "True, but I could smell it on you both."

Brychan laughed. "It is true," he said, grabbing her hand. "I just wasn't quite ready to admit it."

"I'm glad you're done being stubborn," I said.

"And I'm glad you haven't stopped," he said.

"Brychan and I have an offer for you," Dilara said.

"Since Grey can't claim you at Carrowmore, I will. I am still one of your suitors and your betrothed," Brychan said.

"I don't understand," I said. "You guys are in love."

"Yes, but the greater good of our people is worth the sacrifice," Dilara said. "And by our laws, you have first right to him."

"Thank you," I said. "But that won't be necessary. Besides, I could never stand in the way of true love. If I did, how could I stand in front of my people? What would there be to fight for?"

"Are you sure?" she said. She looked between Brychan and me, and I could feel her resistance. She didn't seem to dare to believe it.

I put my hands over theirs, cupping them in mine. "I bless your love. Someday, when I do something you don't agree with, I want you to remember this moment and forgive me."

Brychan laughed. "You? You're going to do a lot of things that will surprise everyone," he said. "But we will support you for all our days."

"If you will still have us," Dilara said. "We would like to stay on as your personal guard."

"I would be honored if you would walk with me to Carrowmore on my birthday," I said. "I would feel safer with you two there with me."

"I was hoping you'd allow us to be there for you," Brychan said.

I smiled and placed Brychan's ring in his hand, closing his fingers over it as I whispered in his ear, "I think you might be needing this back." I turned to both of them. "Now go make love under a tree somewhere," I said.

Dilara laughed; this time, Brychan blushed.

I sat alone the rest of the day in the cemetery and watched the clouds float by. There was a peacefulness sitting with the dead. They weren't anxious, nervous, or scared; they were calm, almost welcoming. Perhaps they knew what I was planning; perhaps they were trying to help me feel peace with my decision to join them.

As nightfall crept in, I smelled Jutta approach. She was quieter than anyone I'd ever met. I didn't hear a single footstep or rustling of weeds as she moved. Growing up in the Bloodrealms taught her that.

"Good evening, Jutta," I said.

"Are you going to sleep out here?" she asked as she stared at the Bloodmoon. It was nearly blood red. It would bleed soon . . . and so would I. The next day, at midnight, I would be claimed.

"I was thinking about it," I said.

"Would you mind if I joined you?" she asked quietly.

"I would love your company."

She sat down next to me. My skin warmed as heat radiated off her body. I hadn't realized I was cold until she sat down.

"What is on your mind, Jutta?" I asked.

"It's just hard getting used to sleeping in a bed and not hiding from every sound and everyone," she said. "I'm tired, but I feel too scared to sleep."

"No one here will hurt you," I said.

"I know," she said. She stared up at the stars as a shooting star filled the sky. "What's that?" she asked.

"A shooting star," I said. "Make a wish."

"I'd never seen stars before you rescued me from the Bloodrealms," she said as she stared up at them. "I wish for you to be my big sister."

Guilt washed over me. After tomorrow night, I wouldn't be anything more than a legend, soon to be forgotten. She needed someone to watch over her, and I wished it could be me.

"Jutta, I want you to ask Brychan and Dilara to teach you to fight," I said. "They are the best warriors I have. You tell them I told you to ask."

She nodded.

"Thank you, Ashling," she said. "I always wanted a sister."

I wrapped my arm around her. She nuzzled in and rested her head on my shoulder. I listened as her breathing slowed and she fell asleep. I kissed the top of her head and looked back up as three more falling stars filled the sky with wonder.

"I wish for a future," I said and closed my eyes to sleep.

I woke to the sounds in the castle, and the first thought in my mind was, *my last day.* When twilight fell, I would face Vigdis. I would see Grey one last time, then I would die. I shook my head, trying to ignore my fear.

"Good morning, Jutta," I said gently.

She yawned, stretched, and looked up at me with a sweet smile. "Thanks for letting me hang out with you," she said.

I ran my fingers over her short hair. "Let's eat like queens," I said.

She giggled. "Race you!" she said. She was already halfway back up the hill to the castle by the time I stood up to stretch. I laughed and walked slowly to the dining hall.

"Happy birthday!" they all screamed.

I nearly jumped out of my own skin. There in the hall stood my entire pack, every last beautiful soul, except for Grey. They had a ridiculously cheesy birthday banner hung from the ceiling and a huge chocolate cake.

"Cake for breakfast? I'll have a piece of that," I said with a smile.

Mother cut a big chunk of cake and carried it over. "I made it just how you like it," she said. "Sour-milk chocolate cake with cream cheese frosting."

I took a bite and let it melt on my tongue. It was exactly how I liked it. Mother had made that cake for my birthday for as long as I could remember. The only time she missed was last year, when we were with Dagny in Norway.

"It's perfect," I said.

"Just like you," Mother said as she sat down next to me.

Jutta grabbed a fork and helped me with my piece of cake.

"There is an entire cake over there," Mother said, smiling.

"I know," Jutta said. She smiled with chocolate-covered teeth. "But it tastes better this way."

I laughed. "She has a point," I said, stealing a bite from Mother's plate. "Definitely better."

"Are you ready for today?" Mother asked.

"No," I said, smiling weakly. "And yes."

She twirled my curly hair in her fingers and closed her eyes. We both knew I would pick Grey, just as she would have gladly picked Baran. Love wasn't fifty–fifty; love was giving your whole self to the other person no matter what.

Father walked over to us and sat down across from me. He handed me a small black velvet box. "Happy birthday," he said.

I slowly ran my fingers over the soft fabric before opening it. It felt decadent. Inside was a black dagger. I pulled it out and held it in the light, and red light cascaded down on my white skin.

"It is blood glass," he said.

I stared at it in horror. I was holding the blood of a dead man or woman. "Where did you get this?" I gasped. "Who died for this?"

"It is my blood," he said. "Since the day you were born, I have spent my life trying to protect you. I read every book in my library searching for the answer. In all our legends, I kept coming across the same passage. It said, 'Only blood can stop evil.'"

"How can it be your blood?" I asked, touching his hand to make sure he wasn't a ghost like Shikoba. His thick fingers were warm to the touch. He was as real as he had always been. I breathed a sigh of relief.

"For eighteen years I have been bleeding myself to make this for you," he said.

"How?" I asked.

"The process is quite grotesque," Mother said as she reached out and held his hand. "Every night your father would go out to the Bloodmark stone; using the golden quill, he would slice his wrist and pour his blood into the dagger mold. The same way you protected Rhonda."

I shuddered, remembering the cut on my palm. I carried the scar still. I'd almost died saving her. I looked at my father and realized he almost died every day trying to save me.

"It will protect you tonight. Carry it with you," he said.

I stared at the dagger. I was truly holding a piece of my father in my hands. It was a sacred weapon. He had planned this day for my whole life, knowing I would need a weapon to protect myself. It was proof of his love. After all these years, I finally understood him.

"I will, Father. Thank you."

He patted my hand and wandered away to talk to Brychan and Channing's parents. I wondered if they had renewed hopes I might choose one of their sons to claim me now that Grey was gone.

I hated those words. *Grey was gone.* It was like bitter poison in my body and mind. Everyone believed he was as good as dead.

"Ash," Mund said, interrupting my thoughts. "You should address your people before we set out to Carrowmore."

I looked around at all the wolves I did and didn't know; they had all come to join our fight for hope. I'd brought the humans in to protect them, and they fought alongside of us. I was proud of my army of my people, and now it was time to give them a new future.

"Have all my people gather here in the courtyard, and I will speak to them," I said.

He nodded and sent messengers to gather all my people. I sat quietly, watching them all. I could feel their fear and yet there was so much hope among them. Today was the beginning of their new lives, but the end of mine.

Once we had congregated in the courtyard, Mund walked back over to my side.

"Everyone is here and accounted for," he said. "Every human and wolf."

"Please get Tegan for me," I said.

He looked at me strangely. He knew I was up to something. He knew me too well, but he did as I asked and returned with Tegan and Nia.

"Tegan, I would ask Mund to stay behind, but you and I both know he won't listen." She laughed and Mund looked rather disapproving. "So I shall ask this of you, Princess Tegan Boru: Should an ill fate fall upon me while I am gone, will you rule over our people with strength and love?"

She burst into tears. She knew I wasn't coming back. She crushed me against her and Nia so tightly that Nia squawked in complaint. "Ashie, I will guard them all with my life," she said.

Mund stared at us. "I will bring her back," Mund said. "So don't get too used to your power, my sweet." He chuckled to himself. She nodded, but I could see she knew better than to trust his strength over my sacrifice.

"Take care of Jutta for me," I said.

I gestured to Kane and Quinn to come over. They knelt with us in the grass. "I'm not taking you with me to Carrowmore," I said.

"What? Why?" Quinn asked.

"Because I am leaving Tegan in charge, and I need you both here to protect the castle and keep Flin from ruling anything beyond his own bowel movements," I said.

"Don't let Flin touch a hair on my wife or daughter's heads," Mund said.

"We will protect your people," Quinn said. Kane nodded in agreement.

I stood before all my people and looked out at the sea of faces. "I, Ashling Boru, daughter of King Pørr Boru and Queen Nessa of the Rock, stand before you as your Crimson Queen. Tonight, I make my run for Carrowmore. In my stead, I name Princess Tegan Boru as your ruler; should we fail, she will be your queen."

Most people nodded in agreement with my choice. Tegan was well known for her intelligence and kindness. I knew she would rule fairly.

"Old Mother and the Crone will stand by me at Carrowmore when I am claimed under the Bloodmoon. Together, we are the Triple Goddess. I ask my mother and father, Redmund Boru, Brychan Kahedin, Dilara Tabakov, Channing Kingery, and Willem and Khepri Killian to stand witness; finally, I ask Dagny and his army to serve as our guard. To protect the city, I leave Kane of the Cree tribe and Quinn Boru in charge with the steel wolf army."

I had chosen my witnesses. I had chosen my successor. I had chosen my guard. It was done.

"What about me?" Jutta asked.

I turned and looked into her wide, teary eyes and scared face. "You, Jutta, are now part of the Boru, and I ask you to look after Nia and Fridrik. You're a big sister now; keep them safe for me," I said. "You know what kind of trouble those two can get into."

She giggled. "I think I can handle them."

I turned back to my people. "Your new lives await."


I sat alone in my room. I would never get to tell Grey all the things I needed him to know, so instead I would have to try to explain everything with a letter. I remembered all the love notes he had once slipped under the door of this very room for me. All of his sweet words that filled my soul with love. There was something endlessly powerful about the written word.

I pulled out parchment from the drawer and delicately dipped a quill into the inkpot. I took a deep breath and began to pour out my soul.

*My dearest Grey,*

*I know you don't understand my sacrifice, that you ache even still, but I have chosen this, and I have to tell you what my heart is screaming. I could not bear a world without you in it, and this was the only way to protect you and all my people. It is a sacrifice that I consider my greatest honor. I live in all of you.*

*I knew on that fateful day when we met there was no one else upon this earth who could love me like you do. One glimpse in your eyes and I was irrevocably yours. You have ravaged my heart. You told me our love was endless, and I believe that. Even in death, my love will never fade away.*

*I won't let you go. Just stare at the sky and you'll find me. We are one soul with two hearts and you forever have mine. I love you, Grey.*

*Always,*

*Ashling Killian*


Tears ran down my cheeks as I folded the letter, hiding my heart for only him to see. I took the candle and melted a pile of black wax on the letter to seal it. I picked up the Boru seal, but it didn't feel right. I wasn't a Boru. I was a Killian. I glanced at the Tree of Life amulet Eamon had given me that lay on my desk, and I pressed it into the wax.

It was the symbol of hope and Old Mother, and it would be our symbol forevermore. Two trees growing intertwined together in life, just as our souls had bound to each other.

I lay the letter on my pillow on the bed and picked up his pillow and smelled it one last time. His musky scent was fading, but it was still there. I breathed out and put it back down.

It was time to change into what was left of the cloak dress that Lady Faye had given me. It was torn to shreds and looked utterly ridiculous, but it had saved many lives. I was proud of that. I took Grey's mother's necklace off and laid it on my bed. I wanted him to have it, not Vigdis. I sighed and looked down at myself.

"You can't be crowned queen in those old rags," Old Mother said from behind me. I turned and smiled sheepishly.

"It's all I have left. I used it all," I said with a shrug.

"I know, dear," she said.

She held her wrinkled old hands over my head and closed her blind eyes. She breathed slowly as she put her palms together. My torn, old brown dress transformed on my body into an intricate brown leather corset with black leather pants. The leather caressed my body and exposed my collarbone. There was beautiful embroidery down the front of the corset and around the edges of the pants. It was truly exquisite. She reached up and touched my hair and gold feathers appeared woven into my red curls.

"Now, that is a wardrobe for the Crimson Queen." She smiled.

I touched the supple leather. "Thank you," I said as I strapped a leather sheath to my thigh and slid Father's dagger into it.

"Thank you, Ashling," she said. "I know I have asked more of you than any of my children before, and I want you to know I see the burden . . . and I see you."

I rushed into her arms and hugged her. I let her strength pulse through me; I needed her love.

Mund knocked lightly at my door and slowly walked in. "Ashling, Baran made this for you, and I thought you should have it today." He held the most beautiful leather shoulder armor I'd ever seen. I held out my arms and Mund slid the armor over my arms and strapped it tight. The layers of leather that went down my shoulder looked almost like leather flower petals. It was beautifully designed with the Tree of Life symbol growing up my arm. I'd never seen anything like it.

"Now you're a warrior, just like Baran," Mund said.

I bit my lip so I wouldn't cry as I stared at myself. I wasn't wearing some ridiculous gown to show my status or queenliness; I was going to war.

Old Mother ran her fingers over the armor and my skin tingled. I looked at her and she smiled. Somehow I knew it wasn't just leather anymore. It held Old Mother's magic.

"He's proud," Mund said. "And so am I."

I wrapped my arms around him and hugged him tight. "I love you, Mund."

"I love you too, Ash," he said.

"It is time you took your place in our world," Old Mother said.

With Mund at the center, we walked arm in arm to the courtyard. It was dark once again, and only hours stood between me and my claiming. Stars filled the sky, and the moon burned blood red. Midnight approached.

As I walked to my parents, the courtyard hushed and everyone stared. I no longer felt scared. I looked upon my people with pride. I knew my duty, my sacrifice, my own heart.

"You're beautiful," Mother said as she kissed my left cheek.

"I love you," I whispered.

Old Mother walked around to Father, Mother, Mund, Brychan, Dilara, Channing, Willem, Khepri, and the Crone, touching each of their outfits. I knew she was binding their clothing to their bodies, making their clothes one with them as she had done for me.

"You grew up too fast," Father said as he kissed my right cheek.

I quickly shifted into a wolf. The corset and armor disappeared and was replaced by my red fur; only the golden feathers in my hair remained behind my left ear. My four paws touched the earth, and energy pulsed through me. I let my true being fill me with strength. Death was only the beginning.

It was over one hundred miles to Carrowmore from the Rock. I'd run to Dunmanas Bay many times, but I'd never been that far north . . . at least not since my birth.

"We run for Carrowmore as fast as our feet can carry us. When we arrive, we will walk six times around the circle in silence, praying to the stones," Father said. "On the seventh time around, we yell to awaken them."

I howled at the Bloodmoon rising in the sky. It would bleed on us tonight. I sang all my hopes to the moon. I thanked Old Mother for every precious moment I was given on this earth, every moment with my family, my friends, Baran, and especially Grey. Every moment was a gift.

Wolves shifted all around me and joined their voices to mine, filling Ireland with our dreams. They all dreamed of the future I would bring; they just didn't realize I would have to die to give it to them. I glanced back at Old Mother, who was now a white-and-gray wolf with the same starry eyes. The Crone was much smaller than I, and her fur was dark gray. I started running; my parents matched my pace, one on each side, with Old Mother and the Crone behind us. They gave me life, and now they delivered me to my end. Mund, Brychan, Dilara, Channing, Willem, and Khepri surrounded us as we ran out of the gates into the unknown. The wolves and humans left behind howled and shouted as we left.

I heard the soft padding of our feet as we ran on the earth, the collective breath and pounding hearts. I heard them all. Old Mother, the Crone, Mother, Father, Mund, Dilara, Brychan, Channing, Willem, and Khepri—we were one pack, one being. I let the rhythm of our steps fill my mind as I ran to my love. All I could think of was Grey. I ran faster and faster, knowing I was getting closer to freeing him. I could feel him. I could smell him . . . and I could smell her.

Hate seethed through me. I slowed to a trot and shifted into a human as we began our ascent to the cliffs of Carrowmore. My leather armor and corset wrapped around me once again. I heard the pack shifting around me. In my mind, all my focus was on Grey.

I didn't say a word on the barefooted hike to Carrowmore. I felt peace with my decision. Grey was my choice in life, and now he would also be my choice in death. Mother and Father walked on each side of me. They would mourn me soon. I shook my head, blocking the pain I was about to cause from my mind.

My hands shook as the stones came into view. A circle of thirty boulders, one stone for the leaders of every major pack, surrounded the center dolmen. The dolmen was created from five upright stones that held up a capstone, creating the doorway into the afterlife. Carrowmore was a passage tomb. Our people had celebrated our dead here for thousands of years.

This is where I was born, on the very earth where Calista died. Every piece of the prophecy Calista foretold had come true, and now I stood before the stones under the Bloodmoon to be claimed.

The sky looked like navy velvet; not a star dared join me tonight. They all hid from the blood-red moon. The air was still and only silence filled the night.

I began walking around the stones as I prayed for the lives of my people, for the safety of Grey, and for the grace to fulfill my destiny. With each lap, my small pack walked with me in silence. I could feel their fear and frustration. All my memories flooded through me, filling me with raw emotion. It felt like every nerve in my body was opened. Six times we walked around those stones, and the stones called to my soul. They wanted me. Welcomed me. On the seventh lap, my pack began to yell to the stones, and I joined my voice with them, screaming as loud as I could. I felt fierceness inside of me as I awakened the gods.

# 35

## *Carrowmore*

*I stopped at* the opening of the stones of Carrowmore. My pack still yelled behind me, but I couldn't hear them anymore. All I heard were the stones talking to me. I knew once I entered the circle I would be there until I was claimed. The stones were alive, and they wouldn't allow me to leave. I wanted to turn and run all the way to Dunmanas Bay and pretend I was still an innocent child, but I wasn't innocent anymore. I had seen too many evils.

I didn't want to step into that circle. I was staring at the place I was about to die. Knowing death awaited was a surreal sensation. I didn't want to die without Grey by my side, but nothing could save me from my destiny. The stones called to me, pulling me inside with a will greater than my own.

"Be careful, *m'eudail*," Mother said.

Willem put his hand on my shoulder, and his sadness poured into me. "Baran walks with you. I feel him still. He surrounds you," he said.

I nodded.

"You can still change your mind," Brychan said. "I will claim you."

I gently touched his cheek and smiled sadly at him. He would always be one of my heroes.

"I will claim you with all my heart," Channing said.

"I know," I said.

I turned and walked slowly into the circle of stones, only a step or two inside, and I felt my wolfness seep away. I felt like something was draining me, like I was weaker . . . human. I turned to Old Mother; without asking my question, she knew.

"On hallowed ground, we are mortals," she said.

Fear rattled what false strength I had, and I clenched my fists. I forced myself forward. The grass was cold and damp under my feet, and with each step I took the stones began to hum like a vibration of a Celtic melody. It was a song with no ending, like death . . . it was my song. The song felt slow and methodical, like being lowered into a grave. I shuddered at the eerie sounds that surrounded me as I walked to the dolmen. No one else seemed to hear the song, but it terrified me.

The Crone and Old Mother stopped behind me, faced the balanced stones of the dolmen in the center of the circle, and whispered Celtic prayers in Gaelic. I didn't know what to do except wait for the Bloodmoon to bleed.

I looked back to find my mother. She stood with her arms wrapped around herself, trying desperately to hold herself together. I couldn't feel her in my mortal form, but I could see the anguish on her face. No mother should ever have to watch her child die, and that was exactly what I had asked of her. I didn't want to leave her. I didn't want to not look upon her beautiful face ever again, but I had made my decision to save Grey and to save them all. I was born to die here. I took a deep breath. Mother was safe outside the stones with Father, Mund, Brychan, Willem, Khepri, and Dilara. They would all protect her.

And my armies stood guard over my people in the mist of the Rock of Cashel. I knew Dagny and Hyrrokkin would protect my castle. I was thankful for that. I was thankful for many things.

The moon began to bleed high in the sky, bathing us in red light. I stared down at my pale skin and watched it glow like red silk. It was as though I was already covered in my own blood. I shivered at the thought.

"It is time," the Crone said, pointing to the stones with her staff.

I carefully climbed to the top of the stone dolmen about ten feet off the ground and stood above everyone. The Crone and Old Mother stood to each side of the dolmen and prayed to the stones.

"My queen!" Father yelled with pride.

"Bear witness to the Triple Goddess under the Bloodmoon. I am the Crone, the end of life." She knelt in the grass, bowed her head, and rested her hand on the stone.

"I stand before the stones as the creator, the Mother," Old Mother said. She bowed down, resting her hand on the stone.

Silence filled the night, and even the wind dared not blow as the earth held its breath for this moment. "I am the Maiden," I said. "I am Ashling Killian, the Crimson Queen." I bowed to one knee.

I swore I could hear the earth awaken and the stones crackle with life. Lightening struck the ground all around us over and over again. My hair stood on end with the electricity that pulsed around us. I stood up as the lightening continued to snap. I stared up into the sky, waiting for it to strike me dead, but instead it stopped. I searched the horizon for Grey and for Vigdis, but they were nowhere to be seen. Had she simply killed him instead?

My heart sank. How could I bargain for his life if he was already dead? My heart was lost to my misery and with it the last fibers of sanity I had. I came here to save him, but how could I bargain for his life if he wasn't here to save?

"She must be claimed," the Crone yelled. "The stones scream for her soul to be claimed."

"Who shall claim you, Ashling Killian?" Old Mother asked.

I wanted to scream Grey's name, but he wasn't here to claim me.

He was a victim in this stupid game. I didn't know what to do. Without Grey here to freely claim me or to have his life bargained for mine, I had no purpose. My hands shook and I chewed my lip.

"I don't know," I whispered.

"Ashling, I will," Brychan begged.

"As will I," Channing said.

"You must be claimed," Old Mother said. "The stones demand it."

I knew she was right. The stones would never let me leave without being claimed. I could hear their rage at having to wait, but who could claim me now? I looked to my family and knew they would do it, but I needed to kill Vigdis. If she didn't die, even my claiming wouldn't stop her from destroying the world.

Thunder surrounded us, but lightening didn't strike. Suddenly I heard Brychan, Willem, and Mund scream in pain. I turned around to see them pinned to the ground by giants. The thunder of more footsteps filled the night as ten more trudged up the plateau and surrounded my pack. I watched in horror as Father, Khepri, and Dilara stood helplessly outnumbered.

"Old Mother, protect us," Mother begged as she stared at Mund as he writhed in pain.

"Inside the stones even I am mortal," Old Mother said.

A voice rang out from the darkness. "I shall claim her," Vigdis said, walking out of the shadows. She caressed the gray flesh of one of the giants as she walked by. "Why hello, sister," she said, smiling at my mother. "Sorry I'm late."

"You are not welcome here," Mother said.

"Oh, but I have something she wants," Vigdis said.

The ground steamed with her every step as she entered the circle of the stones. Her body scorched the sacred ground, leaving blackness on the earth everywhere she touched, like the blackness of her soul.

Two giants followed behind her, dragging a body to the edge of the circle. I didn't have to look to know it was Grey. I knew we'd lost our lives before we ever started them. They tossed Grey's limp body into the circle at Vigdis's feet.

I looked back to Vigdis and studied her twisted face. Her tiny body was covered in black lace, and her black hair was pulled back into a tight bun. Not a single hair was out of place.

"You have no place here," I said.

"Oh, but I do," Vigdis hissed. "I'm here to claim you."

"I will never choose you to claim me," I said.

I could see her smiling through her lace veil, and I knew she saw through my lies. "You don't really believe you have a choice, do you? My Draugr army is attacking your little castle as we speak. I left them there to the beautiful sounds of your people dying." I held my breath, listening to the horror she was unleashing on the world. The Draugr weren't living beings—they were the merciless undead. All the faces I had left behind flickered through my mind. "And with the snap of my fingers, all of your little protectors will die."

I heard Mund gasp for breath under the weight of the giant's foot and Brychan muttering curses.

"Stop this at once, witch!" Father demanded.

"You can't save anyone now, Pørr, least of all your own daughter whom you yourself brought to slaughter," she said.

"You can't claim her without permission," Dilara spat.

Vigdis laughed as she looked right at me. "I claim you or I kill everyone you ever loved, including this boy—you choose whether this little boy lives or dies, but I remind you, you have already chosen so many deaths for your people. Maybe it is time you stop killing them out of selfishness. Selene, Svana, Eamon, Baran, Paul . . . how many more will die at your hand before you submit? All you have to do is simply save the boy you love and give yourself to me."

"Ashling, no!" Dilara said.

Vigdis knew I would choose my peoples' lives over mine, that I would choose Grey. She knew I would die here. That was why she and

Verci attacked the castle. It was never to take me or even to kill my people. It was to capture him . . . because only if they had Grey would I freely choose Vigdis to claim me to save his life. I finally understood their game.

I closed my eyes, trying to raise the strength to die.

Grey groaned on the ground. He looked up at me for the first time with only admiration in his green eyes. "I love you, Ashling," he said with a crooked smile. He looked around the circle at all who stood by watching. "Ashling, don't let the witch win; let me die with grace."

Vigdis struck Grey in the face and my face stung, reminding me that our pain was always shared; even in this mortal circle, our soul was still split between our bodies. My eyes watered, but I tried to hide the pain. "Don't try to be valiant," she said to him.

Grey smiled at me and the dried blood on his face cracked. "You are worth it," he said. Even as we were both preparing to die, he was still utterly charming. I couldn't help but smile at him with wonder. He was my one true love from the first ridiculous time I set my eyes on him.

Vigdis struck him again. "I will claim your soul!" Vigdis screamed at me.

"No," I said. "Not yet." I needed to look into Grey's eyes just a little bit longer.

"He can't claim you, little girl. He's mine now," she hissed. "And if you don't want me to dismember him right here, you better forsake your pride and let me claim you. You have lived long enough."

I loathed her. For all she'd done against my family, Baran's family, and the entire world. She was a plague upon the earth, fueled by hate. She was a disease.

"You must choose," Old Mother said gently. "No matter what you choose, you live on; this is only your beginning, but the choice must still be made."

I breathed out, readying myself. "I give you . . ."

"I claim her as my daughter," Father's voice boomed over the stones, interrupting me.

"I claim her as my sister," Mund said.

"I claim her as my friend," Brychan said.

"I claim her as the sunshine," Mother said.

"I claim her as my world," Grey said.

My whole body tingled with their words. Words had the power to destroy and to fuel. Their words engulfed me in energy and covered me in their will to survive. With all their claims to my soul, I felt loved. Truly loved. More loved and blessed than I ever had. They were all trying to give me an escape from my destiny.

As I stared at Grey, I touched my cheek where Vigdis had struck him, and I finally understood our connection. Even on this hallowed ground where we all stood as mortals, Grey and I were still bound, and I could feel his pain. If I gave myself to Vigdis to save Grey, it was a certain death for him anyway. As Mund had said, neither of us could live if the other died. When she took my life and drank my blood, Grey would die, too. There was no bargain to save either of us. We were both going to die here. I couldn't save Grey, nor could he save me. Our souls were locked together in eternity—in life and in death. The prophecy was never just about me . . . it was always about us.

All that was left now was for us to die to save our people. I smiled at Grey and he nodded. Did he know we were both about to die?

"Who claims you, girl?" Vigdis hissed. "It can't be your mommy."

"Burn in hell," Mother said.

Vigdis yanked Grey up on all fours and pulled his head back to expose his throat. He groaned, and his breathing slowed as Vigdis unsheathed her sword. He still smiled at me. The most handsome little smile.

"Grey," I whispered.

"If you want him to live, then I take you. Make your choice," Vigdis demanded.

She held Verci's sword above her head, waiting to deliver the final blow that would take Grey's life from me.

"I claim the girl with the snow-white skin and crimson curls as mine . . . forever," Vigdis yelled. Grey struggled, wanting to get to me. She sliced the blade into his soft flesh just enough for his blood to slowly drip down his neck, and his scent filled me.

"He can't save you now. Bow to me, my little slave!" Vigdis said.

"Never!" I screamed and leaped off the stones and landed on the soft ground. A wildness came over me and filled my veins with uncontrollable rage. My red hair danced around my face like flames as I watched her breathe in and out. I watched the blade at Grey's neck digging deeper into his flesh, threatening to take his life from me. I saw everything. For the first time, I truly saw everything.

I saw the game. It was all just a game. I didn't need to play by their rules anymore . . . not Vigdis's rules, my father's rules, even Old Mother's rules. I didn't need a man or a woman to claim me. My soul belonged to me and no one else. I gave my heart to Grey, but I didn't have to give up my soul for anyone. In fact, it was the one thing impossible to give away, even if I tried. A person's soul could never be torn from them, for a person exists as their soul; the body was just a temporary vessel. I stood before my enemy, before my friends, my family, my pack, my love, and the dead.

"Vigdis, you can still choose a different path," Old Mother urged.

"I will rule you, Old Mother; you will be my slave," Vigdis said.

"You have forsaken yourself," Old Mother said.

"I will kill them all," Vigdis said. "I claim you, Ashling!" She smiled through her veil.

"I claim my bloody self!" I snarled.

My body shook with rage and pride. I felt the energy and strength of all the souls who died before me filling my veins. I closed my eyes, feeling Old Mother's infinite power blazing through every cell of my body. I felt the beat of every heart in my pack. I heard their thoughts once again. I knew their souls. Everything had changed. When I claimed myself, the prophecy was fulfilled, and I felt my power flowing back into my veins. Nausea filled me as my body adapted to new sensations and I panted for breath. I felt the change in my pack—we were immortal even here on hallowed ground. I opened my golden eyes and stared right at her.

"These are my people," I said. "And our souls belong to no one but ourselves."

Vigdis screeched like a banshee in the night. As she sliced the blade through the air, our entire world seemed to slow. Grey's eyes were wide.

"I love you forever!" he said. I couldn't hear him, but I read his lips. I yearned for one more kiss. In that millisecond, every moment we'd ever spent together flashed through my mind. Our first run in the woods, our first kiss, the first time I heard him sing, our night on the beach, the first time we'd made love—every experience flowed into me and filled me with his love.

"I will see you soon," I said, knowing once the blade sunk into his flesh, I would die, too. Our love was endless; our deaths were just the beginning of our love.

My father slammed into Grey and shoved him out of the way as the blade cleanly swept through Father's strong neck. Father's head fell with a thud on the ground and rolled to my feet. His vacant eyes stared up at me, no longer belonging to the man I both feared and loved.

# 36

## *Crimson Queen*

*"No! Þorr, no!"* Mother screamed.

Rage and horror seethed inside me. I stared at my father's body and detached head as his blood stained the earth at my feet. There was nothing left of the man or the legend.

"You will die for this!" I yelled. Vigdis scrambled back to her feet with fear in her eyes.

"I live in the otherworld—you can't kill me!" she screeched.

Grey lay stunned on the ground, holding the flesh of his neck to stop the bleeding. The two giants behind Vigdis thundered into the circle after Grey. I growled at them as Old Mother and the Crone shifted into wolves and raced into the fight to protect Grey. I heard my pack fighting the giants, trying desperately to save Brychan, Willem, and Mund. They were outnumbered and I heard their screams, but I could feel them winning, and all I could see was Vigdis. She was mine.

I stalked her like prey, one meticulous step at a time. Anticipating her every move. Every battle I had fought had led me to this moment . . . Adomnan, Æsileif, Verci—they had all died at my hands and so would Vigdis. I would end her life and return her to Old Mother so she could turn to love again. I would end this war.

"I'm the queen of the undead," Vigdis said. "And I will kill you just like I killed your father."

"Back away from my daughter, you soulless witch!" Mother said.

Vigdis laughed and charged at me, screaming like a banshee. Her dress moved around her like black fog over the ground. My mother screamed and snarled as she shifted into a wolf and charged into the circle of stones toward us.

I couldn't let my mother die. I'd already lost Baran and Father. When Vigdis was only five feet away, I leaped straight up into the air as I unsheathed father's blood dagger. As my body came back to the ground, I plunged the blade into her neck, dragging her to the ground.

Vigdis hissed and screamed as she swung the sickle sword toward me. My mother sank her teeth into Vigdis's arm and tore it from the socket; her lifeless fingers dropped the sword. She watched me with pure hate.

"Your reign is over," I said. "There is no room for hate in this world."

I twisted the blade, cutting through her throat as Mother bit into Vigdis's side and tore out her entrails, ripping her apart while she hissed blood. My pack fought the giants all around us, but finally, as Vigdis breathed her last breath, only silence filled the night. As soon as Vigdis died, the remaining giants dropped dead, and I had no doubt the Draugr did as well. Her evil spell over the earth was done.

I felt eyes on me. I looked back over my pack to see them all watching. Blood covered Carrowmore. Mother and I shifted into our human forms and our clothes wrapped around our bodies once more. I walked slowly to Father's headless body and broke down.

"Oh, Father," I said. I fell to my knees and cried. "I love you."

Mother laid her head on my lap and wept. She'd lost Father and Baran. She'd lost both of her loves, and I'd lost both my fathers. I ran my fingers through her messy hair and let my pain seep out with my tears. Grey gently picked up Father's head and knelt with us as he placed it with Father's body.

Grey bowed his head to Father, and tears ran down his cheeks. He tried to wipe them away, but more came. "Thank you, King Pørr Boru," Grey whispered. "For my life and for your daughter."

I pulled Grey toward me and Mother, and we broke into millions of pieces of sorrow. We cried for Father, for Baran, for everyone we had lost, and for the love that we still had. I could feel Father's energy around us. He was trying to heal our pain, but I resisted. I wanted to embrace my agony and loss. I didn't want to feel whole when I'd lost so much. I felt like I'd let them all die. I deserved this punishment. I deserved to live in grief and pain.

"I can feel him," Mother said. Her voice was soft. "It's like a warm hug."

"I feel him, too," Grey said. "It's amazing."

I held my breath and opened my heart, letting my father and his love come and heal my soul. His love was so big . . . so much bigger than me, bigger than I had ever known. I could feel him all around us. Just like his voice once echoed in the halls of the Rock, now his love did, too. He no longer hid his love; he'd set it free, and it was intoxicating.

After all we had been through together, after all the years I thought my father hated me, he died to save the man I loved. There was no deeper way he could have shown me his love. No greater sacrifice. I felt his love in death in ways I never could have felt it in life.

"Thank you, Father, for loving me and letting me choose Grey," I cried. "I will remember your sacrifice for all my days."

My pack kneeled around us as Old Mother and the Crone knelt down, placing their hands on Father's head.

"King Pørr Boru, you have died with honor, and with honor, your soul shall live forever," Old Mother said.

All around me I heard, "Amen."

There was a silence. I could only imagine how they all felt in that moment because my emotions were so strong they took over every fiber of my being. I loved him. He was my father, my leader, and my king. Life would never be the same without him or Baran.

"And you, Ashling Killian, have claimed your own soul and are now the Crimson Queen," Old Mother said, pointing to the moon. Every drop of blood had seeped out of the moon. It now shone bright and brilliant in the sky and cascaded beautiful light down onto us.

"The moon has accepted you as queen," Old Mother said. "Lead us well."

"I will," I said.

Everyone bowed down around me, and I felt a rush of pride as I looked upon them. I had given them everything and they were finally free, but they had given me so much more. They were all my family. Grey grabbed my hand and squeezed it as he smiled at me.

"My queen," he said with so much love I felt I could fly.

Old Mother turned to Grey. "Grey Killian, you are now crowned as King Killian beside the Crimson Queen. You are her equal, her protector, and her love. May you ever stand vigilant over her heart. You are bound to the earth and all of its inhabitants for all of your life and death."

Grey bowed down to Old Mother, "For all my days, I am hers." Grey stood and took my hand, pulling me to my feet. "I will love you and honor you and all our people. I will stand by your side. I am ever yours."

"I love you." I smiled. I turned to Old Mother and the Crone. "Are the people of the Rock safe?"

"Death has come," the Crone said. "But with Vigdis's end, so did the Draugr fall."

"How many?" I asked, biting back tears.

"Thirty souls were lost," the Crone said.

"Willem, Khepri, please rush to the Rock and see to the living and wounded. Carry the dead back here, and we shall return them to Old Mother. All those who can travel shall bear witness to King Boru and all our dead returning to the earth." I turned to Mund; I could feel his anxiety. "Mund, you go, too." Mund nodded. They turned and disappeared over the hill.

Grey held my hand as we watched our small, broken pack. He hadn't left my side. His warmth was like a blanket against the pain. I nuzzled my face in his neck and breathed him in; his strength filled me.

"Brychan, Dilara, Channing, can you please build the pyres for the dead?" I said. "We will place King Boru on the dolmen, at the doorway to the afterlife."

"What shall we do with her?" Brychan asked, disdain dripping from his lips as he looked down on Vigdis's torn body.

"We burn her, too," I said.

"Does she deserve that right?" Channing asked.

"Everyone must be set free. It is not for us to decide what happens to them in the afterlife," I said.

Brychan scoffed.

"However, her fire shall be separate from Father and the others," I said. "We shall burn Father on hallowed ground, surrounded by all his people. Lady Vigdis shall be over there," I said, pointing outside the circle of stones. "We will still set her free with as much grace as we can."

"That I can agree with," Brychan said.

I grabbed him and hugged him tight. "Thank you, Brychan, for everything you have done from the moment I met you," I said. He lightly kissed my cheek.

"You are my queen," he said. He walked off to gather wood for the fires.

"So you claimed yourself?" Channing said, running his hand through his blond hair.

"Are you jealous?" I said.

"I really thought you'd choose me." He laughed. "In the end, you didn't truly need any of us, even him," he said, gesturing to Grey.

"You're wrong, Channing. I needed all of you," I said. "Every one of you gave me the strength to claim myself. It is because of all of you that we won our freedom."

He nodded, though he still looked bewildered.

"Channing!" Brychan yelled. "A little help, please?"

Channing shrugged and wandered off to help. I watched as Old Mother and the Crone comforted my mother as she quietly mourned for my father. It was surreal losing him.

Grey lightly ran his fingers over the scarred flesh on my shoulder. "You saved so many lives getting this scar," he said. "It's beautiful. An honor." I looked at him like he was an alien and he laughed.

He was right. It was an honor, a reminder, a piece of me that would forever be different, a symbol of my love for my people. I would always look at that scar and know I saved so many people I loved, and yet I would always mourn the ones who were lost. I wasn't sure that pain would ever go away. Loss was such a deep feeling—so indefinable and raw.

Brychan and Channing moved Father's body up on top of the capstone rock of the dolmen in the center of the circle, and the wood was placed around him. He looked regal even in death. He was still so strong.

How could two of the strongest men in my life be gone in a matter of days? I sighed as I sat down in the grass next to Old Mother and my mother. I had nothing to say, and they seemed to accept my silence. Or maybe they were out of words, too.

Radiant light began to peek over the horizon as the sun dared to wake the day, and the navy sky melted to orange. It was the birth of a new day, a new life. The world was ready for change.

I smelled them on the wind; I could feel their joy and sadness as my entire pack and army ran to us.

"They are almost here," I whispered to Mother.

She wiped her eyes and tried to smooth her dress, but the blood-stains weren't going anywhere. I reached out and gently held her hand. She looked at me and her eyes welled with new tears.

We watched as my pack ran up the plateau toward us. They looked so beautiful to me. I watched all their faces, counting them. I knew Mother was doing the same. Mund rushed up to us with Tegan, Nia, Jutta, Grete, and Fridrik.

Mother took Nia and Fridrik in her arms and fell to her knees.

"Thank you," I said to Mund.

Hyrrokkin, Dagny, Lady Faye, even Felan and Flin were all safe. I nodded to all my people as they began carrying our dead to the pyres that surrounded me.

"Where are Quinn and Gwyn?" I asked. My voice shook as badly as my hands. I couldn't see their faces in the crowd.

"Here!" I turned to Quinn's voice and watched as the crowd part-ed. He walked toward us with Gwyn in his arms. Gwyn had a scar on her face. "She got in a fight with about . . . was it eight Draugr?" Quinn said.

"Ten," Gwyn said with a smile.

I hugged her and Quinn. "Praise Old Mother you're safe," I said.

"We are lucky we only lost thirty before the Draugr dropped dead around us. They were on the verge of breaking the lines and flooding the castle," Quinn said. "Thank you for saving us."

I nodded. "But we lost Father."

"We didn't lose him," Mund said.

When all the dead had been placed on the pyres—even Vigdis's body, far off in the distance—my people surrounded the circle. I looked at all of them; my family, my friends, my warriors. They had all given so much.

I bowed my head to them. "It is with great sadness that we mourn the loss of our king, Þørr Boru, my father. He died to save us all," I said.

A hush fell over them, and I felt their pain. Father had led our people through so may wars and protected so many. A world without him was unthinkable. He had been our rock.

"I can never thank all of you for your faith and sacrifice. We lost so many, yet together we have claimed our freedom. Lady Vigdis's evil has been destroyed and with her all the demons to whom she gave life," I said. "And the moon has accepted me as your Crimson Queen, if you choose me."

I knelt down to them, giving my soul to each and every one of my people. Cheers erupted all around me, chanting my name. They had chosen me. I was overwhelmed with joy and gratitude. I was born to lead them but thankful they had chosen me. All along it was their choices that gave me power.

"Thank you." My voice was barely a whisper on the wind.

I walked around the circle and handed unlit torches to Old Mother, Mother Rhea, Lady Faye, and my mother.

"Together, we give them the freedom they have won," the Crone said. She waved her staff above her head and the torches ignited. Mother walked slowly to Father and whispered to him. I could have listened, but I didn't. It was her message to give.

Mother slowly lit the pyre on fire and the others followed. The fire swept around the circle, and I watched as the flames consumed my father.

I wanted to scream and cry and rip his body out of the flames and cling to him, but calm settled over my heart. My father's spirit was holding the broken pieces of my heart together.

I lit a torch off his fire, and Grey and I walked over to where Vigdis lay. "I give you back to the earth," I said. I wasn't ready for forgiveness, but I would at least set her free. I lit the small fire and stayed a moment to watch the flames engulf her before Grey and I returned to my father. Where I truly belonged.

# 37

*Promise*

*I thought of* Baran and Father and my eyes welled with tears. I lost both of them. I lost so many wolves and humans, some faces I had known and some I would never get to know. I had lost my childlike innocence. Nothing would ever be the same after all I had seen and all I had done. I would never forget, but I could choose to live. I felt peace settle over my heart, a kind of peace that only love could bring. Grey and I had survived and our future was now. I looked at him sitting next to me. He also seemed somehow wiser, and yet so very much the same boy I had fallen in love with. Grey slid one hand into my hair and lightly kissed my cheek as he looked deep into my eyes.

"You are the promise in my heart. I want you to know in the morning when I wake, you are my first thought. I am so proud of you," Grey said.

"Thank you, Grey," I said, smiling at him. "And I'm so proud of you."

"You're mine, love," he said as he kissed my forehead.

"And you are mine evermore," I said. "You know, there has never been a love like ours . . . where when one dies, the other does, too. To be so bound to another, physically and spiritually, it could only happen to us. You were as much a part of the prophecy as I was."

He nodded. "Meant to be . . . inevitable, but we still chose."

"We did." I smiled. I would do it all again to have him by my side. The warmth of his touched engulfed my skin, and I nuzzled into him. I would never grow tired of his touch.

We watched our people leave as the fires slowly burned out. My heart ached when Mother made her way to Dunmanas Bay with Grete, Fridrik, and Jutta, but I knew I would see her soon. We were one pack, one family, one heart.

Finally, only Old Mother remained under the morning sun with Grey and me. We sat at Carrowmore, where I was born, where my life nearly ended, and where my life as the Crimson Queen had begun. I felt the warmth of the sun on my cheeks and smiled. We sat at the base of the dolmen where Father had once been; now only ash remained on those sacred stones, only ash of the legend that was once King Pørr Boru.

Old Mother stood and started walking away to the east. "Old Mother, you're leaving us?" I asked.

She turned and smiled. "I am the wind, child. I am the sun. I am the air you breathe. I am ever there by your side." The wind gusted from the west so hard that I turned to watch Father's ash blow up into the wind and swirl around high in the clouds. When I looked back to where Old Mother had stood, only ash remained in her place.

"The wind," I whispered, closing my eyes as the fresh, cool breeze caressed my skin. Faith was like the wind.

*The end.*

# Stay Connected!

bloodmarksaga.com | aurorawhittet.com

facebook.com/aurorawhittet

twitter.com/aurorawhittet

instagram.com/aurorawhittet

# Pack Reference

**Boru – Ireland**
Ashling Boru
Bridgid Boru
Cadence Kingery-Boru
Donal Boru
Felan Boru
Flin Boru
Redmund (Mund) Boru
Queen Nessa Vanir-Boru
Niamh (Nia) Boru
King Pørr Boru
Quinn Boru
Ragnall Boru
Tegan Kahedin-Boru

**Costas – Spain**
Selene Costas

**Cree – Canada**
Kaneonuskatew (Kane)
Shikoba
Tallulah

**Kahedin – Wales**
Lord Beldig Kahedin
Brychan Kahedin
Gwyn Kahedin

**Dvergar – Iceland**
Adomnan Dvergar
Bento Dvergar
Crob Dvergar
Eamon Dvergar
Fridrik Dvergar
Grete Dvergar
Uaid Dvergar

Vercingetorix (Verci) Dvergar
Vigdis Vanir

**Kingery – Switzerland**
Cara Kingerly
Channing Kingery
Emil Kingerly
Marcius Kingerly

**Killian – Scotland**
Baran Killian
Grey Donavan
Khepri Killian
Willem Killian

**Tabakov – Russia**
Dilara Tabakov

**Vanir – Greece**
Calista Vanir
Lady Faye Vanir
Mother Rhea Vanir

**Asgard – Norway**
Dagny

**Bloodrealms – Valhalla**
Æsileif
Hyrrokkin
Jutta
The Crone

**Norse Lands – Finland**
Odin Pohjola

**United States**
Caoimhe

# Glossary

**Aconite**
*A flower that cures werewolves from silver-poisoning. Also known as Wolfsbane.*

**Barghest**
*Werewolves that consume wolf-children, foresaking Old Mother. Their skin becomes toxic and burns the flesh of other wolves and their offspring carry the same skin toxicity.*

**Battle of Asgard**
*The battle against the Barghest in the home land of the Pojola pack.*

**Beltane**
*Gaelic festival halfway between the spring equinox and the summer solstice ruled by the Irish Boru pack on Old Mother's Lunar Calendar.*

**Bloodmark**
*A pack symbol tattooed in blood.*

**Bloodmoon**
*A red moon that comes once during each season.*

**Bloodrealms**
*Underground fighting world beneath the Seven Sisters Waterfall.*

**Bloodsucker**
*The clan of humans that hunt werewolves.*

**Carrowmore**
*Carrowmore is one of the passage tomb cemetaries in Ireland. In Bloodmark they are the resting place of the humans in the battle of 4600 BCE.*

**Család**
*Hungarian for 'Family'.*

**Crimson Queen**
*The prophecy foretold by Calista Vanir, of the Crimson Queen who would unite the packs.*

**Dire Wolf**
*Larger than normals wolves and werewolves the Killian pack are the only remaining Dire Wolves.*

**Dolmen**
*A stone doorway to the afterlife.*

**Draugr**
*Undead, human-like creatures that blindly consume all living creatures.*

**Elder Gods**
*The original werewolves.*

**Fenrir**
*A junkyard city under the Bloodrealms.*

# Glossary continued

**Foresaken Packs**
*Werewolves that broke their vows to Old Mother.*

**Garm**
*A pack of wolves that no longer are able to shift to human, and prowl the Bloodrealms looking for flesh.*

**Hills of Tara**
*Location of the Vanir and Dvergar battle commemorated by ancient monuments in Ireland.*

**Köszönöm**
*Hungarian for 'Thanks'.*

**Lughnasadh**
*Festival marking harvest, ruled by the Scottish Killian on Old Mother's Lunar Calendar.*

**Megáll**
*Hungarian for 'Stop'.*

**M' eudail**
*Gaelic for 'My dear'.*

**Netherworlds**
*Underground werewolf city in Canada.*

**Passage Grave**
*Ancient graves of stone for Old Mother's preistesses.*

**Samhain**
*Gaelic festival marking the end of summer and the beginning of winter. Ruled by the Dvergar on Old Mother's Lunar Calendar.*

**Steel Wolves**
*A pack of wolves, burned with steel, living underground in Hungary.*

**Stonearch**
*A steampunk mobile city under the Bloodrealms.*

**Szabadság**
*The city of freedom and home to the Steel Wolves.*

**Tha gaol agam ort**
*Gaelic for 'I love you'.*

**Tomte**
*Norweigen born eleves that bare gifts at Winter Solstice.*

**Tree of Life**
*The symbol of the Crimson Queen.*

**Triple Goddess**
*The foretold coming of the Mother, the Maiden and the Crone.*

**Vargr**
*Mythical wolf-like beast twice the size as a Dire Wolf ridden by Hyrrokkin.*

**Winter Solstice/Yule**
*Gaelic festival for winter solstice and*
*celebrates the rebirth of the sun.*

**Wolves of Song**
*A song of mythological wolf warriors*
*said to have been trapped in the*
*Bloodrealms.*

**Yew**
*The skin of the yew plant can be*
*used to bring someone out of shock.*

**Ylva**
*She-wolf.*